GAL EDGE

GALACTIC OUTLAWS

JASON ANSPACH

NICK COLE

Second Edition
ISBN: 978-1-949731-11-8

Edited by David Gatewood
Published by Galaxy's Edge, LLC

Cover Art: Fabian Saravia
Cover Design: Beaulistic Book Services

For more information:

Website: GalacticOutlaws.com
Facebook: facebook.com/atgalaxysedge
Newsletter: InTheLegion.com

OTHER GALAXY'S EDGE BOOKS

Galaxy's Edge Season One:
- Legionnaire
- Galactic Outlaws
- Kill Team
- Attack of Shadows
- Sword of the Legion
- Prisoners of Darkness
- Turning Point
- Message for the Dead
- Retribution

Tyrus Rechs: Contracts & Terminations:
- Requiem for Medusa
- Chasing the Dragon

Stand-Alone Books:
- Imperator
- Order of the Centurion

A LONG, LONG TIME FROM NOW
AT THE EDGE OF THE GALAXY...

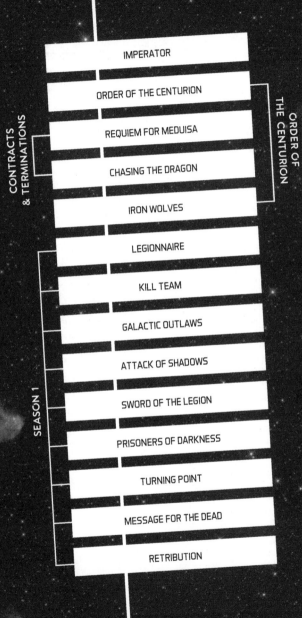

IMPERATOR

ORDER OF THE CENTURION

REQUIEM FOR MEDUSA

CHASING THE DRAGON

IRON WOLVES

LEGIONNAIRE

KILL TEAM

GALACTIC OUTLAWS

ATTACK OF SHADOWS

SWORD OF THE LEGION

PRISONERS OF DARKNESS

TURNING POINT

MESSAGE FOR THE DEAD

RETRIBUTION

CONTRACTS & TERMINATIONS

ORDER OF THE CENTURION

SEASON 1

PROLOGUE
Utopion

Exo sat in the quiet of the bar for a long time after the old leej left him. He wrapped both hands around his half-empty glass of whiskey—a double—and watched the ice melt.

"Another?" asked the bartender.

Exo shook his head. "Nah."

The bartender flipped his rag over his shoulder and began to clean up the old man's empty glasses.

"Hey," Exo said, hitching his thumb toward the door the old legionnaire had left through. "That guy come in here often?"

"Once a week or so. Why?"

Exo blew out his breath. "I dunno. Just… I ain't never heard a story about General Rex like that. Way I heard it he was a war criminal."

"That what they're teaching you new legionnaires now?"

"Ain't teachin' us nothing. It's what I heard is all." Exo rolled his shoulders and popped his neck. "And I ain't 'new.'"

"Well, you heard it from a man who knew him. Always best to believe the leej—"

"—on the ground," Exo finished, interested in his drink again. He took a swallow. "Yeah, I know."

The bartender took away the empty glasses and placed them in a wash unit. He slapped his rag down on top of the lingering condensation rings and began rubbing a shine back into the countertop.

"So what happened?" Exo asked.

"You heard what happened. I was never there. Though I've heard that story enough times to feel like I might've been."

"No. Not all that. Not the hot chick and the... the... killer bots or whatever. To the general. What happened to him?"

The bartender placed both palms flat on the counter and leaned toward Exo. "No one knows."

"Twarg dung."

Exo could tell the man wasn't being honest. Because Exo had that gift, that ability to look someone in the eye without flinching. To burn away whatever was hidden deep inside a man through sheer determination. "Tell me what you heard if you don't know."

The bartender leaned back. "For closure?"

"Sure."

The bartender stooped down to retrieve some fresh glasses, fanning away the rising steam with his rag, then began drying the clean tumblers. With the same dirty rag.

"I got a friend. Friend of a friend, really. Used to be in Dark Ops. Served with the general. And if you ask him when he's had a bit too much to drink, he'll tell you the rumor."

"So what's the rumor?" Exo asked, his patience taxed.

"The general disappeared. And no matter how bad the House of Reason wanted him, they could never find him. 'Cause the general ain't a soldier no more."

The bartender once more leaned in close, returning Exo's killer stare with one of his own.

"He's a bounty hunter."

01
Several Years Later
Ackabar Star Port
Ackabar

The *Viridian Cyclops* settled toward the dry, grit-blasted concrete of the landing bay. Maneuvering thrusters flared from her ungainly bulk. Captain Hogus pivoted the ship so the cargo-loading ports would face the big blast doors that opened out onto the central loading ramp. The only other ship in the massive bay was a forlorn light hauler that looked parted out. Its markings identified it as the *Obsidian Crow*. Perhaps it would provide the *Cyclops* with a few spare parts for the next run out to the edge.

The *Cyclops* was an old Tellarian heavy freighter that should have been out of commission twenty years ago. Its main jump engine took up the entire lower deck, a half saucer rife with spot welds and jerry-rigged bypass cables, leaving scant room for paying cargo. Its bulbous upper deck had been converted to make up for that deficiency; the twin passenger blisters had been refitted for bulk cargo. Crew quarters remained, however, and a cockpit cupola protruded from the left blister. The ship still bore the scarred yellow eagle-and-sword markings of the old Tellarian Spinward Trading Company from the early days of the Republic. That company was long gone from the trade lanes that spanned the galaxy, no doubt absorbed into some Republican mega-contract.

The massive tower of Ackabar Port housed docking bays on nearly every level. A central core contained the heavy cargo and passenger lifts leading down into the city proper. It was the frenetic activity coming from the direction of these passenger lifts that drew the attention of the one-eyed captain of the *Viridian Cyclops*. Civilians and cargo personnel were streaming past, racing in panic toward other ships in other bays.

"Ackabar Ground," called Hogus into the ether, ignoring the chattering of his wobanki first mate. The jungle-brained catman was efficient, but he was always bothering his captain with status reports, announced by the hundreds of red lights and sensor warnings flashing in constant distress across the cockpit. Hogus had learned to ignore most of the flashing lights. He already knew the ship was falling apart; it had been falling apart when he'd stolen it six years before.

He patted the hyperspace computer. As long as that beauty held, he was good. He always patted it twice when he needed to reassure himself that it had held together before, and would hold together for at least one more run.

He flicked on the masters for the landing lights, then brought down the landing gear using the backup levers on the overhead control panels.

Wocks and *ka-chucks* reverberated throughout the battered freighter.

"Freighter landing in Bay Sixteen." It was Ackabar Approach Control. "Please identify via voice. We are cur-

rently experiencing problems with our transponder identification system."

"This is Captain Hogus."

The *Cyclops* settled to the floor of the bay with a sudden drop, her three massive landing gears absorbing her
weight, her hydraulics sensors crying out overstress and
low-power warnings. *Typical.* Hogus stood to crane his
neck back toward the rear of the freighter, visually in-
specting the craft from the rear window spread in the pilot's cupola.

"No fires," he muttered with a smile. "This time."

The wobanki babbled on about a malfunction in the
engine vent housings. Hogus slapped at the cat, who
growled back menacingly.

"Ignore it!" roared Hogus. "She always does that!"

Then to Ground Control, "Ackabar Ground, what
in Tarkedes is going on here? It's like the Festival of
Callus without all the drinking. I'm half expecting to
see a Dolomian bull goring people to death with one of
its heads!"

A bullitar chasing civilians was the only explanation
he could come up with for why everyone was running. As
though this were all just some ancient festival of revelry
known only to the arcane histories of this particular backwater. As though every port to an old smuggler like him
was in a state of perpetual festival.

But the words that came from Approach Control froze
Captain Hogus's blood.

"Republic problems."

The abrupt message conveyed everything.

Hogus knew, at that very minute, that everyone was doing exactly what *he* was considering doing right now. Dumping everything and getting the hell off port and into a takeoff climb, with the nav computer crunching jump solutions for anywhere but here. Sure, Ackabar was technically a Republic protectorate, but it was deep into the outer rim. Practically the galaxy's edge. The Republic couldn't do much out here. Hadn't since the Yranian Revolt. Before that, even.

The wobanki chattered. Clearly he was all in favor of putting the gear back up and preparing for an emergency takeoff. They hadn't seen any Republican corvettes in orbit, but the Legion usually showed up first in drop ships to take control. Then the big destroyers jumped in and set up the blockade. No traffic in or out until all tariffs were paid in full. And warrants executed. Of course.

Hogus had at least sixteen warrants that he knew of.

"Wait just a minute," he mumbled, rubbing his jowly, unshaven chin. "Just wait a minute." He was thinking. Then he was unbuckling his considerable girth and climbing out of the captain's seat in the tight cockpit. He set the auxiliary power inducers to standby. "Might need those," he muttered. He cycled the masters and set them to standby as well.

Down the main corridor of the *Cyclops* he thundered, his blaster banging his beefy leg. The wobanki was still babbling neurotically from the cockpit.

"Well then, get out on another ship! There's money to be made here!" Hogus shouted over his shoulder.

"Captain!"

It was a small voice. A high-pitched soprano. And it brought him to a dead stop. The girl had that effect on him. Commanding him. He mindlessly obeyed because… He didn't know why. He just knew that he was helpless, and that he hated it. He didn't work for her. She was just some patrician brat from a family that wasn't so patrician anymore.

Then he remembered his transport contract was paid, which meant he was done with her. She was no longer his problem. Ignoring her, he took off running toward the back of the ship, though he knew she and her damned bot were following him.

"Captain!"

Demanding.

Authoritative.

Used to being in charge.

His only paying passenger on this run back from that eyesore at the edge of the Republic known as Wayste.

He ran for the cargo door. It was the only one that worked.

"Captain—"

"No time, girl!"

"Captain, what is going on out there?"

"The Republicans are here. They're takin' the capital and the fun's over. I won't charge you to take you out of here. Strike that—I'll charge you half. But there're others that'll want to be getting out of here pretty quickly, never mind the accommodations. And I've got the room at the right price, for anyone wanting to avoid Republic problems, to try and run the blockade that's no doubt strangling this planet as we speak."

"Captain, I do not want to go with you."

Hogus stopped, his bulk coming to a sudden and disbelieving halt. His worn leather jacket flapped open like two massive wings, his blaster bouncing dangerously at his hip. He never kept the safety on because... business.

Who in the— Why would anyone want to stick around and watch the Republic take control? That was...

Was...

The dumbest thing he could imagine anyone ever wanting to do.

"All right then!" He continued on to the hatch controls, slammed his hand on the green square that refused to light up, slammed it again, and waited as the external cargo door began to slowly retreat into the hull above. "Suit yourself. Ride's over. Get off here. Thanks for flying. Buh-bye."

Outside, people were still running toward the massive portage bays where big ships were already lifting away into the swirling purple of the Ackabarian sky. But no one was heading for this particular bay. It was the kind of place where derelict starships and smugglers came to avoid notice and pay lower "fees"—in the form of bribes to the local administrators.

The tiny girl looked up at him, her face worried. She had dark hair. Pigtails. She wore a long dress—torn but clean. Her boots were big and clompy, the kind a Dalovian belt miner might wear in the forests of Iskatoon. Maroon, like the blood of an ox. Her face was pale. And the hint of peach in her cheeks he'd seen when he'd first entertained the idea of transporting her off Wayste three days ago was now gone.

"You told me I could find a bounty hunter here, Captain."

The cargo door was still only half open—it was moving dreadfully slowly. The wobanki had gone on about that as they'd made their approach through the purple, mist-shrouded twilight of ancient Ackabar. He'd tuned his first mate out then. The massive violet eruptions of the cloud storms, breathtaking and dangerous, had absorbed all his attention. He knew that with one electrical strike, the *Cyclops* would short out and drop like an anchor. Hogus loved his ship, but it was a flying deathtrap.

"Uh... yeah. I did. Well, here's as good a place as any to find one of 'em. Bounty hunters, that is."

She favored him with a withering look of contempt, as she'd done the entire trip, even when he'd offered to upgrade her to "first class"—which meant giving her his first mate's suite. For more credits, of course.

It was clear she'd been born better than him. "I assumed, Captain, you might show me where..."

Hogus waited. If she wanted help finding a hired killer in one of the hundred cantinas and taverns where such scum lurked, he was going to make her come out and say it.

"Show me..." She hesitated, as though uncomfortable voicing her request.

The cargo door finally stopped—in a mostly open position—and Hogus ducked beneath it and descended the ramp. Several of the lights along its length were out, in keeping with the overall condition of the vessel.

The stammering girl trailed behind him, her bot scuttling after her. "I assumed you would show me where I might find one," she finally managed.

"One what?" cried Hogus, ducking beneath the ship and opening an access hatch. He struggled, grunting and swearing, to deploy the power cable and get the *Cyclops* connected to the city supply grid.

"A bounty hunter!" she cried. "Where do I find one?"

Hogus was up and racing for the broken venting controls. If he didn't vent the ship's engines within the next three minutes, he'd rupture the hyperdrive container and warp the main destabilizer all to hell. He deployed the keypad from the external access port.

All of the command language was in Jabbari, which he'd had to learn just to fly the damned ship. How a Tellarian ship had ended up with Jabbari programming, he'd never know. The galaxy was a place of mystery and wonder—Hogus's favorite explanation for everything. "Mystery and wonder," he'd crowed from one arm of the Spinward March to the other.

He was thinking about that when the legionnaires stormed the bay. Shooting at everything, of course.

Blaster fire caught Hogus right in the chest, and he went down. Republican legionnaires were excellent marksmen.

"M'lady!" erupted the deep-voiced bot, KRS-88. "I advise we leave this bay immediately. The authorities have arrived, and they seem... murderous."

A squad of Republican legionnaires were now shooting at the *Cyclops* from positions of cover near the primary blast doors. Mainly they were shooting at the cockpit, where the wobanki must still be. Their reflective armor caught the twilight purple of the sky and the arc lights that ringed the bay, and they seemed like bots themselves behind their stark, emotionless battle helmets.

Prisma Maydoon ducked behind a power converter bot as blue blaster fire tore across the bay. Shots nailed critical spots in the freighter, denying it the ability to escape. Burning hot flares erupted from exposed components and blown-out hatches.

KRS-88 scuttled forward on his spindly bot legs, his hulking triangular upper torso sheathed in servitor black. "Miss Prisma, I do suggest we depart now. Emphatically."

"Secure the bay and hunt down any refugees!" intoned the radio-distorted voice of the legionnaire sergeant. "We're moving on to the objective."

A number of legionnaires hustled out of the bay.

A massive Starlifter rose up a few bays over. It angled away from the station, its hammerhead front conning tower rising up like the jutting jaw of some enormous eel. Next came the long spine of the heavy transport's cargo pods, and finally the wide flare of her engines, all eight white-hot and spooling up for full orbital burn to achieve jump.

A missile arched up from within the city. As Prisma looked on, it punched right through the port engine compartment of the Starlifter. Debris—and people—rained down into the port. The ship crashed somewhere beyond the docking bays in the city below. The sound of rending metal was quickly followed by a terrific explosion. Even the legionnaires were shaken off their feet.

That was Prisma's moment. She dashed for the far access doors to the dark machine shops that lined the docking bay. KRS-88 shuffled after her, constantly urging caution. Beyond the machine shops, where hulking drive engines hung suspended from rusting chains waiting to be parted out, they found a cargo elevator. Prisma began tapping in the commands to get the elevator working. A simple locking feature had been engaged by the local net, but emergency protocols allowed override access.

KRS-88 spoke in his menacing basso profundo of sobriety and caution, the very reason her father had chosen this model to oversee her daily life.

Back when he'd been able to choose.

"I do advise we seek the local authorities and alert them to our need for you to be protected from what I can only guess will be rampant hooliganism. These are dangerous times, young miss, and—"

"Crash!" Prisma shouted.

"Yes, young miss?" The bot had been ordered, by Prisma, to respond to the nickname she'd chosen for it.

In front of them the doors of the massive lift opened. It was easily as big as the one she'd seen on the Republican carrier *Freedom.* They boarded, and it clanked and groaned as it descended toward the main sprawl of the city.

"Crash..." Prisma looked about, desperate, seeking something she knew should be there. And knowing it never would be again. Ever. "Tap into the city net and find out where I can find a—"

"Yes, a bounty hunter, young miss, I know." KRS-88 sighed and scuttled forward to interface with the local net. "Your bloodthirsty desire for revenge, young miss, is incomprehensible. This is quite a biologic concept. I admit I am distressed my master is dead, but to kill another would be illogical. It would make the wronged a killer just like the original killers. I do not understand—"

KRS-88 suddenly tilted his almost insectile head.

"Miss, the local net is locked down by Republic Mandate Order 239.0910."

"Shut it, Crash. I need to know if there are any bounty hunters here."

"Querying now, miss."

Forty-five floors down, the elevator finally settled with a *ka-thunk*. Massive locking mechanisms disengaged, and the blast doors slid open. In front of them, the smooth surfaces of the city, angled and blocked like futuristic pyramids, rose above the narrow alleys leading away from the service lane.

"The city intelligence is quite frightened, young miss. But it did tell me that the Republic is searching for someone identified as Tyrus Rechs. Among many other terrible things, this Rechs seems to have a lengthy and outstanding list of warrants relating to activities often associated with bounty hunting."

"Like what?"

"Young miss?"

"What did this Rechs do? What are his offenses? Why does the city intelligence think he's a bounty hunter?"

"Well..." began KRS-88, as though warming gustily to some new mindless task. "It seems he has engaged in unlawful murder. Several counts. Illegal administration of the law. Again, several counts. Discharge of a blaster. Of course, several counts. Robbery. Assault of Republican personnel. Tax evasion. Hate crimes. Failure to appear to summons. Miss, all of these have several counts. Oh, and acting as a known bounty hunter in violation of Republic Mandate 20.0020567F. Pursuant to the Republic's Law Violations Act of—"

"We'll go with 'known bounty hunter,' Crash. Since that's what we're looking for."

"Young miss—"

"I know. Bounty hunters are dangerous and violent."

"Yes. I was going to say that. And..."

The bot hesitated.

"What, Crash?"

"It would seem that this 'Rechs' individual... ah... well, the Republican legionnaires consider him a high-value target for their current operations. Local officials have advised all bots and citizens to be on the lookout for him. His last known location is a refreshment establishment known as the Jaris Cantina. I do not know who this Jaris is, but his cantina has been the site of several murders, *and* it has been cited for food safety violations twenty-one times in the last sixty cycles. My! We should avoid eating there.

Apparently the Bandalorian snake fritters are quite vile. Though I do not eat, of course."

"Lead me there, Crash."

The *Indelible VI*'s internal comm light pulsed blue on the cockpit control panel. An electronic chirp sounded with every fifth flash. Captain Aeson Keel alternated stares between the comm display and Ravi, his turban-wearing navigator occupying the seat beside him.

Ravi adjusted the lavish azure turban over his thick black hair. With a thick Punjabi accent, he said, "I am thinking you should answer."

Keel stared at the display a beat longer, leaned his well-worn Parminthian leather chair forward, and flipped on the comm switch. "Yeah?"

A coughing fit came through the forward speakers, followed by a youthful but commanding male voice. "There's barely any air in here for the princess and me."

Keel frowned. Giving them an internal commkey had been a bad idea. "That's because it's meant for smuggling *non-living* cargo, General. I rerouted just enough air from the *Six*'s life support systems to keep you two alive. Anything more and the Republic would get suspicious."

He switched off the comm, leaned back in his chair, and put his feet on the cockpit console. He turned his head toward his navigator. "I thought that would have been obvious. I mean, name me one freighter captain who provides life support to the non-inhabitable areas of their ship."

Ravi didn't look up from his on-screen navigational charts. "I am not aware of any such individuals."

"Exactly." Keel rubbed the stubble growing along his jaw. "How long until Lieutenant What's-Her-Face arrives at the delivery site?"

Ravi paused his work at the navigation helm. "I am saying perhaps fifteen or twenty minutes before lead elements arrive to secure the landing zone. The rocky terrain will deny access to their main battle tanks, so they will likely move by combat sled. Otherwise you would have been having perhaps an hour."

"I'll gladly lose the extra time in favor of no tanks. We'd have to get airborne to use the main cannons to stand a chance. The *Six*'s burst turrets can handle a few sleds if things get nasty."

Ravi nodded. "I am also thinking you should retrieve your blaster prior to meeting the legionnaire vanguard."

Keel's hand dropped to his hip, instinctively reaching for a heavy blaster pistol that wasn't there. "Yeah," he said, feeling unease over the missing weapon. "I left it on the shop table. Still trying to scrub out the last bit of carbon scoring from the pickup. You know, I thought about increasing the particle—"

Chee-chee. Chee-chee. The internal comm chirped again, and the light flashed blue once more.

"Really?" shouted Keel, dropping his feet from the console. He lurched forward and keyed open the channel. "Yeees?"

A female voice, parched and strained, came through the speaker. "As a royal princess of the Endurian system and a member of the Mid-Core Rebellion against the Republic, I appreciate your saving the general and me from the attack on Jarvis Rho. You saved our lives by stowing us in your ship. But I fear it is all for naught. We are suffocating in your smuggler's hold." She emitted the dry hack of a patient recuperating from a bio-strain of tuberculosis.

Keel opened the channel to speak. "Your Highness, I assure you this is entirely mental. You're not actually suffocating." He muted the comm and looked to Ravi. "She's not suffocating, right?"

Ravi shook his head. "The hold shielding prevents my reading any life scans, but I've been monitoring air quality. I can see no toxicity levels in the smuggling hold harmful to humans or near-humans." He made a circle of his thumb and index finger. "They are A-okay."

The cockpit speakers came to life again. "There must be something you can do?" The princess was almost pleading.

"So demanding." Keel chewed his thumb, considering what to do next. Getting in good with a princess could lead to an untold number of advantages down the road. Even if it meant a death mark on his head should the Republic ever find out. But then, they were idiots, and who could they send that could take him on in a blaster duel?

"Ravi, I don't think she's going to stop calling until I pump more air in there. What're the chances a scanning crew notices?"

"Ninety percent, sir."

Keel's eyes bulged. "That bad, huh? How likely are they to notice if I mute both sides of the comm channels and let it blink?"

"Seventy-five percent."

Grimacing, Keel asked, "Well, what are the odds the scan officer would investigate?"

Ravi twirled the pointed tip of his black beard. "There are a number of variables, including temperament, ambition, schedule, threat awareness..."

"Just give me an average."

"Fifty percent."

"Too high." Keel frowned, calculating whether the extra money he would get from the Rebellion, coupled with special consideration from the princess and her boy-toy general, was worth the risk of withholding them from the Republic. If they found out that he had spared two of their biggest targets during the attack on the rebels—an attack that Keel himself had planned and executed—they might fine him, or insist on half pay after they took her into custody. On the other hand, if the rebels found out that he had wiped out their moon base on Jarvis Rho and taken eight VIPs, including the princess and her general, to the nearest Republican outpost, *they'd* probably kill him. Or at least they'd give it the old MCR try, which was about all the pitiful Rebellion was good for.

Maybe the loose ends beneath the *Six*'s decks needed tying up.

Keel stood and walked past the second row of cockpit seating. Just inside the walkway leading from the cockpit to the ship's common area, he pulled open a panel, exposing breakers and wires.

The comm squawked again, relaying the voice of the princess. "Captain? Captain Keel?"

"Switch the comm relay off mute, will you, Ravi?"

Ravi flipped a switch, then looked back at Keel and nodded to indicate that the comm was live.

"Princess," Keel yelled from the corridor, "I think I can fix the problem."

"Bless you, Captain Kee—"

Keel ripped a wire from the open panel. A shower of sparks danced down his vest before extinguishing themselves on the impervisteel deck. The comm light switched from a blue pulse to a steady red glow.

Dusting his hands, Keel sauntered back into the cockpit. "That's that. We can fix the comm system next time we're in port."

Ravi looked scornfully at the captain. "This is a very dishonest thing. You made her to be thinking you were to provide help with fresh air."

Keel put a hand on his chest as if Ravi's words wounded him. "Dishonest? *Me*? Ravi, she's a *princess*. I have to at least make her *think* I'm doing all I can to bend the knee in her presence, or she might not be so willing to pay back the favor down the subspace lane. And cutting the comms is a hell of a lot easier than explaining Republic scanning procedures. You heard her—she was getting psychosomatic. What?"

Ravi's curled mustache moved upward in a tight smile. He laughed his low, quiet laugh, "Hoo, hoo, hoo."

"What?" asked Keel. "What's so funny?"

Ravi finally answered from behind a grin. "You are thinking the princess will help you due to her social power and connections."

"Yeah?"

"Hoo, hoo, hee."

Keel could not abide not being privy to a joke, especially when it was obvious he was the punch line. Staring daggers at Ravi, he waited for the navigator to tell him what was so funny. He'd shoot him right now if it was worth the charge depletion. And if he had his blaster.

A muffled noise from the ship's common area put a stop to Ravi's laughing and Keel's gnawing frustration. It sounded like a scream—distant, but distinct.

Keel spun around. "What was that?" Without waiting for Ravi to answer, he strode fearlessly into the hallway.

"It's our hidden cargo," the navigator called from the cockpit. "The princess and her general. They are yelling quite loudly, and their voices are penetrating through the seams in the smuggling hold."

"That's it!" Keel strode down the corridor leading to the common room. He went straight to his workbench to retrieve his blaster; he was determined to put an end to this trouble.

From here, he could clearly make out the shouts coming from below. "Captain! Captain Keel! Our comms have gone red! We can't reach you! Captain!"

Keel pushed aside an oiled rag and his blaster's bristled cleaning rod. He grabbed his gun belt from its spot hanging on a workbench clamp, strapped it on his hips—askew for an easier quick draw, like the gunslingers of the old public domain western holos—and picked up his x6 heavy shot Intec blaster. He stormed toward the cargo hold, only to swing back to the bench a moment later to polish one last spot of carbon scoring on the blaster's barrel.

Ravi emerged from the cockpit's long corridor.

"Ravi, what're the odds someone hears these two?"

"Assuming their vocal cords don't give out?" Ravi held his arms out helplessly. "I'm not sure what I am to say, Captain. As long as the scanning crew is not deaf, of course they will hear them, yes."

Keel aimed the blaster at the deck plate hiding the smuggler's hold, putting the toe of his boot to the pop-up mechanism beneath the deck's hidden seam. He paused, shook the barrel of the weapon twice as though it were an extension of his finger, and turned toward his sleeping quarters. "I've got an idea."

Holstering his blaster, Keel moved to the dormitories. An automated door leading to his chambers whooshed open upon recognition of his bio signature. An ancient trunk sat at the foot of his bed, its wood nearly petrified, a relic from when ships sailed on water. He popped open the lid and removed an Armonian fleece he kept around for those long hauls from core to outer rim, where the *Six*'s comfort controls couldn't keep up with the numbing cold of deep space.

The blanket was easily sixty pounds balled up, and Keel had to hoist it out of the trunk with both arms, holding it like a soft and cushy bag of duracrete. The fleece's natural fibers were shorn from shepps that had survived on a frozen wasteland for millennia. Climbers of the galaxy's tallest peaks insulated their gear with Armonian wool.

Returning to the smuggler's hold, Keel dropped the blanket over the plate and spread it out like a throw rug. The sound of hoarse shouting from below was instantly silenced. Only the hum of the ship's auxiliary systems could be heard.

Tilting his head as if to say, "Not bad," Keel folded his hands beneath his arms and leaned against a bulkhead, legs crossed at his ankles.

Ravi looked at the fleece. "That will certainly raise the hold's temperature a very substantial amount, Captain. You yourself can only stand to be under that blanket for a quarter hour."

"Stop watching me sleep, Ravi."

"Yes, I know you have said this, but it is frequently very boring on the ship." Ravi pursed his lips and looked at the covered smuggler's hold. "I am wanting to know how long they are to be in this... sweatbox, to use an old prison phrase."

Keel shrugged. It wasn't as if the princess had left him any choice.

"I confess," Ravi continued, "I was thinking you would kill them."

"That was Plan B."

Ravi touched his fingertips together disapprovingly. "There remains a possibility they will suffer from heat stroke if they are left inside for too long."

"Well, let's hope the transfer gets over quick, then. Nobody has to die as long as there aren't any Republican complications."

A pounding reverberated through the *Indelible*'s impervisteel gangplank. Straightening up, Keel looked incredulously in the ramp's direction. "Who's knocking on my ship?" He moved toward the observation screens built into the wall above his workbench.

Ravi followed, his azure chola flowing behind him. "There is an eighty-eight percent chance these are legionnaires in advance of the Republican transfer team."

"Of course it's the Republic."

One of the monitors showed a gray-green thermal view of two Republican legionnaires waiting beneath the ship. One raised the butt of his blaster rifle and slammed it into the outer door. These types never waited patiently.

Keel knew he needed to lower the ramp before they got it in their minds to break out the cutting torches. "C'mon, Ravi. We're going outside."

Standing between Keel and the door, Ravi did not move. "I cannot leave the ship, Captain."

Keel walked through Ravi like the living through a ghost. He stopped at the black-and-yellow button for lowering the gangplank. "What? Why?"

The hologram flickered, and Ravi looked down at his shimmering self until he optically solidified. "Because our TT-3 hoverbot was broken two stops ago at Los Larynth, when you mistook it for a fly. You have yet to replace or repair it, in spite of several promises, though you have found time to obsessively polish your blaster."

"Okay, take it easy." Pinching the bridge of his nose, Keel let out a sigh. "I need you out there. How far off the ship can you go?"

"I am thinking only to the top of the ramp before the internal holoprojectors can no longer render me."

Another thud came through the door.

Placing his palm over the ramp controls, Keel said, "Okay. Let's go."

He gave the door a solid kick, hoping the legionnaires on the other side would have the sense to move out of the way, then pressed the button. A yellow light flashed above the exit while a white mist of vented gases issued from the ramp's struts, making Keel feel as though he stood inside a cloud.

The ramp lowered quickly, which was critical for the times when Keel needed to make a blitzing assault, and even more critical when circumstances called for a hasty retreat.

The mist cleared.

The legionnaires were nowhere to be seen.

03

LS-19 pushed himself up on hands and knees. His legionnaire armor scraped against the rocky surface of the LZ. Heavy breathing nearly drowned out his helmet's bone conduction audio relays. Moments earlier he'd been banging on the hull of a late-model Naseen light freighter.

And then the ramp dropped.

Dropped *without* the all-comm warning message mandated by the Republic's Work & Labor Bureau. That alone was enough for LS-19 to put a lien on the ship on behalf of the Republic.

But he wasn't thinking about liens or broken penal codes. He was sipping in shallow breaths, trying to reorient himself. He'd barely had enough time for his neuro-mapped self-preservation training to kick in, a drilled instinct that had compelled him to leap out of the ramp's path.

Control Breathing.
Control Breathing.
Control Breathing.

The message blinked in the upper left corner of LS-19's visor, superimposed over the optical scans of the rocky landing zone. He squinted his eyes at the message, cursing it for taking his attention away from his surroundings. Hot breath fogged over his screen with every exhalation, blurring his vision, but it was a losing battle for the vapor—the moment it condensed on his visor, the LegionWorks Type-N Combat Envirocontrols whirred, dehumidifying the helmet, ferreting off the moisture to store for later re-hydration, and maintaining an optimal battleset temperature of 71.3 degrees.

Inhale through nostrils.
Use full lung capacity. Employ diaphragm and abdominal muscles.
Exhale through mouth.

LS-19 obeyed his prompter's commands. They had been programmed by Republic scientists dedicated to making sure that the legionnaires remained the premier soldiers of the galaxy. The instructions repeated until his breathing normalized, then the prompt faded away, leaving only the familiar OpNet HUD on his visor screen.

LS-19 examined the belly of the freighter, some three meters from the ramp. Seams were visible in what should have been a solid plate of impervisteel. It was probably a bad torch-weld from a breach, given the ship's age, but it also wasn't unheard of for the Naseen light freighters to be fitted with illegally concealed weapon systems. He gripped his rifle tightly and rocked to his feet, careful to stoop so as not to bump his helmet against the ship's underside.

The L-comm burst to life with the voice of his team leader, LS-87. "Nineteen. Status?"

"Adequate for duty. What's your status, Lieutenant?"

"Uh, I'm fine." There was a pause. "Oh! Adequate for duty. Maintaining scan overwatch at recon sled, uh… three."

Idiot, thought LS-19. Like most legionnaire officers, LS-87 had been appointed by some planetary governor. He wasn't a soldier, just a politician playing war until his handlers felt the time was right to bring him back homeworld to stand for election.

It didn't used to be like that.

"Eighty-nine, status?" LS-19 asked. LS-89 had been with him when the ramp came down. He may not have gotten clear.

The team commander echoed the call into the L-comm. "Eighty-nine, status?"

Two clicks of static came back in reply, marking an affirmative. LS-89 was alive, but his comms must've been damaged. His face had to be a bloody mess if he hit his bucket hard enough to knock out his mic relay. Still, the trooper lived up to his nickname. He was lucky.

"Is anyone else picking up those static clicks?" the team commander called.

LS-19 stifled a groan. "Acknowledged, eighty-nine," he said with veteran calmness. "Confirm loss of audio output."

Click-click.

"Confirmed audio output loss. Confirm status as adequate for duty."

Click-click.

"Confirmed. Advise: are you under duress?"

LS-19 strained his ears in anticipation, scanning the perimeter with his blaster rifle. He loosened the clasp around a stun-clap grenade should a two-click affirmation sound.

Click.

"Confirmed negative duress," the team commander said, apparently remembering audio-loss procedures at last. "Be advised, the uh, ramp is deployed. I do not have visuals on crew from this vantage point."

LS-19 cursed. "That fool loadmaster could've flattened Lucky and I both. No comm warning received."

"Copy," the team commander said. "The, uh, ship-top comm tower is steady red."

Pressing a button at the base of his helmet, LS-19 muted his comm. "Might've been good to know that *before* we went knocking, you useless kelhorned space rat! I swear to Oba, Republican appointees should apologize to trees for having to reoxygenate the air they deplete!"

He imagined that Lucky was uttering similar curses. Neither legionnaire appreciated being under the command of a point—a politically appointed team leader. That even the vaunted legionnaires were unable to keep out the ambitious and woefully unqualified from grabbing commissions spoke volumes about the Republic's decay. The legionnaires' officer corps jeopardized every soldier under their command. Lieutenant Clueless in the command sled was, sadly, typical. The worst of the bunch always paid extra to get appointed to the legionnaires. It was a surefire way to get elected.

LS-19 found Lucky. His armor was covered in red dust and there was a five-centimeter dent in his helmet. The legionnaires nodded to one another and moved swiftly to the base of the ramp, ready to take on a hostile target with overwhelming firepower.

Trusting Lucky to draw a bead on the turbaned human farther up the ramp, LS-19 aimed his weapon at a human wearing typical smuggler's gear.

Scum.

LS-19 flicked his helmet's external comm speaker to live with his tongue. "Hands! Hands!"

The human tilted his head to the side and raised his hands slowly, as if the command was an inconvenience. Clearly this was the ship's captain.

"Good. Neither one of you moves!"

"Take it easy, huh?" The captain's tone was wounded, yet somehow patronizing. "I didn't bring you *armed* rebels."

The legionnaires' weapons remained steady. "Identify yourself and your starship. Transponder and voice."

"Aeson Keel, captain of the *Indelible VI*. And I can't send ship ID by transponder. Our comms are red." He pointed at the steady red comm attached beneath the collar of his slate gray shirt. "See?"

The troopers lowered their rifles. "All right," LS-19 said. He pointed at the turbaned man. "Who's he?"

Keel looked over his shoulder as though he wasn't sure who stood behind him. He looked calmly at the legionnaires' expressionless helmets. "That's Ravi."

"I don't care what his name is. What's his *function* on the ship?"

"I am the *Six*'s navigator."

"Fine." LS-19 relaxed his guard slightly. The steady red was a good enough reason for the ramp nearly crushing him. The captain would have assumed that the big red comm light would have been noticed by legionnaire overwatch.

It should have been.

Lucky shifted from one foot to the other, scanning the horizon.

"Comms are down, so you can't transmit the cargo manifest," LS-19 said. "Convenient."

Keel shrugged. "You gonna inspect 'em for concealed damage?"

"Stow it and bring down a datapad, then."

As Keel went up the ramp to comply, LS-19 darted out his tongue, silencing his helmet's external speakers. The helmets were soundproof, allowing legionnaires to speak secretly over L-comms inaccessible even to friendly Republican officers and soldiers. The legionnaires answered only to a chain of command that led to the top of the Republic's Prosperity & Safety Council. "LS-19 to Command Sled. Lieutenant, what's Command AI reporting back about ship ID and captain?"

"I, uh, missed the name. Please repeat."

LS-19 allowed a sigh to escape over the comm. "Ship name: *Indelible VI*. Captain: Aeson Keel."

"Roger," the team commander replied from the recon sled. "*Indelible VI*. Captain Aeson Keel. Will upload to commsat and maintain overwatch."

"Negative on overwatch, sir," LS-19 said. "Site is secured and LS-89 is no-go on his L-comm. Protocol requires an exchange of post."

"Right. Yeah. Okay, I'm proceeding to relieve LS-89 on foot. Eighty-nine to relay data to commsat on assumption of post."

There was a hint of annoyance in the lieutenant's voice. *He* was the team commander and should have made the call. But he didn't. Probably didn't know to. So LS-19 had been forced to take charge. He didn't like having a leej who could only answer in clicks serving as his backup.

Four men and two humanoids shambled down the ramp. All were dressed in tattered olive-green uniforms popular with rebels in this sector of space. Their arms were tied together at the wrist with synth-wire, and strapped around each prisoner's leg was an ener-chain receiver, designed to send a paralyzing jolt of electricity through all of them should one choose to break formation.

Keel came last, a heavy blaster pointed at the back of the final prisoner. He tossed the datapad to LS-89, who fumbled and barely caught it while Keel halted the prisoners at parade rest outside the ramp.

Dropping his pistol to his side, Keel said, "Terms were payment on delivery. So pay up."

"You'll have to wait for the main elements to arrive," LS-19 said through his bucket's speakers. He looked over the horizon for the lieutenant's approach. No sign yet.

"Fine," Keel answered. "But you've only got fifteen standard minutes before you start owing for detention."

Lucky joined LS-19 to review the manifest. The silent trooper pointed a finger repeatedly at the datapad. LS-19 leaned in to look.

"Captain Keel!" LS-19 shouted, holding his rifle with heightened alertness. His HUD instructed him to raise his weapon another degree to optimize his ability to aim and fire. "The shipping docs say you were tendered eight prisoners by the bounty hunter Wraith. Where are the other two?"

"Oh, no. You're not gonna pin that on me." Keel marched over to the legionnaires with a furrowed brow. "Here." He pointed at an R-verified notation on the datapad. "See that? 'SLC.' Means shipper load and count. I delivered what was put in my hold, and I'm not liable for any overage, shortage, or damage. Go back to whoever captured these rebels to ask for the rest."

The legionnaires motioned their rifles menacingly at Keel, careful not to point them directly at him, but letting him know that things might easily change. Very easily.

LS-19 amplified his speaker output. The increased volume made compliance 1.4 times more probable. "Captain, surrender your ship for immediate search and seizure."

"Oh, give me a break." Keel glanced up at the navigator, who remained on the ship's ramp. "Search it all you want, but seizure? Not happening. I've been around the block a few times, Leej. The impound fees are more than I'm getting paid for this job."

LS-19 repeated his order, enunciating each word perfectly and leaving no doubt that he meant what he said: "Surrender your ship for *immediate* search and seizure."

"And what if I don't?"

The captain was clearly stalling, but the legionnaire had his answer ready. "Should you refuse, you will immediately become guilty of Republic Ordinance N.779.631-2: resisting a lawful representative of government. If in the view of said representative the aforementioned resistance requires the use of lethal force, such force will be rendered and deemed justified by its deployment. I won't ask you again."

"I had a feeling something like this would happen." Keel shook his head. "You just never know what you're going to get when dealing with the Republic nowadays. I guess you guys are pretty serious about all this, huh?"

"Ninety-two percent," Ravi called down from the ramp.

Keel understood his navigator at once. Ravi was telling him the likelihood the legionnaires weren't bluffing. These were the go-getter type, determined to ignore basic shipping procedures on the off chance they might uncover a clandestine smuggling operation—or the two missing rebel VIPs. Things would have been so much easier if an officer had been handling the transfer instead of these frontline troops. Still, it wasn't as though he hadn't planned for this possibility.

"So I need to come up with two more bodies, huh?"

Ravi's lip twitched in understanding at his captain's meaning. He contrasted the position of the legionnaires' rifles against Keel's blaster, factored in Keel's reflex and fire time—which was considerably faster than most humanoids in the known galaxy—and filled in the legionnaires' reaction time using the average reflex time of the Republic's foremost shock troopers. Multiplying by 1.09997543 to account for the potential injuries sustained by the silent legionnaire in his dive to avoid being crushed by the landing ramp, he computed the odds.

They weren't great.

"Thirty percent."

Keel hissed, boring holes into the legionnaires, his every muscle and sinew primed to draw and fire.

The legionnaires shared a look before turning their attention back to Ravi.

"Thirty-seven percent," Ravi said.

"Still not enough," Keel said, hoping the legionnaires would do something to better his odds.

LS-19 pointed his weapon at Keel. "What's he talking about?"

"Ten percent," said Ravi.

"Shut up!" The legionnaires swung their weapons toward the hologram.

"Sixty-six point nine percent."

Like the whip-tail of a gungrax, Keel's blaster was up. He fired at the black synthprene bodysuit exposed at the neck beneath the nearest legionnaire's helmet. The heavy red blaster bolt blew through the trooper's neck and hit the visor of the second trooper's helmet. Both legionnaires clattered onto the rock-strewn landing zone, smoke rising from their bodies.

Keel smiled and holstered his weapon. "One shot!" He shook his head, impressed at his own marksmanship.

"Yes," Ravi said. "And if you were to be taking two shots like I suggested in case of this situation, you would have had much better odds."

Keel shrugged, still all smiles. "I already *knew* I could do it in two shots." He looked over at the stunned rebel prisoners, their mouths hanging open in surprise. They, at least, ought to have been impressed at his shooting display. "One shot!" he crowed.

The rebels looked unsure what to say.

"Oh, like any of you could've done better."

Keel walked down the row of rebel prisoners. They seemed afraid—probably imagining their coming execution. "Listen up," Keel said, gesturing to the two dead legionnaires behind him. "I'm going back on my ship. *Without you.* Take the legionnaires' weapons and set up a defensive perimeter for when the rest of the Republic's force shows up. I'm going to wait for the Republic to transfer me my credits, then I'm taking off."

A rebel with captain's insignia spoke up. "Surely you don't mean to just leave us?"

Keel pretended to consider for a moment, then nodded. "Yeah, pretty much that's exactly it."

"What the—" The helmet-filtered voice belonged to a legionnaire who had just reached the landing zone. Keel looked up in surprise, swiveling his blaster toward the newcomer, who had lieutenant bars on his armor. The legionnaire quickly looked from Keel to the two dead legionnaires, then turned and ran, frantically keying his bucket comm. "LS-87 to Liberty-Actual!"

Keel gave a half frown. The legionnaire's communication wouldn't go through; the *Six* had begun jamming the L-comm network from the moment Keel took his shot.

The legionnaire ran in zigzag patterns across the terrain in an effort to… dodge? Keel raised his blaster with the indifferent posture of a barfly playing a casual game of darts, and squeezed off another bright red blaster shot. The bolt hit the trooper between his shoulder blades, sending him tumbling end over end. He came to a sudden stop against a crimson boulder.

Keel holstered his blaster and addressed the prisoners. "You can have his weapon, too. Good luck. You're gonna need it."

The *Six*'s ramp began to rise as soon as his feet touched it.

On the ship's monitors, Keel watched the rebel prisoners. They stood, dumbfounded, then ran to grab the N-6 blaster rifles. They began to liberate one another from the bindings on their wrists with a vibroknife taken from a legionnaire's chest webbing.

Keel switched out his blaster's charge slug, then scowled at the back of his navigator's turban as he followed him to the cockpit. He flopped into the pilot's bucket and began flipping switches, running through the ship's takeoff sequence. "What was that?"

Ravi raised an eyebrow, his own hands moving across the control console, the shipboard computer activating switches as the holographic fingers hovered over them. "What was what?"

"That." Keel pointed a thumb to some vague place outside the ship's hull. "There were *three*? You couldn't have *warned* me?"

With a shrug, Ravi reached up and diverted additional airflow into the smuggler's hold. "I am thinking the ship would have told me if you had not ripped out so many of her comm wires and such."

Keel looked at Ravi blankly, unable to argue the fact.

Ravi continued to cycle through the pre-launch checklist. "Shields online."

After keying in a 140-character passkey, Keel leaned back in his chair to watch his monitor. The spinning credit symbol from his off-moon bank account rotated as a secure connection was established. "Ravi, with the money I just got for unloading these prisoners, I'm going to have Olivet Systems do some R&D on how to shoot and kill a hologram."

"Yes, this is a wonderful use of resources, sir. I am wishing I had—"

The screen flashed, then began to play the animation for a lost connection: bold red arrows moving toward the four corners of the screen.

Keel knitted his brows. "Lost signal? That's not s'posed to happen unless the Sharon moon explodes..."

BOOM!

The ship rocked violently, sending Keel out of his chair and onto the deck. He looked up at Ravi, whose holoprojectors rendered him steady, though the cockpit lurched around them. "Who's shooting at us, Ravi?"

The hologram frowned as he looked at sensor screens. "It would appear that the Republicans found a way to get a main battle tank to the landing zone after all."

04
Ackabar City
Ackabar

On their way to the Jaris Cantina to find the dangerous bounty hunter Tyrus Rechs, Prisma and KRS-88 dodged squads of Republican legionnaires. In the swirling nepenthe of the skies over the port, landing transports full of armored legionnaires and specialized units shuttled down to the surface to clear out resistance hot spots and support mop-up operations now that a full interdiction was under way.

"Young miss," announced KRS-88. "We are in clear violation of several local and Republican laws. I advise we surrender immediately so that your safety—"

"Not listening, Crash," called Prisma over her tiny shoulder as she darted away from the looming servitor bot her father had assigned to her. "We have to find this bounty hunter. He might be just what we need."

"Do we, young miss?" the bot intoned deeply in automated condescension.

"Yes, Crash! We need a... hero! I need—"

"Young miss," interrupted KRS-88 as they hid in the shadows of an alley, waiting for a squad of nearby legionnaires to finish blasting away at a group of Gomarii slavers farther down the street.

The squad clanked off at port arms to pursue the fleeing slavers.

"Young miss..." began KRS-88 once again. "Bounty hunters are not heroes. They are dastardly criminals. Reckless murderers even. Why, they're—"

"That's what I need, Crash. I need someone like that. I need a murderer too." She stumbled. Halted. Stared hard at the ground beneath her giant, ill-fitting shoes. "I need... justice," she whispered.

Justice wasn't what she wanted. But it was the only thing left to her.

"I'm only trying to protect you, young miss. That's what your father would have wanted me to do. That's all."

She knew the bot could sense her emotional levels. It had learned to gauge ranges in order to be of better service. And, of course, it had been there. It had recorded everything that had happened.

Prisma stared coldly at KRS-88's seven-foot black metallic frame. She set her mouth hard against anything that might come from it. Anything that might betray her. Anything that might cause her to break down once again.

"As you wish, young miss," murmured the bot.

At the Jaris Cantina they found bodies. Twelve Gomarii slavers. Discarded blasters everywhere. The smell of burnt ozone lingered in the air.

Only a potbellied bartender remained, forgotten broom in hand, staring in disbelief at the carnage and wreckage that surrounded him. He looked stunned, and Prisma could understand why. His place of business was shot to pieces, and it seemed many of his customers were dead.

He stared at the shining credit Prisma had set on the bar. "That bounty hunter come in here all quiet-like," he said.

He sighed, with a wistful expression that seemed to acknowledge the vastness of the galaxy from end to end. Then he took up the credit and turned it over and over, as if in some kind of trance.

"He just come in all silent. But I knew, and everyone else did too, that he was real trouble. Bad trouble. Wearing that old-school legionnaire armor. But all marked up from times before. From the tribes. Didn't even take his helmet off. Carried a big, old piece of slug-throwing iron on his thigh. Like back from the Savage Wars. Not a normal blaster like everyone carries. Why, look at the holes he put in Deke Cansain alone! Fifteen of 'em. There's nothing left of the poor man's face. On second thought, little girl, you really shouldn't look at that. That'll just make you old before your time. Who in the hells of the Arcturus Maelstrom uses a hand cannon like that anymore? Recoil and all, and he's still putting slugs in everyone light speed fast. Smoke and blasts like an old shotgun I seen once on a dorbi hunt. Killed 'em all and then asked where..."

The bartender got real quiet all of a sudden. Then, as if remembering where he was, he started pushing the broom idly, for all the good it didn't do.

"Go on," Prisma prompted.

The bartender, his face twisted from radiation, stared at the credit again.

"You don't see too many of those lately," he said, indicating the credit. "Republic wants everyone on the net. They can keep track of your money there. This... this is a lot of money. Real money. I can do a lot with this. But it ain't worth telling you where he went. I'd have to leave Ackabar if I let you know where."

"So you told him where to go next?" asked Prisma.

The man's mouth worked silently for a moment. As though he were chewing his words over and over, again and again. Fearful they might cause him to choke.

Then, stuttering, "O-of course. H-he stuck that cannon right in my face. So I had to. Had to."

"Well," said Prisma as she climbed up on a stool next to the bar and leaned into the man's tormented face. "They're probably all dead there too now. Know what I mean?"

The bartender looked around at all the corpses. Whatever had happened here... it had clearly left him shaken. There was just so much damage and destruction. The look on the man's face clearly communicated that he'd snapped.

He nodded slowly, then whispered, "Junga's."

"What's a junga?" asked Prisma.

"*Who.* Junga is a who. *The* who. Runs the crime syndicate in this parsec and a few others. Probably 'ran' is more correct. But maybe not. Junga had some heavy lifters working for him. But I won't lie—that bounty hunter moved like a Xanthan eel. But you know... faster. If that's even possible. That one's dangerous. Everybody-gets-killed dangerous, to be real clear about it. Really, listen, kid. If I was you, I'd go in the opposite direction of Junga's. Seriously."

But of course Prisma wouldn't. And didn't. Despite KRS-88's numerous protests, including the ones with his biggest words, she followed the trail of mayhem and bodies that shadowed the bounty hunter.

Junga's hideout was deep in the Breakers. Way back amid the wreckage of a thousand years. A place where people who didn't have business, didn't go. The Breakers was the area of Ackabar where old ships were broken apart for salvage and spare parts. In a way, it was a museum of the history of space flight. Freighters from twenty years ago lay alongside old light huggers from a thousand years gone. Big, bright colony ships lay like the skeletons of beached whales. Only the ribs and transportation spines remained of what had once been the height and hope of technology for the first optimistic pilgrims that took the outbound trek.

Before jump drive came along and changed everything.

Junga's fortress was like a massive pirate's treehouse cobbled together from forgotten starships and odd bits of junk. It climbed the superstructure of an old colony ship; bunkers and walkways led up along the spine to a looming tower hanging underneath the main ventral spine of the ancient derelict. The tower looked foreboding and dangerous, like a stand of trees in a forest one steers clear of on a winter's day.

"Miss..."

"Don't, Crash. We're going up there. We have to."

At the entrance to the catwalk, crossing out into the fish bones that remained of the ancient starship's superstructure, lay the bodies of two dead Gomarii mercenaries in full battle plate. The lone eye that wallowed in each misshapen head was milky and unfixed.

Prisma knew that, inside, she would find the man who would make everything right again.

She was wrong about that.

The bounty hunter Tyrus Rechs didn't always use a slug thrower. But when he did, he left a lot of big smoking holes in anyone who stood between him and his target.

The bounty for Junga Dootabanu wasn't anything special. He was just another lizard slithering across the edge of the galaxy on vice, corruption, and graft. Just another bottom-feeder the locals were paying to put down, since the Republic was probably too busy getting a slice of the action to do the job themselves.

That should mean something, thought the man inside the ancient legionnaire MK1 armor. The well-made kind from back in the Savage Wars, not the mass-produced reflective junk that looked slick but didn't even stand up to blaster fire. Just a shiny uniform for kids to get killed in and feel like they'd done something noble for a galaxy that was anything but.

"What?" he asked himself. "What should mean something to me?"

He did that a lot lately. Talked to himself. But he was all he had, so he did.

Live long enough, and it's just you.

Someone he'd once known, someone important, had told him that. Or had it been a warning?

He was threading the maze of Port Authority passenger corridors that would lead to the lift hub and then down to the city of Ackabar. The Republic hadn't shown up to ruin everything yet. That would be in about five minutes. But that didn't concern him. He had a job to do. That was all that meant anything anymore.

And he had two tails.

Two of Junga's thugs, most likely. Blasters who watched the port. Probably more of them all around. But the two that were obvious were what concerned him at this moment. Were they interested for the sake of being interested? Or were they waiting?

The bounty hunter was carrying a heavy blaster, charcoal-dusted to keep down reflection. It was the same heavy firepower issued to at least one member of every legionnaire squad—the kind that put out thirty blasts in four seconds. The kind that was wildly inaccurate even if you knew what you were doing. He used it to keep everyone's heads down. A kind of crowd control.

Then there was the big old hand cannon on his hip. He used that for terminations. And captures; clients frowned on disintegrations.

This was a termination.

Fifty thousand credits. All of it sitting in a bank vault on New Kessia. IRL. Not digital. Proof of death, and collect in real life.

Does that matter?
What?

The credits. Do they matter?

"Hey!" shouted one of the tails.

In an instant, the look on his mean little face changed from the smirk of the smoothest outlaw this side of Dalore, to the wide eyes of a startled murder victim.

The bounty hunter had turned down a maintenance corridor and screwed on the big fat blaster silencer he kept in one of the armor's many cargo pouches. He didn't like using it. Not unless he had to. It didn't suppress all that well for all that long. Limited shelf life. Totally illegal.

But he'd had to.

He ventilated both of the tails in the blue, shadowy depths of the maintenance passage. Like some Vulcar tyrannasquid, luring its victims down into the shifting dark blues deep beneath that violent sea and greeting them with death.

Someone might have heard a series of low, metallic hisses. If they did, and they were military, they'd know exactly what the hisses were. But most people didn't.

A half second later the bounty hunter left the maintenance alley alone.

He switched on retinal tracking inside his suit's HUD and started a redundancy scan. No doubt the tails had a handler. If the same face appeared in the next few passages more than three times, that would be the handler.

Sure enough, a Hool—hulking, psychotic—revealed itself within the time it took him to double back through a few of the major passages. The Hool was trying to discreetly hide its poisonous spines beneath an old, gray traveler's cloak that had seen better days.

The bounty hunter had killed a lot of Hools back in…

Back in…

Back in the…

Before the Savage Wars ended.

Nasty beasts.

The galaxy was a dangerous place. Always had been. Someone had once said that to him long ago. *Always had been.*

At the port spire, he walked through the transportation hub. Dim Altari pop trance competed with the wash of digital ads that floated along the concourse. It was like walking through a jungle of spam. The bounty hunter timed it just right and hit an elevator before it closed. That wasn't the timing part. The timing part had been making sure there was another elevator open nearby, so the Hool could follow him down.

Inside the elevator, the helmeted bounty hunter deployed a diamond fiber chain from his utility belt and attached it to the hatch in the ceiling. He gave the chain a quick tug, and the hatch clattered loudly onto the floor. His old armor was cybernetically enhanced. They didn't make them like that anymore. If you had a blaster, you didn't need to be strong. But back in the day, during the Savage Wars, hand-to-hand wasn't uncommon. In fact, it was very common.

The galaxy was a dangerous place. *Always had been.*

The bounty hunter stepped beneath the opening and turned on his thrusters using his wrist pad. His head was the joystick that controlled flight. He had two minutes of flight time in the jump pack, but he only needed a short burst.

A moment later he was standing on top of the speeding elevator within an immense cathedral of shadows and machinery. Hundreds of other elevators were rising and falling like some mad piston engine out of time and gone awry.

He spotted the elevator the Hool had taken, and he leapt out into the void. No thrusters. He needed to conserve thrust, and since the lift was above him and falling along a nano cable, a well-timed jump might be all that was needed. He required only a slight adjustment, a short burst from the jump pack, and he landed on top of the other elevator with a metallic clang. His armored boots smartly gripped the surface with magnetic stabilizer assist.

No doubt the Hool would be wondering what was happening on top of its elevator.

If it was a smart Hool, it'd start shooting.

Which it was.

Blaster fire melted the hatch, and three shots followed in quick succession as the elevator rapidly fell into the darkness below.

The bounty hunter switched to IR and dared a quick glance down into the plummeting car. The Hool was down there and moving like a wraith. Its cloak was thrown back, and its quills, quivering with deadly poison, were up and out.

Any sane person who'd run the length of the galaxy would think very seriously right now about not tangling with the homicidal and near-perfect murdering machine that was the average Hool. The lethal poison alone would deter even the most heavily armed. One drop was instant death. No medical treatment. No second chances. The average Hool carried about five liters. They called it blood.

But armor doesn't care about poison.

The bounty hunter dropped down into the lift.

The Hool hissed through needle-sharp teeth and attacked. Its spines flared in anger and its poison sacs engorged, ready to flood its victim's nervous system with mass quantities of lethal neurotoxin.

The bounty hunter smashed the alien in its snarling face with the butt of his heavy blaster.

It went down hard.

He seized the Hool's ridged throat within his armored grip... and squeezed.

"Looking for Junga," he said.

The thing gurgled and howled.

The bounty hunter checked the status display on the elevator. They would reach ground level in just a few moments.

"Junga," he whispered coldly. The voice that came through his helmet sounded like the glaciers of Catabatic grinding against one another for a thousand years at a time. "Where can I find him? Now!"

"*No baba gobaki, Junga!*" the thrashing thing pleaded. "*No baba gobaki, Junga! Hassoon,*" it guaranteed.

"You're lying," growled the bounty hunter. He raised the heavy blaster with one hand and jammed the muzzle into the Hool's gut.

"*Aiyeeee aiyeeee...*" it cried.

They were almost to the ground floor. Port security would get involved. That would not be good.

"*Asssim! Assim!*" the Hool bleated. "*Junga gotaki-ru… Jaris Cantina. Assim! Assim! Icka hassoon. Icka hassoon.*"

Software analytics assured the bounty hunter that the Hool was lying. Lying about something. But Jaris Cantina was a start. And… they were out of time.

Ground floor.

He broke the Hool's neck, hit the button for the top-most floor, and exited. Some freighter jockey tried to push his way in. The bounty hunter pushed him back out onto the concourse and continued forward as the elevator door closed and the carcass of the Hool was carried skyward.

Then everyone around the bounty hunter started to scream. The first Republican assault corvette had appeared over Ackabar. Already, landing transports were descending toward the port tower. Then two more appeared. Sirens began to wail.

It was like the end of the world. All over again.

06
Private Freighter *Indelible VI*
Bantam Prime

The bright green flash of the Republican MBT's main cannon lit up the cockpit an instant before the weapon boomed. The *Indelible VI* shuddered as its shield absorbed the blast, causing the comm relay wires in Keel's fingers to fall back into their panel, twisted together like a ghunnah's nest.

"It's never easy," Keel mumbled to himself. "Why can't it ever be easy?"

Ravi turned around in the navigator's chair. "It is very likely because you yourself are the cause of all these complications."

"That was rhetorical!" Keel found the white-and-marigold striped wire he'd been searching for and jammed it into the comm port, causing a brief spark and subsequent pop. The comm display went from steady red to pulsing blue. Keel gave a half grin.

BOOM!

The ship rocked from another blast. Keel hopped into his chair. "How much more of this can she take, Ravi?"

"At the current rate of bombardment, there is a seventy-five percent chance of shield failure within the next two direct hits. However, they are clearly shooting *under* the ship, at the rebels, so a shield failure would likely only mean damage to our landing struts."

"Well, at least there's that." Keel punched open the comm. "This is Captain Keel. Stop shooting at my ship!"

"Captain!" It was the princess. "Captain, thank you for increasing the airflow. Did you know the comms went out? The general and I—"

"Not to cut you off, Your Highness," Keel's voice took on the delicate and sophisticated airs of a courtesan, "but I need you—*desperately* need you—to get off the channel so I can ask the Republicans outside to stop shooting at my ship."

"Republicans? Did they follow us?"

Keel muted the comm. "Gah! Get off the channel, lady!" He looked to Ravi, who only shrugged.

Composing himself, Keel spoke gently into the dashboard input. "No, Your Highness. I don't think they know you're here. We're caught up in the middle of some sort of local skirmish and I need to let the Republic know we're not involved."

There was a pause. Keel could sense the princess and her general conferring through the static.

"Very well, Captain."

The blue faded to the soft green glow of standby. "Finally. Ravi, punch up all the Republican comms you've got. Except legionnaire. We don't want them to get curious."

"Okay, you are good to transmit."

"This is Captain Keel of the freighter *Loose Dutchman*. Stop shooting at me!"

"How did you get this comm clearance?" The voice belonged to a woman. Its icy firmness made clear that she was not the sort who took well to orders from civilians.

"It came with the cargo upon tender of freight."

"And what—"

Boom!

The thunderous cannon drowned out her voice and rocked the ship.

"Hold fire!" she snapped. "And what cargo might that be?"

"The rebels under my ship that *your* legionnaires were too sloppy to secure after the prisoner transfer. And that's *not* my fault!"

"I was under the impression Wraith himself would make the delivery."

Keel rolled his eyes. "Probably had more important things to do. He subcontracted it to me."

"Indeed." The voice on the other side of the comm was deliberate, pensive. "Your freighter's shields are quite remarkable to have absorbed four direct hits from a Republican Armorworks main battle tank."

With a devilish grin, Keel said, "You don't take a job in a war zone without a little extra padding, Officer..."

"Lieutenant Lynn Pratell. We'll have those rebels soon. Then we will impound your ship until your subcontracting claims are verified by the bounty hunter."

Keel glanced at his navigator. "I didn't think this through fully, Ravi."

Ravi paused, and Keel sensed his navigator was biting his tongue. "The legionnaires you... dispatched... were clearly only an attachment assigned to a Repub-Army force, if this R-A lieutenant is giving the orders. Perhaps the rebels could be directed to become more of a threat? As you know, unlike the Legion, R-A officers are typically more interested in avoiding failure than achieving success. If this could be done, there is a probability, meeting your typical risk threshold of sixty percent, that the Republic will be more receptive to your requests. Or perhaps they will blow us up."

Keel stared blankly at Ravi. "What'd you have in mind?"

Ravi keyed the ship's exterior speaker, the one used as a final warning to docking crews prior to takeoff, and spoke to the rebels. "You will have a better chance—thirteen percent—if you move away from the landing strut you are now using for cover. Please to be setting up behind the boulder at mark six. You will be able to fire without interference from the shields, and still have a sufficient barrier to protect you from the MBT. Target all of your fire on the third hover sled. That is typically the command sled in non-legionnaire Republican battle formations."

Watching the exterior cams from the cockpit monitor, Keel saw the rebels hesitate before finally re-staging themselves where Ravi instructed. Then they rolled out from behind the rock and unleashed a volley. The overwhelming fire of their stolen legionnaires' N-6 rifles slammed into the lightly armored Republican command sled, vivid orange-red blaster bolts peppering the hull. One shot penetrated the front windshield and struck the driver square in the chest. Another cut down the sled's roof gunner as he swiveled his turret toward the incoming fire. The black-

and-tan-camoed soldier slumped onto the long twin barrels of his weapon.

A small blast blossomed from beneath the sled—one of its twin-drive repulsor engines had failed and ignited. The nose of the hovering vehicle crashed down hard into the rocky ground as the rear repulsor whined in an attempt to keep its half of the transport craft off the ground.

A stream of crew members, including a red-haired woman in the smart, black uniform of a Republican lieutenant, jumped from the vehicle, dodging blaster fire as they ran for cover.

As the command sled's drooping nose skidded into the jagged stones of the landing zone, the other Republican sleds fixed their sights on the newly effective rebels and returned fire. The air crackled with energy and filled with the smell of ozone as blaster fire thickened. The remaining members of the attached squad of legionnaires moved to the downed command sled, returning fire with their own N-6s while two of them searched inside for survivors too injured to escape.

A rebel found a firing position on top of the boulder, and shot until the barrel of his rifle began to glow a hot orange. Try as they might, the Republic forces were unable to respond with effective fire thanks to the natural cover Ravi had maneuvered the rebels to. Turret gunners dropped back inside their sleds, and legionnaires frog-hopped one another in an attempt to get out of the line of fire. Two of the dreaded commandos ran for high crag, looking to fire down at the rebel attacker from an elevated position.

Their efforts weren't needed.

The MBT's 300mm main cannon slowly turned, leveled itself, and fired. The tank rocked backward as a bright green energy shell hurtled forward at twenty-five hundred meters per second.

"Whoa!" Keel shouted, his eyes fixed on the monitor. It was a direct hit, vaporizing half of the rebel, leaving only his legs on the rock. "Ravi, did you *see* that?"

Ravi just frowned at the monitors, no doubt calculating the swaying odds as he saw them from *Indelible VI's* external cams.

The remaining rebels took cover, pressing their backs against the rock, careful not to leave a centimeter of themselves exposed to the tank. Blasters bolts scorched the ground around the rock as the turret gunners and legionnaires resumed their fire.

One rebel, younger than the rest, practically a boy—his face covered in dirt, but free of stubble—panicked. His eyes wide and white with fear, he ran from the field of battle. His companions threw out their hands, imploring him to stop before he triggered the ener-chains' paralyzing surge of electricity. But when the soldier ran past the shackle's maximum allowed distance, nothing happened.

"I thought you said they were fitted with paralysis shackles?" Ravi said.

Keel shrugged. "Lookalikes. Cheaper. Besides, as long as they *thought* they were in them, they weren't going to try anything."

A legionnaire with master sergeant chevrons dropped to a knee and fired a single bolt that struck the runner between his shoulder blades. The rebel fell forward onto the rocky terrain. Other rebels peeked from cover and lit into the exposed master sergeant, dropping him with a flurry of blaster rifle fire. The MBT's main gun hammered the rebels' boulder, but the dense stone was impervious.

"I'm sorry," Ravi said, "but I do not understand why you freed the rebels and killed those legionnaires. I have seen you talk your way out of much worse."

Keel didn't respond. He watched the battle with the expressionless face of a professional poke-jack player examining his cards.

The two lead sleds separated from the disabled command sled, leaving it burning behind them, clogging the narrow road to the landing zone.

Keel snapped his fingers. "There."

He looked at the comm display. Ravi did the same, raising an eyebrow as it went from green to blue, signaling an incoming transmission. Keel punched open the audio channel. "Keel here."

"Captain Keel." It was the voice of the same lieutenant. She'd escaped from the slagged command sled. "Your freighter is in the path of seditious operatives hostile to the Republic. I'm ordering you to move it, or you will be fired upon in accordance with the Bikaine Act."

"Listen, sweetheart." Keel paused with a lopsided grin on his face, hoping to hear a hiss of disdain from the comm speaker. When the lieutenant remained stolidly professional, Keel continued. "The shields on this baby aren't the only things modified to handle a war zone."

Ravi pressed a button, causing two quad-burst turrets to drop from *Indelible*'s belly with a hydraulic whine. The turrets swiveled and took aim at the two sleds. The hovering vehicles, which had been moving slowly toward the *Six*, lurched to a stop.

"Here's the deal, Lieutenant Pratell. My shields are a long way from broken, but the concussion impact brought down my repulsors, and there are too many giant rocks around for me to take off at full throttle. So if you're thinking of opening fire before my maintenance bot can finish emergency repairs, understand now that while your MBT will eventually punch through, it'll be long after I tear you and your hover sleds apart. Fathom?"

Keel laced his hands behind his head and leaned back in his chair, utterly content with himself. "Watch, Ravi. Watch."

Ravi furrowed his brow. "*Six* is reporting that repulsors are fully operational."

"I'm *lying*, Ravi."

The comm box squawked. "Very well, *Captain*. We will hold our position until you are able to take off. Pratell out."

Keel leaned forward. "Not so fast, *Lieutenant*. I said emergency repairs, not full repairs. I expect Republic compensation for damages incurred."

"Captain Keel, the Republic paid Wraith for this operation in advance. I assume you were amply compensated as well. If not, perhaps you should better negotiate your next contract with the bounty hunter."

Speaking through a smile, Keel said, "You paying me for any damages sustained in transit *is* in my contract. A hundred thousand credits for repairs. Due now. Pay the bill and I'm out of your hair, Lieutenant."

There was anger and incredulity in Lieutenant Pratell's voice. "One hundred thousand credits. Which *happens* to be the ceiling of what I'm authorized to release at my rank?"

"How 'bout that." Keel eased back into his chair and looked at Ravi, who was stroking his beard with interest. An extra hundred grand would go a long way toward setting them up for whatever came next. Maybe Keel would spring for something next-gen when it came to the TT-3 bots that rendered Ravi off-ship. See what a code slicer could do with something smuggled out of Revolution Robotics.

The Republican lieutenant hesitated. "I... I'll need confirmation from Wraith."

"Unbelievable!" Keel threw his hands into the air. "Ravi, blow her sled up."

Ravi gave the captain a look, his finger hovering over the fire button.

Keel waved him off. "No, don't. Why is it that I have to deal with the only Republican officer concerned with saving tax dollars?" He keyed the comm. "Stand by for Wraith."

Rising from his chair, Keel pounded a fist on the top of the cockpit. "I'll have Wraith make contact. The trouble is worth an extra hundred grand. Transmission should come from somewhere in the Arogas system."

Ravi nodded as Keel left the cockpit.

As the captain reached the rumpled wool blanket, he shouted back down the corridor, "And why has every woman I've talked to today made my life so difficult?"

Ravi stared out the cockpit windows at the brilliant flashes of blaster fire between the rebels and Republicans. He heard the door to Keel's quarters whoosh open and closed, then turned on his audio-visual scanner to pick up the conversation inside the lieutenant's command sled. Wraith always communicated face-to-face.

Republic Combat Sled
Bantam Prime

The hair stood up on the back of Lieutenant Pratell's neck as the incoming call chime sounded from her newly appointed command sled's console. Fighting back the tremor raging along her spine and shoulders, she took a breath to make sure her voice would be clear and even. The Wraith only communicated—when he could be reached at all—face-to-face. Grizzled spacers said this was because the Wraith took hold of your soul when communicating. Science and reason had taught Pratell better than that. The soul was a bit of fanciful superstition.

More likely, Wraith wanted to read the face of whomever he spoke to. Use their fear, or whatever other tell he was supplied with over the holoscreens, to his advantage. So Pratell would remain calm and impassive, calling on all of her academy poise.

She cleared her throat, wondering for a moment if the sled's drivers took this as a sign of weakness or fear. "Bring him on screen."

The interior cabin lights dimmed as a hexagonal screen flickered to life, revealing the spectral visage of the Wraith.

The bounty hunter was positioned in front of his holocam so the screen was filled by his legionnaire-like helmet, a modification of the MK-100 series from a decade prior, the last set of *useful* armor. It was a ghostly shade of gray, reminiscent of that worn by the fabled Victory Company. Pratell could *feel* Wraith's eyes examining her, boring into her from behind the jet-black visor akin to the sunshields built into space fighters' helmets. A glint of light from the holocam reflected in his mask like a sunspot.

One of the drivers swallowed audibly. Both men worked the console in front of them, pretending not to notice who was before them.

If the rumors are true...

They gave sidelong glances to Pratell, probably spying to see if she, too, marveled at the sight of the infamous bounty hunter. Perhaps the last man in the galaxy who dealt openly with the Republic on his own terms.

"Wraith," Pratell began, cursing herself for the way her voice involuntarily wavered. "A certain Captain Keel is demanding that—"

"Pay him." Wraith's voice was cold and hard, grains of sand propelled into a duracrete wall in a cat-4 duster. He turned away from the camera.

The holofeed cut away abruptly, replaced by the rotating crest of the Republic. The cabin lights increased their glow.

The sled's drivers looked at Lieutenant Pratell expectantly.

"Route the necessary credits to Captain Keel."

"Yes, Lieutenant."

"The moment his ship takes off, cut down every last one of those rebels."

"Lieutenant? Our orders were to take possession of the Mid-Core Rebels for questioning."

"No. No survivors."

07

Lieutenant Pratell stepped from her combat sled and walked toward the remains of the deceased rebels. Their miserable resistance had been overcome the moment that incorrigible Captain Keel blasted off. In the end, the main battle tank wasn't even needed. Republic combat sleds had sped around the rock that sheltered the rebels and torn the seditious criminals apart with their heavy twin blaster cannons. Legionnaires now picked over the dead, searching for any actionable intelligence on the bodies of the traitors.

"Ma'am," came the crackling voice of a legionnaire through his helmet speaker, "I've found a survivor."

Unsure which legionnaire was speaking, she scowled at one kneeling next to the still-smoking carcass of a dead horned githid rebel, its lifeless square pupils fixed on the orange skies overhead.

"Then kill him," Pratell ordered. The very fact that she had to repeat her order caused her blood pressure to rise. It was bad enough the prisoner transfer had failed under *her* watch. Now she would have to defend her administration of orders to an efficiency bot upon return to Fort Bantam.

"Why was it necessary for you to repeat orders?" the bot would ask from behind a half-moon-shaped desk, there to

make the whole process seem somehow more... normal. As if the bot kept hours inside the debrief office instead of powered down in some closet.

"How might you have delivered your instructions so as to leave no doubt of your intentions?"

"Do you find yourself questioning your own orders?"

"How might this hesitation have been detrimental to the Republic?"

"How did..."

"Why did..."

"If you were in the place of..."

Pratell gritted her teeth, almost wishing the legionnaire would challenge her. Give her a reason to shout and yell. To show that her rank was not to be questioned.

"No, ma'am. It's one of ours." The legionnaire speaking was not the one she was looking at. Since her childhood, she had never seemed able to pinpoint where noises came from. Bumps in the night might be from the streets below her parents' high-rise, or behind the closet door. She never could figure out which.

She turned to where two of the three dead legionnaires lay—the ones that had been dead when she'd arrived. The incompetents killed by the rebels.

One of the two, LS-19 according to his armor, was being attended to by a regular Repub-Army medic and another legionnaire. They removed his helmet and applied skin packs to the blaster-ravaged flesh on his neck.

LS-19 attempted to speak, but could only manage a sickly gurgle. A mixture of blood and saliva bubbled from his lips.

"Easy, buddy," his legionnaire comrade soothed, squeezing the dying man's hand. "You'll be top gear in no time."

The medic's brows furrowed in confusion. "He's panicking."

The legionnaire hissed through his speakers. "Leejes don't panic."

"Well, he won't stop tapping his fingers against my wrist. I'm going to sedate him."

"No." The legionnaire—he was marked as a corporal, but Pratell could never remember their numbers or little nicknames—pushed the medic aside and bent close to the wounded man.

Pratell watched with interest as the dying legionnaire tapped rapidly on his companion's reflective armored forearm. She could hear the rhythmic noise of it, like fingers drumming on a table.

"You're sure?" asked the legionnaire attending to LS-19. By now the other surviving shock troopers were gathered around their dying comrade.

"Sure of what?" Pratell had no idea what was going on, but judging by the way the legionnaires behaved, it was important. She received no reply.

The tapping slowed... slowed... and stopped. The arms of the wounded legionnaire went limp and were gently lowered onto his chest.

"Sure of what?" she asked again.

"It's a non-verbal code we learn at academy," the legionnaire corporal said, rising to his feet.

"And what did he communicate?"

"He kept saying... double cross."

A flush of hot anger reddened Pratell's face. She fought back tears of frustration. She knew—she *knew*—the captain was hiding something. She assumed it was just bluffing a false ship ID. But to cut down a trio of legionnaires and paint it as a failure—*her* failure—in order to extort money from the Republic...

She turned and ran to the nearest combat sled. She passed the cockpit and moved to the transport section to activate the comm, not wanting the drivers to hear her conversation. "This is Lieutenant Pratell. I need to speak with Commander Ardent immediately."

The wait seemed interminable before the front display flickered to reveal the bloated commander.

He eyed Pratell suspiciously. "What, pray tell, requires me being rousted from my evening meal?"

"Commander, I have actionable intelligence that the freighter captain who oversaw transfer of prisoners in fact *released* the prisoners, resulting in the deaths of multiple legionnaires. He also extorted... a substantial sum from the Republic and forced a confrontation that resulted in the death of all the Mid-Core Rebel prisoners."

Commander Ardent tugged at the corners of his mouth. "That is incorrect, Lieutenant." His voice was cold, correcting. "The prisoners transferred to us had already succumbed to wounds sustained in the surprise attack. The captain delivered them without incident. The legionnaires were killed in a freak sled accident. Is that clear?"

"But, sir, this captain is a menace to the Republic. The way he brazenly—"

"Lieutenant Pratell!" shouted the commander, his face red and glistening with sudden perspiration. "I have worked and scraped to get within sniffing distance of the mid-core, but look around you. This is still very much galaxy's edge. Officers who fail to complete their tasks are only reassigned farther toward the edge. I will *not* let that happen!" He stood up, his portly gut filling the holoscreen before the cam realigned with his face. "I will *not!*"

Pratell knew better than to press. She held her peace as the commander regained control of his emotions.

"Lieutenant, I thought we understood one another. Your career can't afford a... *failure* of this magnitude. Now, I only want what's best for my most promising officer."

You only want to be sure no one asks why you didn't oversee the prisoner transfer yourself, per our orders. Pratell swallowed the urge to vocalize this barb, opting instead to try one more time—delicately. "Sir, yes, but the *Inscrutable* is between us and the desert moon. If we hail them, they could intercept Keel before—"

"Enough, Lieutenant." Commander Ardent waved away the suggestion. "I won't risk the questions and reports that would follow. Now, I have guests waiting at table for my return. I expect your report to reflect the circumstances... appropriately."

"Yes, Commander."

The screen went black, and Pratell bit her lip. There was more than one way to put down this Captain Keel.

Indelible VI
Hyperspace

"Here, Princess, take my hand." Captain Keel reached into the smuggling hold and pulled the princess out of the sweltering space. The general held up his own hand for assistance from Keel, but the captain promptly turned to focus his attention on the princess, leaving the man in the hold with his hand raised awkwardly.

"Thank you," said the princess. "And please, call me Leenah."

"Sure, Leenah."

The princess possessed a near-human physiology. Her bright pink skin and red tendrils—hanging from her head like hair—were the only features that outed her as a non-human. Keel was unfamiliar with the species, but found the princess attractive enough, especially when she took in a lungful of *Indelible VI*'s cool, filtered air. Keel was sure it had been hot in that hold *before* he had placed the wool blanket over the seams. Her white and teal utility suit was soaked in sweat.

"There's a shower down the corridor if you need to use it," he offered. "Right next to the navigator's quarters. Ravi doesn't actually need his own room, so it's yours until we reach Pellek. Not that it's a long jump." He looked over his shoulder. The general was awkwardly hoisting himself out of the hold, struggling as he threw his leg up.

The princess gave Keel a warm smile. "Thank you, Captain. You've been most selfless. Hiding us from the Republic and now offering your accommodations."

Keel matched her smile with a roguish grin of his own. "I do try."

"There's something I'd like to know," said the general as he dusted himself off. He stood a head shorter than Keel, and was young. Far too young to have such a lofty rank, unless the Mid-Core Rebels were desperate for *any* sort of leadership. Or unless he had a wealthy father or patron who had placed him higher in command than he deserved. Keel made a mental note to stay on the young man's good side if he showed any of the telltale signs of good breeding and accustomed wealth.

He held open his palms. "Ask away, General...?"

"Lem Parrish. What exactly was going on outside while we were stuck in that hold? It sounded like a full-scale war."

With a somber nod, Keel puffed out his breath. "Yeah, it was pretty bad." He clapped his hands together and bent down to put the deck plate covering the smuggler's hold back in place. "But that's water under the crossing!"

"Captain, are we still in any danger from the Republic?" The princess placed her hand lightly on Keel's shoulder.

Standing up to look into her violet eyes, Keel said, "No. We passed the Republic frigate *Inscrutable* without issues. I waited until we were safely in hyperspace before letting you out of your hidey-hole."

"I suppose we owe you a debt of gratitude for saving our lives *twice*, Captain," said Parrish.

"Nah, you don't owe me anything, General. Although there may be some repairs necessary for the shield generators..."

Parrish nodded.

"Maybe I can take a look?" suggested the princess.

Keel rubbed the back of his neck. The thought of anyone but him looking around his ship didn't sit well.

Think of the big picture...

"Of course you can see the ship, Your Highness."

Keel took Leenah gently by the hand. It was surprisingly callused. Probably some sort of evolutionary byproduct. He escorted her toward the refresh room, leaving the general to his own devices in the small common area by the smuggler's hold. "We'll drop out of hyperspace and arrive in the Pellek system soon, though. It's a quick jump. After we dock, I'll give you a tour before heading into Tannespa. There are some supplies I need to get, and then I'll take you on to the port of your choosing."

The door opened with a chime and a pneumatic whoosh. "Thank you, Captain," Leenah said as she stepped across the threshold. "The MCR owes you a debt of gratitude."

"The honor is all mine, I assure you." Keel bowed, eliciting a radiant smile from the princess. She clearly enjoyed the royal treatment.

Good. One more admirer stowed in another corner of the galaxy won't hurt things, that's for sure.

The trick was keeping those admirers from running into each other. Like that time at the under-ocean gaming palace on Kashir. Keel winced at the memory.

Keel returned to the common area, where he found the general at *Indelible*'s workstation, examining a pair of calibrated spanners.

"Careful with those, huh?" Keel said, adjusting the holster on his hip. "I just got them spaced properly for my Intec." He patted the blaster at his side. "Took me the better part of a jump from Ackabar to Wendall Prime, so..."

General Parrish placed the spanners back on the workstation carefully. "You know, Leenah really *would* like to look at your shield generators."

Keel scoffed. "What? Out of curiosity? I can just show her the owner's manual." He put his hands on his hips and leaned his face down to meet Parrish's. "I don't like people looking around my ship."

"She's a good fleet mechanic."

"Who? The *princess*?"

The youthful general smiled, but his reply was drowned out by a ship-wide chime, followed by Ravi's voice.

"Captain Keel, I am thinking you should come up here right away!"

Keel furrowed his brow and strode up the corridor to the cockpit. "You might want to buckle in, General," he said over his shoulder.

As if to emphasize the point, the ship lurched. The *Indelible VI*, like most nimble starships, had gravity and motion equalizers, but quick, jerky motions, like evasive maneuvers or collisions, happened too fast for full compensation.

The cockpit door swooshed open at Keel's approach, revealing Ravi working the flight controls frantically. They were out of hyperspace, newly arrived to the Pellek system. Bright flashes lit up the cockpit. Searing green lasers, fired from an extreme distance, were impacting harmlessly against the shields.

Keel jumped into his seat and flipped an array of switches. "Fly or shoot, Ravi?"

"This is depending on who is firing at us. I am not comfortable firing at legitimate authority figures, as you—"

"Ravi! Focus!"

The holographic navigator twitched his mustache. "*Six*'s sensors have identified four K-13 Preyhunters flying toward us from the planet itself."

"Those are old starfighters," Keel mumbled to himself. Preyhunters were two-winged snub fighters with a single blaster cannon at the end of each wing. They were capable of atmospheric and space flight, and though old, they had shield tech and a single baryon torpedo apiece.

He pulled the ship up and looped it around until they were heading straight for the enemy craft. With a double tap of a red triangular button, the forward cam feed superimposed itself over the cockpit window with a magnified view of the starfighters. They were beat up, their brown-and-yellow finishes chipped and dinged to reveal the gunmetal gray hull beneath. "Yeah, that's them."

"Who?" Ravi asked.

"Pellekanese pirates. See?" He pointed out a magnified logo on one of the ships—a golden oak with a horned Ridoran skull in the foreground.

"Yes, I am seeing," Ravi said. "In such an instance I am comfortable manning the weapon systems."

"Good. I'm a better pilot anyway."

The flashes continued to erupt harmlessly around the cockpit as the four Preyhunters fired. But the distance was shrinking, and after the pounding the shields had taken from that Republican MBT, the laser blasts would begin to do some damage before much longer.

"Ravi, how many concussion warheads do we have left?"

"Three of six."

"Only need one. Fire right at the middle of the formation."

Ravi primed *Indelible*'s missile launcher. "They will be having ample time in which to dodge."

"That's the plan, Ravi. Divide and destroy."

With a perfunctory nod, Ravi fired the concussion missile. It streaked toward the oncoming Preyhunters, its single blast drive making it look like a pale blue comet. The pirates took evasive maneuvers, scattering like a nest of spooked gronks.

"It's a wonder they didn't slam into each other and save us some trouble," Keel said as he looped the *Six* into a corkscrew turn to follow the leftmost Preyhunter. The maneuver lined up another starfighter underneath them. "Ravi, belly guns!"

The *Indelible VI* shuddered from the rapid fire of its twin quadburst turrets. Blazing red energy blasts ripped through the Preyhunter's left wing, leaving scorched holes and exposed circuitry.

"Did you get 'em?" Keel asked, keeping his focus on the pirate in front of him. The pilot rolled and banked in an attempt to escape.

"Down, but not all the way out, Captain."

"Let me take care of his friend first..."

On the forward window, *Six*'s targeting computer laser-projected the image of the enemy craft drifting through the ship's crosshairs. The image brightened and flashed as a high-pitched beep indicated a lock. Keel fired the forward blaster cannons slave-linked to his flight control. Red blaster-bursts spit out in rapid succession, slamming into the Preyhunter's single ion thruster. The small snub fighter erupted into a flaming ball of incandescent gas.

"Ha ha!" crowed Keel.

"The other two are behind us," Ravi said, his face betraying no emotion. "I am attempting to hit them with the tail turret."

A barrage of enemy laser fire caused the *Six* to shake as its shields absorbed the energy.

"That's not good." Keel decelerated and steered the ship down, as it were, at a ninety-degree angle. One of the pursuing craft failed to compensate, presenting itself to Ravi in a lazy, wide arc. The navigator fired, making the pilot's mistake a fatal one.

"The other ship is still being in hot pursuit, Captain. I am thinking this is the ace of the pirate crew."

Keel continued his dive, spiraling and rolling in an attempt to avoid the unrelenting laser fire. "Thank you, Ravi, for pointing these things out."

The *Six* again shuddered as blasts found their shields. For a split second, the main lights dimmed across the starship.

The onboard comm chimed. "Captain, is everything all right? Is it the Republic?"

"Can it, General!" Keel shouted. He turned to Ravi. "Gotta shake this guy. Hold on."

A visual appeared in the upper corner of the cockpit window. The princess, wrapped only in a white towel, her naked pink shoulders visible. She struggled to remain on her feet as *Indelible* waggled and swung its way in and out of laser fire.

"C-captain!" Leenah shouted before falling head over heels. Her feet and a billowing towel were all that remained visible on the feed.

The Preyhunter fired again. *Indelible* rocked violently, and the lights winked out again. When they came back on, they were noticeably dimmer.

"We have lost shields!" Ravi said, almost in disbelief. "You were supposed to be dodging!"

"It's not my fault!" Keel protested. "She *distracted* me."

"We will suffer a potential hull breach if such a deluge of laser fire is to strike—"

"I know! I know!"

Keel's mind raced for a maneuver that might shake the stolid attacker. "Hang on. Just hang on."

His mind made up, he put all power into his engines. The sudden burst of speed pushed him back in his seat. He couldn't imagine how Leenah might be sliding around on the refresh room's floor. Actually, he *could* imagine. *Was* imagining. He shook the images from his head. He needed to focus or they'd all be vaporized.

As the *Indelible VI* sped off, the Preyhunter adjusted its own speed, not letting its quarry escape. The reality was that the *Six* could easily outrun a K-13, and Keel expected the pirate pursuing him to think that was just what was happening.

He guessed right.

The Preyhunter's pilot fired repeatedly in a desperate attempt to disable or destroy the escaping Naseen light freighter. Keel dipped and rose as though he were tracing the pattern of a wavelength. The Preyhunter followed every move, each time just missing the freighter.

"Now!" Keel yelled to himself. He pulled the freighter up hard, maintaining such a sharp turn that he doubled back and zoomed directly toward the oncoming Preyhunter. Lulled into the belief that this was just another patterned dodge, the pirate exposed the belly of his starship for a split second. He realized his mistake and compensated, but the opening was all Keel needed. He and Ravi both fired, vaporizing the ship moments before the *Indelible VI* shot through the ball of flame where the pirate once was.

Adjusting course, Keel continued at full speed toward the last position of the final, damaged Preyhunter.

Ravi stared at his captain for some time before Keel, who was smiling at his own exploits, looked his way.

"What's that look?" asked Keel.

"Had even one single shot connected during your head-on run, the odds of our destruction were eighty-four percent."

"*Had*, Ravi. I didn't give him the chance. No need to worry."

"I am finding it difficult to do anything but worry, sir." Ravi probed with the *Six*'s sensor arrays. "The remaining Preyhunter is attempting to reenter Pellek's atmosphere. It should be within homing missile distance before it can escape." He switched off the missile's launch safety.

"No, no," Keel said, waving his hand. "I want him to go down there. We're gonna follow him, see where he lands. Kill his family. All his friends. His dog, if he has one."

"Oh," Ravi said, his voice rich with sarcasm. "A detour for vengeance. How enjoyable. Yes, this is precisely the sort of thing we should do with no operable shields and two known rebels. I am wondering why I have not thought of this before. And what if we are knowing these pirates? Lao Pak is Pellek..."

"We should kill his schoolteachers too, if we can find them."

"I will be refraining from all the killing. I cannot leave the ship, if you are recalling?"

"I'll kill them for you."

"Please to be leaving me out of this."

"Suit yourself, Ravi. Suit yourself."

08

"Captain Keel, where are you going?"

General Parrish was on the captain's heels the moment he stepped from the cockpit. He had apparently been waiting for Keel just outside the single-man blast door separating the pilot and navigator from the rest of the ship. They'd landed, and the youthful rebel would now be demanding answers.

"Outside." Keel tightened the holster around his thigh before removing his Intec blaster. He took out the weapon's charge pack and inspected it in *Indelible*'s bright overhead lighting. Satisfied, he shoved the charger back in place with a slap of his palm. "Ravi, is there a welcoming party?"

The navigator spoke through the comms. "Just the lone Preyhunter at the adjacent landing pad. The pilot appears to be doing its post-flight cycle."

"Lao Pak?"

"I am seeing no sign of Lao Pak or the rest of his pirates, Captain. But there is a seventy-four percent chance he is scrambling to meet us. We came in very fast for landing."

"That was the idea." Keel lifted his palm to engage the quick disembark ramp. "That little twerp is going to pay for double-crossing me."

General Parrish placed himself in front of Keel. The captain looked down at him, a frown on his face. Had the young general always been this short, or was he only now noticing?

"Captain Keel... Lao Pak? Pirates? I need to know what's going on." It was a thin request more than a command. An order given by someone not used to making them. Or at least not when the person on the receiving end had no compulsion to obey.

Keel just barely resisted the urge to roll his eyes. The general, the princess. They could still be worth something.

"That's right, General. Pirates ambushed us once we completed the jump to Pellek. We followed a survivor to Lao Pak's little pirate den. He's *supposed* to be a friend. I'm going out to thank him for the welcoming party." Keel slapped the ramp release and closed his eyes as the white cloud of gases hissed with the quick drop of *Indelible*'s plank.

"Do you need backup?" The general showed a gleaming, chrome-plated pistol on his hip. It was an expensive model, shot accurately enough, but was woefully underpowered.

"No." Keel stomped down the ramp, calling over his shoulder, "But you can come if you want."

The general drew his pistol, holding it upward in both hands like he'd seen Planetary Police do as he ran down the ramp after Keel. His footsteps echoed in time with his rapid heartbeat. The planetary atmosphere was arid and seemed to wick away the moisture from the creases of his mouth. He could feel the heat of the sun through his boots. The landing pad itself was clearly made from scrapped freighter hulls, pounded flat and welded together. Captain Keel's ship landing here was like putting a priggot seed on a dinner plate. This sort of a pad was made to support the truly massive deep space haulers.

No telling what a pirate might reel in.

Parrish looked around with curious interest. There was a spaceport off in the extreme distance, barely visible behind shimmering waves of heat. Closer was some sort of... compound. That must be the pirate den Keel mentioned. A gross amalgam of portable duracrete buildings, repurposed freight sleds, and the occasional cargo hold of some derelict, all welded or riveted into an oddly symmetrical structure.

Stepping in a half-circle, Parrish observed old, single-man anti-fighter emplacements. Unoccupied. In fact, the whole compound seemed abandoned. Which was a good thing.

Gathering his wits, the general looked for Keel. The captain, blaster still in its holster, was walking with balled fists toward a damaged Preyhunter starfighter.

The Preyhunter's triangular canopy opened straight up, revealing a particularly surly looking Drusic. The black-haired sentient primate filled nearly every cubic centimeter of the small snub fighter's cockpit. It snorted as Keel approached, then let out a growl. It had alarmingly sharp eyeteeth.

Parrish fumbled with his blaster while Keel closed the distance between himself and the ship.

"Look, Keel..." the Drusic said in a deep, rumbling voice. "Lao Pak sent us up. Nothing personal. Besides, you won. Shot us to hell." The pilot extended a massive, hairy paw as a peace offering.

Grabbing hold of the gigantic mitt, Keel swung himself up onto the nose of the Preyhunter so he stood directly above the muscular Drusic. "Nothing personal? Then neither is *this*!" He threw his elbow into the Drusic, just above the primate's eye, and followed up with a barrage of punches to the creature's face.

Keel knew that all this effort was only enough to daze a being of this size and toughness. So he was prepared when the Drusic let out a primal scream and raised both fists in the air. He jumped nimbly backward.

Confined by the cockpit, the Drusic rose to a semi-standing position. It brought down both fists like twin sledgehammers on the spot Keel had occupied only seconds before. The Preyhunter shook from the impact. The Drusic lifted its boulder-like fists for another attack, revealing two dents in the already beat-up starship.

Keel jumped up, grabbed the open canopy, and brought it smashing down over the head of the Drusic with such force that the ore-glass shattered. Of course, the thick skull of the Drusic went a long way in helping that to happen. The pilot slumped unconscious in the cockpit. Keel keyed in a rapid sequence on the Preyhunter's control dash.

"Captain Keel!" a voice called in the distance. Not the general's. Someone else. Keel turned to see a pirate approaching with a pair of Hool bodyguards at his side and the general in tow. They had already apprehended and disarmed the youthful rebel.

"What poor Ishm'mark ever do to you, huh?"

Keel jumped off the nose of the Preyhunter. He squinted in the sunlight at the leather-draped pirate, his black hair in long braids. "Lao Pak."

"Not so fast, Keel." Lao Pak took a worried step backward, bumping into one of his menacing Hools. "You slow down now. You keep coming this way and I have Seepa prick your friend. Terrible bad way to die."

The Hool hissed and bristled its venomous spines. A dry, panicky *glug* came from Parrish's throat.

"So kill him," Keel said, advancing toward the pirates.

Seepa jerked Parrish toward him, but Lao Pak raised a grease-stained hand. It was trembling. "He no important?"

Keel knew what Lao Pak was thinking. The pirate had overplayed his hand. That, or Keel just didn't care about this particular crew member.

"Okay, Keel. Ha-ha time over. No more kidding. I let your friend go... this time."

With another drooling hiss, the Hool threw Parrish to the ground. The general scampered toward Keel.

"So okay, Keel? We friend now? Like old time?" Lao Pak continued his nervous withdrawal, repeatedly bumping into the snarling Hools, who looked nowhere near as keen to retreat. But these idiot monsters didn't know who they were dealing with.

Keel reached toward his blaster, eliciting a yell from Lao Pak, who ducked in expectation. But the Hools apparently knew enough about Keel to have their surplus N-4 rifles ready. They leveled them at Keel.

His hand hovering above his blaster, Keel stood ready to draw. Ravi could tell him what the likelihood was that Keel could drop them both—but even without the numbers, the captain felt confident. Mostly.

Not yet.

Keel relaxed his arm. "Why'd you try and blow up my ship, Lao Pak?"

The cowering pirate straightened and mouthed a quiet prayer of thanks. "Keel, that not personal, you know."

"If one more person tells me it's not personal... You *shot* at my *ship*!"

Lao Pak held up his hands. "Only a little. Big money bounty, Keel! Had to try." The pirate looked behind him at the compound. "Came on black channel. Everybody see it.

How can I say no to hundred thousand credits? My crew mutiny if I no try." He shook his finger at the sky, like a professor giving a lecture. "Being pirate king very hard."

The price caught Keel's attention. "Wait. A hundred grand? For who, the princess or the general?"

Lao Pak pointed at Parrish. "He general? Of what, nursery school?"

Parrish blushed and threw his shoulders back. "I'm a general of the Mid-Core Rebellion." His tone was proud, a bit wounded.

"Oh." Lao Pak gave a dismissive wave. "He just another pirate."

An aggrieved look came across the general's face. "The MCR are *not* pirates."

Behind Keel, the Preyhunter's engine primed. No one except Keel seemed to notice.

Good.

Lao Pak smiled, revealing several gold teeth. "You say no pirate. I say..." He began to count on his fingers. "Kublar, New Penda, Rhyssis Wan..."

General Parrish looked down. "Those were a long time ago. The MCR has changed. We're a united force for good."

"*You* say." Lao Pak looked to Keel, as if appealing to him for help in the discussion. "I say MCR pirates. Only they lie about it to feel better. Republic say traitor, so who care?"

"*I* say," Keel interjected, trying to regain control of the conversation, "you are going to tell me whether the bounty was for the general or the princess. Or both." Another hundred thousand credits sounded pretty good. Even if he did end up having to give a cut to Lao Pak.

The pirate shook his head. "Mid-Core general not worth money. Too many fakes. Have money for MCR? Here, you general now. Look at you." Lao Pak put his finger on Parrish's face, leaving an oily black smudge when Parrish pulled away. "You family rich, I bet. You give money to be general. But so young, probably you not even fight." A contemplative, philosophical look came across Lao Pak's face. "*Is* your family rich? Where they live?"

To his credit, Parrish refused to dignify that accusation with an answer.

"So the princess..." Keel said, steering the discussion back to his own interests.

The general laughed. "It wouldn't be *her*."

"Why not?" asked Keel, facing Parrish with his hands on his hips.

Lao Pak stepped forward. "It you, Keel."

"Shut up, Lao Pak. Why not, Parrish?"

"Because she's not a *real* princess. She's from the Endurian system. They're *all* princes and princesses there. Have been for years. They all get the title. Equality, you know."

That explained what Ravi had been laughing about.

Keel put his hands on his hips and glowered down at the general. "You two certainly *carried on* like she was an important princess."

General Parrish took a step back. "You seemed more interested in helping when you thought..." He shrugged.

With a growl, Keel asked Lao Pak, "How much is the going bounty for a rebel princess?"

The pirate tugged thoughtfully at his wispy mustache. "I can find out. *If* we friends again. Not as much as for you, though."

Keel nodded. "Well, find out. I don't have all day. Wait! What do you mean for *me*?"

"See, that's why I had to!" Lao Pak exclaimed. "Big money from black channel. Dead or alive, she say."

"And you figured killing me would be easier."

"No!" Lao Pak sounded wounded. "Not *kill*. I wanted your ship, too."

Keel's hand went again to his blaster.

Lao Pak shouted, "No! No! You kill my pilots! You beat up Ishm'mark! Blow up my starfighters! We even! You pay me back!"

The damaged Preyhunter suddenly roared to life. The delayed takeoff sequence Keel had entered into the console was now active. The starfighter blasted away from the landing pad and barrel rolled through the air. Its Drusic pilot was flung from the ship as the Preyhunter shot toward the pirate compound, leaving a vapor trail behind it. With a sound like a glacier breaking apart, the craft penetrated a duracrete building and exploded.

Keel used the distraction to draw his pistol and shoot both Hools in the head, dropping the bodyguards in a crumpled heap.

Hools. Good riddance.

Lao Pak screamed and threw his hands up in the air.

"Relax," Keel said, holstering his blaster. "Nothing personal. *Now* we're even."

"That not even! That worse! Hools expensive!" Lao Pak folded his arms across his chest. "You lucky everybody else shot down or have shore leave in Tannespa."

"Fine." Keel looked back at his ship. "I'll give you the *princess* to turn in for whatever the Republic gives you for her." He looked to General Parrish, expecting an objection, but if the general had any, he was keeping them to himself.

"That nothing," said Lao Pak. "They give nothing. I sell her to Gomarii slavers."

Keel shrugged. "Fine. But first you need to tell me who put a bounty on my head."

"Oh, you need your friend Lao Pak's help?" The pirate looked around, taking in the destruction. "Maybe you pay for help? Cost me so much money."

"Lao Pak…"

"Okay, okay. Like you don't know." Lao Pak reached into his coat, then paused with his hand inside. "I just grab datapad. Don't shoot me, okay?"

The pirate pulled a rugged datapad skinned in a thick protective case. He tapped the screen a few times and held it up for Keel to see. It was a bounty notice, featuring a picture of the *Indelible VI* and a male silhouette with Captain Keel's name beneath it. No photo. That was good. The enormous, flashing words—"100,000 credits"—were not as good.

Keel shook his head. *How did this happen?*

He strained to think of some unhappy crime lord who would be angry enough to hang that many credits over his head. Sure, there were plenty of individuals in the galaxy who were less than fond of him, but with Wraith in the picture… they wouldn't dare put something like this out. Would they?

A separate black silhouette sat in the upper corner of the bounty notice—a holovid. Usually these were heavily encrypted and distorted recordings; black channel bounties were illegal, and those putting them out were well advised to remain anonymous. But sometimes, if you squinted hard enough, you could pick up some details.

"Bring that up," Keel ordered. "I wanna see if I can piece this together."

Lao Pak gave Keel a crooked smile. "You want see the *decrypted* holovid?"

Keel raised his eyebrows. "You've got someone who decrypted black channel encoding?"

"Oh, yeah. He real good." Lao Pak tapped his dirty fingernails across the screen, shielding it from the sun with his other hand. Keel and Parrish came around and looked over his shoulder to watch.

An image of Lieutenant Pratell appeared on the datapad. Her red hair was let down, contrasting with her formal military bearing. However, her black uniform—a dead giveaway with the encryption broken—was clearly visible. "This contract is open to all bounty hunters and privateers located in the Pellek system," she said. "It is my belief that one Captain Keel is arriving shortly in a heavily modified Naseen light freighter. I did not make visual contact, but am transmitting holos of the ship, designated *Loose Dutchman*, though this is probably a false identification. Captain Keel, a seasoned liar, is responsible for a number of deaths and should be considered highly dangerous.

Again, the bounty is one hundred thousand credits. Dead or alive. Expiration: thirty-six standard hours."

"Is that a Republic officer?" Parrish asked in wonder. "This needs to get to the MCR. It would be a major communications victory if we could prove that the Republic has gotten so crooked that they're using black channel bounties to wipe out enemies. I mean, we've known this for years, but with proof..."

"She not bad-looking," observed Lao Pak. "What you do to her? Marry her and run away with all the money?"

Keel frowned. The lieutenant must've figured out what he was up to. Still, the fact that she had come after him on the black channel meant that the Republic didn't deem it worth investigating; truth and justice ceased to matter once a government became invested only in itself. And with only a thirty-six-hour window, he'd be fine. If she pressed beyond that, he'd leak the transmission and ruin her career.

"This new kid you've got decrypting black channel files. Is he here?" Keel hoped he hadn't blown him up when the Preyhunter flew into the pirate compound.

"No. He at Tannespa. I tell him find cheap girl, get drunk. But guess what he do instead? He alone building new bot when I tell him to decrypt message. He smart but boring."

"Where in Tannespa?"

Lao Pak's eyes shifted from left to right. "So what you do to that girl, huh? Why she hate you so much? You easy to hate, but she *really* hate you. You break her heart? Cold feet and leave at wedding altar?"

"Lao Pak," Keel said evenly, "you're changing the subject."

"This better subject! What she see in you anyway? You not *that* handsome."

"What's the kid's name?"

"I forget."

"Lao Pak..."

The pirate grimaced. "I tell you, you steal him for your crew. Cost me even more money."

Keel held up his hands. "Relax. I'm not gonna steal him, I just want to see if he can modify some TT-3 bots for Ravi."

"You promise?"

"Cross my heart."

"Ha! You lie too much for promise to work." Lao Pak's dirty fingers tapped furiously across the datapad, leaving a greasy smear. He entered passkey after passkey, digging further and further into the system. Keel couldn't hope to keep up.

"You good buddy with Wraith." Lao Pak winked at Keel. "I send you to kid for TT-3 bot, but you do this job for me, split sixty-forty. You get big portion."

"What's the job?" Keel tried to look at the screen, but Lao Pak hid it against his chest.

"Not in front of boy general."

"Go wait in the ship," Keel ordered.

Parrish looked as though he wanted to object, but quietly walked back toward the landing pad.

"So what's the job?"

Lao Pak spoke in a hushed voice, though the only beings around them were two dead Hools. "Big, big, big job. I tell you money first."

Keel nodded. Starting out with the money had a way of cutting to the chase. "How much?"

"Two hundred and fifty..." Lao Pak let the number settle on Keel's mind before adding the game changer: "... million."

"*Million*?" Keel looked instinctively for the absent Ravi, to confirm that his ears did indeed hear such a staggering sum. "For what?"

"Spot and report. Some big shot warlord who just return from beyond galaxy's edge."

"*Spot and report*? You're telling me I get two hundred and fifty million, and I don't even have to *apprehend* the guy?"

"You no get two hundred fifty," Lao Pak snapped. "You get half. We partners. And you just find him. Big Republican admiral want to meet with big shot, so no apprehend, no kill. Think you can keep gun in holster?" He laughed. "There is first time for everything."

Keel made a face. "Republic? Is this another black channel job?"

"No. This big. Big, big, big. This come from contact of contact of contact. Straight from admiral. No one know. *I* not supposed to know. But pirate kings, we know lots. They want to find Wraith for this job, but won't risk open contact. He hard to find in person. But *I* know *you*. That the other reason I not tell pilots to kill you. I trade your bounty if you convince Wraith to capture whoever the admiral is after."

Keel was only half-listening to Lao Pak's rambling. *Two hundred fifty million...* That many credits were always worth investigating. Besides, it wasn't like he and Ravi had anything lined up now that the raid was finished. And he didn't even have to catch the guy, just locate him. Although he did kind of enjoy the catching part.

He was about to ask for details when his comm chimed, and Ravi's voice buzzed, "Captain Keel, I am wondering why the general was just telling me that you are to be letting the Princess Leenah be sold by Lao Pak?"

"I may have overdone it a bit down here," Keel said, looking back at the smoke rising from the pirate's compound. "Besides, she's not a real princess. And you knew it!"

"Yes, but she has already repaired *Six*'s shields."

Keel shook his head. That couldn't be right. "What?"

"Yes. It is unlike anything I have ever been seeing. I am thinking they are stronger now."

A mechanic like that might be useful. And she wasn't bad on the eyes. Better-looking than Ravi, anyway.

"Okay, Ravi. We'll keep her on board. Send the general back out. Tell him I need his help." Keel looked to Lao Pak. "Looks like you get to add a general to your pirate crew. I'm sure he'll fit in fine."

Lao Pak shook his head. "No! I want mechanic girl. You cause lot of damage. Cost me too much money."

"Shut up, Lao Pak."

The pirate kicked the blaster rifle of one of the dead Hools at his feet and crossed his arms in a pouting scowl.

"Okay, fine. I take little boy general. Teach him to be man. But this make us friends again."

Keel gave a lopsided smile. "Best friends. Now, supposing I can get Wraith to join me on this, who is this warlord we're after? I need a name at least. And where do we start looking? It's a big galaxy. I need more information."

"That not my fault. You talk too much. Interrupt me before I finish. I send you name. Goth Sullus. I never heard of him. He not so big shot, huh? Pirate king not even know his name, how tough can he be? But he disappear, so admiral say you find some dead family, dead family lead you to target. Family name..." The pirate checked his datapad. "Maydoon. I—"

Keel cut in. "How will finding a dead family—"

"You listen, you get answer! You flap gums, you hear only Keel mouth smacking. No, maybe I not tell you. You bad listener. Lao Pak have better idea. I send info to Ravi. He smarter than you. Also, I tell Ravi where to find Garret. He the coder." Lao Pak raised a finger. "But you no steal him!"

"Lao Pak," Keel said, turning toward the *Indelible VI*, "I'm glad I didn't kill you."

09

Ackabar Star Port Slums
Ackabar

The legionnaires scrambled for cover and started to return fire.

Tyrus Rechs ducked behind the cover of a large servitor bot diligently trundling its master's goods across the city's main concourse. The thing was hulky and slow, beeping and burbling in its arcane servitor code language. Blaster fire tore it to pieces in seconds.

Rechs sighed. "Why'd they have to be such good shots?" he mumbled as the servitor bot exploded in a hot shower of sparks. But of course he knew the answer.

He released a shock grenade from his belt, squeezed it, then tossed it over his shoulder.

"Five," he counted as he dropped and rolled left.

Blaster fire followed him, ricocheting off the undercity concourse. One shot glanced off his chest plate and reflected skyward.

"Four."

He came up firing on full auto. There were six of them. He took down two with direct hits. Smoke rose from the holes burned into their newly issued armor by the high-intensity blasts.

Rechs triggered his jump jet and bounced back the way he'd come. A short hop, but away from them. He fired as he rocketed to the side and backward, hitting another and continuing his countdown through "three" and "two" as they tried to track and fire on him.

Then the grenade went off and fritzed out their armor's defensive capabilities.

Rechs knew their HUDs were now down, as were their pneumatic and gyro-assist subsystems. These kids hadn't learned to move in unpowered armor on a dust-red world for six months without supplies. Or fought a battle inside the crushing gravity well of a super gas giant. Even with powered armor, that had felt like breathing heavy water. But all that had been years ago.

Tyrus cursed himself for counting badly. Time and age were conspiring against him. Gaining ground. Winning a little more, every day.

And maybe they didn't make grenades, or anything for that matter, the way they used to.

He landed in a fury of grit and dust as he cut the rockets and shot the rest of the stunned legionnaires down.

There was a long moment of silence.

A moment where one should feel something about the corpses at one's feet.

You should feel... something, a voice reminded him.

I don't.

And...

And I haven't for a long time.

Then he was off and closing in on the Jaris Cantina as more evacuees rapidly became refugees. As more and more

Republican corvettes filled the storm-tossed skies above Ackabar. He needed answers. Taking out Junga shouldn't have been this hard. But who could've guessed the Republic was going to pull a tax interdiction raid? Things were getting more difficult with each passing moment.

Of course the cantina hadn't gone smoothly. He'd had to kill almost everyone to get the location of Junga's hideout from the one guy he managed to leave alive. And the info from Tels Aracnic—the info that had started this whole job—wasn't holding up. The rhino-lizard called Junga was supposed to have been at the cantina. Was supposed to be holding a macrocore that contained information the client needed. Needed badly. The client also needed Junga dead.

This contract was going from bad to worse.

Other bounty hunters would've walked.

Rechs had pursued the target straight to a fortified lair in the Breakers. He knew better than to approach head-on. But that was exactly what he was doing now. Because time was running out.

The four Gomarii guards at the front were tough.

Two died in a firefight so fast it was like sudden heat lighting. The other two deployed directional personal energy barriers and locked shields. The bounty hunter rushed them behind a stream of concentrated blaster fire. He hadn't been able to punch through their barriers in the least, but his barrage kept them from shooting back. The energy barrier shields prevented all blaster fire from passing through for as long as they were active.

One Gomarii stepped back and deployed a spear from a weapons baton. The charged tip was a mass of seething energy.

He'd faced these before, way back in the Savage Wars. If it struck Rechs's armor, that would be all she wrote. Game over, man.

So don't let it hit ya, he told himself as he squared off for hand-to-hand combat.

He raised the heavy blaster rifle in both hands and slammed the shaft of the incoming spear into the other Gomarii.

A sudden and savage *bang* indicated contact; the struck slaver was flung off the walkway, spinning into the canyons and alleys of the dead starships below. Sparks from the energy spear's tip rained down on the bounty hunter and the surviving slaver.

The Gomarii stepped back and slammed the energy spear's butt into the ground, loading a new charge, then crouched behind his force shield, close to the edge of the platform. *Too* close. Rechs leapt forward, pushed both feet against the shield, and kicked off from the butt of the blaster he'd planted in the dirt. The slaver tumbled backward, off the lip of the platform, out into open air, and down onto the rusty ruin of a gutted Class IV hauler that was nothing more than spars and rusting iron bones. A small explosion sounded from the dead ruin.

Rechs scanned the makeshift catwalks leading up into the old skeletal ship where Junga and his gang had made their lair. A Republican first-era battleship—Ohio class. Behind the bounty hunter, over the city, the Republican corvettes were still hovering, and more and more assault troop transports shuttled down to the surface.

Rechs knew his window for getting out of here was closing. Getting back to the ship would be tough. Running the orbital blockade would be insane. But what other choice did he have?

The Republic had made it clear long ago that he was a dead man walking.

He ran, pounding up the narrow steel that had once been part of ancient ships that flung themselves between the stars. The catwalks moaned and sang in the early evening winds that plagued this stormy and unforgiving world. Ahead, Junga waited for him—of that the bounty hunter was sure. And the reception would not be polite.

The first guards he met were dug in, with a clear kill zone for anyone coming up the ramshackle walkway. A small bunker had been established near the main entrance to the old life hab of the colony ship. But the thugs who guarded Junga weren't legionnaires. They hadn't lived and breathed with a blaster in their hands. They hadn't fought for the Republic in countless unremembered actions on worlds far and wide. Instead they were drifters, and assassins, and the occasional merc who'd gotten by on just waving a blaster around to intimidate the peaceful folk of the galaxy.

Which was why the Legion had always needed hard men to do hard things. They were the line that protected the galaxy, the Republic, from the lawless chaos that was always waiting out near the edges.

Or at least, they had been, once. A long time ago. Not anymore.

These guards of a minor criminal overlord had no idea how fast a trained legionnaire could move and shoot on the fly—even if the armor he was wearing didn't have target assist. Legionnaires had to learn to do all that before they were equipped with that fancy little gimmick, or all the other toys they became masters of.

Rechs shot all three guards, then turned just in time to see a sniper from atop another gate watching, silhouetted against the purple of Ackabar's darkening sky. The lone red eye of the sniper's scope drew the bounty hunter's aim from across the ramshackle courtyard. Rechs pivoted and fired. Three shots smashed into the wall around the sniper, and the fourth hit the scope in a shower of sparks. The guard was gone. Most likely dead, or at least dying.

"Entrance," mumbled Rechs as he searched the junk wall for the secret door that would lead into a labyrinth where the Minotaur named Junga was waiting to be slain. Just like some old forgotten myth from near the beginning of all things.

Rechs was talking himself through the op, where once he'd talked to squads, and companies, and armies, and legions. Was it somehow a comfort? Talking to oneself when one was all alone? Did it give him a sense of not being alone and outnumbered? And outgunned, too?

He dismissed those wonderings. He'd always been alone. Even when he'd led troops into battle for the Republic, even then, he'd been alone. He preferred it that way, for reasons he didn't think about anymore.

The entrance was an old radiation shield door from a Galactic Lightship. One of the first to reach the inner worlds back in the day. Big, fast beasts that got up and went like no tomorrow. State of the art. Back then.

He remembered standing beneath one on a world he could no longer name. Feeling hopeful. Feeling like everything was beginning again. It was the same feeling as being in love. And there was someone... someone who went with all those memories. And smoke. And music. And laughter.

But that was long ago.

He strode to the massive door, determined, like his mere presence should cause it to move aside.

There was a security code.

It was in Maktow. Digital pictoglyphs swam across the screen as the thing chittered at him.

"No time," he grunted.

He ripped the ancient door from its anchor bolts.

That little maneuver cost him more than he liked. In his HUD, an indicator signaled that the gyro power from the battery was low. The armor's available power was below thirty-five percent. And no spare power slugs. The old armor didn't hold a charge like it used to.

Peering through the entrance into a cavernous darkness below, he detected multiple targets. All of them carrying blasters. Waiting in the dark and shadows. Beyond their trap, ground radar showed him the graphed lines of a massive set of stairs rising up to two large doors deep within the remains.

This oughta be fun, he thought grimly as he rushed through the open doorway.

Blaster shots were immediately everywhere. He took cover in the vent housing for the main engines of the old battleship. The superstructure of the massive nacelles that had once housed the mammoth engines rose up and away above. Blaster shots exploded across the cold engine systems all around him, knocking off caked coke hundreds of years old.

He engaged one of Junga's mean little thugs, hiding in a housing opposite his position—nailed him with a single shot. He killed two more, targeting them in the shadowy darkness with light-enhancement software.

Then a lucky blaster shot destroyed his rifle. The explosion rattled his hands through armored gloves. As he threw aside the heavy blaster, he heard, through the helmet's sonic amplification system, the enemy leader crowing to his whelps that they had him right where they wanted him.

Rechs drew the old hand cannon from his hip and switched to automatic. He felt the weapon connect with the ammo feed in his right gauntlet as the load indicator blinked to life in the upper corner of his helmet's screen. Then he was knocking them down with ten-round bursts.

Each set of staccato explosions tore Junga's thugs apart worse than any blaster ever could. But they continued to fire back at him. The few shots that struck the bounty hunter's armor merely ricocheted off into the dark vaults above. Only a direct hit, close up, would punch through. Well... in theory. Fact was, the armor was old. It'd been through a lot. Who could tell when it would fail? And where? Best not to get hit at all. Or as little as possible.

"Captain," purred a voice in Rechs's comm. "Someone is trying to steal me."

More of Junga's men appeared at the top of the massive steps that led out of the ancient engine housings. Once long ago, the flames of hell had surely blazed through this space when the old Ohio-class had fired up for battle back in the old frontier wars. The frontier then. Not now.

"Well... don't let them," he growled. He zeroed in on a fast-moving thug.

"It's just one, Captain. One person is trying to steal me."

"Lyra!" he barked in frustration. He didn't need this too. "Don't let whoever it is steal the *Crow*."

"I understand, Captain. I will endeavor to do my best. Containing... now."

"And—" Blaster fire exploded near his helmet; he ducked just in time. "Stand by to pick me up. My location."

"Oh, I don't think that's such a good idea, Captain," said Lyra hesitantly.

He leaned in and targeted the runner. He led him with a burst and cut the legs out from under the thug. Rechs paid for the exposure with more close and untrained blaster fire all around him.

"It's gonna have to be, Lyra. This one is getting hot."

"Captain, may I remind you of my landing on Noba V? My attempted landing, I mean."

"Lyra! You're a ship!" cried Rechs. He took cover behind some old injector nozzles at the bottom of the stairs. New reinforcements were overwhelming his position with blaster fire. He had to keep moving along their line. Now he was popping up in different spots to take random shots, and not hitting every time.

Armor integrity was dropping. As was mobile power.

"Finish this up soon," Rechs grunted to himself.

"What, Captain?"

"Lyra, get the *Crow* in the air and maneuver to my location. You might have to fly through the superstructure of an old Ohio-class battleship. You can do this."

He was down to half his ammo. He switched to five-round bursts. The targeting enhancement system was having trouble compensating on the larger bursts, and he was wasting ammo.

"I'll try, Captain." But the ship didn't sound too sure of herself.

Like there's any other option, he thought as he took out a leader of some sort. The guy had been shouting and waving his arms, trying to get a bunch of cowardly murderers to rush Rechs. Blowing his head off provided an effective counterargument.

But still, they were closing in on the housing. They were the type, collectively, who knew how to take advantage of any situation. How to harass and intimidate the weak.

Then they're in for a surprise, thought the bounty hunter.

Now they came on, sensing an advantage, or perhaps just knowing they didn't want to face Junga as failures.

Firing as fast as they could, they closed their semicircle about him in the darkness of the ancient drive engine. At close range, their blasters would tear his armor to shreds.

The critical mistake they made was when the end of their semicircle—seven bloodthirsty and desperate criminals in total—came close enough for Rechs to roll away from the disintegrating fuel inducer housing they were concentrating fire on and right into one of his attackers: a Tennar holding four blasters in its tentacles.

Like greased lightning, Rechs was up and behind the humanoid squid. He punched it once in the throat, then struck right through its main heart with the industrial diamond blades he deployed from the knuckles of his gloves. Then he pulled the body close and used it as a shield.

In its frenetic death throes, the Tennar squeezed the triggers on all four of its blasters. Wild shots went in every direction around the engine compartment, some striking other hired guns, others dancing off into the high darkness of the superstructure.

In the face of this wild, untargeted fire, near at hand and danger close, the rest of Junga's thugs began to duck and seek cover. Rechs seized the advantage provided by this moment of chaos. Grabbing one of the neurotic tentacles, he secured a blaster. Then he was squeezing off shots on the rest of Junga's cowering thugs, taking them all down, one after the next, his movements automatic, mechanical, lethal. When the last enemy fell, Rechs tossed the lifeless body of the squid off into the darkness and advanced up the stairs.

The door at the top had once been the main engine fuel cutoff gate within the engine housings. Now, Rechs was certain, it was the door to Junga's inner sanctum.

Time to finish this, he thought. *And there's not much of that.*

With the armor's diagnostic emulator, he scanned the blaster he'd taken off the Tennar. He found he didn't like its targeting alignment or power. It was the kind of weapon some second-rate thug on a back-end world carried, hoping he'd never have to use it as anything more than a fashion accessory.

But guys like this, thought Rechs as he looked around at all the corpses on the deck, *guys like this are always dying to use it on someone. It's what gives them power.*

And then that voice inside him whispered, *If that's what you need to sleep… just keep telling yourself that.*

Rechs hadn't slept well in a long time.

There were too many dead who liked to talk to him when he closed his eyes.

Too many things done that he had to live with long after the doing.

Far too many.

Lifetimes' worth. Plural.

"Hey!"

It was the voice of a small girl. Plaintive and helpless, with an edge of fear, like all the other voices he'd ever heard on all the countless worlds he'd ever soldiered on. Flown to. Flown from. Killed for. Or just killed. Forgetting where it all began. Knowing its end was somewhere ahead.

Soon.

"Hey!"

Rechs turned amid all the carnage he'd wrought. The dead at his feet. The burnt flesh. The gore.

A little girl and an old war bot stared at him. In the depths of an old battleship that was now some gangster's hideout.

And suddenly she was crossing the blackened main engine chamber. She was the opposite of everything real. Everything terrible. She was small. Young. Determined. The war bot skittered after her.

He remembered the war bots. They'd been with him at Kungaloor. When the rains came and the *Goliath* went down in flames and thunder. When the line was so thin. He remembered it all in that moment, as if he could reach out and feel that long-ago rain on that first of all alien worlds he'd been to.

No...

Kungaloor wasn't the first. It was later. The first was all red desert and sand. And winds. Winds that would flay you alive. And the winds sang. He remembered that. They sang to him.

That was the first.

She was talking to him. The little girl. Earnestly. Honestly. No guile. Not yet.

We learn that when we're older. This one was still young and innocent. A believer in right and wrong.

The galaxy hadn't ruined her yet.

But it would. It ruined everyone.

He was holding the almost worthless blaster. Not pointing it at her. Not pointing it away. As though either option was just that... an option. Yet another in a series begun long ago.

"Are you a—"

She halted when he finally turned his helmet to look at her.

Prisma was struck by the bounty hunter's fearsome appearance. Armor and weapons. Killing tools. Faceless because of the helmet. A cold and ruthless killer of others. He looked just like the ones that had...

Her legs went out from under her. No—they just wanted to. Wanted to buckle and not remember what had happened. To be small and insignificant once more. To hide.

But she didn't. She held. Held her position as best she could. Held her feet and fought to continue doing so.

"Are you a bounty hunter?" Her voice came out as small as she wanted to be. Because the galaxy was big, and it had a way of making everyone feel so very small, so very helpless. Especially when your father was being murdered right in front of your eyes every time you closed them. There was no justice. Not really. For some, but not all. And that's no kind of justice, really.

Justice is a form of mercy. For the innocent. Isn't it?

She was suddenly full of anger and fire. Cold fire.

"I'm looking to hire a bounty hunter."

"What...?" murmured Rechs.

This was all too surreal. He wondered if he was having another one of his episodes. Another reality-gone-askew moment in a life too long lived because you were too good at not dying. A little girl, familiar in some haunting way he couldn't name just yet. Maybe the war bot had something to do with that. Inside the tomb of an old Ohio from a long-lost war no one remembered, one of many, all of it colliding with what he'd become. What he'd never been meant to be.

What he was.

A bounty hunter.

The thing you will be, you are now becoming.

And then... there was something in that. No. he wasn't that. That was just... something for now.

"Some men..." she began, as though she were about to recite some speech and she'd memorized all the words just right. In all the long hours alone when there was no one to blame but herself. As though the speech would make it all right. Except that when she began it... all the words ran away and left just her, Prisma, holding the bag that contained all the grief. Standing there all tiny and far away. Feeling rage, and anger, and fear, all of them competing to master her when she'd told herself she was their master. They laughed at her now.

"... they came and killed..." The fracture appeared in her because it had always been there. "... my father."

But what she meant was, *my daddy*.

That's what she meant to say as her shoulders began to shrink and KRS-88 scuttled forward to somehow comfort her. As if a bot could ever be capable of such a thing.

The tears were falling now. Streaming down her cheeks.

"And I need someone to go kill them because..."

She sobbed again, making that silent ugly crying face she said she'd never make again every time she found herself making it. She moaned softly between breaths, begging the galaxy not to be as cruel as it was. Begging for everything to be different. Begging the universe not to be made of stone and low men.

"He was my daddy!" she cried. "I know he wasn't perfect. But he was mine. And they took him." And then she was sobbing in full, arms at her sides. Helpless and uncontrollably sobbing.

Rechs let the weapon drop and bent down on one knee. He felt every pop and buckle in his old frame, his old armor.

Every injury. Every hurt. Everything missing where there should've been something left besides scars.

She fell like a tiny pole into his armored front, and he held her. Because he was once good. Because she was lost. Because he was an adult. Because she was a child. Because the galaxy was cruel. Because she needed comfort. And safety. And justice.

Through his armor, the armor that had protected him from the worst the galaxy could throw at a man, he could feel the shaking grief. And humiliation. And fear.

And so he just held her.

Which was the most human thing he'd done… in years.

And then the Legion showed up, supported by basics.

"There he is! Blast 'em!" cried the officer in charge.

Armored troops flooded the massive engine compartment of the ancient battleship. At least two squads.

"Oh, my!" rumbled the war bot as blaster fire struck the steps all around them, exploding in sharp bursts of static electricity and smoke.

Rechs picked up the little girl and ran through the portal leading into Junga's inner sanctum.

"Crash!" she screamed.

"Move it, Tin Can!" Rechs called to the bot as he turned and fired twice. He hit nothing, but he kept the legionnaires too busy to shoot back. "Stay here and you're parts!"

They dashed through the ancient main flow shutoff valve, return blaster fire ricocheting off the walls.

10

Rechs, with the girl under one arm, pounded down one of the main engine's intake flow channels. The mincing war bot followed as best it could. The space had been converted into some kind of smuggled goods storage warehouse. Containers of actual Republic goods, probably pirated from bulk haulers, lined the walls.

Pursuing legionnaires tried a few shots, but Rechs skidded around a corner, poked his blaster back out, and fired wildly to cover the war bot.

Three quick turns later through the maze of scavenged ship conduits and shadowy maintenance tunnels, with legionnaires trailing them, they reached a canted main corridor that had probably once run the length of the battleship's spine. Dust and shadows were all that remained of a starship that had been filled with life long ago.

They'd gained some breathing space after Rechs had discouraged the lead pursuers with well-aimed blaster fire. The corridors behind them were dotted with dying legionnaires. But in the distance, the boots of the legionnaires still clanked in discordant cadence against the deck plating.

"Oh!" rumbled the war bot. "This ship still has an active intelligence. I'm in communication with it now."

"Flight deck," said Rechs to himself as he set Prisma down. Taking out Junga was off the table now. Too many legionnaires running around. And in all likelihood, Junga was on his own freighter and trying to run the blockade.

He had to get the girl out of here too. *Why?* asked some ancient part of himself. A very young-sounding part. He didn't bother to reply.

"Will you?" she said, almost devoid of emotion now that her storm had passed. "Will you help me get revenge?" she whispered softly.

Not now, he wanted to tell her as he spun about, trying to get his bearings, still absently holding the substandard blaster.

"I'm talking with the ship, sir," said the bot. "And he says—"

"This way!" cried Rechs. "C'mon, move it!"

He grabbed the girl's hand and headed up the spine of the ship. If they didn't get off the main passageway, they'd be easy targets for the pursuing legionnaires.

"Sir, the ship is indicating that the flight deck is—"

"Spit it out, Tin Can!" shouted Rechs as he scanned the dark cross passages ahead. He'd been on an Ohio once, long ago. Maybe even this one. He knew the flight deck was... There were *two* flight decks! He suddenly remembered. Both were on the ventral wings. And he also remembered... something else. Then it was gone. And all he knew was that it was somehow important, and not important now. Or anymore.

"Sir, the ship says both flight decks are missing. They've been salvaged."

The first blaster shots went wide, sailing off in front of them down the massive dark passageway where crew and troops had once thronged day and night. Rechs could still see them, as if they were still here, still racing to battle stations at Engador, or off the Jether's Folly asteroid field.

Focus!

He jerked hard on the girl's hand and pulled her down a dark side passageway. Switching on low-light imaging, he saw that the passage led to the lower decks. Gunnery stations would be down there, if one went all the way to the hull.

"Is there still power to the ship, Tin Can?"

"Yes, sir. The ship says he's hooked into the main grid so that salvage crews can continue their work of tearing him to pieces."

"Tell the ship to start the main power-up sequence for launch."

"Sir... This ship, sadly, will never fly again. He says he's incapable of starflight."

"Tell him to do it anyway. Power in the main start-up sequence will give me access to the security panels. If I can find one."

"Ah! Brilliant idea, sir. The ship tells me that he's powering up. And that it feels like old times," announced the war bot proudly.

One deck down, Rechs skidded to a halt in front of a panel set in a bulkhead. He ripped off the security shielding, revealing a touchscreen with a keypad. *Alphanumerica, we used to call it.*

"Don't think about it," he told himself when he tried to recall the numbers, the password sequence. *It's there. Don't trust your mind. Let your muscles do the remembering.*

Then he chuckled with disgust. His mind wasn't what it used to be. Which was good in a way. Maybe he didn't like all these memories. Maybe they reminded him of all the things he'd left behind. The things that were missing.

His fingers flew across the pad. Until the last number. The last digit. His finger hesitated over the nine. Unsure.

And then he just punched nine, because, he thought, what else could he do? What other option was left but the gamble of a guess?

One day the house will win.

"Let it not be today," he muttered.

The main functions screen appeared.

Seconds later he had some of the blast doors between them and the legionnaires irising closed.

That should hold them for a few.

He brought up the ship's schematic and cycled through the layout until he found what he was looking for.

"Lyra," he said into his comm.

"Yes, Captain. ETA your area three minutes."

"Good. I need you to fly right into the superstructure of this ship and find the main gun bore. It's what they used to fire the old planet-killer weapon out of. Halfway down its length there's a maintenance platform. Try to get the *Crow* as close to that platform as possible!"

A long pause.

He heard the unmistakable sound of a laser torch cutting through a distant bulkhead. The legionnaires.

It wouldn't take them long. Those torches could cut through anything, durasteel and ceramic even, like it was warm butter.

He remembered the year he'd had nothing but a laser torch for a weapon during the Savage Wars. It had been like a sword, or a ceremonial sabre. It had been both elegant and brutal. And he'd killed more than he cared to remember with it.

Why?

Because the galaxy had been that close to going into permanent darkness.

"Follow me," he told the little girl and the bot.

As they moved, he heard a distant bulkhead clattering to the deck, then the metallic clack of legionnaire boots coming for them.

They followed the maintenance tube forward, then crawled through an oxygen grate and out into a curving hall that would lead off toward the bore of the main gun. The planet-killer.

MG42. That had been its military designation.

The Republic didn't build those anymore.

But back then... we did, he thought. *We built weapons to kill planets.* As bad as things had become, they weren't as bad as they were then.

Rechs stopped at a T-intersection. One way led to the bore platform where Lyra and the *Crow* would soon be waiting. The ship could at least get the girl out of here.

He checked the low-quality blaster once more, as though still not believing he was carrying such a useless weapon. It was anathema to him. Every weapon he'd fought with had always felt a part of him—but not this. Maybe that's why he'd been dragging it along. Keeping it as far from his body as possible.

"Listen, Tin Can. Take her and follow this passage." He indicated the one on the right. "Find door M3. Tell the ship to lock it once you're through. My ship is coming. It'll get her off the platform."

"Ah! Excellent, sir! And what about me?"

"Once she's in the ship, it can take you both somewhere safe." But that was a lie. There really wasn't anywhere safe anymore.

"You're not listening to me," said the girl. "I want to hire you. I want you to kill—"

"Shut up!" he shouted. He fixed her with an emotionless turn of his soulless battle helmet. "You don't have enough to pay me to get your revenge! And you need to get over that. The galaxy is full of that kind of stuff. *Full of it.* Get over whatever happened to you. It happened, I'm sorry, but get over it. Trust me. You don't need revenge as bad as you think you do. It'll just eat you up and spit you out. There'll be nothing left of you at the end of it."

Trust me.

She stared up at him. Her eyes were hard and angry. Stared right through the helmet he'd hidden himself in for so long.

"I'll never get over it," she said. "He was my—"

"You will!" shouted Rechs desperately. He could hear the legionnaires coming for them. He needed her to move now. "You will. You'll fall in love someday and you'll forget all the bad things that ever happened to you. We can't remember every terrible thing that's been done to us. Otherwise we'd never make it. We couldn't go on. And we have to. Trust me, you'll survive this. You have so far. You will. Tin Can—" He looked at the old war bot someone had turned into a servant. Remembered seeing these things ripping Zengaari raiders to shreds in the half-light of a carbon-dust-storm-shadowed Cyclon. "Get her out of here now. Command override 'Reaper 19.'"

The tall war bot grabbed the girl's hand instantly, without hesitation or reply—as if the polite, watchful servant had never been. As if a deadly machine—a monster, used to obeying orders—was all that remained.

"What're you doing, Crash?" the girl screamed. "Let me go!"

"Take her to the platform," ordered Rechs. "Get her on my ship and get out of here. I'll try to buy you as much time as I can."

"As you command, General."

The bot lumbered into the darkness of the right-hand corridor, dragging the screaming and kicking girl like some immense boogeyman, the nightmare of all fragile and good things.

The legionnaires were coming closer. Calling out blind spots to one another. Moving tactically. Moving smart. Coming for him.

It's you they're here for, he thought. *Give her time to get clear, and they might forget about her.*

He pressed himself against the wall, blaster held against his chest plate, readying himself as he'd done countless times before. Readying himself to die killing others.

The first footsteps came near. Rechs waited. Then pivoted smoothly and fired. Two shots. Both were badly sent by the wonky blaster, but one hit, spinning the advancing legionnaire into the wall.

Now he kept up a steady stream of inaccurate fire.

"He's pinned down!" called one of the Rep-Army sergeants. "Try and flank him!"

Of course, thought Rechs as he sent more shots down the dark passageway. They returned fire, but were more interested in cover. They were smart that way. They knew he was dangerous.

He tried to calculate whether the war bot and the girl had reached the platform yet.

A legionnaire poked his head out far down the hall, in the left-hand passage, then quickly ducked back. They had him from two directions now.

In a moment now they'll set up a crossfire. Then I'm done for.

That was when his blaster broke.

A small high singing note warned him it was about to happen. Then the smell of something burning. Probably the crystal focuser fusing. He tossed it to the side and drew his hand cannon from his hip, slick as a pit viper.

The indicator in his HUD told him there wasn't much ammo left.

He put five rounds into a legionnaire who had decided to rush during the two-second pause between the blaster fritzing out and his drawing of his third-to-last weapon. All center mass. The legionnaire fell to the deck.

But others were stepping over him, swarming Rechs all at once. And at the same time, more legionnaires appeared in the cross passage, hemming him in.

He drew his rocket-powered grappling hook from his combat harness belt and fired it at the first legionnaire in the cross passage. When it entangled the man's weapon, Rechs flicked the thumb switch to reel it back in.

Still firing with his hand cannon at the advancing legionnaires in the main corridor, he secured his grappling hook with his other hand and caught the N-6 battle rifle smoothly.

Now I've got something to work with.

He fell back, firing. There were more legionnaires behind those dying just in front of him. He dropped back, corridor by corridor, running, firing. Making them pay all the way to the platform.

He lost count of how many he'd taken out, but obviously the first two squads had been reinforced. Still, he managed to stay ahead of them.

When he arrived at the maintenance hatch that led onto the platform inside the gun bore, he overrode the panel, stepped through, and locked it shut behind him.

He'd made it.

The girl and the old war bot were standing near the edge of the abyss—the massive gun bore of the ancient weapon that should've never been built. Through bore, the running lights of a ship were slowly approaching. His ship. The *Obsidian Crow*.

Behind him, the legionnaires started on the door with a cutter.

Two minutes.

"Kick it in gear, Lyra. We're running out of time."

"I'm really not good at flying, Captain. You know that." But the ship's speed did increase. "And Captain, I cannot land."

That was true. The tiny maintenance platform wouldn't even hold one of the three main gears of the *Crow*.

"Just get as close as you can."

The flat ship came nearer, its bulbous cockpit sticking out from the top forward portion, and then suddenly stopped. Its screaming engines shifted into the lower tones of throttling down. The legionnaires were halfway through the door.

"Bring it in closer, Lyra!" Rechs yelled into his comm as he turned to face the door, blaster ready.

I can take out a few, he thought. Surrender never even occurred to him.

"Captain, this is as close as I feel comfortable with at this time. I just run the systems. I do not fly. You know that. We've discussed this—"

"Put the prisoner on!" growled Rechs.

The legionnaires were three quarters of the way through the hatch.

"That's an odd request, Captain," replied Lyra. "But very well. It's a wobanki. So of course... you know how they are. He's patched into your comm now."

"Attention, prisoner. You've tried to steal my ship. I can have you jettisoned in deep space according to Republic law."

The cutter was having problems getting through the last few bolts in the door. Then it stopped. *They're switching out*, thought Rechs. *The fresh one will cut faster. It's a small break. But it's the only break I've got.*

"I can only guess you were trying to get off planet because of the Republic," he said quickly. "I am too. So how about instead of jettisoning you, I hire you as my first mate?"

"*Taju janki tegu...*" yowled the wobanki.

"It pays!" shouted Rechs indignantly. "I'll pay you."

"*Tabu janki? Tabu janki!*"

"Well, we'll discuss amounts later. But right now, I need you to get that ship, especially the lower access hatch and boarding ramp, as close to this platform I'm on as possible. Do that, and yeah... *tabu janki. Bugu tabu janki.*"

It didn't matter how much the wobanki wanted. If Rechs didn't get himself and the girl off this platform in the next few seconds, they'd be dead. And the legionnaires no doubt had a surface-to-air trooper somewhere nearby. One of those guys equipped with an MLAR anti-ship missile could knock a light freighter out of the sky in seconds.

The wobanki yowled wryly, which was the wobanki way of indicating it could do something. It was also the wobanki way of meaning many other things.

The cutter started up on the door again.

"All right then. I'm instructing the ship to release you from your harness. One move to escape before you get us off this platform, and I'll have the ship eject you."

He hoped Lyra knew he was bluffing. The ship couldn't eject, but the ship was a bit of a literalist, and it might choose this moment to speak up and correct his error. It had done so before. But thankfully, it remained silent. It was probably glad someone else was going to fly it.

The *Crow* moved haltingly toward the platform in a series of thrusts from the maneuver jets and main engine yaw thrust controls. It rotated around to bring the cargo ramp, which was already lowering, down to meet the platform. Expertly done.

And it still wasn't close enough.

The whine of the cutter stopped. The legionnaires were through. In a moment they'd kick it down and come out blasting.

Rechs grabbed the girl and activated his armor's rockets. A short hop, and he was off the platform, across the empty void of the gun bore, and landing on the ramp.

"Oh, my," intoned the war bot. "What about me?"

"Crash!" screamed the girl as Rechs tossed her up into the hold. "Don't leave Crash!"

Legionnaires squeezed through the ragged cut in the door and began firing. Rechs returned fire from the boarding ramp.

"Don't leave him!" the girl demanded.

Hell, thought Rechs.

As the *Crow* began to maneuver for departure—the wobanki, thankfully, was not waiting for additional orders—Rechs grabbed one of the platform struts to hang on to, targeted the war bot with his grappling hook, and fired.

"Get us out of here!" he screamed above the whining engines as he anchored the hook in the old war bot.

The ship spun, and a moment later it was pointed back down the bore exit. Rechs knew the wobanki would now be reaching for the throttles on the forward panel. He gripped the strut tightly and reeled in the bot with the last of the armor's power as legionnaire blaster fire found the bottom of his ship.

He grabbed the bot and fell backward as the cargo door closed, bringing them up into the main hold. The primary engines ignited, and the *Obsidian Crow* raced away down the gun bore of the ancient battleship, headed out. Headed up. Climbing toward the Republican blockade.

Readying to make the jump to light speed.

11

Tannespa had more cantinas than traffic bots, and Keel imagined he must have just about visited all of them, never staying long enough for so much as a sip of Ponteeran ale. The interior of the establishments varied, some dingy and rank, others attempting to exude a core-world sophistication that came across as more tacky than anything else. Results were another story altogether.

Keel had a name for the coder, and a rough description from Lao Pak, who was just as likely making it up given the pirate's attention to detail. That was about it. Bartenders—human and bot alike—didn't remember seeing who "wore a pair of sled gunner's goggles around his neck" and "probably" a green shirt. Certainly the name Garret didn't ring a bell, but why would it? Based on Lao Pak's own admission, the kid wasn't the type to make a flashy show of himself.

It was a surly group of drunken space pirates who gave Keel his first real clue as to the coder's whereabouts. A clue that cost him five bottles of Rypian brandy—or would have, had Keel not paid the bartender to fill empty bottles of the ultra-elite liquor with watered-down spacer rum.

"Bam Tammo's junk shop," hiccupped the inebriated pirate who served as something of a leader, spilling his glass as he wobbled to keep his balance. He drained what was left of the knockoff beverage, hissed, and wiped his mouth. "Yeah. That's good."

"I'm glad you like it," Keel said, hiding an amused grin behind his hand. "It cost me a pretty credit. Where is this... *junk* shop? Come to think of it, *what* is it? Are we talking narco-stims?"

This caused an eruption of laughter from the booth holding the pirates. Keel feigned laughter along with them.

"Nah! Not Garret," slurred another pirate, this one stinking of orange ryhnn, most of which ran in a stain from her lips down her neck. "Oh, you know, Garret. Heesh alwaysh goin' around that place. For the *junk*. To make... his... *schtuff*." She made a point of closing her fist around her thumb so it stuck out between two fingers, as though she'd forgotten how to ball a fist. "Schtuff."

Keel gave a half smile. "Sure." He rose from his seat at the end of the booth. "Tell you what, I'll just ask the bartender. Enjoy the drinks, huh?"

The motley crew of pirates toasted Keel as he left for the bar.

"Bam Tammo's junk shop?" Keel inquired of the Kimbrin bartender.

The barkeep bristled the spikes on his neck and shoulders and pointed south. "Two blocks that way. No sign, but it's full of salvage. Can't miss it."

With a flick of his thumb, Keel tossed a credit chit at the barkeep. "Thanks."

The junk shop was easy enough to find once Keel knew which direction to go. An assortment of spare parts, used-up servos, and disassembled bots sat like buoys on an endless sea of scrap metal. It all seemed to spill out from the squat, box-like shop's entrance, nearly to the street. No signage was visible, just like the bartender had said, but Keel couldn't imagine what else the place might be other than Bam Tammo's junk shop.

Stepping over a dented comm dish that looked like it was pried from some deep space hauler shortly after the Savage Wars broke out, he entered.

The shop was lit exclusively with discarded neon ad boards and partially functioning holoscreens. Bright colors glowed, touting products Keel had never heard of in a dizzying number of scripts, some of which he couldn't comprehend. Most of the ad boards only had a few letters or characters lit up, the remaining burnt-out sections giving the illusion of misspelled words or incomplete sentences. The effect of this... *peculiar* form of illumination gave the inside of the junk shop a certain ambiance, like a seedy space-station nightclub.

Keel sashayed across the shop's junk-strewn floor, his gun belt bathed in alternating lemon and mauve glows. No one came out to greet him in spite of a two-tone chime that sounded when he crossed the threshold. The place seemed entirely empty until Keel heard a faint scurry. The noise came from behind a makeshift counter constructed from the wing of some mid-core spacefighter. The blaster cannon had been removed from the wing's tip, and black carbon scoring and fried wiring gave a hint at the craft's final moments of flightworthiness.

Leaning over the counter to find the source of the noise, Keel found himself looking down at a small, lemur-like creature. Its fur was a crimson-brown, and it had a slender, prehensile tail curled like a question mark just behind its large round ears. The little thing examined Keel for a moment, watching him from beneath bushy eyebrows that shaded large, expressive, brown eyes. Probably some sort of shop mascot or pet.

Keel rested his elbow on the counter and looked around for Bam Tammo. "Hello? How 'bout a little help?"

The shop's pet hopped up a series of stacked crates, scooted along a ramp that read "Special Edition," and stopped on top of the counter. It stood on its hind legs, looked up at Keel, and spoke. "Don't talk like I'm not in the room, huh, pal? I got ears."

"Cute." Keel frowned.

"Yeah, that's what they say about me… especially *your girl last night.*" The little furball began swiveling its tiny hips.

Keel rolled his eyes. He noticed a pair of sled goggles sitting next to one of the crates the creature had just hopped from. "Those yours?"

The creature followed Keel's eyes to the goggles, then turned back at Keel. "Yeah. You buying?"

"Garret?" Keel ventured.

A tiny, mocking laugh escaped the alien, causing its fur to ripple around its stomach. "You know, you're lucky you're so big. Otherwise I might *smack you around* for even suggesting that. Do I look like some gutless kid from Mentarro, working for pirates?"

Keel shot out his hand to grab the creature. With a squeaky howl it ducked and attempted to jump clear, but Keel's reflexes were too quick. He snatched the thing from the air, grabbing it by the smooth fur on the back of its neck.

"Put me down!"

Holding the creature up so he could look it in the eyes, Keel furrowed his brow. The wiry little thing swiped at Keel's face, revealing a predator's dental structure—in miniature. Keel drew his blaster and brought the barrel up menacingly next to the tiny creature's chin. "Settle down or I'll use you for target practice. I take it you're Bam Tammo?"

"Yeah," Tammo answered in a small, high-pitched voice. Its body was limp, all resistance having drained away at the sight of the blaster.

"Wonderful. Now we're getting somewhere." Keel holstered his blaster. "I need information, and reliable sources tell me I'm going to find it here."

Tammo raised long bushy eyebrows that seemed to invite Keel to continue.

"So what we're going to do is start over. Yeah?"

Tammo nodded vehemently.

Keel adjusted his grip, holding Tammo around its torso, fingers wrapped beneath the creature's armpits. "I'm looking for a coder. Works for Lao Pak and goes by the name Garret. You know him."

"Yeah, Garret. I know him. He helps me get some of the more delicate and expensive pieces working." Tammo pointed to a gleaming portable shield generator locked up in an energy case on the far wall. "In exchange, I let him take whatever he wants—within reason—for his own little projects."

Keel didn't care about whatever working relationship the kid had with the little space rat. "Where can I find him?"

Tammo pointed a tiny thumb over its shoulder. "Should be in the back still. He was sorting through some spare hoverbot parts. MCR buys reconditioned TT-16 observation bots for way above market price for new... if you can get 'em delivered without questions."

"Around back. That's all I needed to know." Keel tossed the junk store owner into a pile of assorted springs and power cables.

Tammo popped its head up from the debris, a newly stripped ion coupler dangling from its ear. "Rude! All you pirates are rude!"

Keel left the shop and made his way around back. Turning a corner into a small, weed-infested yard, he was greeted by a blinding flash of blue light. As he blinked away the painful aftereffects, he saw a goggle-wearing humanoid sitting at an open-air workbench, welding together two pieces of armored plating on a full-size observation bot. Lao Pak must have misidentified welding glasses as sled driver's goggles.

"You Garret?" Keel asked.

The welder thumbed off his torch and placed it on the workbench. He lifted up his goggles and squinted at Keel. "Yes." His voice was curious and self-conscious at once. Slick sheets of combed, oily hair dangled around his eyes and ears. Lao Pak was right: Garret was just a kid. Probably too young to even drink on any world except lawless dens of iniquity like this one.

Keel leaned against the shop wall, crossing his ankles. "Lao Pak said you could help me."

Garret opened his mouth wide as if to speak, but no words came out. "Oh, well, the thing is..." he shook his head and smiled meekly, apologetically. "I really have to finish this before my leave is up, or Bam Tammo is going to be pretty unhappy."

"Forget about Bam Tammo. I need something that can render my navigator off-ship."

Garret gave a nervous laugh and a slow, dismissive shake of his head before looking up at Keel with sudden interest. "Hologram?" The coder leaned forward, his interest clearly piqued. "Like, like a shipboard AI?"

"Something like that," Keel said, poking through a pile of discarded charge packs with the toe of his boot. "We used TT-3 bots to render him off-ship, but those were... uh, destroyed. I'm looking for an upgrade."

"What kind of upgrade?" Garret was clearly excited.

"Something that will make him combat effective. I dunno, modify the bots to shoot blaster charges," Keel suggested, stretching his neck enough to cause his vertebrae to pop. "Use your imagination. Sky's the limit."

Garret stood up from his bench, knocking over a spray can of fiber sealant. He didn't seem to notice. "What about an optional permanence renderer? It's theoretical, but Bam Tammo has the stuff that could get it done—in his below-ground cache."

"Sure," Keel said, waving off the details. "Charge it to Lao Pak; we're old friends. How long will this take?"

The coder pushed away an oily strand of hair from his right eye. "Oh... maybe a few days?"

"To get the parts?"

Garret laughed, a sort of breathy, ungainly sound. "No. I can have those in a half hour. I mean a few days to have it all finished, sir." Garret inclined his head, strands of hair hanging down loose from his brow. "I don't know your name."

"Aeson Keel. I fly the *Indelible VI.*" The captain looked around, verifying that he was alone with the coder. "And that's too long. I'm jumping system tonight, and I don't know when I can get back."

Garret shook his head. "I can forward them to you on a shipping crate, or—"

"No," countered Keel. "You can finish them on board. C'mon." He patted Garret on the back, sending the coder stumbling away from his workbench.

Righting himself by grabbing hold of Keel's vest, Garret gave a nervous laugh, shaking his head as though the suggestion were an impossibility. "A lot... a lot of people would be *really*," he leaned in to Keel's ear and whispered, "angry."

Keel gave a lopsided grin. "It'll be fine. You're with me."

"I really don't think—"

Garret's objection died there as Keel grabbed a fistful of his coveralls and pulled him toward Bam Tammo's shop.

Keel navigated his way through inventory-filled racking and repulsor pallets to the front of the store. He whistled. "Hey, Tammo!"

The furry creature appeared from behind a stack of holodrives. It smoothed its fur and stood on its hind legs. "How may I help you, *sir*?" Tammo asked, his voice thick with hostile sarcasm.

"The kid here is working on something for me." Keel hitched a thumb toward Garret, who shuffled uneasily, looking down and rubbing the back of his neck. "Give him whatever he asks for."

Tammo leveled a cold stare at Garret. The coder, for his part, kicked the ground, looking like he wished to be anywhere but here.

Keel put his hands on his hips, his stance askew. "Before the tech becomes obsolete, huh?"

The staring contest broken, Tammo and Garret began rounding up parts.

Keel strode next to Garret, who pushed a repulsor pallet loaded with boxes and crates. The coder had been sharing his backstory, while Keel answered with what he hoped were enough "uh-huhs" and "hmms" to provide a passable show of attentive listening. A trio of drunken pirates strolled by singing a space shanty, all of them leaning on one another, too inebriated to stand on their own.

"So," Garret concluded, "that's basically it. I bought my life from Lao Pak when he raided a passenger transport. Been working for him ever since."

"Lao Pak killed all the others?" Keel furrowed his brow. "That doesn't sound like him. Surefire way to grab the Republic's attention."

Garret let loose a breathy laugh. "No. I just *thought* they were going to kill us, so I begged to be spared." The coder looked up with melancholy in his eyes. "Everyone else, he let go..."

Keel rolled his eyes. "You can jump ship as soon as Ravi's upgrades are complete."

At the mention of the upgrades, Garret's eyes lit up. "I'm really looking forward to that. The project, not jumping ship. Most of what Lao Pak has me do is routine maintenance and decryption. Plus whatever the crew asks for. Usually holostream updates and better climate controls. But this stuff is exciting. I haven't done anything along these lines in... well, a long time. Before I started working for Lao Pak, I was hired to reprogram an old Savage Wars–era war bot into a personal servant unit by some rich family. That was a challenge! The trick was—"

Keel gave a dismissive smile and nod. He was busy watching a pair of delphins arguing with each other on the front porch of a game hall. But when he became aware that Garret had stopped talking, he looked over to see that the coder was stopped in his tracks. A burly human with a bushy red beard was standing in front of the repulsor pallet, holding it in place.

"These for my new racing skiff, string bean?" asked the interloper as he examined the various crates.

Garret shook his head and gave his wispy, open-mouthed laugh. "N-now Drex… Lao Pak said that I couldn't—"

"Is Lao Pak *here*?" shouted Drex. Keel assumed this was a member of the pirate's crew. "Skiff races are next week, and I need those repairs finished or I won't be able to qualify."

"But," Garret protested, looking meekly at the ground, "you still haven't… haven't paid me from last time. Skiff parts… a-aren't cheap, Drex."

Drex swatted Keel's chest with the back of his hand. "Get a load of this guy, huh?" the pirate said, chuckling. He turned his attention back to Garret, even as Keel's eyes stayed fixed on the spot where the pirate had touched him.

Drex tapped his fingers on Garret's forehead. "Hello, code-rat. If I spend all my divvy on ship repairs, I won't have anything left for the cantina."

"No, you're right, Drex," Garret confessed, sheepishly laughing with the large pirate. "I'll order the parts and get the skiff race ready by qualifiers."

"Upgrade the optical sensor gyro, too. Skiff felt unbalanced when I took the turns at Mos Orba."

Garret nodded. "Okay, Drex. Sure thing. I-I just have to do a job for Captain Keel first."

Drex looked Keel up and down. "What do I care about some long-haul space pilot?" He poked Keel in the chest. "You'll have to find a new code-rat. This one's busy."

With a blur of motion, Keel grabbed Drex by his wrist and wrenched it behind the pirate, twisting it until he could hear the meaty bones and joints popping. Falling to a knee, Drex screamed out in pain, then abruptly stopped at the sight of Keel's blaster pointed at his temple.

"This one important to Lao Pak?" Keel asked Garret.

The coder stood stock still, his eyes wide and his face pale.

"Yeah," Drex pleaded, seeming to pick up on the reason Keel asked. "I lead his boarding crew. He needs me!"

"Wasn't talking to you," said Keel.

Garret blinked, and raised his shoulders as he ducked his head. "Oh, I... I don't know, really. I mean, I think so. I think... I think Lao Pak—I don't really know."

Keel shrugged, then clubbed the pirate on the back of his head with the grip of his blaster. The burly brigand went down in a heap. Keel pushed the repulsor pallet over the unconscious body.

Looking back, Garret said, "Drex is going to be angry about that."

"Why? I didn't kill him. C'mon. Docking Bay 49 is right up this way."

The coder had gone quiet. Probably worried about what he'd gotten himself into. Keel resolved to make him feel at ease. It wasn't good for him to be jumping from one form of indentured servitude to another—compelled work tended to provide inferior results. "Why do you let guys like that push you around, kid?"

"Oh," Garret shook his head. "It's not so bad. Besides, it's not exactly like I can do anything about it."

Keel patted his re-holstered blaster. "That's what these are for. Equalizers. You know how to use them?"

"No."

Keel nodded. He hadn't expected otherwise. "I've got some training bots on board. You can practice when you're not working."

"Thanks," the coder said. He didn't seem much more comfortable than before.

Attempting a new angle, Keel said, "Tell me about that job reprogramming a war bot. Didn't think there were any of those left."

"They're hard to come by!" Garret found his enthusiasm again. "Like I said, the family was *rich*. I was probably the fourth code slicer they subcontracted."

Keel laughed. "Rich family like that... I take it Lao Pak tried to get you to share their hyper-coordinates? This is us." Keel pointed to a brown and battered docking bay door and helped Garret maneuver the pallet sled.

The door whooshed open, and Garret moved to the front end of the sled, facing the captain.

"He never asked, so I never told him," Garret said, peeking over his shoulder at the *Indelible VI*. "Naseen freighter. How modified is it?"

Keel gave a grin. "Let's just say that even if you're in a corvette, you don't want to underestimate her."

"Nice. Yeah, that family brought me to their villa to work on the bot in a luxury 'vette. *Prisma's Future*."

Keel waved for Ravi to lower *Indelible*'s ramp. "Sounds like a nice job, if you can keep it."

"It was," Garret confirmed. There was a look of something—nostalgia?—on his young face. "The Maydoons treated me really nice."

Keel stopped cold in his tracks. "*Maydoon?*"

12
Republic Towers Building
Corsica, Mid-Core

Keel saw the smile on Ravi's face after the navigator pressed the button for the three thousandth floor of Republic Towers. How long had it been since the hologram had been able to manipulate anything other than the sliced controls of the *Indelible VI*? Yes, Keel felt he had *more* than come through in finding Garret. The coder was a technological miracle worker, making a reality of things that were only posited as theoretical in the various corporate trade holos.

"Not bad, huh?" Keel said.

"Yes, I am most pleased," Ravi confirmed. And then he eyed Keel in a way that made him feel like a prey species being watched by a predator. "I am curious to see how well the technology holds in *combat*. It has been some time, and of course, I can't be hit back..."

Keel furrowed his brow. "Ingrate."

They were on Corsica, a mid-core world close enough to the galactic core that its residents could *almost* pretend they were in league with the galaxy's movers and shakers. The 3,500-story Republic Towers building was the crown jewel of the planet's capital city—a lone obelisk offering a foretaste of what the future held, a future where galaxy's edge would become the new mid-core, where worlds like Corsica would finally ascend into the proper respectability of the *true* core.

The name "Maydoon" had turned out to be quite a sufficient lead, thanks to Garret. Garret didn't know the current whereabouts of Kael Maydoon, the man who had hired him to reprogram a war bot to serve as some sort of housebroken bodyguard, but he was certain that if they could find the bot, they'd find its owner. And since Republic Towers was where Garret had been hired, Keel was confident that this was the place to start their search.

Leaning against the back wall of the speedlift, Keel watched the coder and princess both shift in their places. "It's a good three-minute ride to our floor."

"Two minutes, forty-five seconds," corrected Ravi.

"I am excited to be off ship, captain." Leenah seemed genuine. "I wonder if there are any operatives sympathetic to the MCR who might be able to..." She paused as if to gauge Keel's reaction. "I mean, I should probably head back some time."

Keel shrugged. "You're not a prisoner. I like having you on the ship—when you're working, I mean. Why not stick around for a while? See a bit of the galaxy?"

Something made Keel believe she hadn't really seen all that much of the galaxy—apart from her home planet and a few rotting MCR mobile headquarters. The Mid-Core Rebellion didn't seem to fit her. They were idiot insurgents, just as likely to kill you as free you in the name of liberty. For all their talk of moving on from their atrocities, Keel was unconvinced.

Regardless, Keel was determined to keep the pink-skinned humanoid on his ship as long as she was willing. For all the credits he'd put into the *Six*, he couldn't quite remember a time it operated so well as since Leenah began going over it with a tension wrench.

Leenah smiled at Keel. "Well, whatever happens, I'm thankful. You saved my life, after all."

"Oh, yeah," Keel said somewhat absently as the speedlift accelerated. "Well, you're welcome."

A comm indicator beeped.

"It's Lao Pak again," Ravi informed Keel before the captain had the chance to check his comm.

"Ignore it," Keel ordered.

"At some point he will no longer wait for you to answer why you took his best coder." Ravi held up a finger for emphasis. "And this *after* he specifically made you promise not to do the very thing you have done."

Garret's face blanched. "H-he's not... *mad*, is he?"

"Of course not," Keel said, giving the coder an incredulous look. "We're old pals."

"But," Garret protested, "Lao Pak kills deserters. It's his favorite thing to do in the world."

Leenah cleared her throat. "Is he the one that the general stayed with to see about joining the rebellion?"

Keel let out a nervous chuckle. "That would be him," he said, giving Ravi a don't-say-anything look.

The hologram shook his head disapprovingly.

The princess pulled on a pink tendril hanging down from her head. "I'm sure once the general explains the rebellion's need for a stronger fleet to resist the Republic, Lao Pak will be more than willing to help."

"That doesn't sound like Lao Pak at all..." began Garret. He looked to Keel, as if asking permission to elaborate and dispel what was obviously an incorrect opinion.

Keel gave a fractional shake of his head, indicating that Garret had talked quite enough. "I guess we'll see," the captain said, attempting to sound upbeat. This lift ride couldn't be over fast enough. He looked to Ravi, who seemed to be enjoying watching his captain squirm. "But who knows? Lao Pak can be persuasive. The general might end up joining *him*. The boy general turned pirate prince. Story writes itself, really."

"He doesn't usually give you a choice," Garret said under his breath.

"What do you mean?" Leenah asked.

"Okay," Keel laughed. "Let's just... stay focused, huh?"

"Wait," Leenah insisted. "Did General Parrish stay behind voluntarily?"

Keel winced. "In the sense that he didn't have any other choice... yes."

The princess's eyes grew wide. "You *left* him! You abandoned him to a vicious pirate!"

"I had to abandon *someone*," Keel said, hovering somewhere between defensive and incredulous. "Lao Pak needed some compensation after I... well, he couldn't just let everyone go, and I couldn't kill him. Well, that's not true. I *could* have killed him. But there's a lot of money for all of us with him alive."

Ravi raised an eyebrow. This was the first time he'd heard Keel suggest the crew keep any of the bounty.

"But... but..." Leenah seemed to be searching her Endurian brain for just the right word. "This is... *knavery*!"

Keel shifted his eyes from side to side. "That's a very princessy word, Your Highness. You can call it knavery, but the rest of the story is that I saved your life—twice! Lao Pak wanted *you*—and your friend, the boy general, was more than happy to see you go. He didn't seem to think too highly of you once you'd served your purpose in getting him rescued off that little rebel base, Your Majesty."

Leenah looked down, and Keel knew that he'd hurt her. "Look, Leenah, I—"

The princess waved him off. "No, I understand. It would seem I owe you thanks for my life yet again, Captain Keel."

Only the smooth whir of the rising speedlift could be heard.

Garret was the first to speak again. "You know, Captain Keel rescued me, too. I was basically an indentured servant under Lao Pak. I think he's a good man."

Ravi let out a one-note laugh. "Ha!"

"Thanks, pal," Keel grumbled.

The speedlift chimed to indicate its arrival at level three thousand.

"If we're all friends again, let's remember the plan," Keel instructed as an indicator light told riders to stand back from the lift door. "We're just a friendly spacer outfit looking for work. Garret here remembered an old contact at Trident, so we're all going fishing for a contract together."

They stepped off the speedlift and into a grand waiting room. Luxurious leather sofas and exotic woods studded the area. Paintings and sculptures, both physical and holographic, were seeded tastefully along the considerable walk to a lone reception desk at the end of the room. A massive trident, wrought and shaped out of pure silvene, was fastened to the thirty-foot-high wall behind the desk, its prongs pointed down.

The entire floor was leased by the Trident Corporation. On its info-site, the company identified itself as a "multifaceted holding company specializing in the acquisition of small to mid-sized companies with an emphasis..." Et cetera. Left out was Trident's employment of a coder through the dark market to undertake a reprogramming job that was indisputably illegal, according to the Robotics Conduct laws that had come about near the end of the Savage Wars. But these dark market brokers had set up on Corsica, instead of a place like Tannespa or Ackabar, which meant that the appearance of respectability was crucial to their success. The powerful and wealthy—and the Maydoons seemed to be exactly that—weren't likely to go to the seedy underbelly of the galaxy, where a double-cross was more likely than anything else. Instead, they would come to Trident.

A young woman in a gray business dress, her blonde hair pulled back into a tight bun, sat behind the desk. She looked up to appraise the foursome moving toward her, arching a single, thin eyebrow before returning to her work. The approach would take time, so vast was the room. And though it was large enough to double as a hangar bay, Keel's team and the receptionist were the only beings in the room.

"Why should we ask for a contract?" Garret whispered. He shook his head nervously. "I thought we were just going to ask where to find Maydoon."

"We are," answered Keel with a roll of his eyes. "But we're not just going to come out and *say* it. They'll get suspicious. Think we're out to track down a rich client and rob 'em. Bad for business."

Joining in the whispered conversation, Leenah said, "No one's told me what the three of you are planning on doing with this *Maydoon* individual once you find him."

Keel looked at the princess, considering what to say. She looked earnest.

"Yes, Captain," Ravi said with a wry smile. "What *are* we to be doing?"

Keel frowned. He didn't relish the idea of having two conscience-minded beings on board. Ravi was about all the moral compass Keel could stand. "Oh, you know... just tell him someone's looking for him."

Somewhat perceptively, the princess asked, "You're not going to kill him, are you?"

Keel made a show of being wounded. "Me? What makes you think I would kill him?"

"It just seems like you've killed a lot of people since I've met you," Leenah observed. "I heard you and Ravi talk about the legionnaires you shot. I nearly broke my neck while you were shooting pirates out of existence..."

"You do seem a bit violent," Garret agreed.

"Those were all *justified*," Keel insisted. "Even *Ravi* was willing to kill the pirates."

"Weren't they your friends?" the princess asked, giving Keel a pointed look.

Garret also looked to Keel for an answer.

"Well, not those *particular* pirates. Just the guy they worked for." Keel pointed a finger at Leenah. "And you're one to talk! A princess in open warfare against the Republic."

Ravi laughed. "Hoo, hoo, hoo."

"Laugh it up, Ravi," Keel said. "Who knows how many people you killed during the Savage Wars before you finally... never mind. Let's just go see Garret's contact."

They walked the remaining distance to the front desk.

The receptionist examined the party, her face expressionless. After a pause so long that Keel wondered if he'd have to say the first word, she asked, "Yes?"

Keel nudged Garret in the ribs. The coder rubbed his side as though the captain's elbow really hurt, then stepped forward. "I... *we* wanted to see Mr. Kimer."

"You don't have an appointment," the secretary replied with a finality that suggested that while she could be mistaken... she wasn't.

Garret glanced at Keel with uncertainty in his eyes. "H-he... he said I could stop in any time and..."

The secretary didn't even look up from the holoscreen built into her desk. "No, that's not accurate. I can't let you in to see him."

"Actually, you know what?" Keel said, his voice conversational and friendly. "You're busy. We're all old friends, us and... Kimbler—"

"Kimer," corrected Garret.

"Right. We go way back. So just... watch your holodrama or whatever, and we'll go see Kim... Kimbl... our old pal. Garret, you remember how to get to his office?"

The receptionist pushed herself up from her desk. "I'm sorry. You have your answer. I suggest you come back another time."

The coder gave a nervous nod and turned to leave.

Keel grabbed him by the collar and grinned at the receptionist. "We'll just drop in. It'll only take a minute."

With a hard voice, the receptionist said, "I said you have your answer. Don't go back there."

"No, it's fine," Keel said, striding toward the high double doors just beyond the reception desk. "Thank you, though. I can see you take your job very seriously. Good for you."

In a blur, the woman swung herself around the desk and made herself a barricade between Keel and the door. She stood coiled, in a martial defense stance Keel didn't recognize.

"I estimate a ninety percent chance she will attempt to physically halt your progress should you proceed," Ravi said.

"Really?" Keel asked the receptionist. "You want to hit me *that* bad?"

The young woman whirled her arms and raised her front foot slightly off the ground in a combat posture. The motion pulled up her sleeves, revealing a pair of black lotus tattoos on her forearms.

"So, probably one hundred percent," Ravi said. The hologram stepped toward the woman, his palms up, his posture non-threatening. "There is little to be gained in resorting to physical violence, miss. I—"

The receptionist performed a jumping roundhouse kick that passed through Ravi's holographic head. Keel drew his blaster, aiming from the hip and locking eyes with the receptionist. She looked coldly at the captain, though it was clear to Keel that she was attempting to make sense of what had just happened with Ravi.

"As I was saying," Ravi continued as though nothing had happened, "you will do little more than get a good workout against me. And as for him," Ravi nodded toward Keel, who had placed himself out of her physical reach. "Him you do not want to fight. Most definitely not."

A mocking smile crept over the receptionist's face. "I'm a sister of the Lotus. I've trained my hands and feet to kill since I was seven years old. He doesn't want to try and get past *me.*"

"I am sure this is all true regarding your training regimen," Ravi conceded. "But the fact remains that you weigh perhaps one hundred and fifteen pounds, while he weighs nearly twice as much. Such a size and strength advantage would result in significant trauma should he land even a single blow, while your skeletal and muscular structure at best could generate force enough to—"

A chime sounded at the front desk. "Sentrella, who's out there with you?"

Before the secretary had the chance to react, Garret blurted out a reply. "Aldo! It's me, Garret Glover! I wanted to see about any work you might have…" He ended his sentence with a nervous laugh.

Dead air followed, as if the person on the opposite end of the comm was taking time to consider. Finally, the voice answered with warmth. "Garret! It's certainly been a while. Come on back here! Like I said before, there's always work for a coder such as yourself."

Sentrella, the receptionist, straightened herself. "And the others?" she asked, staring at Keel ruefully as he re-holstered his weapon.

"Others?" Aldo Kimer asked. "If they came with Garret, let them through. Garret, just come right in, buddy."

Sentrella stood aside, but did not open the doors.

"Thanks," Keel said, grabbing hold of one of the silvene handles. "I've got it." He held one of the doors open as the rest of his crew passed by.

"Sorry," Leenah mumbled as she scooted past the receptionist's glare.

Keel gave a half smile as he let the door close behind him. "Told you we were old friends."

"Okay," Garret said, pointing to a door just ahead and on the right. "That should be Aldo's."

Though Keel had clearly heard Aldo say that Garret could come right into his office, the slender coder paused at the door and knocked timidly.

The door slid open and Kimer said from inside, "Come on in, Garret."

The office was a museum of core-world pastiche. Each corner, holoportrait, bookshelf, and piece of furniture was perfectly matched to the opulent décor found in the deep core worlds. Kimer himself sat behind a massive desk in the middle of the room.

Leenah and Garret took the two open chairs immediately in front of the desk, leaving Ravi and Keel to stand in the background.

Aldo Kimer looked as though a hefty portion of his credits were reinvested into his appearance. His black hair was slicked back without a strand out of place, and he wore a custom-tailored spindark-silk suit. His face was free of spot or blemish, and his features bore the too-perfect look of the surgically altered. He looked up from behind a cigar, its smoke just now filling the room. "Who are your friends, Garret?"

Keel held out his hand and approached the desk. "Captain Aeson Keel. It's been a while between jobs, and Garret said you might have something for us."

Kimer stood to shake the captain's hand, then sat back down. "I'm sorry, Captain. I'm not sure what to say. I'm a great fan of what Garret can do as a code slicer, but I'm afraid I don't have any of the sort of work you would be accustomed to as a spacer. Perhaps you'd have better luck at the port authority?" Kimer reached into his desk drawer and pulled out a datapad. "I have a contact there. He might be able to supply you with a harvest run or surplus system-to-system courier move."

Keel grabbed the back of Garret's chair and tilted the coder to the side, causing him to spill out and stumble over to the side of Kimer's desk. The captain flopped down into the chair and set a booted foot up on the desk. "Let's not play coy, huh?"

Kimer recoiled at Keel's boot, but said nothing.

"We both know what sort of company Trident is," Keel said, waving a hand at the office. "And we both know what you do. No amount of expensive suits or smuggled cigars can hide that." Keel removed his foot and leaned forward. "But you might not understand just what you have in front of you—other than Garret, I mean."

"And what is that?" Kimer looked miffed. Probably more from Keel calling him and Trident out than anything else. These types always tried to keep up the appearance of respectability. This was the sort who scolded their children for lying after a long day of fraud and blackmail.

Leaning back again, Keel pointed to the princess. "She's a mechanical genius who can bypass any security system known to man." Leenah opened her mouth to speak, but Keel nudged her with the toe of his boot. "Ravi here," he pointed his thumb at the hologram behind him, "has cognitive abilities bordering on prescient. Ravi, what're the odds Kimer is thinking of calling in his secretary right now?"

"Based on body positioning, perspiration, eye contact, and the likelihood of a 'trouble' button mounted beneath his desk, I would say... twenty percent."

Kimer frowned and furrowed his brow, but didn't contradict the hologram. "And what of you, Keel?"

"With me you've got the best pilot in the galaxy. And fighter... and a whole lot more." He looked to Leenah and winked. The Endurian princess turned a brighter shade of pink, which had the peculiar twin effect of making Keel's heart race while also bringing about a certain feeling of embarrassment at his own brashness.

"I'm listening." Kimer leaned forward and steepled his fingertips. "What sort of action did you have in mind? Maybe boosting?" He shook his head. "No. Your type is more of a fence or a runner. Surely not an enforcer crew?"

"Maybe that Maydoon family has more work for us?" Garret blurted out.

Keel closed his eyes and swallowed a sigh. He watched as Kimer's face went from puzzled, to wary, and finally... frightened.

"Sorry," Kimer said, his hand moving toward the call button beneath his desk. "I don't have any work for you. Check the port." He stood up, his face ashen. The name "Maydoon" had had quite an effect on the man. Gone was the suave confidence he'd exuded when they first entered his office.

His office door slid open. Sentrella stood outside, beckoning for them to leave. "Let's go," she ordered.

"I just remembered," Kimer said, somewhat breathlessly, "I have another appointment. Good day."

The *Six*'s crew rose to their feet. "If you change your mind," Keel said on his way out, "you wanna know how to reach me?"

Kimer shook his head vigorously. He looked as though his mind were far away. "No. That's—no. Good day, Captain. No."

13

Aldo Kimer stood at the gallery window at the side of his office. He told himself that he would only watch the Corsican sun go down and then get back to closing up. But when the titian and golden hues faded into a distant purple glow on the horizon, Kimer didn't stop looking. The dark market broker stood motionless for so long that his motion-sensing office lights all went out. The glowing red of a passing speeder's taillights filled the office, casting Kimer's long shadow against the opposite wall.

A sheen of perspiration broke out on his forehead. He wiped his brow with four fingers, half expecting to see them covered with his own blood when holding them before his eyes. He mumbled a self-instruction. "Grab hold of yourself, Aldo…"

Irrational. That was what Kimer knew he was being. The coder bringing up Maydoon—of all people, *Maydoon*—was probably just coincidence. The Maydoons were obscenely wealthy. They treated their contractors as if they were foreign dignitaries. Who *wouldn't* want another job like that? The captain, Keel, was a man of the galaxy, but he didn't *seem* to have any reaction when Garret gave the name. But then again, Kimer had been so entirely overtaken with fear at the speaking of that cursed name that he hadn't thought to look for anyone else's reaction until several seconds had passed.

No. It wasn't worth it. He had barely escaped with his life the last time those black-and-red armored... *monstrosities* showed up looking for Maydoon. He wouldn't risk more of the same trouble. Besides, Trident had outgrown Corsica years ago. Rent would be higher on a core planet, but with the reputation he'd built, he could afford it. His clientele might actually *appreciate* him being located on a core planet. Even if it was only the lower core.

He moved to his desk to check the status of a drivescrub, though he knew it had already finished erasing itself while he was looking out of his office window. Looking for monsters. For killers. He was sure that the visitors were portents of his own demise. He was going to die, tortured for more information, though he'd already yielded everything he knew to soldiers so hard and cruel that—on reflection—he had never stopped worrying about them. That's what was really on his mind. He was anxiously waiting for them to return and tie up him. The final loose end.

No.

He shook his head. He was being silly. Jumping at shadows in his own mind, like a frightened child.

A ring of sweat dampened his silk collar. Kimer moved past silvene-and-gold-accented furniture to the private fresher adjoining his office. He splashed cool water around his face and neck, then stared at his reflection in the mirror. The room around him seemed to darken, as if every light but those around the mirror turned off. Kimer stared intently at his own face, watching with morbid fascination as beads of sweat formed from his pores, the cooling effect of the water no longer active. In his mind flashed a dark memory of the armored men in black and red who marched into his office only a few weeks earlier. Men who looked like legionnaires—but not. More menacing, if that were possible. His heart raced as his mind recalled the shadowy figure who'd entered behind the soldiers—and the dark, oppressive feeling that had sprung up in his chest as a result. The figure who had spoken without speaking, who'd had Kimer breaking his cardinal rule: *Never roll over on customers.*

But Kimer spoke that day. He told the man things he wasn't even asked—anything to appease. Anything to get the unnatural visitor and his wicked entourage to leave him. Leave him and never come back. He remembered telling them—with an attention to detail his customers always complimented him on—how to find Maydoon. How to circumvent the security system that he'd set up in exchange for hundreds of thousands of Maydoon's credits. He spoke freely, knowing that in so doing, he was issuing a death warrant for Maydoon... and his entire family.

And now they were coming back. Coming back not in force, but subtle. Like serpents. Posing as a freighter crew. Seeking to catch him unawares. Seeking to hurt him. To kill him. Punish him.

"Sentrella!" he gasped, trusting his secretary was still at her desk to hear the comm.

"Yes, Mr. Kimer?" The receptionist's voice was calm. "Are you all right?"

"I need you to accelerate my departure. Have a ship come for me now. We can transfer the rest of the data remotely." Kimer looked at his reflection. He could *see* his pulse in the veins of his neck. "And... and I don't want to set up in the core. Not yet. I want you to find me somewhere remote. Something at galaxy's edge. I don't want to be found, Sentrella."

Sentrella's answer was slow in coming. "As you wish, Mr. Kimer."

Kimer turned the water back on and brought it up in violent splashes, rubbing his face vigorously, not caring about the way the water was ruining his expensive shirt and suit jacket. Unconcerned with how the sopping clothing wrecked the smuggled cigars in his breast pocket. His knees threatened to buckle as he left the fresher and moved past his desk to an amply stocked wet bar. His hands went up to the top shelf and pulled down a bottle— it didn't matter what it contained. Anything would do.

Through the bar's mirrored backsplash, Kimer watched himself pour. His hands shook, and the neck of the bottle jiggled and clinked against the glass as Kimer attempted to hold both still. He was a nervous wreck.

The glass filled almost to capacity, Kimer set down the bottle and again watched his shaking hands in the backsplash. He saw a glimpse of movement, shadows drifting through shadows that caused him to drop his drink into the bar's sink. The glass shattered on impact, and Kimer sliced his finger in a reflexive attempt to save it.

"Damn!" Kimer cried out, venting a frustration that went well beyond a simple cut. He squeezed tightly around the slice, causing blood to swell from the wound.

The broker reached for a bar towel—and froze. In the mirror, he saw an armored humanoid almost hidden in the shadows behind him. Keeping his body pressed against the bar, he turned to face the intruder. "Who are you?"

The figure moved forward. The color was different, a ghostly sort of gray instead of black and red, but the armor was nearly the same. A bullpup blaster rifle rested in the mercenary's arms, and Kimer could see his reflection in the black visor of the specter's helmet.

This was Wraith. They'd sent Wraith to kill him.

"Sentrella!" Kimer screamed, knowing his receptionist would hear the call and burst into the room.

Wraith took two steps toward him when the door to Kimer's office whooshed open.

Sentrella leapt into the air, screaming "*Kaiyee!*" as she sought to deliver a flying kick.

The mercenary sidestepped the attack and sent an open palm square into Sentrella's chest. Her momentum was redirected downward. Kimer could hear the air escape from her as her back slammed onto the floor.

Wraith took another step toward Kimer. Kimer called out to the woman on the floor. "Sentrella! Stop him! I hired you to stop this from happening again!"

Before Kimer's bodyguard/receptionist could come fully to her feet, Wraith half-turned and sent a blazing blue energy blast into her. Sentrella convulsed, the paralytic stun bolt shutting down her voluntary motor functions, then dropped once more to the floor.

The blaster rifle now aimed at him, Kimer pushed himself back against the bar, knocking over a snifter of priceless port wine, which poured out blood red on the polished hardwood floor. "Hey, whoa." Kimer held out his hands, palms up. "Wraith... look... Wraith. Please. I can work with you."

The mercenary stopped several paces away from Kimer, but kept his blaster rifle leveled. Why did he pause? Did this mean Wraith *wasn't* here to kill him? He did use only a stun blast on Sentrella, after all. Kimer clutched at hope. "I... I wanted to work with you for a long time. Never had a way of reaching you. My clients... some of them heard about you. From Republic friends. Always asked if you could be hired. Bump off a husband. Run down an embezzler. Take out a rival crime syndicate..."

The spectral mercenary said nothing, and Kimer felt as though he was looking past him. Into his very soul. "Just, rich people problems," Kimer offered weakly. "You know... you know."

"Tell me," Wraith said, his voice harsh and cold from behind the audio filter of his legionnaire-like helmet.

"T-tell you what?"

Wraith adjusted something on the side of his blaster rife. A knob? A kill switch?

Oba—is he going to kill me now? Did he change his mind?

"No, no!" Kimer shook his outstretched hand as if waving away the danger. "Don't shoot! Please. Yes. Maydoon. Yes. I'll tell you. It's not like he can come after me now."

Wraith stood silently.

"Maydoon hired me for a job. He had me reprogram a war bot for domestic use. To protect his kid. The kind of thing that'll get someone stripped of their office. I hired a savant, who got the job done. We all got paid. That was it."

Wraith seemed to bore a hole in Kimer's center from behind the mask. He gave no indication. No reaction.

Kimer looked around his office helplessly. The puddle of port wine was a mess. Sentrella was breathing, but her shoulder looked out of socket. "I... I don't... There was—I had another code slicer. Not as good as the kid, but good enough. I had him put something—a tracker—in the bot. Insurance, you know?" Kimer shook his head rapidly. "These wealthy types. The core dwellers. They'll sell you out if you don't—"

"The tracker," commanded Wraith.

"How to track it? I—it's technical. You have to deconstruct the archaic Republic internal comm code. Not hard to do if you know the language. Fewer people do now, those bots are ancient, but yeah. It's always announcing its location. Always. Until its power supply is completely depleted."

Wraith brought up his bullpup blaster rifle, aiming for Kimer's head.

"No—no!" Kimer shouted, cringing as he curled into a standing fetal position. "I told you! I told you!"

"The rest," insisted Wraith.

Tears welled in Kimer's eyes. "I'm not— He...he's *evil*. I know that sounds crazy coming from a guy like me. He's evil, though. He came in here with legionnaires. Only they weren't. They looked like you only black and red instead of gray. I didn't want to give up Maydoon. He had a family—a daughter. I didn't want her to die. I didn't want to tell." Kimer slid down the bar and sat in the spilled wine. He looked up at Wraith, tears in his eyes. "I *had* to."

Ackabar Star Port
Ackabar

The *Obsidian Crow* shot past a hammer-headed Republican ground assault corvette and dove down along the larger ship's spine, passing open docking bays and tiny legionnaires scuttling for assault shuttles.

"*Tenku no chobba Tenku!*" cried the wobanki as Rechs slid into the captain's seat and scanned the star field through the metal lattice of the flight deck.

Still in his armor, Rechs smelled of burnt ozone from all the blaster fire down in Junga's junk fortress. He dialed in the master deflector array and booted up the jump computer. "You better not have scratched my ship, kitty kat!" he muttered in reply as he took over the flight controls.

They had three Republican fighters on their tail, screaming in hard and firing warning shots. Rechs eyed the tactical targeting computer. Lancer-class fighters. Pilot and a gunner. Two big jump nacelles for engines behind the jutting canopies for the pilots. Standard gold-and-white Repub Navy.

He pulled off his helmet. There was an audible whoosh of air as it disconnected from the suit. A dull *clang* as he tossed it into the navigator's seat behind him.

"*Hachoo obbi tonada?*" asked the wobanki.

Rechs had forgotten all about the small girl and her war bot.

"Tell 'em to strap in. This is gonna get tricky."

He yanked the *Obsidian Crow* into a twirl to avoid the pursing fighter's now targeting-to-disable blaster fire, and cut across the hull of the Repub assault corvette. Rechs scanned the swirling purple clouds of Ackabar and the glittering city below. Turret fire from the corvettes was now starting to track and lead his flight path. They had yet to find their range, though. He needed options...

"Ship."

"Here, Captain," she purred.

"We need a jump solution from low-Earth orbit in the next two minutes, or we've had it."

"Captain, you know the average jump solution takes ten to twenty minutes to compute for safety," the ship announced. "But I'll do the best I possibly can despite your use of arcane navigational terms. Low-*Earth* orbit indeed."

Rechs ignored the AI's snark. He was too busy trying not to smash into the main port hub of Ackabar while dodging fire from the assault corvettes. Never mind those fighter pilots all over his six.

The *Crow* circled the giant monolith of a star port once, staying close to the mushroom-shaped hub and docking bays. The Lancers were trying to line up for a clear shot, but there were too many Republican corvettes attempting to continue the planetary tax interdiction assault—never mind the departing star craft full of civilians attempting to flee said tax interdiction.

Young Repub Navy pilots might have mistaken the *Crow* for an old light freighter, with its standard pancake configuration and pilot's metal-laced cupola peeking out just aft of the two leading edges. But in truth it had only recently become an old light freighter. It had been a brand-new Terran navy bomber back in the day, as they used to say.

"Whatever it takes, Lyra," Rechs shouted over a deflector overload relay alarm that suddenly began to ululate. "Because we won't be around ten minutes."

As if on cue, blaster fire smashed into the *Obsidian Crow*'s dorsal thrusters.

"Why aren't the deflectors reorienting, you addle-brained cat!" Rechs growled at the wobanki as he sent the ship spinning down toward the city floor. But the wobanki had gone aft to take care of the passengers.

"He didn't set them properly," the ship replied.

Rechs shook his head once at the obviousness of this statement. He snapped a series of contacts in place that angled the deflector shields into the standard dogfight configuration.

Now the assault corvettes were shooting at him. But their pulsed energy fire was slow-moving, and he could easily avoid it. That the shots slammed into the civilian populace below didn't seem to be of much concern to the Repub gunners or their superiors.

The Lancers were all over the *Crow* as Rechs throttled back and took the ship into a series of mammoth gas-refining catacombs beyond the dockyards. The ship's shields shook at the powerful impacts from the Republican fighters' blaster fire. If he trusted Lyra—or if Lyra even trusted itself slightly—Rechs could've turned over the helm and run back to the defensive omni-cannon.

Alas, the ship had no confidence in its ability to fly itself.

And it was fat and slow compared to the Repub fighters that trailed it into the cyclopean gasworks, jockeying for a freighter kill.

Rechs followed the twisting maze of pipeworks and found the main exhaust vent network. One wrong move and they'd end up all over the walls. He executed a tight turn and slipped the *Crow* into the mammoth exhaust housing channels of the sprawling gas refinery. The Lancers broke attack formation and scattered.

"If the shut-off gate is closed, this is going to be a real bad idea," he said to no one as the dorsal thruster overheat warning sensors lit up like a fireworks display.

"Lyra… lock those down. I'll use ventral."

"By your command, Captain."

Rechs switched on the running lights, because the carbon-blasted gas-refining furnace was as dark as the night sky at midnight beyond the galaxy's edge. It was like flying beneath the murky water of some swampy river. The ship streaked past blackened mausoleums of infernal despair, or so it seemed for a moment to the old bounty hunter. Like some Ancients' ruins he couldn't remember fully, but that haunted his dreams nonetheless. A place he had once been long ago. He'd seen such places... but he couldn't remember where. Or when.

"Stow that!" he muttered to himself as his hands swam across the controls. He checked the jump computer. The ship was still loading in the solution.

"Tarravil?" he barked.

"It's the only safe jump I can compute under these circumstances, Captain," replied Lyra.

"Tarravil it is," Rechs sighed.

The wobanki slid into the copilot's chair next to Rechs.

"Any good with an omni-cannon?" Rechs asked.

The wobanki purred and shook his head.

Never mind then, thought Rechs.

"All right. Let's find a way out of here."

He picked a gas relay channel he hoped would lead to the refining gate, then throttled up.

The Republican fighters were already swarming into the massive chamber behind him, unloading bright blaster fire across the walls and the ship's rear deflectors. Shots reflected off the pipeworks and careened into the swallowing darkness, illuminating the blackened machinery as they went. One of the fighter pilots misjudged his speed and the turn he'd need to make to follow Rechs into the vent tubing. A moment later there was a deafening explosion as the Lancer kissed the sides of the pipe housing and disintegrated. The tube was lit up by the explosion as debris outraced the speeding freighter.

"*Chabu o'bong bong!*" the wobanki cried.

Rechs held course down the tunnel. The vent gate was either open, or it was closed. They'd find out in seconds.

A moment later they shot through the titanic opening and out over the main refinery.

A Republican superfreighter was lowering into position to confiscate all the product it deemed untaxed—which would probably be everything it could get its hands on. Rechs spun the *Crow* over onto its belly and dove away from the gargantuan ship. Emergency proximity alert warning lights flared across the freighter's length as collision alarms bellowed ominously throughout the factory.

But the storm-tossed skies above were clear.

The remaining Lancer was too late in turning, and moving at too high a speed to do anything other than spend itself all across the underside of the superfreighter with little damage or effect.

"Get us ready for departure," Rechs ordered the wobanki as he opened up the nav computer. A moment later he pointed the *Crow* toward the barely visible stars and pushed all engine throttles forward.

The *Obsidian Crow* shot skyward at incredible speed, disappearing into the neon atmosphere swirl above as more Republican assault ships swam downward toward Ackabar.

14

Punching through Ackabar's violent atmosphere revealed the chaos of the immovable force suddenly meeting a hundred objects desperate to escape. All manner of freighters and star liners, along with other private ships, were hurtling past the Republican corvette blockade, and Lancer squadrons were scrambling to disable the fleeing ships with accurate turbo-fire before they could make the jump to light speed and escape Ackabar—and the Republic.

"Captain," the ship said. "I'm receiving a transmission from the corvette *Victory* to stand down and back off our throttle... or we will be intercepted. I suggest—"

"Let 'em eat static!" Rechs shouted as he spun the *Crow* on its yaw axis while trying to make for the calculated jump point the ship had selected. A train of Lancers had picked up his tail and were throwing everything they could at the *Crow*. Evasive maneuvers that messed with their targeting computers were the only possible reply.

Two massive Republican cruisers moved in to block access to the jump. Whether they were running a course intercept algorithm to defeat prospective jumps, or it was by blind luck, Rechs had no idea. But it didn't matter—they were there now. *Great.*

"*Nachu tenda?*" asked the wobanki.

"Of course I do," Rechs growled. "How could I miss them? They're right where we want to go!"

More Lancer fire slammed into their collapsing rear deflector. He spun his captain's chair about to face the master bus panel. He snapped off several internal systems, including the life support generator, and re-routed the excess power to the deflectors. "If we don't get in close to one of the big ships, they'll keep shooting at us."

The life support alarm began to shriek, as did the proximity alert.

The Lancer pilots were good. Not great, but good enough. The lead pulled alongside and above, flipped his fighter over onto its belly, and motioned for Rechs to shut it down. There was only a brief moment of contact, as both ships were shooting toward the waist of the first big corvette.

Rechs had no intention of backing off the throttle.

Suddenly, he executed a near-vertical turn and sent the *Crow* screaming amidships. Turret fire from across all decks of the corvette began to fill the space ahead of the speeding freighter. Rechs got a target termination blink on the near-space proximity map. One of the Lancers had just gotten knocked out of the fight by the corvette's gun batteries.

Rechs stood and looked out the aft viewing panel of the flight deck cupola. The fighter was an exploding vapor cloud with debris trails streaking out in all directions. Another fighter shot from the expanding debris cloud half a second later. In the background, the big corvette heeled over in pursuit, hurling large-caliber blaster fire at the *Crow*.

"Bring us about and take us around behind the engines!" Rechs shouted.

The ship streaked past the massive dull glowing engines at the aft of the corvette. Holding on as the inertial dampeners fought to maintain gravity aboard the freighter, Rechs moved the master deflector to their starboard array.

Ion streams from the powerful cruiser's engines buffeted the *Crow*, and the wobanki did everything he could to hold course through the sudden energy storm. Then they were out of the thermal tempest and in clear space.

Rechs waited to see if the fighter pilot was dumb enough to follow.

He wasn't. The Repub fighter pilot had peeled off and was now coming back around, over the cruiser's engineering hull, to reacquire the *Crow*.

Ahead, Rechs could see that the other cruiser was angling in to cut them off, its engines on full burn. It had most likely computed their jump point by now and was moving to shut it down.

They were caught between two giants.

Long-range gun batteries opened up from both cruisers, and Rechs threw the *Crow* into a series of automated evasive actions designed to confuse their attackers' targeting computers. A fighter squadron departed from the launch deck of the corvette ahead and came howling toward them.

It's getting a little hectic. Rechs wondered if he'd bitten off more than he could chew this time.

"*Abu watangi murrowe tap*," purred the wobanki, who was busy trying to keep the ship out of the corvette's area target fire.

"No," replied Rechs. "This is all going according to plan."

The wobanki yowled. He didn't believe a lie that bald. "*Choda?*" he hissed softly.

"No surrender," Rechs replied.

Power array batteries went offline after another hit. Now the Republican fighter squadron was within blaster range and coming straight at them.

At least the big turrets have backed off. They'll let the fighters try and take us out.

"Distance to jump?" Rechs asked.

The wobanki cackled out the answer and added his opinion on the odds of success.

"We're gonna make it," Rechs replied.

The wobanki sighed and continued to maneuver the ship.

Rechs climbed out of his seat and shouted, "Lyra! Charge up the omni-cannon."

A moment later the bounty hunter was pounding down the curving corridor inside the *Obsidian Crow*'s main hull, racing toward the access hatch that led to the lone gunnery turret.

Rechs crawled into the gunnery ball and flicked on the master controls and the inter-ship comm. "Keep us moving toward the jump point, but make your turns lazy and slow so I can lead them. Keep your speed up though," he told the wobanki. "I need the belly of the *Crow* facing them at all times, Catman!"

The ship heeled over in obedience as the wobanki cried, *"Tu mangu Skrizz."*

Rechs spun up the antique tri-barreled omni-cannon and started to unload on the nearest Lancer. It disintegrated as he drew a bright line of blaster fire across one of its jump nacelles.

"Good for you... Skrizz," Rechs muttered.

The catman yowled in victory—whether at the destroyed pursuer, or the use of its proper name, it was impossible for Rechs to determine. Most of the galaxy found the wobanki cats to be enigmatic to the point of bizarre.

Rechs doled out a few short bursts from the cannon as the squadron swarmed all over the slower freighter heading toward the jump point.

"More fighters inbound," the ship announced.

Rechs grunted as he sent a full burst into a Lancer that tried a strafing run on the turret. Rechs laced it with fire from wing to fuselage, and it exploded violently against the black velvet of space. The look on the pilot's face, even at that unreal speed in the heat of battle, was clear enough to Rechs in the last second before the fighter exploded.

Everyone dies alone.

The wobanki announced they were clear for jump.

Three more fighters closed in for the kill.

Rechs shut down the cannon.

The big corvettes were hurling hot bolts of charged energy across their path, but the wobanki was now twisting and twirling the ship well in advance of the trajectories of plotted fire.

For a moment...

Just for a moment...

It was all so beautiful to Rechs.

The big ships.

The dancing fighters.

The debris and expanding vapor clouds of destruction.

The stars.

The galaxy.

It was all he'd ever really wanted.

"Jump now," he whispered into the comm.

And then the battle was gone as everything shifted over to light speed by orders of sudden mind-numbing magnitude.

Within the *Crow*'s passenger lounge, if it could be called that, Prisma stared wide-eyed and straight ahead. She'd never been in a battle before, much less one in space. Her tiny knuckles had turned white from the death grip she'd maintained on the safety bars that surrounded her after she'd been tossed into a crash seat by the wobanki.

She'd been fearless in her pursuit of a bounty hunter to obtain the justice she so badly craved. But back there, during the battle, as the junky old freighter she'd found herself in was getting hammered by blaster fire, and the enemy fighters were swarming so close to the outer hull she could hear their hollow ghostly engines thrumming through the superstructure, and the electrical snaps and discharges were sounding all throughout the strange dark ship as the deflectors fought to disrupt and distribute the blaster energy from the Republican fighters...

Back there she'd begun to fear.

And in those moments, she missed her daddy more than she'd ever thought possible.

She wanted to say, "I really need you now, Daddy."

And she'd been trying not to cry when she realized she could never say that again to him.

It was in that moment that she realized: this fear wasn't about a battle. It wasn't about almost being murdered in space. It wasn't about death at all. It was about being lost and alone forever no matter what happened... in a galaxy that was too big to care about little girls all on their own. It was about knowing that there's no place like home. And that home doesn't exist anymore on any known map.

And then, in the middle of that howling battle, as the lights and life support failed, in the comfort of near darkness... she did begin to cry. Just one tear, as some Republican fighter swept in close overhead, screeching blasters that made that death-rattle hiss of discharged energy.

In that moment she desperately wanted her daddy to hold her and tell her there was nothing that could ever get them. Not ever. Like he did when they left the capital for the edge. For Wayste, where he would be the governor, and a daddy who was always there. His time away from her was done.

She'd been so afraid of leaving the known for the unknown back then. But excited, too. As the carrier they'd been transported to powered up toward jump, lumbering away from the center of the Republic, from the bright jewel that was the center of the galaxy's core and all that was known to her, she'd been so afraid of, and excited by, the unknown. She could still feel his big hand holding her tiny hand.

"What will we find out there?" she'd asked as she leaned into his dress uniform. The one with the diplomatic medals sash.

"Our future," he told her softly. Squeezing her hand in that way that only daddies know—a way that makes you feel as if there's an anchor on which the galaxy hangs. A way of holding close, and holding on, to all that matters. Creating a barrier the galaxy can never ever blast its way into.

Or at least that's how it had felt.

"I'm afraid," she'd mewled like a common house kitten.

"Never. Ever. Be afraid," he'd told her slowly. Pronouncing each word as though it were its own sentence. Its own island. Its own world, galaxy, reality.

Its own truth.

"Never, Prisma."

And she'd promised herself she wouldn't. No matter what happened. Even after the times when she'd been so afraid during... what had happened on Wayste.

And after. When she'd been on her own and all alone.

And then on the junky ship that took her away from Wayste.

And on Ackabar, in the middle of all that chaos and searching for someone to give her revenge.

And now.

In a ship being pounded by Republican fire and feeling like it was going to come apart at any second.

She'd wanted to scream at the galaxy that she was just a little girl and nothing more.

She squeezed her eyes tight shut when life support went off and the lights went out. She promised herself she wouldn't whimper, but she must have, because Crash asked, looming silently in the dark next to her, "Are you all right, miss?"

"Yes," she managed. She felt her features contorting into her ugly crying face, and she was grateful for the darkness.

I will not cry.

I will not cry.

I will not cry.

She could hear the bounty hunter shouting commands from the flight deck. Then running past them, his boots sounding exactly like the metallic clank of the legionnaires who'd chased her in that long-abandoned ship.

Then the whine and blur of some weapon firing back. Distant explosions rocking the hull. All of it feeling like the end of the galaxy all around her.

And then she'd felt the shift.

That sudden lightness of being that everyone who dares space flight knows as... the jump to light speed. That overwhelming, otherworldly thick silence that was there... and not there.

To Prisma Maydoon, yet one more of the galaxy's orphans, hyperspace was a kind of safety. A running from danger. A safe and hidden place beyond the reach of the galaxy.

I never want to leave hyperspace, she thought, and wondered how she might stay here forever. Cocooned in the old rubber and cracked vinyl of the crash chair that had been designed and newly installed long before her grandparents had even been considered. She breathed in its warm, close, industrial fuel scent, and found the dust of its being from an age long before as some kind comfort she'd never imagined knowing.

The comfort of all ships that had stories from long ago somehow reassured her that she, too, would one day have her own stories. It was a feeling she would take with her for the rest of her life. No matter what, and who, she became.

They can't get you here, she told herself.

And she asked…

How does one manage a life in hyperspace forever?

There was no answer to this from the galaxy. She was just a small girl, and the galaxy was too big for any one person to know everything and to mean anything in the grand scheme of it all. Especially a little girl who wanted nothing but…

She couldn't remember what she'd ever wanted. Except that she really could. It just hurt too much to carry with her now.

Now, the only thing she ever wanted was…

Revenge.

She had wanted her daddy back. But in lieu of that, she would take revenge.

Revenge would be enough.

Revenge would do.

The life support came back on. The soft hum and whir of ventilation. Even heat. Lighting flickered back to that bare shadowy deep blue that humans needed to not go stark raving mad.

"Oh good, miss," rumbled KRS-88. "It seems we've escaped instantaneous death."

The old bot seemed content with just that. As if continued runtime was all the galaxy needed to offer it. Just one more day in which to follow its programming in a seemingly endless series of days. That was all it needed to be happy, or at least content.

If happy was even a thing for bots.

Who knew?

Who really knew?

From down the curving corridor came the bounty hunter. He didn't have his helmet on now. His armor was beat up and covered in blast marks—and, she noticed for the first time, it was adorned with strange and arcane markings. A patch with the letters "NASA" on it. Some old flag she didn't recognize.

He is stranger than anyone I have ever known, she thought as she studied him.

He looked tired.

He sat down with a *thump* in one of the bolted chairs that swiveled in the small, dark lounge. His armor creaked and scraped as he adjusted himself to lean back, one leg out, one leg back. An arm hooked over the back of the seat he'd taken.

His hair was iron gray. Blue, washed-out eyes the color of a sky she'd once seen, watched her. If there was kindness in them she could not tell. He had a small beard. Gray salt and once-dark pepper.

"Now," he asked her. "Who exactly are you?"

And then... not "why," but:

"Who do you want me to kill?"

15
Maydoon Compound, Bacci Cantara
Wayste
The Past

When the shooting started, Prisma did what she was told to do. She ran as fast as she could, and then she hid.

They'd only been on Wayste for three days. Three days since the landing at the old star port out past "the Barrens," as the locals called the dead lake where the occasional rare ship set down in a sudden blast of sand and thrust-driven debris. A Republican shuttle had dropped them off in just such a manner and left in a hurry of grit and dust.

It was just the three of them standing on the burning, dead lake at the edge world no one really ever came too. Kael Maydoon, his daughter, and their bot.

"When will the official greeting committee for your sector governorship arrive, sir?" intoned the massive KRS-88 in his deep-bass voice modulation of courtesy, respect, and decorum.

"It's not that kind of governorship," replied Kael Maydoon absently.

"What kind is it, Daddy?" Prisma asked in her tiny soprano, her voice piercing the desert silence now that the shuttle had leapt back up into the sky to rendezvous with the carrier. A small wind came out of the vast glaring desert from beyond distant iron-gray mountains, tossing her hair across her face. Toward the west they could see Bacci Cantara, the only actual city on Wayste. In reality it was more of a settlement than a city. Prisma was holding a tiny case. It contained everything she'd found valuable enough to take with her.

Kael bent down, one knee hovering above the parched and cracked dirt that spread away in every direction. Over his shoulder a tired, old moon hung low above the bright, burning horizon. Every crater of it was visible in the clear silence, even though it was so low to the atmosphere. *It must be very near to this planet*, thought Prisma. If there'd been an ocean on this world, it would have been very turbulent. But there wasn't. Prisma had learned everything she could about Wayste on her datapad.

"It's the kind," Kael Maydoon began gently, his smile broadening across handsome yet worry-lined features, "where we can be together now. Finally, Poppet."

Prisma smiled.

He held her close and whispered, "Finally," again. As though he were pronouncing some law or new statute that the galaxy must obey because the Republican Council had declared it a law for all time. A special ordinance just for the two of them.

He was a handsome man. His hair was brown, tousled and turning gray at the temples. The gray was definitely well before its time. Laugh lines, and other lines some might call worry, creased his face and especially his eyes. Those eyes were gray, and one could tell at a glance that they had seen far too many things that could never be unseen. One could tell that about him. Even in the most casual of conversations.

But not Prisma, even though she knew the lines were there and saw them sometimes when she caught him unawares. When he was reading. Or staring out at any one of the many alien horizons on all the worlds on which he'd served the Republic's diplomatic corps. In those moments she could see the haunted look he so desperately tried to hide with a quick smile, a soft chuckle, or a friendly question meant to distract.

Of all the things Prisma would ever learn about him, even things that were at odds with what she knew, or thought she knew, to the end she would've told you he was the kindest man who ever walked the galaxy.

She would think that until the end.

Despite everything that would happen.

Deep down inside, he was a kind man. Her daddy... was a kind man.

He stood. They had arrived at the back end of the Republic, in some no-name sector no one cared about back on Utopion, or any of the other glittering capital worlds that held sway. And even in these circumstances, Kael Maydoon looked every inch the Republican diplomatic governor arrived to administer and oversee. Crisp white uniform and silver diplomatic sash with all his medals. Short, silver-trimmed cape. Polished high black boots. No weapon. No blaster. That he'd come in the name of the Republic, in peace, was enough to guarantee his safety in a galaxy ruled by just one government.

"C'mon now," he said to Prisma. "Let's go see our new home. We've got a lot of exploring to do. A lot of living to catch up on."

What they found after the long walk into Bacci Cantara wasn't much of a city, or even a settlement. It was nothing more than a few streets and some fair-trade establishments the desert rats came in to do business with. The governor's mansion was a wind-battered old bunker that served as the official seat of power for the Republic. At the edge of Bacci Cantara, up along the town's main street, past cantinas and other enigmatic businesses, it waited beneath a high, rocky cliff that would provide shade in the late afternoons of the burning days on Wayste.

Their new home.

Kael Maydoon produced a credentials data globe and inserted it into the ancient lock to the right of the massive security door that guarded the entrance to the bunker. A moment later the house unlocked, and the impressive security door swung wide open.

"That's a big door, Daddy!" Prisma whispered as it swung out into the hot desert air.

"It is, Prisma. Nothing will ever get to us through that. This house is a very safe house. The Republic wants us to be safe, because what we do here is very important to the galaxy. So we have to be protected. No matter what."

Beyond the doors, within the dark of the bunker, two giant bots, bigger than KRS-88, lumbered forward to greet the new sector diplomatic governor.

"Long live the Republic, sir," rumbled the first war bot.

Prisma had seen many bots in her time on ships and other worlds. These were older models than any she'd ever seen. As though they'd been kept because no one had gotten around to replacing them yet—or perhaps because no one had come out this far, so near the edge of the galaxy, to swap them out. Even so, they were still very fierce-looking. Huge iron fists. Deployable tri-barrel blasters and micro-missiles. Squat heads. Broad-shouldered torsos. She'd once heard Republican soldiers refer to bots like these as "hulks."

"I am HB-2505..." rumbled the first war bot loudly. "And this is my companion, HB-2506. We protect and defend the governor and this residence. Standard protocols are in effect. Do you have any special instructions at this time, Your Grace?"

Kael Maydoon seemed uncomfortable with this title. "No. N-none," he stuttered. He'd been caught off guard. Hesitated. But he regained himself, and the moment, as he issued his first directive. "Raise the flag and prepare this residence for occupation, two-five-oh-five. The Republic is here to serve the sector and the people of Wayste."

"By your command, Your Grace," rumbled the automated killing machine as it turned toward its tasks. The two big war bots lumbered out the main door.

Though it was not big, or grand, the governor's residence was everything Prisma had ever wanted in a home. A place to do all the things she'd dreamed of doing. A place of their own. And the most important thing was, they would never have to leave again. Here was where they would be a family.

Finally.

She took a deep breath, her tiny shoulders rising. And then she exhaled, letting everything, all the worry and fear... go. It was as if, to Kael Maydoon, the weight of the galaxy, held on his daughter's shoulders, flew through the massive doors that would keep them safe, and ran off into the desert.

Kael Maydoon felt that he saw this. He'd seen many strange things across the galaxy. He saw this, and he told that evil spirit to never come back. To never bother his daughter again.

He remembered something then. Something Prisma's mother had made him promise.

"Be a family, Kael. No matter what happens."

His voice was a whisper as he said these words and watched that evil spirit disappear into those iron-gray mountains along the distant horizon. His eyes were wet. Then he smiled and quick-changed back into the man he wanted the galaxy to see. He'd become a master at wearing such disguises. Life and death often depended on it.

Prisma was looking around at the Spartan living quarters. All the new surfaces and spaces to be explored. She knew there was a room just for her somewhere within it. He'd promised her that. A place for her to keep her collections. She was forever collecting.

"A family then," he whispered to the silence as Prisma ran off to find her new room. "No matter what happens." And he smiled.

Two days.

Those two days before the shooting started were the best two days of Prisma's life.

The townspeople of Bacci Cantara came, bringing local foods and imported delicacies, along with gifts for the new Republican diplomatic governor. That first night there was an impromptu party under the few stars this far out near the edge. The low moon rode across the sky like a burning, bright world of fantasy, making everything blue.

The local people were so kind.

Her father shined, answering all the questions about their future, as far as the Republic was concerned, with the ease and promises of a better tomorrow. And later, as the last of the townspeople faded into the blue darkness, as the slow-moving moon fell into the distant, shadowy horizon, her father turned to her. He said, "We're off to a good start now, Poppet."

Which was what he called Prisma, sometimes.

She had no idea why.

If she could've had him back, after he was gone, she would've asked, "Why did you call me Poppet?"

But the ghost of him never appeared to answer, or apologize. That answer was lost, as are so many other important things in the galaxy. Especially out near the edge. But she never forgot the question.

"We did good today, Poppet."

"Did we?"

"Yes. Very. They trust us. They're hopeful that the Republic is going to expand operations here, in this sector, and they hope that means more credits for them and their families."

"Is the Republic really going to do that?" Prisma asked.

He paused. The vast desert floor beneath them spread off into the darkness. A forgotten planet somewhere in the backwater of the galaxy turned once more on its axis in its long revolution about a star no one much cared about.

"Yes. I'm going to do my best to make the House of Reason see why they need a military base here. Why they need to watch the edge."

"Why do we need to watch the edge, Daddy?"

He didn't answer. Instead they went inside and set the security protocols for the hours of sleep and dreams. The big war bots would lumber around the perimeter all night long. Watching and waiting.

She told Hulk One, which was what she called the leader, "G'night!"

It stopped to regard her, turning its low, squat head, its glowing, red eyes coming to rest on her. "Thank you, miss. Good night to you also." And then it resumed its tireless patrol.

Later, her father turned on the fire in the sunken living area. He had a glass of Faldaren scotch. He stared into it, and occasionally the crystal fire.

Prisma could tell that he was thinking about something.

"Why do we need to watch the edge, Daddy?" she asked again.

He started, suddenly. As though he had not been there in that room, on that planet, with her. He smiled at her and put down the glass.

"There are things out there. Things that need watching."

This sounded mysterious to Prisma.

She liked mysteries.

She read them all the time on her datapad. Mysteries about girls who crash-landed on dangerous planets and found pirates and ancient treasure from the Savage Wars. Artifacts, too, from inside Ancients' ruins. She liked those the best.

"Like... what?" she prompted when he didn't expand. He just seemed to be staring off at something again.

He hummed to himself as though he were thinking about whether to proceed. She knew what this meant.

"If it's monsters..." she said, "I promise I won't have nightmares."

He nodded at that.

He took a sip of his scotch.

"Beyond the galaxy," he began. "Way out in what the old freighter pilots and scouts call the..." He paused. Looked unsure about whether this was appropriate before-bed conversation.

"Oh, please," she begged. "I'm almost a woman, Daddy. I need to know things."

A smile tried to appear at the side of his mouth. But it just never made it. He just nodded once as though telling himself there was nothing truly to be afraid of. Just Kael Maydoon being ever cautious, and really... afraid of boogeymen who would never return from out there. So he continued.

"Oh... lost civilizations that are far older than the Republic, and..."

But he stopped again and almost laughed. Except it sounded like he was choking. He took another sip of the scotch to clear his throat.

"And what?" Then she guessed. "Monsters?"

Secretly, she loved mysteries about monsters. She didn't tell anyone that. But monsters were sooooo epic.

"There are always monsters, Poppet. Even here inside the Republic. More than you can imagine. But sometimes there are things worse than monsters."

"Worse than monsters?"

He nodded solemnly. "Worse."

"How?" she asked.

"No, Prisma. It's too late for that. I want you to sleep, and you don't need your mind going all light speed at this time of night. Always try to think of something good before you go to bed. Not mysteries."

"But I love them, Daddy."

He smiled. "I know you do."

"Then that's a good thing to me. So tell me!" she pleaded one last time. He was actually quite helpless when she begged.

But he seemed to think on this.

"I will," he promised. "Someday."

But that "someday" would never come.

And Prisma went to bed that night trying to think of what mysteries could be more incredible than monsters.

What, she thought, was out there beyond the edge of the galaxy? What needed watching?

But the question really should have been: "Who?"

She drifted off to sleep promising herself that she would go out there, beyond the edge, and find all those mysteries. Just like the girls she read about on her data-pad. She would have adventures and see things. And that would be her life.

What a life it would be.

Yes, maybe she would even find monsters. Though lost civilizations were pretty interesting too. Lost civilizations and monsters *together* would be *epically* perfect. To see that was to see the greatest mystery one could ever hope to see, she thought—and as her mind surrendered to sweet sleep, and then dreams, she hoped that would happen to her.

But why, she wondered as sleep took her for the last time she would ever be a child. Before the shooting started the next day and she'd have to run for her life.

Why did the "Big Dark" need to be watched?

What was out there?

Everyone saw the big ship come in. It wasn't a freighter. It was big like a small warship. Gray and bristling with weapon mounts. It came out of the bright clear sky and over the desert, moving slow like it was looking for something. The old bell that was the lone historical relic of Bacci Cantara, an actual old bell inside an old church someone had built long ago, started to ring. It was activated by an automated warning system that was operated by the star port's AI.

Prisma was at the library. Her first day exploring on her own. Of course, she was always with Crash—the bot Daddy had purchased to keep an eye on her while he did Republic business, trailing along and constantly telling her to "Be careful, miss" and "I don't think we should be gone this long, miss" as they explored what little there was to see of Bacci Cantara.

They'd met some interesting people. People Prisma had promised herself she would delve more into. Get to know. Hear their stories. She liked that. She liked meeting new people. Hearing their stories. Getting to know all about them.

But then everybody, the whole town, stopped suddenly as the solemn bell began to toll. The orbital proximity monitoring system had detected a ship. And a few minutes later, the large angular ship came through the clouds and settled on the ancient dry lake bed Bacci Cantara called their star port.

"Traders from Venice?" Prisma heard some old desert rat ask as she went to the edge of the high road to get a better view. When she saw the ship, a cold shiver ran through her, but she chalked that up to coming out into the sun from the cool interior of the library.

"Nah..." replied another man along the road, holding his hand up to shield his eyes from the bright sun. "Nothin' ain't due for two weeks. This is sumpin' new, and that means extra credits, I'll bet. Gotta get my minerals samples all in order." And then that guy ran off. In fact, most everyone was running, scurrying really, everywhere. Not in fear, but in hope and expectation. As though some galaxy circus had just hauled into orbit high above.

"Miss," interrupted KRS-88 over the general hubbub of excitement. "I do believe we need to seek out your father. This... unusual experience falls under a specific set of parameters he has personally instructed me in. I insist."

Prisma saw the men disembarking from the ship. They came out from underneath, and even from this distance they appeared large. Armored in black, they looked like the pirates she'd seen pictures of in her girls' adventure novels on her datapad.

She'd seen real pirates, too. Pirates the Republic had captured and brought in for a big public trial. Like that time when an entire liner had been murdered despite the ransom paid. These pirates looked like those pirates. Blasters. Armor. More blasters. Dirty, just like every pirate she'd seen in the news, or on the entertainments. Except this time it was real life, which is a thing one never expects to actually happen. And the truth was... they were scarier in real life. This was that sudden very real moment where one finds oneself beyond the safety parameters of the ride inside the galaxy circus. Or in the novel you'd been safely reading.

Prisma had experienced this same kind of moment once before, when she'd gotten away from her father on the big Republican carrier *Freedom*, which had brought them out to the edge. She had snuck onto the flight deck where the fighters were launched on patrol, and she got too close to a Lancer spooling up for departure. In that frightful loose-energy moment, she'd been made acutely aware of how small she was and how big the launching interceptor was. It thundered and roared just past her in an ear-splitting howl-scream as it leapt away from the carrier. Some deckhand had seen her and pulled her out of the way just in time. In that moment, she'd realized just how close to death real life could be.

This felt like that.

The dark men, venting from beneath the ship onto the desert floor, fanned out into a rough wedge and started walking across the dry lakebed toward Bacci Cantara.

"Let's get back!" Prisma said suddenly.

And Prisma was running as fast as she could. Not totally knowing why. Only convinced that somehow losing her daddy was suddenly real and possible.

The shooting started just after that.

Prisma came up short as she rounded a deserted street. Far away she could hear the resounding whine of distant blaster fire echoing over the silent desert world. Just a few shots. Then a volley. Then more.

Then nothing but an ominous silence where there had once been something.

Crash scuttled up beside her.

"Miss, that's blaster fire. I think Bacci Cantara is under some sort of attack."

Prisma rolled her eyes at the obviousness of this statement.

"Prisma." It was her father on her comm. "Prisma!"

She answered.

"Daddy! There's shooting. A ship landed. It looks military, but not like the Republic. It's different!"

"Prisma, I know. I need you to listen to me, and I need you to do everything I say." The tone of her father's voice scared her. It was hard, yet she could hear the fear.

There was more shooting nearby now. Some kind of battle was taking place just a few streets away. And Bacci Cantara didn't have that many streets. People were running past her. A woman screamed that someone had been killed. No, that wasn't right. She screamed that "they" were killing everyone.

"Prisma, I don't want you to come back," her father shouted over the comm. "I want you to hide in town somewhere. Wherever you are. Under no circumstances do I want you to come back here. And whatever happens, do not let these men get you, or find out you're my daughter. No matter what. Do you understand?"

"Daddy, what's—?"

"Do you understand me, Prisma? You must do what I say right now. I love you. No matter what: *I love you.*"

Right there she began to cry.

This was serious.

"Prisma. You are..." His voice broke and caught in his throat. "Prisma, you are strong enough to do this. Everything will be okay in just a little while. I promise. But don't come back here until they leave."

Then...

"Do you understand?" he shouted.

She tried to say something, but her mouth wouldn't work. Her lips were trembling uncontrollably.

She heard boots now. Heavy boots on the old laser-cut sandstones of the streets of a place no one in the core worlds cared much about. A place no one was ever supposed to find. That's what her daddy had told her many times, though she hadn't really understood what he was saying then. She'd thought they were just hiding from his career with the Republic and his endless work.

Now she knew they were hiding from these men.

She ducked behind some old shipping modules.

"Prisma…" She heard her father's tiny voice over the communicator as she moved for cover.

"I understand, Daddy," she whispered. "They're coming."

"I love you," he said again. And just before he cut the link he whispered, "Always."

And then he was gone.

The boots of the men, many of them, came on against the laser-cut sandstone, making a dull hollow thump that was like the marching band music for some terrible piece of music no one ever wanted to hear.

Prisma peeked around the corner of a module.

Long tattoos, like the edges of severe blades, curled about the men's massive arms and bulging biceps. Their blaster armor was a patchwork assembly of a reflective black leather variant. Even Prisma knew that criminals preferred this kind of armor. It let them pull their "jobs" more easily. Especially the ones that required stealth.

They looked, to Prisma, like zombies. Dark circles under their eyes. Knotted, long, dirty hair. Pale skin and those tattoos like big curling hydra-pythons.

But there was another one among them. A man in a dark, hooded robe. He moved at their center, seemingly oblivious to their scanning movements and military hand signals. His arms were tucked within long sleeves and held in an almost reverent position. His bowed head was hidden beneath his cloak.

Prisma felt a wave of intense cold run through her. As though her skin, all the way down to her bones, had suddenly turned to ice water. They were headed for the governor's residence.

They were headed for her daddy.

When they reached the end of the street, Prisma pushed off from behind the cargo modules and followed them quietly, at a distance.

All Prisma could ever really say for a long time about what happened—all she saw in her mind—was a very specific moment, and that was when the massive security door had just come off its hinges. She'd been creeping closer to the pirates, or whatever they were, that had surrounded the governor's residence.

They stood before the angular, squat desert building in a rough semicircle, blaster rifles ready. The man in the dark, hooded robe was behind them and off to the side, as though he wasn't really with them. As though he was very far away from all that was about to happen. He was a ghost that hovered nearby. A ghost which everyone saw, even though they didn't want to.

Prisma had passed the people of Bacci Cantara on the way to the residence. People she would never know because they were dead in the street.

"Really, miss," rumbled KRS-88. "This is absolutely the opposite of what your father has instructed you to do. I shall be forced to tell him of your rebellious behavior when we meet him again. I regret this deeply. Perhaps at this evening's meal, before dessert."

"Crash," hissed Prisma. "Shhhhhhh. You're going to get us killed."

"Oh... yes. You are quite right, miss. I'm not very good at this sort of war thing. I'm just a service bot. Pomp and circumstance at your service. Again, young miss... this seems an excellent way to get killed, and or disabled. Please, come away from all this... this... excitement. It's unseemly."

Prisma ignored the bot's warnings and crept forward. Toward the gang of pirates. Then closer still. She could hear one of them, a gravel-voiced man, yelling at her father.

"Come out and face Goth Sullus, you Republican scum! Things can go easy—or they can go real hard!"

A moment later—a moment after the giant of a man lowered his blaster and turned back to the man in the dark, hooded robes—the massive security door just came away from the building. As though the pirates had used some sort of hydraulic jaw, or some trick only they knew to violate such barriers.

Prisma would always remember that. The loud shriek of rending metal. The pirates scrambling to get out of the way of the flying-outward door.

A security door meters thick.

State-of-the-art Republican defensive perimeter security hardware.

When the dry dust of Bacci Cantara cleared, the door lay on the courtyard in front of the governor's residence.

"I'm coming out!" she heard her father say. His voice sounded small and distant and pathetic.

Where are the two hulks? Prisma screamed inside her head. *They should be defending us.* Later she would find out that they had been destroyed. Shot to pieces. They'd been blasted into melted ruin on a side street where they'd tried to set up an ambush on the pirates.

"I'm coming out with it," her father said.

What was "it"? That was something Prisma would wonder later. Later, when she sat in the ruins of the home she'd almost had. And on the ship she took to get off the planet to find a bounty hunter who would kill for her.

The pirates were moving forward, weapons aimed. The man in the hooded cloak still faced outward toward the dry desert world that seemed only to be filled with silence. An afternoon wind whipped and caught at his robes, making him seem like some mythic wraith that troubled the legends and bedtime stories of a thousand worlds.

The whining report of a lone blaster shot rang out— and Prisma's life changed forever.

As though her soul were suddenly frozen in that terrible high-pitched whine of a blaster report moment.

Then the gravel-voiced giant exclaimed, "Got it!"

Now Prisma could see the big man approach the hooded figure almost fearfully. Not reverently, Prisma would later remember. The man was in fear of his fear. He held out her father's credentials data globe. The man in the hooded cloak took it, palmed it, examined it as though he were some second-rate star carnie gypsy about to read a fortune. Then it disappeared within the folds of his wind-flapped garment.

He nodded once.

"Let's get out of here, brothers," shouted the giant pirate. "Tactical movement. Watch the corners and alleys. We're not off this dust bowl yet, leejes."

And in time they were gone.

Prisma waited.

The entire town was silent now. Only the sound of the moaning wind, rising and falling, moving and keening through the old buildings, remained. As though it were the only thing left to mourn all the dead.

Slowly Prisma crept forward from her hiding place. She would remember running. Oversized boots pounding against the hot afternoon sandstone pavement of the courtyard and the now dead place called Bacci Cantara. She saw her father lying on the ground. The blaster hole in his chest. His beautiful gray eyes staring skyward. Not seeing her at all now.

"Get up, Daddy," she said. Her voice small and desperate. She shook her head once, back and forth, and began to cry. She begged him to get up.

His hands lay at his sides. The fingers open to the sky. As though he had finally surrendered all that one can grasp and hold in this life to something inevitably greater than himself.

Heaving with sobs, she dropped to the ground and took one of the hands. She tried furiously to rub life into it.

"Please... Daddy, please..." She could barely understand herself through her own tears. But she understood enough to know that she hated the sound she was making. And to hear herself begging was to hate it all the more.

"Please, Daddy... I can't be alone now. Not yet."

Far below, out on the vast dry lake bed, the big ship's engines ignited and grew to an ear-splitting roar.

Please.

She must've said that a hundred times by the time the ship rose into the sky, turned its back on Bacci Cantara forever, and surged off toward the stars and all the other mischief it must make before this tale is over.

A wan wind and a scattering of grit washed over her, and still she cried, helpless now, letting his cold hand fall back onto the dirt of that place.

Tears left dusty tracks on her face. Her shoulders shook, and her chest heaved in violent spasms.

Please.

Please.

Please come back.

And...

Why?

Night fell. Prisma sat next to her father. He was just a body now.

Gone.

Taken.

By whom, asked some voice deep within.

She watched her father's eyes stare up at the few stars coming out along the galaxy's edge.

By whom?

"Please," she whispered, her voice raw and scratched. Her eyes dead and far away. "Please come back now."

By whom?

Her tiny mouth formed the first word, making no sound. Then the second. Who had killed her daddy?

Who?

Someone named...

"Goth Sullus."

16
Obsidian Crow
Hyperspace

Tyrus Rechs listens to the young girl's tale of woe. He has listened to many such tales of tragedy and loss before someone has asked him to kill for them. Sitting there amid the ticking and humming that is almost nonexistent and yet somehow constant in an interstellar starship, he is lulled into a kind of meditative trance.

Though he has never been to Wayste, he knows that world. He has known all the worlds that were ever like Wayste. In the end, to him, they are all the same.

And though he has never met the girl's father, he knows him also. Knows the type. A bureaucrat who got caught up in something he didn't have the credits, influence, or brass to buy his way out of. All bills come due eventually. The kid's story seems like nothing more than a bill that was finally required to be paid. The tragedy on the other side is someone else's business.

Oftentimes Rechs's business.

He listened to the last of the story. How the light freighter *Viridian Cyclops* came in to do trade out at the old desert star port. How this little girl was the only survivor of the massacre at Bacci Cantara. How she traded everything she had to the pilot in order to be taken to the nearest sector capital. Ackabar. So she could find a killer.

So she could obtain justice.

"Will you kill him for me?" she asked him innocently at the end of her story. As though she'd just asked a parent—someone who'd raised her, loved her, taken care of her; anyone other than the armored stranger in front of her—to take care of some spider that had frightened her.

She repeated the question.

He was tired. Getting more tired all the time. And this story bothered him like most never had. Probably because she was just a little girl. Somewhere ahead was the end of the galaxy for him. Even he, Tyrus Rechs, who'd lived a very long life, knew that all things must come to an end for everyone. All bills must be paid. All debts reconciled on the ledger of the galaxy.

"Will you?" she asked for a third time in her tiny soprano voice. It seemed to be the only thing in the near darkness of the hurtling ship.

There had been no crying while she'd told the story. Just silent tears filling up her large, dark, unblinking eyes.

Rechs suspected there had been enough of crying—when no one was looking. The galaxy constantly demanded that you get yourself together and lock it down in order to move on. And she'd had to learn that before most. You had to lock it down because that was the price of admission and the only way one could survive day after day in a soulless galaxy that was quickly becoming an out-of-control dumpster fire.

Dumpster fire.

Those were old words, he thought to himself in the silence between him and the little girl, with the big war bot looking on. In the darkness and dim lighting he liked to keep as a constant blanket inside the *Crow*.

A place outside the galaxy in which to hide.

He stood up, feeling his muscles begin to stiffen and even ache. He'd take a shot of Androx. It wouldn't do much, but it was something. Something to keep surviving.

"Just keep... moving forward," he thought he said to himself. Instead he'd said it aloud.

"What?" asked the little girl.

Prisma Maydoon, she'd announced herself as. Maydoon was an old name Rechs barely remembered. He'd heard it once. Long ago. Some admiral, or something. Back in the early days of the Repub.

"Nothing," he muttered as he turned to go.

"So will you? Will you kill... Goth Sullus?"

He didn't say what he wanted to say. Didn't even shake his head just slightly like he felt he should've. To indicate something. To pass some kind of judgment for her to understand.

You're too far gone for all that, he reminded himself. *Just tell her yes... or no. And keep moving on.*

"I can pay," she whispered.

There was that too.

There was always that.

"No," he mumbled as he walked off. Into the darkness of the other places within the speeding ship.

"Why?" she asked plaintively.

But he didn't answer. He was gone, and all that seemed to remain within the silence of the ship was her question. Echoing off the bulkheads of his mind. Asking him to kill... and other things.

Later, via comm, the wobanki woke him in his bunk with a status update in its babble-speak nonsense.

"Lock in a course for En Shakar," he replied. "Then execute the next jump." He cut the link and watched the status display above his bunk.

The dull, almost nonexistent hum of hyperspace was gone. He hadn't even noticed the *Crow* falling out of the jump into Tarravil. He'd been too tired.

On the display panel he watched as the ship confirmed course change and spooled up for a new jump. He closed his tired eyes and rubbed them. He hadn't even gotten out of his armor. He really should, he thought, as he swiped a bottle of pills from the shelf next to his head. He stared at them, then shook a few into his mouth.

They hit, and he closed his eyes. A moment later the ship lurched into hyperspace, but he was already gone. En Shakar was a long jump out into the big, dark nowhere along the edge.

Indelible VI
Hyperspace

Captain Keel ducked his head to avoid a piece of overhead conduit as he made his way deep into the mechanical aft of the *Six*. As soon as Wraith had shared the tidbit about the war bot, Garret had set to work reverse-engineering a tracker. He'd finished it within an hour. Now the crew was on its way to Ackabar.

A violet glow lit up the confined space ahead. While they were jumping from Corsica, Leenah had said the ship's timing pulsars seemed out of sync. Keel had hardly seen her since, with the exception of a few visits to the galley for meals and the occasional passing in the cozy passages. They were nearly to Ackabar, and Keel felt the need to check in on her. He was growing accustomed to having a larger crew. And Leenah certainly was useful.

"How's it going?" he asked, looking down at the princess, who was straining to tighten a bolt.

The pink-skinned alien looked up and wiped her brow, leaving a dark smear of dust and grease across her forehead and along her hair-like tendrils. She smiled. "I *think* I just about have the sub-light timing synced properly. It was off by almost one thousandth of a second. When was the last time you had it serviced?"

Keel couldn't remember. "It may have been a while. Probably the last time I was in the core. Usually Ravi—"

Leenah cut him off. "I didn't think you were the type to let a thing like that go. Flyboy like you?"

"Like me?" Keel echoed with a smile. "What is it you think you know about me?" He sat down and let his legs dangle into the service pit where the princess worked.

"You flyboys *always* obsess about your rides. It's often the only thing your type thinks about."

Keel turned down his face thoughtfully. "I was more of a ground-based operative to start with. It just turns out I took to flying naturally once I gave it a try."

"Well," Leenah said, pulling off her heavy gloves, "it's still well within the range of what's considered acceptable for high-performing starships. It's just not..."

"Perfect?" suggested Keel.

"Ideal," Leenah answered. She vaulted herself out of the maintenance hatch and took a seat next to Keel. "And in your line of work..." She left her sentence incomplete.

They sat together quietly for a while. Staring at the violet thrums that flashed on cue with the timing pulsars. They seemed to light up the darkened section of machinery like fireworks on Republic Day.

"So..." Keel said, "you still set on rejoining the MCR? There's a lot more money if you stick around."

And there it was. He was asking the princess to stay. Expanding operations. Taking on the aid of others, though he'd started his career swearing off the very thought. It was Ravi's fault, really. Keel had been a fine loner until meeting *him*.

Leenah gathered a fingertip of dust from the hull floor and held it up for inspection. "Looks like it's been a while since you did a vacuum purge."

Keel nodded. That, too, was on his list of things that needed doing. But cleaning out the ship and cycling it through several shipwide airlock ventings took time, and that time never seemed to come. Maybe after this job was finished.

"Listen," Leenah said. "I've been thinking about what you said. About the MCR. How it started and what they... did. I admit it's not as noble and romantic an organization as I first thought back on my home planet. But they've changed. Really. One of the first things they tell you when you join is that the MCR of Kublar and the like isn't the MCR of today."

Keel shrugged. "Sounds like what the Republic says every time the galaxy finds out about some clandestine revenue seizure. Always sorry until the next time."

Another silence fell between the two. Keel finally got up. "Well, Ackabar has no shortage of insurgents. You should be back at home patching up whatever shoddy tech the MCR stole from the scrapyard in no time, if that's what you want."

Leenah hugged her knees. "Can I still work on your ship until then? You said I do good work."

Keel rubbed the back of his head. "Yeah, you do. Sure thing. The *Six* is all yours until you get the chance to join up with the terrorists again."

"They're not terrorists. They're freedom fighters."

Keel began to backtrack through the sophisticated—if dusty—machinery toward the modified freighter's lounge, then stopped. "You know, I understand killing for self-defense. Even for money if the target has it coming—like those insurgents on that base I plucked you and the general from. But I don't buy into freedom fighters *or* Republic governments killing for *ideals*. Then everything becomes okay, a means to a greater end. And all that's *really* left in the end is a body count and a new list of targets."

Keel turned to continue on his way.

"Is that what you were doing on Jarvis Rho?" Leenah called to him from her place in the *Six*'s guts. "Ridding the galaxy of rebels—*insurgents*—who had it coming?"

Keel halted and faced her. "Maybe."

The princess rose and walked over to him, her face seeming to fight back a swirling panorama of emotions. "And the one who launched the attack. Wraith. Your partner. That's you, isn't it?"

Keel didn't reply.

"And so," Leenah continued, looking down as she spoke, as if she were working out the solution to a logic puzzle. "You figured, *she* might be worth keeping around. So you took off your armor and put on your human face and came to rescue the princess." She looked up at him.

Keel's face was locked, his jaw set tightly. He wondered if, somewhere behind his eyes, a hint of the remorse he now felt was showing. "Look. Every day something comes to snuff you out. Either you don't let it—you let 'em know that you're not gonna die—or you make it so your dying only makes things worse. That's how the galaxy works."

"Does it have to be?"

Keel felt... perplexed by this question. He remained silent.

"They say, after the joining ceremony and debriefings, that most people last a year in the MCR. Thirteen months is cheating death. Two years is a miracle—unless you have a command. You found me three weeks after I'd jumped to the other side of the Republic. I was so new to Rho that I hadn't made a single friend beyond the general. And I'll let you guess why *he* wanted to make friends."

Keel nodded. Leenah was attractive. And the boy general seemed like the type who loved himself. Those types always set out to make love into a conquest, if only to justify how wonderful they were. "So..." he said. "Let's say I *am* Wraith. And say the MCR are still galactic terrorists feeding disillusioned youths into the Republic's jaws. And I won't play for either side. Where does that leave us?"

"Ravi told me on Tannespa, before he got his new bots, that deep down, you were a good man. I believe him. I *trust* Ravi." Leenah looked back at the violet glows behind her. "I'm a good mechanic. Would my leaving the ship make life better or worse for you?"

"Worse." Keel took Leenah's hands and squeezed them gently, not to make her heart flutter, but to assure her that what he was about to say was the truth. "Lots worse."

"Then... I'll stay."

Garret was working at Keel's blaster-smithing table when the captain arrived. Keel frowned at the way his own tools and instruments were pushed to the side or placed on shelves or hangers, none of which were the correct shelf or hanger for the tool in question.

"Good work on the TT-3 bots, kid."

Garret beamed at the compliment. "Thanks. You know, I've got something else I've been working on. It's about the war bot."

"Yeah? What?"

Setting down his spanners so he could move his hands freely, Garret held his arms wide. "A war bot is *big*, right? And they've got a ton of weaponry. When I finished reprogramming Maydoon's model, it was armed with something less than a full payload because it was going to be used as a servitor bot. But it can still level a company of soldiers, easy."

"Sounds fun," Keel said.

Garret let out a breathy laugh, as though the dry comment was the funniest thing he'd heard all day. "I'd say not. High-velocity blaster in its arms, tactical micro-rockets, grenade launchers... lots of fun."

"We need to make sure it doesn't use those against us."

Garret clapped his hands, making a damp sound like two fish slapping together. "Exactly. And that's what I'm working on. A control cylinder that can override its primary directives. I've got the hardware all set, but I need to test it. So I've coded a war bot AI in a partition I set up on the *Six*'s main drive. You see—"

Keel nodded. "I think I've followed about as much as I'm able. Good thought, good job, keep it up. But if you feel like taking a break, we should be dropping out of hyperspace soon. You should check it out if you've never seen it in person."

"Yeah, sounds good," Garret said, sounding somewhat absent. "Be right up there."

"Does that invitation extend to me?" Leenah emerged from the ship's maintenance hatch and carefully dogged it shut.

Keel gave a half grin. "Sure."

The swirling blue of hyperspace came to an abrupt stop, and a myriad of stars sharpened to tiny points in the darkness as the *Indelible VI* dropped into subspace. The orange-and-green planet of Ackabar took up most of the ship's cockpit view. But it was the flotilla of Republic destroyers and corvettes that grabbed Keel's attention.

"Looks like Ackabar's status as an independent world came to an end," he commented to Ravi as he silenced the various comm chimes that pealed upon their return to normal space.

The navigator nodded. "There is a high probability that it was absorbed through Republic tax enforcements. We will face a success rate of ninety-three point six five three eight eight nine one four—"

"Ravi, we've been over this," Keel interrupted. "I'm not a bot or an AI. Give me a round number. Telling me the odds to the tenth power doesn't really make much of a difference."

Ravi twitched his mustache at this. "It *might* make a difference…"

"Not one that I can see." Keel reached out and took the incoming Republic hail. A destroyer helmsman wasn't the type of sailor you wanted to ignore—no matter how fast your ship was.

"This is Captain Ethan Bowlerro of the freighter *Woodchip*," Keel said. He pointed to Ravi. The hologram transmitted the doctored identification.

Leenah leaned forward to look at Keel, filling the space between the pilot's and co-pilot's seats. "What if they recognize the ship or false ID?"

"It'd be a first." Keel moved his hands across the comm dash. "Never been in trouble for falsifying identities."

"Yet," Ravi added.

The Republic helmsman asked over the comm, "Freighter *Woodchip*, are you importing cargo?"

"Hoping to find second-hand driver generators for resale," Keel said smoothly.

"All exports are restricted until a Republic planetary governor is installed," the helmsman said, the tone of her voice suggesting she'd repeated the phrase several times already. "All traffic to or from the planet is prohibited until further notice. An emergency refueling station is provided at the following nav coordinates."

"The bot's not down there," Garret said, his gaze fixed on a datapad. "It *was* here, but it looks like it jumped out. No sign of it since, so it's probably still in hyperspace."

Ravi turned to face the coder. "Perhaps you can give me the coordinates? I may be able to determine a probable destination based on exit vectors."

Garret nodded.

Keel swiped through comm messages on his dash. "Well, may as well see what Lao Pak has to say."

The pirate king appeared superimposed over the canopy view. Garret jumped with a start and hid himself.

"What are you doing?" Leenah asked.

"If Lao Pak thinks I'm working with Captain Keel, he'll kill me."

Keel looked at the coder attempting to hide in the second row of seats. "He'll kill you either way unless we make good on finding Maydoon. If Lao Pak smells a payoff, he's the most forgiving pirate in the galaxy. But you can relax. This is a recording."

"Keel!" Lao Pak screamed into the camera. "I have good news! Now that you have Wraith on board with big plan, admiral say he work with us. He want Wraith contact him. I send you message later when I have encoded channel."

Keel shrugged. "See? It worked itself out. Here's another message."

"Keel!" Lao Pak screamed again. Only this time someone shifted behind him.

"That's Drex," Garret said, his voice trembling.

Keel recognized the pirate he'd leveled while taking Garret to his ship back on Tannespa. He had a good idea what was coming next.

"Why you steal my coder?" Lao Pak screamed, his face turning red with anger. "I tell you no! I say, 'No take coder!' You promise! Now you die, Keel! I buy more Hools. Lot more. You dead man flying, Keel. You die so bad, Ravi die just from watching."

The message ended abruptly.

"He'll get over it," Keel said, unconcerned with the pirate's empty threats. That's all they were. Honor among thieves was all fine and good, but with enough credits on the line, everything was negotiable. "Got anything, Ravi?"

The navigator tapped a finger against his lips. "Yes. I am having something. Vadoria."

Keel moved the ship into position to make the jump to hyperspace. "Good, let's plot a course for—"

"Or En Shakar," Ravi said. "There is a fifty percent chance of either. Well, technically there is a forty-nine point seven three one six eight eight eight eight seven one eight percent chance the ship jumped to Vadoria, and a fifty point two six eight three one one one one two eight two percent chance it jumped to En Shakar."

Keel looked at Ravi blankly.

"But since you have again instructed me not to be so precise," Ravi continued, "I am thinking you should flip a credit coin."

"A coin." Keel repeated. "Thank you for that, Ravi."

Leenah laughed at the exchange. "Maybe we should just stick around here until the bot shows back up on Garret's tracker?"

"For how long?" Keel asked. "The Republic isn't going to let us just sit out here indefinitely. If the bot is headed far enough toward the core, it could be *weeks*."

"Less than that!" Garret shouted breathlessly. "I just picked up something! The war bot is on En Shakar."

17

"I know! I know!" muttered Rechs through gritted teeth. "En Shakar is a rough approach. It gets better below the storm."

Outside the canopy, ice and sleet swirled and rattled against the hull like a typhoon of broken glass.

"*Anchu baba no tengi ru?*" chattered the wobanki.

"Of course it'll hold. Atmospheric stabilizers go bad all the time on lots of ships. Just watch for the outer marker. We don't make that turn, we'll be all over the ice."

"*Tantaar!*" the catman screeched.

"You'll need a new identity if you ever hope to work inside the Repub again. You're most likely a wanted cat now. Trust me, leejes record everything on their buckets. You got a bounty too."

"*Dubba dubba En Shakaru?*"

"Watch that nav! It's off the grid. That's why it's safe here."

Or at least as safe as any place in the galaxy can be these days, thought Rechs. The Republic was getting a little crazier every day as it tried to hold on to what it could not.

Times have been worse. Back before the Big Jump. Way back.

But he blocked out those old memories and fought to keep the *Crow* on final for the run up the canyon approach to Mother Ree's.

The storm tossed the freighter hard, and Rechs reached over and brought in the compensators just to hold the glide path. They whined in obedience as a relay surge alarm began to annoy the flight deck. The ship was always doing that.

They dropped below the perpetual storm that tormented the upper atmosphere of the tiny ice moon, and Rechs spotted the massive jagged scar carved into the blindingly white face of snow-covered En Shakar. He backed off the throttles and dropped the nose of the *Crow*, aiming for the canyon, searching for the outer marker.

"*Beelie beelie markaru!*" shouted the wobanki triumphantly.

Rechs knew the catman was nervous. He should be. There was no star port for repairs within sub-light range if they botched this. And sending out a distress signal was likely to attract the Repub.

"Now you'll see some flyin'," Rechs whispered as he concentrated on lining up with the beacon inside the ice canyon.

The freighter shot down beneath the plane of the planet's surface and disappeared into the translucent blue ice of the shadowy canyon. It was like entering another world man had never been meant to see. When he had the beacon locked in on auto, the ship flew between the jagged edges of a narrow ice crevasse and disappeared within the optical illusion.

Rechs switched on the running lights, revealing a world of glittering diamond, hidden in the subterranean darkness. Far below was a massive, silent sea, trapped beneath the ice of frozen En Shakar; huge thermal vents flared and roared far down in its crystal-clear depths. Leviathans moved in a pod way down in the darkness, passing between the shafts of light that came through rents and cracks in the ice.

The wobanki chittered.

"It's down here. Trust me." Rechs pointed off toward port, drawing the wobanki's attention to the tiny atoll that erupted through the surface of the sunless sea. From its crescent shape erupted a volcanic mountain, and carved into its side was the monastery of Mother Ree. Tall and beautiful like she'd once been, long ago.

Rechs dialed in the maneuvering thrusters. "Get the landing gear out and tell them who we are."

Letting the wobanki do the talking might make things go a little smoother, he thought—and wondered if she would ever forgive him.

Who? asked that old voice from long ago deep within him. *The little girl in back? Or Mother Ree and the young woman she once was?*

But Rechs didn't answer questions only he could hear. At least not when anyone else was around.

He angled the *Crow* and fired the landing thrusters, doing his best to bring the ship in just right for a three-point landing. He got the two rear landing gears onto the platform first, then the forward main. *Good enough.*

Through the metal-ribbed canopy, Mother Ree's disciples in white thermal robes were already appearing on the landing platform. They had no weapons; she'd never allow that.

He wondered if he should dress in his armor. Threaten them. Intimidate them.

"You can't hide in there forever," she'd once said to him. "Someday you'll have to come out, Tyrus. Someday you'll have to be vulnerable. Just like the rest of us."

Now, years later, he would have to obey that young woman—the young woman who'd promised him that reckoning.

"All right, let's go get this over with," he muttered to the wobanki as he climbed out of his seat.

"*Blasteroos?*" asked the wobanki.

"No. It's not that kind of place. Not those kind of people. We're just dropping the kid off. Then we're outta here."

Rechs banged on the door of the cabin he'd given the girl for the trip. Just two quick strikes as he passed on his way to the boarding hatch controls.

"This is where you get off!" he shouted. In the darkness of the lounge he passed the idle war bot. "If she's not out in five, I'll order you to remove her, hunk-a-junk."

The bot clicked and whirred as it came up from its downtime power setting. "Yes, sir," it replied.

At the hatch, Rechs watched the boarding ramp lower itself to the surface of the monastery. When he'd heard the *ka-thunk* of locked hydraulic struts, he cycled the hatches and strode down the ramp. The wobanki followed agilely, its long tail swimming back and forth as though tasting the cold oxygen far beneath En Shakar.

And then Rechs saw her. She was older now, but he recognized her nonetheless. Recognized her eyes. Sparkling. Glittering like the ice high above. Blue and alive with that fire he'd seen long ago—when she'd been no longer a girl, but not yet a woman. When she'd been a prized harem slave.

If he'd thought, in all the long years since then, that she bore him some ill will, some promised fate or fantasized doom, he was wrong. His gunfighter's eyes saw only the aging woman catch her breath at the sight of him. No one else saw it. Only him. And then she was moving forward, arms out, with the warm smile of a woman who has lived and loved. Those fantastic, glittering blue eyes held back a tear, which made them shine even more.

She reached out and clasped his face between her hands. "Oh," she began, her voice wavering. "General Rex. Tyrus, you've barely changed." She drew him to her and kissed him on the cheek, with her eyes closed. Like the young woman she'd once been had always wanted to do.

Tyrus held her—awkwardly at first, and then just as he'd wanted to all those years ago when she'd fallen in love with him. When she'd been someone else. When the galaxy had changed again.

Back on some rock the Repub wanted the Legion to erase.

Jungle Planet Andaar

The Past

A long time ago...

"We'll hold the line here, General Rex. Long as we can," Lieutenant Hilbert gasped. "Just get her to the rendezvous, sir. Get her off this hellhole. And sir—don't let them kill her."

And then... "For the Legion, sir."

A long-dead legionnaire had just vowed to General Rex, as Tyrus Rechs was then known—General Tyrus Rex, the T-Rex of Andalore—that he and what remained of his company, just four other men, would hold the line for as long as they could in order to get the high-value target to safety.

So the Republic could kill her.

On this distant world, his squad of leejes was surrounded by the galaxy's version of the perfect killing machines and tasked with doing the impossible. One more time. Again. For just a little bit longer.

He saluted them all, each in turn. The Legion salute.

"For the Legion."

The five remaining troopers, shot to hell and dying before his eyes, seemed to stand a little taller in that moment when their general honored them. After all, it wasn't every day a living legend of the feared Legion saluted you. Even if you were about to die.

Lieutenant Hilbert, whose men would one day call him "Pappy."

Sergeant Reyal.

Corporal Tacas.

Specialists Ahamalee and Ren.

They stood… and saluted their general back.

"For the Legion."

Then Rex grabbed the hand of the daughter of Ambassador Krayvan and disappeared through the smoking hole in the outer defenses of the pirate's fortress. The Cybar were coming for them, and this time they would get through. The rendezvous with the Repub rescue shuttle was five clicks to the rear. Five clicks through a burning swamp. Time to get moving.

He towed her after him and out into the festering, blazing jungle. Republic warships had just nailed the area with an orbital strike. Rex's armor was offline, but it would reboot after the strike, once it had dealt with the EMP effects. He had his hand cannon for a weapon, and that was it. The silk bikini-clad girl who would become Mother Ree had managed to grab a battered N-16 assault blaster from the gloves of a dead leej.

He dragged her through the fetid jungle, pushing through the tall grass toward the swamp and the river. Large sections of the jungle had gone up in walls of hot flame, and black plumes of oily smoke rose into the air. But the primary threat was the half-biologic, half-mech killing machines known as the Cybar. A lifeform undiscovered until now. They had been a surprise to the five hundred leejes who survived the assault landing.

The leejes of the 101st.

Rex had led them against the pirate stronghold on this planet. Officially, that was their mission—to knock out a pirate base. Unofficially, it was to secure the girl he was now trying to save, so she could be returned for execution at the Sector Orbital Fortress on Demaron V. Nearly a thousand men lost, all for one girl. All so she could die in the right place, at the right time.

When Rex and the girl reached the river, they found the remains of a pirate raider, a converted medium freighter, sinking into the mud of the shallow yellow river. The bodies of the dead crew drifted away with the sluggish current.

"What now?" said the girl at Rex's side. Though she had been brave, and tough, and had fought alongside the leejes sent to rescue her, everyone has a limit. And she was close to hers.

"Hang on," grunted Rex through his armor. Inside, his HUD tried to reboot, but it was malfunctioning. He hefted her onto his shoulder and waded out into the muddy yellow river. In unpowered armor. But the Cybar were coming, and maybe the river would be some kind of defense. He could hear their scouts thrashing through the tall grass like Dongolian dust devils, but worse. More murderous and maniacal somehow.

"We'll get through this," he told her as the mud sucked at his boots and the water tried to carry him away.

"Then what? You'll take me to Demaron to be killed?"

Rex didn't say anything, because there was something big in the water with them. Some other lifeform on this planet no one had bothered to survey because it was overrun by ancient killer robots long before anyone had even heard of the Galactic Republic. He hoped it wasn't some kind of alpha predator.

Gargantuan muddy brown humps slithered through the river. It was some kind of sea serpent swirling about them and causing the water to whirlpool and froth. Rex could only think of the eels mankind discovered on one of the first worlds they surveyed after the Big Jump. Murderous and vicious beasts. But in time they became great traders and scientists. You just had to get past the deadly neurotoxin they paralyzed their victims with, before they dragged them down into the coral-laden depths of their emerald water world.

But this thing coiling about them in the water was much larger than those eels. Like some prehistoric beast of fable and legend.

Rex wouldn't be able to use his gun in the river.

The girl in his arms shrieked when it came close. The mammoth coils bumped against them and almost knocked Rex over. He went down on one knee in the sucking mud, and she went underwater with him. He could hear her gasping and choking on the dark water. It took all his strength to force his unpowered armor up out of the muck and raise her back above the waterline over his head. His helmet was almost submerged, but he got her out of the water, and a few feet later he could feel the rise of the sand ahead.

They collapsed on the sandbar, both of them gasping. Along the far bank they could hear the mechanical monotone chatter of the Cybar. It was like being pursued by a pack of ghostly mechanical wolves.

The armor was still struggling through its reboot. It was taking forever, and Rex wondered if maybe it was finally done for. He knew they didn't make 'em like this anymore. He slapped one armored fist into the side of his helmet, and the armor reboot cycle finally engaged like it was supposed to.

For the next hour, the two of them tried to stay ahead of the Cybar. They ran through the smoking jungle on the far side of the river. They came across twisted debris and dead pirates from the battle that took place overhead. Three Republican corvettes and three hundred pirate raiders of various designs had fought in the skies above.

That alone had been enough to make it a major action. But no one would ever know, because the Republic was merely covering up all their dirty secrets with dead leejes these days. And this girl was yet one more secret that needed to be cleaned up.

And that makes you nothing but an assassin, Rex told himself as they ran.

A Cybar came out of the jungle at them. Rex didn't have time to bring his hand cannon to bear before it had three iron tentacles wrapped around one of his arms. Another was flailing like a metal whip, trying to crush his helmet. The Cybar's face, a bizarre hydraulic jaw assembly beneath actual eyes from some big jungle cat, leaned in. He fought to push the thing off him so he could shoot it.

The jaws opened and bit into the armor effortlessly, tearing away a section of the shoulder plating. Rex smashed in the "face" of the neurotic monster with a head butt that seemed to do little other than sound a loud metallic ring above the burning *crackle* and *snap* of the blazing jungle. And the thing was growing more biomechanical tentacles and wrapping them around Rex's armor.

"Should I shoot it?" screamed the girl.

Rex weighed the option as even more tentacles sprouted and whipsnaked around his armor. The beast was dragging him to the ground, and he couldn't do anything about it.

"Do it!"

She fired on full auto. Shots hit his armor and rebounded. Not a pleasant thing when you're inside old Mark I armor, but it was better than being holed by a blast. Others hit the Cybar, and it emitted a ghostly shriek and frenetically leapt away. A moment later it was scrabbling through the dead fall of the burning jungle debris and lunging for the barely clad girl.

In one fluid motion, Rex drew, tracked, and fired.

The Cybar died rolling toward the girl's feet.

Target Z987 had been the girl's designation in the briefing. He tried to remember her name. Maybe he hadn't learned it on purpose. Maybe that made it worse.

You're just an assassin now.

No, he thought to himself. *I'm no hired killer. There are... reasons.*

Except right there in the jungle, he couldn't think of any reasons that made sense for why he'd been doing the Republic's dirty work. It hadn't started out that way.

It had started out as something noble. Something worth fighting for.

"It's changed," he muttered.

"What?" gasped the panting girl.

The leejes had been calling her "the Fox" ever since seeing a picture of her during the briefing holo. She was tall, lithe, with red hair and pale skin. Piercing arctic blue eyes. No wonder the pirate who'd botched everything and carried her off the starliner on her way to be executed had chosen to add her to his harem instead. No wonder. She was an epic beauty.

But to Rex she was just a girl.

Not even a target.

"What is..." He paused. He knew he was crossing some boundary. Some line. Some river on a map that meant a lot more than just a navigational feature. And he'd learned long ago that you didn't always come back when you crossed certain rivers. What was the old saying? *Let the dice fly.*

He nodded to himself. She was staring at him. Her mouth open. Her skin dirty with ash and blood. The blood of leejes she'd dragged out of harm's way in the middle of psychotic firefights with real live alien monsters. The very same legionnaires who'd been sent to kill her.

"What's your name?" he asked her.

She shook her head. There was some sudden anger there. And then a helpless smile. An innocent smile despite everything. She had begun to believe that the galaxy had forgotten her. Forgotten her name. She'd been close to the edge.

"Mara," she whispered.

He stepped close to her and took off his helmet. She saw a man with iron-gray hair and burning blue eyes. His skin was tan and hard, and if she'd had to guess, she would've told you he was middle-aged, barely.

If she had been told he'd once seen the Pacific Ocean of a long gone and fabled Earth, she wouldn't have believed it.

"Mara, you won't be executed. I promise."

She let the N-16 fall to her side, and she exhaled like some sudden weight had been lifted from her slender shoulders. She gave one uncontrollable sob, then stood on her toes to reach up and grab his battered armor. She closed her eyes and kissed him on the cheek.

Yes… in the months of fleeing to come, she would fall in love with him. But he would never allow that love to blossom beyond this one princess's kiss for the knight in battered armor who happened along the way. He would get her away from the Repub fleet that had come to kill her. They would run, and he would find a place for her to hide far out on the edge of the galaxy.

And all it would cost him was his place in the Republic, becoming Public Enemy Number One for the House of Reason, and having the galaxy's highest bounty placed upon his head.

But in that moment, with a jungle world full of lunatic monsters burning down all around them, Mother Ree— who had once been a beautiful young girl named Mara— found the love of her life.

She would always think about him.

Mother Ree's Sanctuary
En Shakar

"I see you're still rescuing young girls from the clutches of the Republic, Tyrus," said Mother Ree, looking over her shoulder at Prisma.

"Some things never change, I guess," Rechs mumbled.

They were ahead of the rest, and the brief space provided them enough room to have a moment's private conversation on their way into the interior of the monastery.

"She doesn't need to be rescued," he said. "No one's looking for her. Her father was just murdered by some local warlord. She needs a new life now. And I can't give her that out there. But you…"

"You haven't changed much," said Mother Ree as she walked arm-in-arm with the bounty hunter. "But of course it would be foolish of me to think you would."

Behind them, deep within the ice caverns that led into the inner sanctum of the hidden monastery, followed Prisma, the wobanki, KRS-88, and a coterie of disciples.

"I can change," Rechs whispered morosely. "Some might even say that you were responsible for the biggest change in my life."

"Ah, yes," Mother Ree crooned. "Famed legionnaire general betrays Republic and absconds with daughter of traitor." She paused when she saw that her teasing was making him even more withdrawn than normal. "You really did give it all up to save me, Tyrus. I know that now. I never fully understood it then... At the time I just thought you were my knight in shining armor come to rescue me. I had no idea the Republic would want you dead because of it. I was a young girl and I didn't understand the ways of the galaxy—or even life. I only believed in good and evil and happy endings."

She looked at him, her eyes serious now. Watching him as she spoke. "In the years since, I've come to appreciate your sacrifice. And all I can say now, and I know it'll never be enough... is thank you, General Rex. I still believe in good and evil... and happy endings."

They entered the grand colonnade of the outer monastery. Massive pillars of sculpted ice led out across a cobalt blue river of running translucent ice diamonds. Small icebergs disappeared into the darkness. On the far side, two grand and ornately carved doors signaled the entrance to the inner sanctum. Behind them, Prisma could be heard oohing and aahing. KRS-88 told her to mind the edge.

"It wasn't all your fault, Mara," Rechs began. "My leaving the Republic... it was a long time coming. You were just..."

And then words failed him.

"What was I *just* to you, Tyrus?" Her eyes searched his like they had so many years ago. Seeking some perfect answer when she begged him not to leave her in safe hands that would hide her from the Republic for the rest of her life. "I loved you, Tyrus. You know that, right?"

They continued on. He was almost leading her, as he had so long ago when she was a mere slave girl fleeing an invading force sent to kill her. But she was not so old that she didn't feel him squeeze her hand once. Firmly.

They passed through the inner sanctum and entered the gardens. The wobanki begin to yowl, and Prisma gasped at the sudden lush beauty.

"The Hidden Gardens of Revelation," Mother Ree announced with quiet pride.

They were standing on an immense platform. Below them, stretching seemingly in all directions, was a garden paradise. The cavern blazed with a light descending through the layers of jagged ice above. In the distance, Rechs could even see a smoking mountain.

"This is... amazing," Prisma said. She came forward, staring in awe at the vast forest. Birds rushed from tree to tree, calling to one another in constant joy. The smell of jasmine and sandalwood hung heavy in the air. From a distance came the sounds of drums and flute. "What is this place?" she asked, her voice filled with wonder and awe.

Mother Ree knelt down next to the young girl.

"A place where one can find the answers we hide inside ourselves. And a place where some come to hide for the rest of their lives. It is where they find peace in a violent galaxy. Hidden beneath the ice here is a whole continent just like this, a continent we've created with bioengineering techniques and philosophy. The Republic will never find you here, girl, and you will be safe for the rest of your life. If you want to stay with us."

Mother Ree put her hand on the young girl's wiry shoulder and felt her flinch. But she also saw the girl's wide brown eyes gazing in amazement at Mother Ree's garden.

Prisma shook her head. Then, slowly, she turned to face Rechs.

"No. I don't want to hide. And I don't want to run away. I want that... that... the man who killed my daddy... I want him dead. And I won't ever... ever... I won't ever stop until he's dead. I'll get out of here any way I can. I'll join the Legion. I'll learn how to kill. And then I'll find him..." And now she was sobbing. But she continued on. "I will kill him for taking my daddy away. I will kill them all!"

Mother Ree pulled the small girl close, and Prisma, like some pole that wouldn't bend despite all the winds the galaxy could throw at it, finally allowed herself to surrender and be embraced as her shoulders shook and the galaxy refused to change.

Rechs is deep within the hidden forest. He has wandered long and far away from the rest. And even though evening has fallen through the ice above, it is still warm and fragrant down here in this living forest beneath an icy planet lost out in the Big Dark.

He hasn't done this for a long time.

Life, a very long life in fact, has been spent jumping through space within the silence of a ship. Alone with his thoughts and memories until they became a kind of prison. And then there was all the searching through a thousand seedy spaceports along the edge, looking for...

For...

Bounties? But that didn't seem true, even though it was. It seemed like a lie he'd been telling himself all along. A cover. There had been another reason for it all.

Another voice was there, and then—then it was gone. Maybe it had been whispering in the days since he'd met the girl. He just hadn't been able to hear it. Until now. It spoke the answer that always came up when he asked why he was doing what he was doing: that if the Repub wouldn't keep law and order on the galaxy's edge, then it was up to him, and bounty hunters like him.

Leaving the Legion and betraying the Republic had freed him to operate beyond their weak and ineffective laws.

Isn't that why you've been out here in a thousand spaceports and a million cantinas leaping through the Big Dark? Haven't you been cleaning it up on your own, one wanted thug at a time?

"The galaxy's a pretty big place," he told the burbling fountain in the night. Some lone forest bird gave a short and mournful call in the twilight. The forest was almost utterly silent now.

The truth was, he hadn't been thinking much. Not for a long time. He'd become a puppet. All strings and wires for the impetus to distribute justice. A killing puppet. Except who was pulling the strings? What original reason had you out here... waiting all along? Waiting near the galaxy's edge for someone to show up.

But you haven't really been doing that, have you, Rechs?

The voice that talked to him sometimes in his head—asking him questions he didn't want to answer—was speaking here in the forest as though it were right next to him. So much so that he turned to see who it was that spoke.

There was no one there.

"I've been waiting."

For whom?

And that was the answer he didn't know.

But the question was true. That he *did* know.

18

Dawn was just a few hours away. Rechs had walked the forest all night, trying to remember something he knew was important. Something that had surfaced in the dark waters of his mind.

Toward the middle of the night, deep in the strange forest smelling of the heavy scent of cut wood and pine, he searched his mind and tried to think of what his earliest memory, or thought even, was.

"The first thing you remember?" he asked of himself. It sounded like an order.

Everything in his mind was a jumble of ancient starships and leaders no one remembered, or cared about, anymore. How many emergency klaxons had he heard, and felt within his bones? How many fresh new hells had threatened them at each turn as they crawled farther and farther out into the Big Dark?

How many bullets had he heard buzzing past his helmet?

And blaster shots too, for that matter.

How many?

And on how many strange planets had that all once seemed so alien and strange?

He walked the quiet forest path not really seeing the things in the dark that his gunslinger's eyes could detect. Instead he saw a million jump cuts from a thousand dramatic moments that made up his life. He felt the end nearing, the final scene coming at him. Like some ancient movie projector winding out toward that last white strip of bright light. Closing time.

How much is too much for any one man?

And yet, one phrase kept repeating itself every so often, surfacing like some ancient leviathan in the deep, dark waters of a forgotten sea.

Hang out on the edge. Wait.

In the silence of this place, way out on the trails beneath strange trees, he heard that. Like some buried code in his hard drive. Like a mantra, or an order, that had been guiding his life all along, and he'd never known it. Even before the Legion—and hadn't the Legion been a convenient way to watch the edges? Hadn't it?

He'd heard it.

What was it? What did it mean?

When the Legion hadn't been enough, he'd just gone rogue and patrolled the waters alone, like some shark lurking beyond the safe harbors out in the dark waters, waiting for prey it knew would show up one day.

He tried the name of the man the girl wanted him to kill.

"Goth... Sullus."

There wasn't anything in it that sparked some sudden flash of revelation.

And yet, way down deep, there *was* an unexplained feeling to the name. Some streetlights-coming-on-and-you-were-expected-home feeling that was so ancient, yet so familiar. As if, had the name been different... all would've been revealed.

He'd felt that way many times about many things.

About planets from which one could barely see the stars of the core. About lonely star ports that hadn't seen another ship in twenty years. About the wind moving through the rusting metal of those long-dead starships beached on the sands like dead monsters from another age.

Those thoughts were like some unquiet and accepted ghost passing through the rooms of his mind.

"There should be... more."

He waited on the walkway that overlooked the strange garden outside Prisma's cell.

In time, the strange birds awoke, giving their first tentative morning calls one to another. High above, the distant star began to cast itself across the frozen surface overhead. Soon a wan, almost fog-shrouded, light filtered down, awakening the garden and all its wonderful smells.

Life, thought Rechs. *Life is so much more than looking down the end of a blaster rifle.*

He'd wasted it all.

And not...

Hang out on the edge. Wait.

That was important. And somehow the little girl who wanted revenge was the key to a tune he could barely remember. Or a lock that needed to be found before it could be opened.

It started with a question when the little girl came out from her monk's cell within the inner sanctum. Tyrus Rechs was waiting for her. Quietly sitting on a small stone bench nearby.

She stared at him with hard, angry eyes, knowing he was going to leave her behind. She was tired and sleepy, but the anger was there... and it always would be.

"Do you know what you think about when you kill a man?" Tyrus asked as she sat down next to him on the bench.

She merely stared at him, then wiped sleep from her eyes. One fluid movement. Fast. Gunfighter fast, noted Rechs. Her movements were unexpected and sure.

But still she didn't answer him.

"You think about the next man you have to kill. Sometimes within the next second. Sometimes for the years you wait for him to finally come for you. That's what you think about. You think about the next man you have to kill."

She tilted her head and seemed to consider this. But nothing more. The distant chanting of the monks had begun for the morning.

"Once you start killing," continued Rechs, "it never stops."

She turned her head now and watched him. Challenged him.

"In that moment when your target goes down… all the triumph you thought you were going to feel, all that you'd imagined you were going to feel… you don't feel any of that."

"No?" she asked, her voice soft and scratchy.

"No," replied Tyrus matter-of-factly. He stretched one leg out in front of the other. Along the length of that leg, hidden beneath the tactical pants, were a dozen scars. Tyrus couldn't remember how he'd acquired them all. He just knew they were there. And at times, like now, he felt them even though he could not see them. "No," he said as an afterthought. And then, "You don't."

Silence.

"Because it doesn't bring them back?" she tried. And then added, "The ones you kill for."

It was an honest question delivered in a little girl's voice, but to Rechs it contained all the truth that could be known even if one spent lifetimes searching the galaxy. And so he just nodded in reply.

"I want to leave you here," he said. When she didn't protest, or even shake her head, he continued. "I want you to grow up here, where it's safe. These people will take care of you. And what happened to you on Wayste… it will never happen again, Prisma."

Still she watched him.

"Killing this man… you'll never be safe again. And you won't stop. You'll find a dozen other reasons to go on killing and settling up scores until the reasons why are all just imaginations in your head. Do you know why you'll do that? Why you'll become that way?"

She shook her head slowly. Barely.

"Because that's how you become a bounty hunter. It's not that you like the killing work. That's just to begin with. It's that, in the end, you don't *mind* it. That's where vengeance leads. It leads to your own death even though you don't realize it. You're dead inside, except you're still walking around."

Some bird hopped down onto the sandstone floor of the subterranean monastery. It hopped forward once, twice, three times, then leapt away and back into the high vaults of the quiet place, telling all its friends what a brave warrior it was, as it chirped and squawked. Or maybe it just babbled like an idiot.

Birds just don't care, do they?

Rechs turned back to the little girl. "As a bounty hunter you do what other people need doing and you don't mind it so much. In the end there's nothing left of who you once were. Trust me, Prisma. Stay here and grow up... and fall in love and live... and be a little girl while you can. Please. Don't become like me."

She listened to him and considered his words. And like all little girls who must have their way, she consulted the compass she called her heart and once more shook her head. Barely. She began to mouth a word, and it would always be "no" in all the languages that communicated information from one life to another across the span of the galaxy. It didn't matter what she said, the bounty hunter saw it, and it would be "no" to all that was good. Life. Love. The pursuit of happiness. She would have revenge, and it would consume her.

He made a face. A small, quick face that grieved for all that might've been.

And at that moment, Tyrus Rechs had the most profound thought of his very long life.

We start out knowing all the answers, and in the end we realize how little we know. Just the important things. And by that time... no one listens anymore.

Hang out on the edge. Wait.

"I will hunt this Goth Sullus for you, Prisma."

He watched her eyes. Eyes like a cat that would not change. Only waiting. Watching. Considering. Weighing.

"And I'll take you with me, girl. You'll see."

Her eyes searched his face cautiously.

"I'll teach you what I can. And everything I've warned you about will happen to you. Whoever you were, whoever you might have become... it dies if you leave with me. So you should stay."

She gave nothing away. No joy. No hope. No resignation or even second thoughts. Nothing.

"Do you understand that?"

She nodded.

"You will do everything I tell you, girl."

She nodded.

"If I tell you to run, you run."

She nodded.

"If I tell you to shoot, you shoot."

She nodded again.

For a long moment he held her eyes, watching for any falseness. Any weakness. He found nothing. He'd looked into the cold eyes of predators from one side of the galaxy to the other and seen the same thing he saw in this little girl's eyes before him. He knew a killer when he saw one. She'd already killed this Goth Sullus, whoever he was, a thousand times over in her heart. Or what was left of it. Looking into this little girl's eyes, he found another killer. Just like him.

"Now you pay me. For the job, Prisma."

She looked at him. Her eyes conveyed her lack of money. Then she remembered something.

"My... He left a lot of credits in a kind of bank and told me how to get them. They're there."

"No, Prisma. Pay me with your most precious possession."

She thought about this. Then she got up and went back into her cell. She came out holding something. She stared down at it... then she held it out for him to take.

It was a picture of a woman, and a baby.

Rechs studied it.

"This?" he whispered.

"I never knew her. This is all I have."

The woman in the picture had Prisma's eyes. Maybe someday the little girl in front of him would grow up to be as beautiful as this woman was. No doubt the baby was Prisma.

Rechs placed the picture in his shirt pocket.

"Payment accepted."

He watched her watch the place where the picture had gone. He would give it back to her when the deed was done.

It wasn't the anger. It was the absence of life he found inside those eyes. It was the cold deep already growing inside of her. Like some yawning and bottomless chasm on some lost and lonely dead planet that had been flung from the orbit of a loving star long ago. Now it just wandered the Big Dark, a danger to everyone.

The wobanki was prancing to and fro across the landing platform underneath the *Obsidian Crow*, dumping vent ports and unhooking the materials hoses from the local access. Monks assisted as best they could, but this was not the most advanced of star ports. It was little more than a landing platform with some basic services.

The ice and wind howled all around the ship, and the running and platform lights threw great starbursts of illumination across the scene. Rechs was wearing a heavy coat and hood. The fur trimming whipped and tossed in the face of the storm. It would be a rough departure for sure. But that was to be expected. Far below, he could see the hidden paradise of the gardens and monastery deep beneath the ice.

"Ready for departure?" he shouted at the frantic wobanki.

The wobanki yowled in the affirmative.

Across the landing pad, Prisma dragged his clamshell weapons case to the boarding ramp. The large war bot scuttled after, indicating he should be doing that for his mistress. But the girl refused to let anyone help her with the first task her sensei had given her.

Rechs shook his head. Even he knew this was a new low for him. Turning a child into a killer. *You're not really going to do that?* the voice inside his head asked.

Or was she some kind of bait?

Or a touchstone to that phrase that kept floating just out of reach in front of his mind's eye?

"Hang out on the edge. Wait."

What had started as a distant whisper was becoming clearer with each passing moment. As though the plot in some entertainment was coming into focus.

What does it mean? he asked himself.

The voice chose not to reply, and the storm suddenly howled and threw sleet across the platform.

"Start the master de-icers," he shouted at the catman.

"You're taking her?" asked Mother Ree from behind him.

Rechs turned. She was wrapped in a deep white heavy robe. The wind pulled at her clothing, but her ancient features were set in stone and unmoving.

He nodded.

She moved closer. "There's no magic in this galaxy. No strange force that gives people powers, Tyrus. I can't read minds or move objects, but I can tell... I knew you those six months we fled nonstop from Republican patrols on every planet this side of the Falda Nebulae. You're taking her after him."

Her voice was a hard spike driven into him like an accusation.

When he didn't respond, she continued. "She's just a little girl, Tyrus. Are you so far gone you can't see that?"

She was right. There was no defense. Just some puzzle slowly falling into place deep inside a man who'd lived far too long.

"At best you'll get her killed quickly," Mother Ree said. "At worst... she'll become like you. An empty shell. A puppet whose strings are pulled by revenge until even the revenge is just a ghost. But you can stop, Tyrus. You, and she, can stay here and live."

That would've hurt if it weren't true. The part about being a puppet. But it *was* true... and it went deep to a place he'd never bothered to understand. Maybe because it was such a mess. Maybe because it was buried under a thousand years of messes.

"Yes," Mother Ree continued. "I loved you, Tyrus. Loved you madly when you rescued me like some princess in a fairy tale. Those six months were the best of my life. Being rescued and running for our lives... But I knew all that was never really about me."

She stopped. And what she said next was neither hard nor bitter. It was merely pitying. And somehow that was worse than all the other things it could've been.

"It was about *you*, General Rex. It was about you heading toward some conclusion that began long ago. Something you can't even remember now. No, there may be no magic powers in this galaxy that let people see into other people's minds, or sense things, but I know this is true—I can see it on your face. This is about something you began long ago, and you think she's somehow part of it. Princesses in need of rescue are just a convenient excuse for you to... to..."

He looked off. The storm was getting worse. Time for departure. But really, he had no defense against her. She was right about everything.

"And that's not the worst part. Not knowing exactly what it is you're looking for. No, the worst part of it is, it's not even about... her. Is it?"

You were going to say "me," he thought. "*It's not even about me, Mara." That's what you were going to say.*

Long ago, he'd had an idea how much pain he'd caused her when he left her here in the care of people who would protect someone the Republic probably still wanted dead today. But now, looking in her eyes as she pled with him... now he really knew. And it was much, much worse than he'd ever imagined.

He shook his head. He hadn't meant to. His involuntary response to all her accusations had just busted through his rigid discipline and controls.

"You're heading toward some kind of ending, aren't you?" She had to raise her voice to be heard above the howling storm. "And she's part of it?"

"I don't..." His voice was dry and cracked. He swallowed and licked his lips. "I don't know," he confessed. "But there's something I've... something I've been waiting for. And... and she's part of it. I need to take her with me to find it."

Mother Ree shook her head in disgust. Except it wasn't disgust. It was that other worst thing. It was pity.

"You're using her, Tyrus. Just like you used me, used the excuse of rescuing me, to abandon the Republic and go off on your own. To reach the edge and—"

"Yes!"

He shouted the word, and the admission instantly stung her. As though he'd said something so terrible it couldn't possibly be true because it was so selfish and craven. Except it was true. And that had stunned her worse than she had ever imagined it would.

"Where?" was all she could mumble in reply. Even though what she wanted to ask was... *Why?*

"Telos."

"What's there?"

"The men who were with this Goth Sullus worked for the Brotherhood. At least, that's the way she described them. I know their markings. Part of a bounty hunter clan. On Telos there was a big battle long ago. They maintain a base deep inside the wreckage of an old ship. We'll try to pick up their trail there."

She interrupted him. Not caring about trails and cabals. "But why take a little girl on a quest to kill some man you've never met? You're not really a bounty hunter, even though you're the most feared one in the galaxy. You're the devil no one talks about because you're some kind of bad luck charm for nightmares. But you were never a killer for the sake of a job. You've gone from a knight in shining armor to some cursed memory of that chevalier on a quest it can't remember. Why her, Tyrus? You don't even know what you're looking for. I knew that back then... and it's still sadly true now."

He opened his mouth to say he didn't know why, except that maybe, the little girl was some sort of clue in and of herself. A lucky rabbit's foot that would help him find the lock. And if he found the lock, he'd blast it open, because that had always been his way. But nothing came out of his mouth, because all of this was some new low about himself he'd never considered.

The low of using others for a reason you can't name.

"Mara..."

"Don't!" cried Mother Ree.

"I don't know what it is, but yes," Rechs said. "The kid's somehow part of it. Something to remind me why—or what—I'm looking for."

Mother Ree changed. The pity was gone. So was the anger. She'd learned long ago that one best not take those things with you one parsec more than you had to. Life was hard enough as it was. Keep your baggage light. So instead she had chosen love. Unconditional love for the man in front of her. It had worked before, even when it made no sense. It would work again.

"I'm so sorry, Tyrus."

She leaned in close, put her arms around his head, and pulled him down to her. She held his face in front of hers and stared into what remained of his soul.

"I feel as though this is goodbye." Her voice quavered. "And I don't want it to be. Just know that. Know that, Tyrus, somewhere in all the galaxy you were loved for nothing more than that you were just you."

And then he kissed her. Just as he should've done all those years ago.

The *Obsidian Crow* lifted off despite the fever pitch of the storm. The stabilizers held as the flat ship pivoted and the engines ignited for departure.

Climbing through the toss and buckle of the storm, the wobanki asked, "*Nanchu deytanku jabberwongi?*"

"Telos," replied the bounty hunter.

The catman dialed in the coordinates for the next jump.

19

The *Crow* dropped out of light speed just outside the main debris field of the old Telos battle site. The scarred hulks of disintegrating warships careened and bounced off one another in a constantly colliding maelstrom of metal and ruin. At their center was an old dreadnought that dwarfed all the other wrecks. Its name escaped Rechs, but this was his destination. He took the controls from the wobanki and flew toward the drifting hulk deep inside the debris field.

"*Ilatango dura?*" the wobanki asked.

"Because this is where we'll find the Brotherhood?" Rechs replied.

"*Ruthbroodaru?*"

"Of Vengeance. The big ship in the middle is one of their hideouts."

The catman erupted in a series of mournful yowls, the meaning of which was all too clear.

"No," Rechs said. "You're not getting out of here. They know me. We'll be just fine."

Again the wobanki yowled a question.

"Because," Rechs replied, "the mercs that were with the man who..." He nodded toward the rear compartment.

"Well, they were Brotherhood of Vengeance based on the description she gave me. Besides being bounty hunters, they also sometimes work as guards and mercenaries for the less than legal business concerns along the edge. They're classy that way. The clan that operates out of here will know which clan is working for Goth Sullus."

"*Sutaokru meto no-taki!*"

"I know they work with the Gomarii, but I won't sell you to them. You're part of my crew now. You'll be just fine. Now bring in the extra power to the spatial deflectors. We're gonna take some hits going into that debris field."

"*No sutaokru meto*," the wobanki grumbled.

"Trust me. I'm in with these guys… sorta."

Two ancient Rigelian fighter-bombers swooped in from above, forward auto-cannons blazing. As the *Crow*'s deflectors absorbed the strafing run, the lights flickered out across several panels at the rear of the flight deck.

The wobanki howled and began rerouting power to critical systems.

"Got it!" rumbled Rechs, reangling the deflector shields.

Two more fighters were coming in from behind at attack speed. He knew there would be six. Standard Brotherhood hunting patrol. And they wouldn't be interested in discussions, wouldn't even open the comms. Salvage was easier if no one survived.

Time to get out of the open, Rechs thought.

He rolled the *Crow* one-eighty and dropped down into the elliptic of the battlefield, barely missing the ruined remains of a smashed Republican cruiser's tumbling bridge section. Memories tried to crowd in, but he fought them off. He was hunting now. The past would have to wait.

The *Crow* wove through the spreading remains of an exploded destroyer. Fire from the fighters stabbed out ahead of the freighter as Rechs maneuvered to keep them off his tail. He took the *Crow* in close to the bigger wreckages, and the Rigelian fighter-bombers re-angled their thrust foils into horizontal maneuver mode for slower flight, while the pilot canopies rotated into the bomber targeting configuration. One passed close enough that Rechs could see the pilot dialing in the targeting array spread.

Best guess, thought Rechs as he swerved to avoid the flower petals of space-frozen steel where some torpedo had long ago erupted from the skin of a destroyer, *is that the pursuit craft are going to saturation bomb the debris field... with the* Crow *in it.*

"Lyra!" Rechs shouted.

"Here, Captain."

"I need you to spam jam their targeting computers, otherwise you're gonna get holed in all kind of places."

"Activating ECM countermeasures now, Captain. Power to radar disk... booting up for cyber warfare now."

"Are we under attack?" It was Prisma, leaning in through the hatch to the flight deck.

"Buckle up, girl!" Rechs roared. "This is gonna get real hairy."

Prisma hesitated, watching the star field spin and whirl as colliding debris and the prehistoric remains of behemoth starships smashed into one another. A fighter-bomber streaked just over the *Crow*'s flight deck canopy, its ion engines howling like a stuck pigasaur.

"I said buckle up, Prisma! Now!" Rechs shouted in his command voice. "Unless you wanna get sucked out into the Big Dark if we take internals."

Prisma turned to leave the flight deck, but Rechs grabbed her and shoved her into the navigator's chair behind him. "You ever play games on your datapad?" he asked.

"Uh-huh!" said Prisma as she raced to draw the straps across her tiny body.

Another fighter-bomber made a strafing run across the deflector shields, its blasters sending hot bolts of energy into the *Crow*.

"*Tabu tanaka!*" the wobanki screamed.

"Forget it!" Rechs yelled, dragging the ship away from the hot blue streaks coming from the enemy craft. "We don't need hyper-destabilizers! Re-angle the deflectors to the aft display. I'm increasing speed."

Rechs's fingers swam across the controls.

"Prisma, I'm bringing down a targeting computer. This is just like any game on your datapad. Land that reticle over any ships that appear inside the display, then fire."

"What am I firing?"

"Aft point defense turret."

Below the ship, a tri-barrel blaster deployed from a secret hatch, powered up, and began to chase targets.

Rechs moved the throttle forward and dove into the heavier parts of the debris field. One of the pursuing fighter-bombers clipped a tumbling photon inducer from some obliterated Republican corvette and went spinning off into the field. It smashed into the tumbling wreckage of a shot-to-pieces dragoon fighter and exploded violently.

"Five," Rechs muttered to himself.

The *Crow* flung itself through the debris field at dangerous speeds, trying to avoid the erratic and unpredictable drifting remains of the ancient battle. The proximity alarm went off, and Rechs scanned for the approaching target. A massive piece of twisting metal, still flinging debris from itself like some comet spraying ice, rolled into view. It was getting larger by the second.

Rechs pulled hard at the controls and drove straight at the hazard. It was an old trick. Head where something that's moving currently is, and you won't hit it when you occupy the same space. Trying to avoid it usually meant you'd meet it head-on by meeting it in the place you'd steered to avoid it. The odds and the galaxy were weird that way.

The pursuing fighter-bombers were wise to this as well, except for one of the rearmost pilots, who managed to collide with the fighter-bomber next to him. Both ships were vaporized instantly.

"Three." Rechs reduced throttle and angled in toward what remained of the massive dreadnought. One of the last great ships the Republic, in its brief heyday, had been able to build. Now the only ships the endless bureaucracy of the Republic managed to produce were cheap mass-production corvettes.

Rechs diverted power to maneuvering thrusters.

"Got one!" Prisma shouted.

Rechs checked the near-space tactical. It was true—she *had* gotten one. Now there were only two fighters closing in for the kill.

Some distant part of him wondered if she realized she'd just killed someone.

And...

Do you realize you're the one who taught her how to do it?

"Good job, kid. Now stay focused!"

He spared a glance at her as the *Obsidian Crow* raced for the dead hulk of the dreadnought. Prisma was leaning forward into the targeting display, oblivious to all the chaos on the flight deck. She was biting her lip.

"Breathe, kid," he reminded her.

He watched her tiny torso rise and fall once. She'd taken just one breath.

The remaining fighters began to hurl proximity torpedoes at the fleeing light freighter. The *Crow* bounced and bucked against the explosive storms of focused energy erupting all around the hull.

And then a massive tractor beam from the old dreadnought grabbed the *Crow*, and the pursuit was over.

Which was just what Rechs had wanted.

"*Tabu rust reeversaroos?*" the wobanki asked as the ship began to shake violently.

"Negative. This is how we get them to stop shooting at us—and get them to haul us inside their secret base."

The remaining fighters took up escort positions astern, blaster cannons ready, and the *Crow* was towed slowly onto the hangar deck of the massive ship. The wreck soon swallowed everything in the cockpit's field of view.

So this is what remains of it, thought Rechs. The forward command structure had been blown off in the battle. He remembered that. He remembered going to life support. Remembered giving the order to abandon ship. Remembered the deck-to-deck fighting as Savage marines tried to board the doomed ship.

That was all so long ago.

And he had been someone else.

Indelible VI
En Shakar, Approaching Mother Ree's Compound
Keel gently guided the controls of the *Indelible VI* as a storm of ice and sleet battered the shield array. It was delicate work, but nothing he hadn't seen before.

The storm gave way as the ship descended, the cockpit window briefly spidering with webs of ice crystals as moisture from one vapor cloud rapidly froze on arrival of another arm of the storm. Flying became easier in low atmosphere, and Keel nosed his freighter toward a lonely docking bay, the only sign of life he'd managed to pick up on sensor array.

A yawn crept from Keel's mouth as he engaged an auto-run. It was early morning on En Shakar, but not for the crew of the *Six*. They were out of sync with the planet, and Keel would rather be in his bunk, snoozing away.

The cockpit door opened, and Ravi stepped inside. "Do you know what you are to ask?"

Keel rubbed his chin. "I was thinking maybe of asking about the weather, then casually inquiring whether they'd seen any killer war bots."

"Under the circumstances," Ravi said, his brown eyes twinkling, "this approach may be as good as any. But I have found something interesting in my analysis of L-comm voice logs from Ackabar."

"Yeah?"

"A war bot was identified multiple times on planet during a series of combat engagements. The bot was associated with—prepare yourself—Tyrus Rechs."

Keel laughed. "Tyrus Rechs? Sure, Ravi."

"You don't think it was him?"

"I don't think there *is* a him. Just a bunch of legends. The real Rechs probably got dusted decades ago. And even if he didn't, he'd be dead of old age by now. Nah, I'll tell you what happens with legends. Some wannabe calls himself Rechs, gets some traction with the name, blabs at some cantina, and soon half a dozen other people are calling themselves the same thing. I'll bet you your share of the credits that this fake Rechs the legionnaires on Ackabar were talking about is already dead and buried."

Ravi inclined his head. "I would perhaps agree if not for the reports that Rechs escaped several squads of legionnaires and is suspected to have avoided the Republic blockade. *With* a war bot and an unidentified human female."

Keel sat up straight. "Maydoon?"

"Perhaps this is so, but it is my suggestion that when you leave the ship, you see if the name 'Tyrus Rechs' gets a reaction. If so, we can expand our search for Maydoon without giving out *her* name."

"Good call." Keel stood and filed past the seats to exit the cockpit. "I'm gonna kit up for this one."

"Ready?"

Keel waited for Ravi to nod his approval before lowering the ramp of the *Indelible*. A swirl of cold air blew up and into the ship. Keel shuddered. Frozen planets were something he could do without.

He put on his helmet, transforming himself into Wraith.

"If I may so say, Captain," Ravi said as he followed Keel down the ramp, "you missed a most breathtaking sight as I guided the *Six* toward the landing beacon. It was as if I sailed a diamond-bottomed boat over a perfectly clear ocean."

"I'll see it on the way out," Keel said. "Here comes the welcoming party."

A procession of robed men and women seemed to glide forward to meet him. Leading the way was a middle-aged woman with silver hair. She stopped several feet in front of Keel and Ravi, and smiled.

"Welcome, travelers."

Keel gave a brief nod.

"Thank you," said Ravi, bowing. "I am Ravi. This is... Wraith."

"I am called Mother Ree. I greet you both in friendship... and peace." Mother Ree moved closer and gently pulled her hand through Ravi as though running it through the mists of a waterfall. "You are an enigma, Ravi. For there is nothing to you and yet... there is *much* to you."

Ravi stood motionless, but Keel sensed a certain bewilderment hidden behind the face of his navigator.

"And you." Mother Ree stopped in front of Keel, staring up at her own reflection in his helmet's visor. "Wraith. You come here, a man hiding inside his armor. And not the first. Would the man inside find peace at my monastery? Would Aeson Keel show himself?"

Keel looked to Ravi, words escaping him. He turned back to Mother Ree. "How? How did you know...?"

"Remove your helmet, Captain Keel, and I will tell you what you wish to know about Tyrus Rechs and Prisma Maydoon."

Keel hesitated.

"That is your quest, is it not?"

Keel removed his helmet. "Yeah."

Mother Ree peered into Keel's eyes. There was an intensity in her look that made Keel feel as though she could see into his very life. Watching the events that had made him.

"The galaxy reveals its secrets slowly," Mother Ree said, her voice melancholy. "It shows me Wraith. And inside Wraith it shows me Captain Keel. And inside Captain Keel... it will not say."

Keel shifted uncomfortably, but found he could not pull his gaze from Mother Ree. She had him entranced and yet... she was not a witch. There was nothing dark or impure about her. She was a creature of the light, and Keel was unable to comprehend her. So he listened.

"There are two paths before you, Captain Keel." Mother Ree held up a palm. "On one, you will find that which you seek. And that which you've worked toward will come to be."

"And the other?" Keel was surprised to hear himself ask the question.

"The Wraith, and the man inside the man, become one. And you live a peaceful life, forever free of the struggles and cares of the galaxy."

Forever free.

Free.

Keel swallowed and opened his mouth to speak. No words came forth.

From the corner of his eye, he spied a man in priestly robes slowly backing away from the gathering of Mother Ree's disciples.

"Cal Camp?" Keel asked in disbelief. He drew his blaster and aimed it at the robed figure. "Camp!"

The priest's face registered terror—which gave way to a shocked death mask as Keel sent a blaster bolt squarely into his chest. The man slumped down in the arms of a priestess.

The voices of the other disciples rose in fury. Mother Ree silenced them with upheld arms.

She turned and faced Keel. "You have chosen to leave, then."

Keel holstered his blaster. Whatever trick the silver fox had played was a good one, but he felt in control of his senses. "C'mon, Ravi."

Keel strode to the corpse of Cal Camp and pulled out an optical scanner. The thumb-shaped device issued a green flash of light and a single beep. Keel laughed. "How about that, huh?"

Ravi's eyes bulged at the sight of the dead fugitive. Cal Camp was a notorious murderer. The Child-Killer of Kandalar. The Monster of Mirshra. Wanted throughout the galaxy. The combination of bounties and planetary rewards would add up to almost two million credits, now that Keel had proof from the scanner. "The odds... are staggering."

"How staggering?" a jovial Keel asked.

Ravi held his arms out at his sides. "Given the restrictions you have dictated, I am saying less than one percent."

Keel grinned. "Go ahead and be specific, just this once."

"Three billion and six to one."

Keel moved back to Mother Ree with a spring in his step. "You can thank me later, Your Holiness, because I just killed one of the most notorious murderers in the galaxy today."

"I no longer give thanks for the taking of life," Ree said, not unkindly.

Keel winked. "Truth be told, I'm in it for the money, not the thanks." He clapped his hands together. "So! How do I find Maydoon and make myself some *real* money?"

Mother Ree inhaled deeply, then took time to let it out slowly. "There are many events in play. More than you could possibly imagine. The end you seek will happen at Tusca. Go there, and you will find Maydoon."

"Tusca," Keel repeated. "Just like that?"

Mother Ree's face was sorrowful. "Take care of this gift, Captain Keel. It is a secret that I am forbidden to share with any but you. I could violate this trust for no other reason—not even for the one I love."

Keel didn't bother to respond. He bent down to retrieve his helmet and marched up the ramp of his starship. "C'mon, Ravi!"

The hologram bowed to Mother Ree, then followed his captain.

20

The Brotherhood was all hands on deck in the old dread-nought's one remaining hangar as the *Crow* was hauled in from deep space via tractor. A motley collection of savage bounty hunters, from almost every race in the galaxy, dark circles drawn under their eyes and curling bladed tattoos on every limb, watched the light freighter pass through the hangar deck's force field and atmospheric barrier. In some parts of this derelict ship, power had been restored; in others, grim, guttering torches burned where once deck lighting would have sufficed.

All of the bounty hunters were dressed in the black leather ceramic-weave armor of the Brotherhood. That was the one thing that was the same about all of them—apart from the drawn dark circles and blade tattoos. Beyond that, there wasn't a thing alike in any pair of them. Hair, weapons, scars, all were singular—and yet some-how they were all part of a universal uniform adherence of which only they knew the arcane standards of. All of it designed to communicate exactly what kind of nightmare you were unlocking should you choose to mess with the

Brotherhood. They war-whooped and hollered as the *Crow* dropped her landing gear and set down in the hangar.

Most bounty hunters operated independently and alone. But long ago the founder of the Brotherhood, a man Rechs had once known, had formed a small posse to pursue a renegade zhee who'd murdered a trader's daughter on some planet whose name Rechs could never remember. The trail of blood and vengeance those seven bounty hunters had left across the spiral arm in the Altara cluster—which was the frontier in the pre-Repub days—was so infamous that countless entertainments had been made to tell what supposedly happened, and how it all culminated in the violent confrontation known as The Coke Plant Shootout. That Rechs had been one of those men, known by another name then... that was a part left out of most movies. And something even Rechs barely cared to remember.

He remembered Riley, though. The man who had gone on to form the Brotherhood out of what remained of the posse, not including Rechs. He remembered that Riley had been cruel and hard, and yet there was a fairness in the infamous killer. Riley was eventually hanged with an actual rope by a detachment of Terran Navy Spartans on Vaalcava IX. But that, as with most everything, happened long ago.

"What do we do now?" Prisma asked. She looked out the cockpit at the sea of seething killers waiting to plunder their prize.

Rechs grabbed his helmet and inspected it. He looked at the wobanki.

"Get your weapon, Catman. They won't respect you if you don't have one. If you have to pull, pull fast and fire. Don't think twice. I'm sorry, hairball, but that's the way it is here."

The wobanki levered itself up out of his seat and went aft to retrieve his gear.

Rechs turned back to Prisma. "Tell your bot to stick close to you."

"I'm right here," announced KRS-88 politely.

"Anyone tries to touch her," Rechs said to the old war bot, "I authorize any means necessary to protect her. Override order nineteen."

The war bot's voice instantly switched to something out of a nightmare—as though it were slowed down to the point of dripping Denariian syrup. The voice of a drowned ghoul. "By your command, General Rex." The old war bot stared intently at Prisma.

"Prisma," Rechs said, "there are laws... laws of the bounty hunter. You're becoming one now. It's time you learn them."

Prisma nodded solemnly.

"One: always shoot first. Two: don't trust anyone. And three..."

He watched the tiny girl. Felt as though he was ruining some precious thing that, left untouched, would have lived a perfectly normal and ordinary life of not murdering people for money.

But I'm not doing that, he tried to tell himself. *She's already ruined.*

He nodded once.

Goth Sullus, whoever he was, had done that to her. And as Rechs studied this innocent little girl sitting in the navigator's chair of an old bounty hunter's ship, having just murdered some pilot in space combat, for the first time he wanted to kill Goth Sullus for doing this to her.

He hadn't felt that way in a very long time.

"You're all you have," he told her. "That's rule number three."

The hangar was a sea of angry jeering and drunken threats. The occasional blaster got pulled and fired into the air, or at someone. But when they saw the wobanki walk down the boarding ramp wearing a bandolier of fraggers and carrying a double-barreled blaster, and then a small girl and a hulking eight-foot-tall war bot, a silence fell across the apocalyptic remains of the old hangar deck.

Perhaps this wasn't as easy as everyone had talked themselves into. Suddenly weapons were being drawn and priming switches thumbed on.

But it was the old Mark I armor that really drew the hissing hush from every murderer. That gear was old school. Back during the Golden Age, as some called it, it was full of tricks the legends told of that weren't just myths. And of course there had been all those rumors for years of someone calling themselves "Wraith." Dealing out justice, never mind the competition. If the rumors were even half true about that operator, then now was the time to be very careful. And every hardened killer on the rotting deck of the ancient war machine knew it.

Except that one guy.

Because there's always that one guy who doesn't read the situation. Even among the Brotherhood, there is that guy.

"Hey, Grandpapa! Where do you be getting old relic to play bad boy in?"

The catcall came from a Lahursian, which explained the ridiculously mangled attempt to speak Standard. Not that anyone ever pointed out the snake-like creature's linguistic challenges. When you could strike or draw a blaster so fast your opponent's head would spin, most people weren't going to call you out on your flaws. Unless they weren't all that interested in going on living.

"Me Rabu the Ripped," hissed the Lahursian. The humanoid snake strode to the front of the crowd of hired killers, clearly relishing its moment in the limelight.

Rechs halted before the challenger, waiting. The hand cannon remained in its holster on his thigh.

"Well..." crooned Rabu. "Me Rabu claim all your stuff by battlefield salvage laws. And girl child."

Rechs remained motionless like the dark jungle statue of some nameless warlord long gone and unconsidered. The wobanki's paws caressed the wooden stock of his double-barreled blaster. Cats, like the Lahursians, were among the galaxy's most lightning-quick uber predators.

But everyone forgot about the catman after what happened next.

Like a snake. That was what some of the Brotherhood would say, ironically, when they recalled the event over strong drink later that night. That was how fast the hunter in the old Mark I moved when he reached out and simply crushed Rabu's neck. For a brief, stunned moment Rabu couldn't believe what was happening. He flared his hood—probably some dying automatic response—bared his fangs, and sank them into Rechs's mailed arm. Both fangs shattered, and that was the last thing Rabu felt before he drowned in his own neurotoxin.

It was a horrible and violent death, and though they would never admit it, many of the Brotherhood were emotionally scarred for what remained of their lives.

Every one of them took one step away from the guy in the Mark I armor.

The wobanki purred with admiration.

"Oh my, young miss, do look away," KRS-88 rumbled.

But Prisma could only imagine Goth Sullus's fate at the hand of Rechs. Or at her own hand, if she had a Mark I suit of her own. Finally she'd witnessed real power—the power to fight back. And she found it utterly intoxicating.

Across the deck, off in the darkness, someone began clapping. One lone pair of hands, sounding above the mortified silence that had fallen over the crowd.

"Tyrus... Rechs."

The slow clapping continued, and now the entire hangar deck, once alive with the whine of engines idling for takeoff, and the growl and beep of heavy machinery loading weapons, and men and women scrambling to rearm as shields collapsed and hull integrity was breached, held its breath and dared not move a muscle. Now there was only this sound of slow, sarcastic, and utterly confident clapping.

"As I live and breathe," said the voice within the parting crowd. "Do you realize there's a bounty on your head, Tyrus? Republic's paying a planet's worth of credits for you... dead."

Only a blind man could have failed to notice every killer's hand, claw, or paw reaching for their blaster. Very slowly. All of them figuring how a planet's worth of credits got divided up six hundred ways.

"Goth Sullus," said Tyrus, his bucket's amplification system making him sound spectral.

A man appeared within the crowd. An ordinary man. He wasn't wearing the ceramic-weave armor. No. He was wearing... a bathrobe. A red silk bathrobe that was rather frayed. He had long dreadlocks and pasty white skin. A small bot followed him. It rolled along on two omni-directional balls, and it chirped and beeped softly at everything and everyone. On its head was a steaming bowl of rice from which two chopsticks protruded.

The man swept aside the dreads and moved forward as though he were a dancer approaching some dangerous jungle beast. Which was very wise of him. Because he was.

He smiled. "I don't know of any... Doth Sullast. Never heard of him. Nope. But Tyrus Rechs, man... The Republic would pay well to have very dead. Yes. Have heard much."

If this bothered Rechs, no one could tell. He remained immobile, and it was this immobility that concerned all the murderous murderers on the deck. Everyone was trying to get as close to their blasters as possible. Fingers gently drifting in that don't-upset-the-guy-in-the-ancient-armor-who-just-crushed-Rabu's-throat-like-it-was-nothing sort of way.

But Rechs... he seemed as though he couldn't have cared less about that massive piece of slug-throwing iron on his thigh—the piece that people from the Savage Wars called a hand cannon.

He didn't seem concerned in the least.

The men on the hangar deck were used to people being concerned when they were just about to kill those very same people. They were hyenas that way.

They had grown accustomed to the scent of fear, and they liked it.

Except this time... no fear.

And that was beginning to bother them.

"One of your clans..." Rechs began, his voice echoing hollowly off the darkened reaches of the abandoned deck, "is pulling security for him. They were on Wayste two weeks ago. I'll ask one more time."

And if they were bothered by the fact that he couldn't have cared less about his weapon, then him telling them he was going to ask all six hundred of them "one more time" and didn't bother to add any kind of "or else" to the end of his statement... well, that was just too much.

They were officially freaked out.

"Who's the psycho?" asked some nervous killer in the silence.

The man with the dreads spun about to face the guy who'd talked out of turn.

"Who is Tyrus *Rechs*?" he asked the suddenly ghost-ly white dude. "You've never heard of the Butcher of Andalore? Never read any history about the Savage Wars? Never heard of a little slice of hell called Diablo's Durance? No?"

The man with the dreads cast his beady-eyed gaze about the crowd. Then he returned his attention to the guy who'd spoken.

"Wow. You are just too stupid to live."

He rushed the guy, robe flapping, and gouged out the guy's eyes with long dirty fingernails. The same finger-nails he'd been rubbing across his teeth while he talked.

Just like that.

The others hauled the blinded man into the crowd, though his screaming was heard for some time.

The man with the dreads whirled on Rechs and smiled. "See? I can do that crazy killer thing too!"

"Goth..." Rechs began. He was heedless of showman-ship and antics, making good on his promise to ask one last time. The air suddenly felt heavy and swollen with un-stable thermite. This was where people, a lot of people—everyone in fact—was about to get good and killed.

"I know!" shouted the man in the dreads, cutting off Rechs before he could finish repeating his request for the last time. He began to babble quickly. As fast as he could. As though only *his* life depended on it, and not every-one else's.

"I know you said you'd ask just one more time, and it's pretty clear at this point that you can kill a discount-sized bunch of us real dead, dead, dead if we don't give you what you want. Okay!" He slapped his fists against his robe. "Got it!"

He snapped his fingers. It was like the sound of dead wood breaking in a quiet forest. The bot that had followed him rolled forward.

The man in the dreads picked up the two chopsticks from the bot's bowl and began to tease out some rice. He blew on it and stuffed it into his mouth, making exaggerated chewing motions. He let out a brief maniacal laugh.

"I can't honestly be expected to... to... to... rat out a fellow clan, can I?" He spoke as though talking only to himself.

He looked at Rechs, then returned to his rice.

"No. I really can't. That's quite ridiculous."

He erupted in an insane little titter, then put the bowl down and began to rub his teeth with one finger.

"Listen..." he began, his head shaking, or nodding. Or doing both at the same time. "My name is..." He hesitated, to make clear that he was lying. "Beltazar Gex. I..."

He twisted around and threw his hands wide to encompass the six hundred killers who surrounded him. Six hundred minus the snake and the guy whose eyes he'd gouged out. There was still blood and gore all over his hands. He seemed to realize this, as he walked over to one of the bounty hunters and comically wiped his hands across the man's ceramic-weave vest.

"Sorry," he murmured. He made a sincere couldn't-be-helped face, then returned to Rechs in long, quick strides.

"Where were we? Oh, right—Beltazar Gex. Me." He placed his long fingers on his bare chest beneath his robe.

"*The* Tyrus Rechs. You." He gave a courtly bow worthy of the most ham-fisted of tragedians.

"You are a bounty hunter, too… right?"

Rechs didn't bother to reply.

"Well, I'm going to assume you gave me an answer, and it was 'yes.' Clan leaders know all about you, and we don't spread it around. Not even to the Republic. You see," he turned to the crowd, "*that's* how this works, everybody. Secrecy. Don't talk to the Republic. Everyone knows that. Right, guys?"

There were murmurs of acknowledgement.

"See," said Gex, turning back to Tyrus, "can't give up Othgay Sullyay." He winked broadly. "Because if we did, well, you know what happens next in the Brotherhood. We—or rather they, the rest of the Brotherhood—they come here and… and… well, I don't want to be crass in front of little ears." He indicated Prisma.

He paused as though Rechs might tell her to plug her ears. When that didn't happen, he gave a heavy sigh.

"Well. They would come in here and slit our throats—*after* they removed our hands, feet, claws for some of you, tentacles for others, tongues, and…" He cleared his throat. "Other things. Yeah, the way we do it—and believe me I've been part of this kind of reorganization thing—is we take all those things first and *then* we slit the throats. That's the proper order, and that's how you keep people in line. No talkee, no slittee. See?"

He beamed at Rechs as though all this should make perfect sense.

Rechs drew his hand cannon and stuck it into Gex's cheek.

The man whimpered and held up his effeminate hands.

"I start with you, and eventually someone tells me what I want to know," Rechs growled.

"There's… th-there is… another way!" Gex stammered. "C'mon, man, honestly. This is savage. Straight up savage and… frankly it's unprofessional. It's not like I don't have snipers trained on the little girl. C'mon, what kind of monster am I? Would I really splatter her brains all over the deck just by circling my index finger? Would I?"

Rechs tilted the barrel back from Gex's dreadlocked head. "Another way?"

Gex smiled and snapped his fingers. The bot wobbled over. Gex took up the bowl of rice and the chopsticks and shoveled a few quick bites into his mouth. He smacked his lips as he talked.

"Yeah, totally. We have this… this… clan law, you might call it. Beat our best guy and… you get anything you want. Even info—which is pretty much a sacred cow to us."

"Beat your best guy," Rechs repeated.

Gex shoveled in a few more bites, then set the bowl down on the bot again. He wiped his hand and sidled up to Rechs. He began to clean his teeth with his finger again.

"Yeah. And actually, you'll be doing us a big favor. We'd, uh… We'd…"

He felt around in his bathrobe for a second. Finally found what he was looking for. He produced the joint and stuck it between his thin lips, just above the barest of mustaches. He lit and inhaled.

"Yeah... we'd uh, like to get rid of him. He went a little crazy—even for us. He's down in the weapons vault, so we can't really get to our weapons unless... well... it's not like Montraxx hasn't been awesome for us. And that's saying a lot for a Kungalorian cyclax, big ferocious semi-intelligent beasts that they are. Really they're just big old guard dogs." He took a deep draw on his joint and laughed. Held the smoke, then let it spill out.

"I make my own Black Lotus. It's good stuff. Primo Locus. Take off your helmet and tune in. No?"

He inhaled again.

"So if you would go on down there and please kill Montraxx, that would be awesome. For us... and you. Because then I can freely tell you what you want to know."

Silence.

"Listen... you know how this works. We may all be scurvy, craven murderers, but we, like you, are generally the only justice most people are going to get out here on the edge. We got standards, and we've done lots of good— relatively speaking. You know the Repub don't care. So, and believe me, I get that you'll kill a lot of us, starting with me—I get that. I'm a getter of that. But I will not tell you what you want to know unless the rules are met. You don't get to be clan boss without following the rules. And even though I freely admit I am a no-good backstabbing piece of Nanga filth... I have standards. As unbelievable as that may seem to you and your little crew, I have them.

"And, I might add, we have a man-portable torpedo system. Got it from a Tellari trader. Not even your armor could stand up to a direct hit from one of those. They're guided, did you know that? So. Go kill Montraxx for us and we good, bruh!"

Gex stood back and beamed his crooked smile as the tiny joint smoldered between his long, dirty fingers.

21

Montraxx batted Rechs across the vast hold deep within the ruin that had once been the armory of the Republic dreadnought. As Rechs flew through the air, knocked nearly senseless, he saw the name of the ship printed in large Repub font along one wall. *Justice.*

He hadn't been on this ship at the Battle of Telos after all. He'd been on the *Unity.*

He smashed into the wall of the hold, and the monstrous cyclax roared in triumph. It towered a full story above Rechs, its fangs dripping with thick gobs of viscous saliva. It beat its broad gorilla-like chest and rushed forward to rend the bounty hunter limb from limb.

Rechs's HUD was scrambled and intermittently fritzing out. He smacked his bucket into the wall, and the display centered, aligned, and gave him targeting data on the incoming monster. Which was all but useless—because no bullet or blaster was going to penetrate a cyclax's natural plate-armor skin. Rechs knew that, because he'd already tried. He'd put twenty large-caliber slugs center mass, and the thing hadn't even bothered to wince.

The words "Jump Pack Offline" flashed in his helmet's display.

Great.

Montraxx grabbed Rechs. Instead of throwing him, this time the beast apparently intended to squeeze the life out of him. Its wild animal eyes filled Rechs's display as the creature literally tried to crush Rechs's armor in on itself.

The suit's integrity warning alarm began to sound.

Rechs tried to get his glove up so he could punch in a command on his left gauntlet interface. But the thing crushing him held him so tight that even this simple action was impossible. In desperation, Rechs switched to vocal interface, which hadn't worked for years.

"Activate defensive surge measures, set for one hundred thousand volts!" he groaned with what little breath he had left.

And to his surprise, the ancient suit actually responded to his voice command. Somewhere through the years it must have fixed itself, and he'd never known it.

The howling monster shrieked and flung Rechs away like a pitched fast ball. Rechs hit a bulkhead that was designed to stand up even in the case of ship-to-ship ramming, yet his armored suit went through the massive chunk of ceramic-refined hyperalloy like it was some ancient sheet of flimsy yellowed paper.

And the entire deck collapsed into the abandoned recesses of the old battleship's disintegrating superstructure.

He heard a dull crack within his helmet, or his head, and it was lights out. The last thing he remembered was falling into a deep darkness...

... And then he was back at the Battle of Telos, aboard the other ship that was just like this one. The *Unity*. When the Savages broke through the line.

That day had been for all the marbles. The last major ship-to-ship action in the Republic's fight against the Savage fleets. The Savages' cheap, high-firepower cruisers had gone right through the Repub Navy corvettes and straight at the two big, shiny dreadnoughts, hoping for a knockout blow.

There had been two dreadnoughts there that day.

Both were lost.

It was a trap!

The Republican Navy, under Admiral Caspo, had been lured into the fight at Telos. Caspo had fallen for it for all the wrong reasons, and the main one had been his own firm conviction that the Republic was weak. That only he knew the way out of the galaxy-wide quagmire that was the Savage Wars. A thousand little wars flaring up everywhere because of some anomaly in man's ancient history of starflight. The galaxy was aflame because... because Caspo, a man Rex had known well, had been very right. The Republic was dying, feeding on itself to support an elite class that cared little and invested less.

Caspo had hoped a decisive military action would change all that. More power would be given to the military to right the wrongs and set straight the things that very badly needed setting straight. The ruling council and the House of Reason would see that the path they were headed down led only to madness and destruction, a galaxy-wide dark age.

But instead, the mass-production cruisers of the Savages, armed with every conceivable weapon they could stick on them, came in hard behind a ragtag fighter wave larger than any Rex could ever remember seeing. He'd been on the bridge that day, and he saw the first waves come streaking in. Turret fire barely made a dent in their numbers.

"Rex," Caspo had said to him, "today we finish the Savage Alliance, old friend. Once and for all. Today we save our Republic."

Already the hammerhead corvettes were engaged and getting chewed up. Fighters were buying time for the motley collection of Savage Alliance cruisers to move in close enough for ship-to-ship volleys of heavy turret fire. Soon both fleets were engaged in short-range heavy fire on a massive scale. At any given moment shields on some ship would collapse, and targeted fire would hole the vessel in several places. Command structures and engineering sections went up in sudden explosions, never mind the wholesale death going on in a thousand raging dogfights along the hulls. The bridge aboard the *Unity* was alive with the names of ships suffering catastrophic damage.

"There goes the *Daring*!"

"We've lost *Discovery*!"

"*Constellation* is reporting reactor cascade in progress. Requesting permission to abandon ship?"

"Corvette *Admiral Husla* has been rammed. Casualties on all decks. She's dead in space."

"The *Republica* is abandoning ship!"

Enemy fighters streaked in to hit key system targets on the heavy capitals. Republican fighter screens attempted to take them out before the torpedo bombers could deliver their strikes. But there were too many.

"Concentrate fire on group alpha," Caspo ordered. He turned to Rex one last time. "We'll need the legionnaires, General. Board that big ship there." He pointed toward a massive Bulari command cruiser, bulbous and long like a flattened football with a dorsal torpedo turret hanging from underneath its mass. She was lumbering in toward a burning Republican cruiser, closing in for the kill.

"What about the *Unity*?" Rex asked.

"We can handle anything that comes at us. You and I both know we've been through much, much worse. Knock out that ship, and we can jam the rest of their fleet comm and traffic."

Out there on the line, the aft reactor on a hammerhead corvette exploded, taking a squadron of fighters with it. The explosion rippled up along the spine of the corvette, and the forward command section lurched away. Then the rest of the ship was gone. No survivors.

"Assault shuttle loaded and ready, sir!" announced the Repub deck officer in charge of boarding ops.

Caspo cast a long glance at his old friend Rex.

"We've got to win this one today, Rex. If we don't, then everything we've built is lost. The Council of Reason and the rest of the Republic will see... this is the only way now. It's either that, or the galaxy surrenders to savagery, even if we still do win the war somehow."

The two of them were the senior-most officers on the field that day. They knew more than anyone what was at stake.

"Admiral!" shouted another deck officer at a bank of monitors along the upper level of the command bridge.

"Another fleet dropping out of hyperspace, bearing one-eight-zero from *Unity*. More Savage cruisers and a full carrier group. Fighters incoming!"

"Knock out that ship, Rex. Now more than ever," said Caspo one more time. One *last* time, really.

And then he looked away from the projected tactical display inside the command bridge. He stared straight at Rex.

"Things never change, Rex. The names may change, but even you've come back around to your own true name. Remember Mars? Remember the day the *Uruguay* went down in the sand? That was a bad day, and we came through that hell six months later. We'll come through this too. Go now, General. And make it back safe, my friend."

Rex had gone. He'd boarded assault Shuttle 218 and led a strike against the Savage cruiser *Agamemnon*. The big Bulari command cruiser. On board, the fighting was brutal. Legionnaires were going down all around him. But they took the strategic interface command deck and downloaded a standard Repub hunter-killer infowar algorithm.

Even so, the battle was lost by then. The massive fleet they'd first engaged above Telos V had been just a feint. A soft jab. The knockout punch came from another direction altogether, and it hammered the Republic fleet senseless.

When the Repub Navy was fully engaged in ship-to-ship combat with the Savages, that's when the privateers joined in. Almost every national system fleet had contributed these ships to aid the Savages—and they targeted the *Unity* with overwhelming firepower. It tried to get in close to the atmosphere to keep the continuous waves of fighters off its collapsing shields and burning decks. But when the engines went down and it hit the atmosphere, it took Rex's oldest friend and ten thousand crew with it.

They'd had their differences. Rex and Caspo. But they'd been together from the very beginning in one name or another. And they had seen the Quantum Palace inside the Dead Space. Two of only three who'd made that journey and lived.

Now Rex, on the *Truth,* was in command. Fires were out of control in the main reactor when he gave the order for all Repub ships to evacuate the system. He barely got out alive that day. He and the 131st, or what remained of it, had to fight their way out by hijacking a Savage frigate and forcing the crew to execute an uncalculated jump away from the battle.

But all that—Caspo, Telos, and even the Quantum Palace, which hurt his mind to think about—all that had been a long time ago.

Now the cyclax was hauling itself down through the ruined wreckage of the decks above where Rechs had finally come to rest.

It was coming for him.

He looked around. Suit diagnostics were booting up and scanning for damage. Nano-repairs were being effected as best they could.

He'd come to rest near the skin of the ship, deep inside the ship's destroyed targeting processors. These processors had once crunched the numbers to keep up accurate turret firing solutions across the vast volume of space. The processors were close to space so the computers could more easily burn off the incredible heat they generated.

"Use that," Rechs told himself as he struggled to his feet, searching for some kind of weapon. The cyclax was just two decks above and crawling down through the exposed decking. Rippling muscles in its powerful arms flexed as it pulled itself downward at him like some kind of horrible story-tall spider. Slavering jaws opened and shut as the thing roared in anticipation.

Rechs got to his feet and felt a swift moment of vertigo as he struggled with his balance. He cleared all the warning messages in his HUD. When had he ever paid any attention to those?

Now the beast was right above him. Maybe fifteen feet. Rechs stumbled away just in time.

The thing dropped onto the deck, causing the ruin to rumble and shake. More debris fell from the ceiling above. Rechs pushed his way through the long-dead stacked processors that rose up into the thermal venting. The cyclax lumbered after him, sweeping away the processors as though it were harvesting some sort of strange black metallic and gray plastic wheat in some dark hell that had never seen the sun.

Rechs came up against the hull and ran his hands along it. No doubt this was only the inner hull, but it would have to do. He pulled a thermite grenade from his belt and dialed it to max yield, minimum spread. Then he slapped it on the hull and slammed his mailed glove against it, instantly detonating the small bomb. There was no time for anything else—the monster had closed the distance and was reaching out for him.

The blast tore through the inner hull. The outer hull was already exposed to deep space, thanks to the many rents and wounds in the dreadnought's skin.

The atmosphere vented like a violent cyclone, and Rechs was sucked out into the shadowy and forsaken place between the hulls—or, he thought as he spun and twirled away, between the hells. His suit assured him it had integrity in zero gee, as well as some oxygen. Montraxx, on the other hand... not so much.

But the massive creature refused to die so easily. It grabbed onto the gaping wound in the inner hull for all it was worth. Precious oxygen rushed past it.

And here was the danger. If it let go, it would smash into Rechs and probably punch through the outer hull with enough momentum to take them both out into deep space. Rechs's jump jets would never get him back inside the ship. And no one would come looking for him out there. He'd disabled his tracking firmware years ago.

He hoped the jump pack would work despite the earlier "offline" message. He checked its reserve power level— below fifty percent.

"That'll do," he growled.

He pulled his carbon-forged diamond-edged machete from his back, fired the jets—they still worked—and drove straight at the monster.

He passed between the cyclax's bulging arm and massive leg, and he forced the wicked blade of the machete straight through Montraxx's gigantic bicep. The monster howled—an inhuman cry of pain that sounded like thunder even through the suit and the windstorm of deep space's insatiable demand for all your oxygen. And then the howl was gone—as was Montraxx. It was sucked out into the airless void between the hulls. Never to return.

It would gasp and explode out there in the cold. Its frozen body would rattle around between the hulls until one day the old dreadnought finally came apart at the seams and drifted into some gravity well.

Rechs's jump reserves were dropping like a rock. He pushed the thrusters hard to reach a bulkhead he could hang on to. The jets finally gave out just as he grabbed it.

He waited for the tornado to die, hoping the superstructure in this portion of the ship wasn't so damaged that it would just give way and tear itself off into space. As he held on, he could hear the smashed debris—the debris of the battle he'd lost long ago—still endlessly striking the hull like small micro meteorites doomed to forever live out a melancholy destruction of bare white noise.

"We watched you on closed-circuit!" Gex erupted when Rechs came back up onto the deck in a lift. "Saw the whole fight! Thought you were dead for sure. But we was wrong! See?"

Rechs looked at the *Crow*, and saw the wobanki up in the illuminated cockpit canopy. The cat gave him a paws up. Rechs had told Skrizz to take Prisma inside the ship and lock the hatch while he was gone.

"Goth Sullus," Rechs said. He turned his gaze to the wiry man in the bathrobe bouncing from foot to foot in front of him. The slime devil swept his dirty dreads to one side and smiled. His teeth were rotten near the gums.

H8 user, thought Rechs. Teeth like that were a dead giveaway. *Should've noticed earlier*, he admonished himself. *Should've known he'd double-cross me.* H8 users were like that. Zero reliability. Zero credibility.

"Yeah... about that," Gex said. "Remember when I told you it's not like we have a portable ship-to-ship torpedo launcher that your... your suit wouldn't stand up to even just a little bit?"

Rechs looked around. The hangar deck was dark and empty save for him and the weasel. Rechs switched the armor's imaging systems to IR. Off in the darkness of the upper decks he saw the rest of the six hundred hired killers, minus two, in position with weapons pointed straight at him. They were everywhere. His HUD began to tag all their weapons—including several ship-to-ship launchers.

Gex, sensing that Rechs understood the game, smiled. Like he'd won the junkie lottery of all time. An old Mark I was a name-your-fortune price in the black markets of Denebia. Everyone knew that. But Gex had gained more. He'd salvaged an old piece of Mark I, gotten rid of Montraxx, *and* would be collecting on the most wanted bounty hunter in the galaxy—making this the best day ever in Gex's miserable life.

"Remember when," said Rechs. He knew his armor projected his voice with a ghostly sound, and he could tell it gave even the creepy Gex the willies. "Remember when I didn't tell you that if I die, my ship explodes? Romula nuclear space mine hooked up to the micro-reactor. Callisto Wars. Very old school. Found it a long time ago. Rigged it to the suit telemetry. They don't make 'em that big anymore. The Romula nuclear space mine, that is. Back in the day it would've vaped a dreadnought like this, no problem. Remember, Gex? Remember when I didn't tell you that?"

The sleazy crime lord swallowed hard. It looked as if he were about to choke on his own bile. He was understanding the game more fully now than when he'd first begun to play.

"I remember now." His voice sounded small and hollow and strangled.

"Goth Sullus," Rechs said.

There was a long moment in which Gex was undoubtedly running through any aces in the hole he might have left to play. Apparently he found none.

"About that... okay, here's the actual deal-y deal. Those guys, the guys who're Brotherhood and working for that dude... they're all ex-leejes. Ghosts from Nether Ops. Except they're the ones that got drummed out for some mass murder on Ulori that went bad. Work off a ship called the *Siren of Titan*. Old fast-attack cutter from some war no one cares about. But it's real trick and slick if you're into that sorta thing. So, main guy's name is Daeth. Daeth Hunda. Real bad. Very bad guy, in fact."

Gex stopped as though hoping all that might be enough.

"Last time I ask, Gex. Where is Goth Sullus?"

Gex shook his head. He put one hand on his hip and wiped his forehead with the other. Rechs knew the man was actually considering shooting it out right there and now rather than telling Rechs what he wanted to know. Both ways would end badly for Gex. It was just a question of how soon.

"Okay, okay... truth is..." His voice shook. "Like I said, they're drifters. Not a fixed operation like here." He threw his hand wide as though he were taking some hard-earned pride in the derelict remains of an old warship. "So exactly *where* they are... I don't actually know, my friend. Just know they were crewing for him out of that ship. Got a heads-up, via our internal comms net, that they were headed to Andalore. We always let each other know what we're up to. If you're going to pick up their trail, well, then Andalore's the scene, and that's all I mean."

He slapped his hands together and held them up, indicating he was done.

Rechs turned and strode toward the *Crow*. Already the boarding ramp was extending down onto the deck. He circled his fist at the wobanki, and the engines began to spool up for takeoff.

"Don't tell Daeth where you heard it," shouted Gex over the engine's roar. "That guy's a real psycho."

22

"And all *I'm* saying is that the glass sea wasn't as nice as you made it out to be," Keel said with a wave of his hand. "It was pretty, but you set the bar a little too high, pal."

Ravi shook his head, his eyes narrowed into slits as if Keel had insulted his mother. "You are a very bad judge of beauty."

The mention of beauty made Keel think of Leenah. "The princess give you any idea how much longer it would take to get the hyperdrive repaired?" As they'd exited the atmospheric blizzards of Mother Ree's planet, a hailstone the size of a snub fighter had punched through the *Six*'s shields and damaged the hyperdrive.

"Difficult to say." The comm light blinked. "Lao Pak calls again."

"Pass," Keel announced, as if he were an executive reviewing business deals.

A short while later, the comm light stopped blinking. "This is odd, indeed," Ravi said. "This transmission was seventy percent shorter than the average from Lao Pak. I am wondering why it was so short."

"Pre-recorded?" Keel ventured.

"Yes. I am thinking so."

"Bring it up."

Lao Pak was seated on a makeshift throne—a command chair salvaged from an old Ohio-class battleship. The pirate king began with a foul-mouthed tirade in his native tongue. Keel couldn't understand much, but he got the gist of it: Lao Pak hadn't found room in his heart to forgive him again.

Then Lao Pak composed himself and said, "This message from Admiral. It coded so you can't see his face. He want Maydoon now." Lao Pak shifted in his seat, his eyes darting about the room. "You hurry up."

The screen darkened, and a black channel recording came up, a silhouette of a man, his voice heavily distorted. "I have been made aware that the bounty hunter Wraith has been retained to find the location of the Maydoon family. Instruct Wraith to contact me directly with the location, once it has been acquired. Payment will be deposited upon satisfactory proof of location." The silhouetted man paused. "I... shall look *forward* to seeing just who has taken up the name of *Wraith*."

The cockpit lights came up at the end of the recording. "I'm famous," Keel quipped. "*All* the scheming admiralty of the Republic are dying to rub shoulders with little old me."

"With you?" asked Ravi. "Or with Wraith?"

Keel waved a hand. "Same person."

"Mother Ree was not so sure..."

Keel frowned. "Mother Ree was a kook." He stroked his chin thoughtfully. "I wonder who this admiral is."

"We have Garret on board," Ravi pointed out. "Perhaps he will be able to decrypt?"

"Good idea." Keel activated the all-ship comm. "Hey, Garret, come into the cockpit, will ya?"

The coder arrived shortly. "Captain Keel?"

Keel queued up the admiral's black channel communication. "Can you decrypt this?"

Garret smiled. "It's already decrypted. All these messages run the same cypher 'crypt-strings. When I cracked one, I cracked them all. Hold on."

The skinny code slicer rummaged for a datadrive, unrolled it, and affixed the triangular device to *Six*'s osmosis port. Seconds later, the black silhouette began to lighten in degrees of gray. It pixelated and added color until the image was as clear as if the admiral were standing in front of them all.

Keel's stomach dropped. Of all the people in the galaxy...

"Hey, I know that guy," Garret said. "How do I know that guy?" He snapped his fingers. "It was from when I was still in fundament school. He was a big deal. The hero... *the hero of Kublar*!" The coder smiled as if proud of himself for remembering.

"Admiral Silas Devers," Keel said. He got up. "Ravi, I'm gonna put on my armor and tell the admiral that—"

Chee-chee! Chee-chee!

The comm flashed a peculiar orange. Ravi brought the call up privately, so he was the only one to hear it. "This is Nightshade... yes."

Keel screwed up his face in confusion. "Nightshade? Ravi, who are you—"

The navigator held up a finger. "Andalore. And you're sure of this? And Tyrus Rechs just left? Good. From where?

Even better. Half payment will be transmitted immediately. The rest will come upon confirmation of information. I do not need to tell you what will happen should... good."

Ravi turned to Keel, smiling. "Nightshade is an alias I set up. Information broker with a modest network. Mostly pirates and drunks, but this time a pirate with Beltazar Gex knows where Rechs is headed. Andalore. And we are positioned to get there first, assuming the hyperdrive is fixed in time."

"Gex?" Keel crossed his arms. "*That* scumbag?"

Ravi shrugged. "A pirate *with* Gex, though given the particular way he hesitated in an attempt to hide his ridiculous style of speech, I estimate a sixty-two percent likelihood it was Gex himself."

Garret injected himself into the conversation. "Hey—I just got a reading on the war bot. Telos."

"Yes," Ravi said. "That is what they informed me. They apparently just made the jump to hyperspace. You can use that knowledge to ascertain whatever delay is in your tracker."

"Okay, great!" Garret said. He sounded genuinely excited to do just that. "I just had a thought. Wouldn't this Gex person know your voice, Ravi? It's fairly distinctive..."

"Ah, yes, this is being true. But I spoke to him through a vocal modifier. No problem."

"Andalore." Keel said. The planet was important to that particular sector of Republic space. Some kind of data archive? Keel couldn't recall. "I'm going to put my armor on and transmit the message so we can get done with this job. Set a course for Andalore as soon as we're able."

Ravi looked at Keel with his large, expressive brown eyes. "You are actually going to share this information with Admiral Devers? I—given what you have shared with me about your past, I would not have calculated favorable odds…"

Keel gave a grim smile. "Then you didn't factor in the two hundred and fifty million credits."

Obsidian Crow
Hyperspace

"Pardon my blithering idiocy, Mr. Rechs, but isn't Andalore a sector capital? Going there would seem ill-advised for one who is as desperately wanted by the authorities as you are." KRS-88 clicked and popped.

"Shut up, Crash," Prisma said. She was peering over Rechs's shoulder, studying every move he made as his hands set up the cockpit for the drop from light speed. Rechs moved his right hand forward and grasped the jump throttle. He moved it back slowly and studied the astrogation panel. When the readout confirmed they'd arrived over the jump coordinates, he pulled the throttle full back, and the streaming star field returned to normal.

A massive green-and-blue world spun before them. Off to port a small forest moon orbited.

"*Zergagi aru antanku tak?*" asked the wobanki as he reset the flight master bus and checked the power systems readouts.

"We're sneaking in," said Rechs, scanning the stars.

"Won't they track our transponder?" Prisma asked.

Rechs was surprised at her knowledge of star flight. But what did he expect? Kids were getting smarter every day.

"Normally, yes. But until we reach the inner traffic control hub, we're flashing a stolen mining vessel code. We won't be required to provide full verification until we're on final for Andalore."

"Oh." Prisma seemed to accept this answer—but as usual, she quickly had a dozen more follow-up questions. Rechs was learning that she loved to ask questions. And he didn't so much mind teaching her. Over the course of the jump, he'd decided to begin educating her on blasters, starting with the standard blaster. He'd taught her how to strip it. Clean it. Reassemble it. Calibrate it.

But not fire it. Not yet. He'd told her only the most basic information about firing a weapon. Including the philosophy that guided every bounty hunter—a philosophy that *should* guide every person who ever picked up a weapon, in Rechs's opinion.

"I know you want to kill this man," he had told her as she worked under his watchful eye. "I understand that. But you never shoot with your heart, girl. Or your emotions. Those have nothing to do with what's happening when you decide to point this at someone."

He was holding a T19 needle blaster. He'd used it for assassinations. Easy to conceal. Low blast signature.

Accurate to twenty meters. No recoil. Long barrel. She needed two hands just to lift it and steady it. But he would show her exercises that would train her arm to be steady, strengthen her so she could hold her sidearm in one hand. And he could tell that one day, if trained right, she'd be able to hold one in *each* hand. But not yet. She needed to walk before she flew.

She's just a little girl, that voice reminded him.

And:

"Hang out on the edge. Wait."

Those thoughts came and went as he taught her how to clean, maintain, and prepare to fire a killing weapon.

"You shoot with your mind, Prisma."

She'd made a face then. Given a small little girl's chuckle. It was the first time he'd ever heard her laugh.

"What?" Rechs asked. His voice was gruff and old compared to her perfect embodiment of youth.

"My school studies say there's no such thing as the mind."

Rechs thought about that as he took up the weapon she was cleaning and inspected it. It had been fairly scored with carbon. He was making her clean every edge and groove. Her hands were dirty and her face was smudged where she'd wiped away the sweat as she worked. He noticed she often bit her tongue while she concentrated on a particular problem. That was not a good habit.

He handed the weapon back to her and pointed out an area that needed her attention.

"And what do you think about that?" he asked.

"About what?" she asked as once more she began to clean.

"The mind. Is there one, or is it all brain and meat?"

"Well... the Council of Reason says it's only brain. There is no such thing as a mind."

"I didn't ask what *they* say. I asked *you*, Prisma. What do you think?"

"Well..." She applied her cleaning wires to the part he'd pointed out. She bit her tongue as she drew the wire brush back and forth with determination.

"Breathe," he reminded her. "You always breathe during a gunfight. You shoot better. Think better. And go on living. If you breathe."

She took a deep breath and exhaled. He watched her tiny shoulders rise and fall once more. He'd begun to enjoy this little automatic response even she didn't know about herself. It was a delight to him, and Tyrus Rechs could not remember experiencing many delights in recent years. Or any.

But he knew once... long ago, very long ago... there had been things that had delighted him. People, too. Seeing her do this automatic little thing even she didn't know she was doing was like the memory of all those lost good things. Familiar somehow, and Tyrus Rechs did not know why.

"I think..." She took another deep breath. "I think that sometimes—like when I'm sick and my whole body hurts—my mind says this is okay, Prisma. You're fine. This won't last forever. Or when I'm sad, even though nothing is wrong with me. That's the real me. The inside me that talks to myself even though I feel a certain way. Not my brain. So

I never agreed with my official school studies. But I just gave them the answers they wanted to hear because that's what you have to do in the Republic. Daddy says—"

And then she stopped. Abruptly. She focused on the part of the weapon he'd given her to clean, yet he suspected she didn't see it at all. She scrubbed and held her eyes open until the tear that had tried to form dried.

Rechs waited.

Then...

"I think you're right, Prisma."

She looked up at him. Just a little bit of the tear remained.

He nodded. "That's your mind, girl. That's what you shoot with when everything around you is going from bad to worse. Not with your emotions or your reactions. Your mind. You think before you shoot, and during—and then not so much afterwards."

Tyrus shifted. He was getting sore from sitting. "The most important part about shooting is the before part. Because once you've started shooting you can't put it back in the bottle, as they used to say. *During* the shooting, you shoot with your head because you have to see the blast you can't dodge. You've got to shoot that guy who's going to shoot you... first. Afterwards... you try not to think so much. Because you'll think about those people you shot for the rest of your life."

After a moment's silence she gave a small "okay" and continued her work on the needle blaster. Rechs was sure she would remember everything he'd told her—even though it probably didn't seem important to her now.

He'd never told anyone any of these things.

But he'd thought about them.

Rechs spotted the mining freighter lifting off from the surface of the forest moon. He pushed the memories of Prisma aside. "Take us in close to that ship," he ordered the wobanki.

He swiveled the pilot's chair around and switched on the active scanner. He nailed the freighter with a high-gain burst of EM detection from the *Crow*'s radar dish, and a moment later he had a pretty good readout of the schematics. The ship was automated, hopefully. He studied it for a few minutes more and found exactly what he was looking for.

By now the wobanki had the *Crow* trailing the massive ore hauler and closing in on her stern. The big ship was on full departure burn as it struggled up and away from the moon. Already it was shifting course for an intercept with Andalore Prime.

"What are we gonna do?" Prisma asked.

Rechs tapped in a few settings and moved the throttle forward, flying the *Crow* right in underneath the belly of the big ore ship. He matched forward speed, spun the *Crow* on its axis, and angled the bow in close for a descent toward the hull. "We'll use this ship for cover and get in underneath local Republican detection. Once we find a site down there to hack into the planetary network, we can figure out if our target has been here or not. The *Crow*'s pretty fast, so we may have beaten them here."

"This seems easy," Prisma said.

"It isn't," Rechs replied. He hugged the automated freighter for final approach into Andalore's atmosphere. "And you haven't gotten to the drop yet. Tell me how easy it is after that, girl."

Prisma's mouth made a small circle. Rechs suspected she was considering what he meant by "the drop."

"Strap in, we're going atmospheric, and we're gonna pick up a lot of chop this close to the hull."

Sure enough, the ship began to rattle and bounce. The wobanki and Rechs fought to hold course just beneath the speeding atmospheric hauler. The wobanki seemed rather used to this sort of thing. Despite the occasional warning alarm and the near-constant earthquake going on all across the flight deck, the cat seemed content to calmly call out the distance-to-hull readings. Rechs focused all his attention on keeping both ships from sudden collision.

"*Nachu twivonki meks,*" the wobanki announced.

"Okay... this is where the fun begins," Rechs said. "Twenty to drop. Hold on, and don't throw up. Whatever you do, Prisma, don't do that... because you'll clean it up."

The ship began to shake even more violently.

"Don't worry, Miss Prisma..." KRS-88 whispered. "I'll clean it up for you."

The ship gave a sudden jerk.

"Is this the drop?" Prisma asked cautiously. Rechs could hear the fear in her voice.

"Not even close," Rechs said with a smile. "But don't worry. I've done this once before. It helps if you try to tell yourself you're having fun."

Prisma whispered to KRS-88, who was holding on for dear runtime to the flight deck access walkway. "We're having fun, Crash."

"If you say so, young miss."

A maw opened within the freighter, and shining metallic and silver rocks began to drop, destined for some remote part of Andalore.

"*Nachu funfvon meks!*" shouted the wobanki over the rattle and cacophony of the cockpit. Proximity alert alarms were now bursting forth with shrieking regularity.

"Now!" shouted Rechs.

Rechs backed off the throttles completely. The view outside the canopy pivoted sharply away from the underbelly of the giant automated freighter, and then the *Obsidian Crow* was dropping like a rock too.

It was like flying inside an avalanche.

It was the war bot that began to moan first. The terror in its basso rumble suggested it perceived an approaching end to its runtime. Then Prisma gave a short scream and the wobanki uttered some sort of battle yowl. Rechs just clenched his jaw. He was fighting to avoid most of the small asteroid-sized falling rocks and watch the altimeter at the same time. They had to drop below two thousand feet before he could bring the power back in. The drop had started at ten thousand.

The lush mountains of Andalore raced up at them, and Prisma found herself pushing back into her seat as falling debris streaked past the ship and into the massive canyon below.

"Restart ignition masters," Rechs ordered.

The wobanki flicked a couple of switches—and nothing happened. The wobanki roared. It wasn't a happy roar.

Rechs reached over and slammed his fist against the main engine master restart cycler. The thing flickered to life and the engines came online with a less than enthusiastic hum.

"Thirty-five hundred... bringing in the power now. Full deflectors to ventral array," Rechs shouted above the scream of atmosphere whistling past the canopy.

They fell another thousand feet. Rechs went to full throttle as soon as they dropped below two thousand. Then they shot away from the avalanche of falling rock and into the misty mountains of Andalore.

"All right..." Rechs said. "Let's find a relay station to cut into and find out what's going on here."

23

The parkland in front of the Republic's Sector Defense Administration Campus on Andalore was a richly landscaped parade ground off-limits to the public and dominated by a courtyard of statues, used only for promotion ceremonies and grand soirees with visiting Republican elites. Andalore Prime, the capital of Andalore itself, spread away from the manicured confines of the government buildings that occupied the best property within the city. At most times, the area was quiet, even peaceful.

But at the moment, a small war had broken out.

Republican legionnaires were everywhere and shooting at everyone. Squads of them were coming in via dropship. A Brotherhood fast attack ship was pulling some kind of op on the Defense Admin's main citadel. The big ship had made an unauthorized landing on the platform and had immediately taken out the local security detail. Brotherhood bounty hunters were currently holding the platform and the roof. Whatever was going on inside the citadel was unknown to the legionnaire command structure at present.

Captain Antullus, the point in command of the legionnaire reaction force assigned to handle the situation, had issued orders to go ahead and terminate everyone involved, keeping civ casualties to a minimum, if possible.

In other words, it was a full-scale free-for-all with pros shooting at pros. The Brotherhood were firing down on the legionnaires, who'd been forced by Antullus's bad decision to land in the courtyard as opposed to assaulting the platform by air and controlling the high ground, as per Leej Sergeant Mach's unsolicited recommendation.

In the midst of all this was Tyrus Rechs. The bounty hunter and the wobanki had ended up in the middle of the wild firefight while trying to recon the location and lock down a positive ID on any Brotherhood who might be doing the same. Now they were both pinned down by a heavy crossfire between the two opposing elements, as the leej squad and the Brotherhood snipers on the tower went to blasters with the intent to kill.

The wobanki popped up and unloaded both barrels from its blaster on a nearby legionnaire NCO who was trying to organize some type of flanking assault. The intuition, combat experience, and good sense of that NCO—Sergeant Mach—were thereby lost. Antullus would go on to receive a commendation for his actions, and a promotion to major.

Rechs popped a fragger and heaved it over the pedestal he was crouched behind. That was when he noticed two things.

One, the lumbering war bot advancing through the courtyard dropping legionnaires left and right. The war bot was followed closely by tiny Prisma Maydoon, with a needle blaster of her own.

And two, the statue he'd just thrown the grenade over. It was a statue of *him*. But back in the day. Back when

Andalore had been a hot spot in the Savage Wars. He'd been called the Butcher of Andalore then. Except this statue had a bronze plaque that stated he was the *Liberator* of Andalore.

Rechs pushed a thousand images of that terrible conflict out of his head and waited for the fragger to explode right where the NCO was no doubt receiving medical attention from noob leejes gathered to protect their wounded. It did, and those leejes were thrown into the air by the blast.

Things like that—lobbing a grenade at people who were trying to rescue a wounded soldier, a wounded leej— things like that were why they called you the Butcher.

Things like that, except on a grand scale.

And then he reminded himself that he'd always played to win, never mind the means. At least in combat. There were no rules. And there could only be one winner.

That had been the problem. The House of Reason and the Senate Council were always insisting on rules, and oversight, and acceptable losses. That's what had driven Caspo and so many others to try and take matters into their own hands in their misguided attempts to save the Republic from itself.

The Repub had hated the Legion. It hated the fact that it *needed* the Legion to defend itself. And it especially hated guys like Rechs and Caspo. Guys who'd inspired the phrase, "When you go to war... go Legion on your enemies."

A legionnaire squad took up a position inside the entrance to the park and laid down heavy fire from a crew-served N-50. The big war bot now was forced to take cover as well. Its enhanced impervisteel frame could generally stand up to most light arms, but the powerful N-50 could knock it down. And if the leejes brought out anti-armor, it would be game over for the killing machine.

Two leejes rushed Rechs's flank, weaving in and out of the statues to get close. Rechs leaned against the pedestal beneath the statue of himself and squatted down. He waited for his targeting reticule to fall on the lead trooper, then he fired, blowing off the guy's head. The next trooper dove and managed to roll behind cover as Rechs chased him with a blossom of auto-fire.

The heavy, crew-served N-50 at the park entrance continued to chew up everything that moved.

So Rechs didn't move.

The second trooper popped from cover and shot Rechs in the chest plate with his blaster. Rechs's armor fritzed and rebooted, but Rechs already had the guy in his sights. His hand cannon spat briefly and tore through the cheap ceramic they made leej armor out of these days. That leej was out of the fight and most likely dead.

Play to win.

Brotherhood snipers saw their opening and got off several blasts. Marble and tile disintegrated all around Rechs as he pushed off from the wall and ran for better cover.

He heard a blaster shot strike KRS-88 with a loud *daaaank!*

A low, humming drone sounded from the sky—a Republic buzz ship drifting over the cityscape beyond the park and the tower.

"Everyone down!" Rechs shouted.

Fighting against instincts, he didn't drop until he saw Prisma do so first. She pushed her face against the pavement of a wide walk that wound through the park. She didn't have a wall or statue to duck behind, but her bot provided better cover than any standing structure could ever hope to.

Good girl.

In the face of this buzzing specter of death overhead, the Brotherhood snipers sent hurried shots at the craft's front windshield in a desperate attempt to break through and wound the pilot. The buzz ship waggled only briefly, then steadied and unleashed a torrent of blinding blaster fire. The snipers, along with the building facades they'd used as cover, were reduced to smoking chunks of debris.

Always ready to heap more firepower upon an enemy, the legionnaires at the park entrance focused their fire on the Brotherhood as well. It wasn't needed. As the rapid fire of the buzz ship's blaster cannons slaughtered everyone on the citadel's roof, the whine of the guns reminded Rechs of the slaughter on Andalore. And all the other slaughters the galaxy never seemed to tire of.

Play to win.

Rechs brushed away that faint cobweb of a memory. With the Brotherhood out, the legionnaires would be free to concentrate on him now. He needed to find an exit.

He reviewed the battlemap his HUD provided, looking for some landscaping or statuary to slip through, or an unobserved stretch of parkland to double back on to get behind the Republic troops.

"Crash! Where are you going?"

Rechs whipped his bucket around toward the sound of the girl's voice. The war bot was up and moving across the park toward a memorial hall of fallen heroes. Streaks of blaster fire from the N-50 darted above and behind it, sending showers of dirt and permacrete skyward with every near miss.

"Stand down and return to the line!" Rechs ordered. But the bot ignored his command. It walked at an even pace through the storm of blaster fire.

"Crash!" Prisma shouted as a blaster bolt struck the bot in its shoulder. The bot's armor shrugged the blast off—it took more than a few glancing hits to take one of those beasts down. But the girl... the girl was reacting. Responding without thinking.

Running after her war bot.

"Crash! Crash!"

"Prisma!" Rechs shouted. "Stay down!"

What had he been thinking? He'd brought a little girl into a war zone, and what? Thought that because he told her a few words of wisdom and taught her a few things about a blaster that she'd keep her head under fire?

The girl kept on running after the bot. Whether ignoring him or not hearing him, Rechs didn't know. Growling, he took off after both of them. As he ran past the catman he called, "C'mon," trusting Skrizz to follow.

The bot had entered the warehouse, and Prisma wasn't far behind. She disappeared inside its shadows, and Rechs heard her scream—but just for a moment. It ended abruptly.

Rechs ran faster.

The N-50 tried to lead him. Statuary and paving disintegrated all around him. He didn't bother to dodge or weave.

This is going to be it. You're charging into an enclosed space against an unknown foe.

He kept running.

Stupid. Find an alternate entrance. Toss a fragger in first. The girl got herself into this. Play to win. Remember.

But he ignored those meaner voices and kept running as fast as he could, hoping desperately to catch her.

He reached the door. The wobanki was close at his heels.

Rechs expected to be greeted with a sea of blasters. Part of him wondered if this Goth Sullus had set up a counter trap just in case some bounty hunter showed. Guys like that, local galaxy's edge thugs-slash-warlords, they were smart and crafty that way. Had to be out here. Anything was possible all the time.

Rechs pointed his hand cannon in the darkness and prepared to deal as much death as possible—and hopefully get the little girl out alive.

That's important to you now? asked that voice.

He stopped short. There were only two blasters leveled at him.

One belonged to the war bot. The retractable forearm blaster in its left arm was pointed directly at Rechs; its right hand assembly was clamped down on Prisma's mouth. She looked frightened. Kneeling beside her was a pink-skinned Endurian princess—they were all princes and princesses on that planet. The Endurian was attempting to... comfort Prisma?

Rechs wondered if his mind had finally gone like it'd been promising to do. *How much is real, and how much is just my mind falling apart?*

Part of his mind wondered that. The other part—the tactician; the general; the killer; the butcher... the survivor. That part assessed the situation. And it told him the entire tableau was an act to keep him off guard.

Rechs looked down the barrel of the second blaster pointed at him. It was a bullpup model that promised a good punch. Held by a... legionnaire? But not. Modified armor of an older sort, maybe a decade ago. Victory Company. Kublar and all that mess. The last set before the Republic put the leejes inside those ridiculous, cheap, reflective pieces of junk that were more for show than survival.

"You're shorter than they say, Tyrus Rechs." The legionnaire-but-not spoke like some kind of ghost. His voice modules sounded like sand passing through impervisteel. A dry, punching way of speaking. All business.

Most likely a mustang officer. A real leej. Not some House of Reason point.

The legionnaire—now a mercenary of some sort—was not alone. A skinny kid with glasses, who looked out of his element, moved forward from the shadows, some sort of device in his hand. And a turbaned Sikh stood in the background. That instantly brought up memories of some Savage War battleground Rechs had arrived at too late. The dead and the dying being burnt by the mountainful. It had been medieval.

Bio scans from Rechs's visor said the Sikh wasn't really there. A ghost? He'd seen stranger things. But no—his visor also identified the TT-3 bots that gave away the hologram's trick.

The wobanki caught up and skidded to a cat-scratch halt beside Rechs, panting and obviously waiting for Rechs to make the first move. Its double-barreled blaster shifted from one target to the next. The guns were now even, if you didn't count the fact that the war bot was programmed to terminate company-sized levels of resistance.

"War bot!" Rechs shouted. "Release the girl and turn your weapon on that legionnaire."

The legionnaire-but-not tilted his head as if to say, "Really?"

"Permission to fire?" requested the bot in a low and terrible voice. One programmed to strike fear in the heart of mortals it was about to massacre.

"Granted," Rechs replied, readying himself for the action.

But the bot didn't move. "Denied," whispered the ghostly legionnaire.

The war bot kept its blaster aimed at Rechs.

"Authorization: guild-cyan-six!" attempted Rechs, using an older code, the highest level of clearance he could recall at the moment.

Still the war bot remained in target mode. It seemed only interested in killing Rechs.

The skinny kid said, "It's no good. I had a lot of time during our jumps trying to catch up to you to get this just right." He waggled the device in his hand. "Your codes and clearances? Gone. Big guy's all ours now."

The wobanki hissed at the kid—an unmistakable predatory hunting call. The skinny youth, probably a coder, tugged at the goggles hanging from his neck and retreated into himself, dropping his gaze downward and ducking his head below his shoulders so as to avoid eye contact with the cat. Wobankis could rip your arms off after they opened your guts with their claws. They often found employment with the warlord who liked to be left very alone.

The hologram stepped to the front. "We have come here to talk with you, Tyrus Rechs, and I am wishing to point out that had our intent been to kill you, we have had ample opportunity to do so. But of course... you can see that we have not."

Rechs remained silent.

"Had we instructed the war bot to open fire on you while you took cover during the buzz fighter's attack run, there is a seventy-seven point six percent chance that the surprise attack would have been fatal to you." The hologram twisted his pointed mustache and looked at the cat-man. "Ninety-three percent for your wobanki friend."

Skrizz growled in reply.

Rechs stared coldly at the hologram. "Talking to people who point blasters at me makes me want to shoot them in the face."

The Sikh nodded. "Yes, I understand this. However, even if I were to discount sixty percent of what is told about you as legend—and I suspect that might not be enough—the likelihood of you shooting before asking questions was too high for us to remain unarmed. You former legionnaires let go of many things, but KTF is not one of them."

Rechs lowered his weapon and signaled for the wobanki to do the same.

The ghost legionnaire followed suit. He called out to the bot, "Stand down, but keep hold of Maydoon."

Rechs squared himself and stood in front of the legionnaire. They faced off like two gunfighters at high noon. "You know who I am," Rechs said. "So who are you?"

The hologram's eyes flitted to the legionnaire. Clearly he was interested in hearing how the leej would answer. Maybe a false ID was coming…

"I'm you without the marketing campaign. Name's Wraith."

Rechs rolled his shoulders. "I've heard enough whisper about a *Wraith* for me to believe—if you're him—that you're well on your way to having a few legends told when all is said and done, kid. For whatever that's worth these days."

Rechs looked to Prisma. She'd calmed herself. And she was listening to every word. They were *all* listening. All wanting to see what would happen next.

"Why don't you just let the girl go," Rechs suggested. "I'm the only bounty you'll ever need to collect on. Wealth… and rep-wise."

Wraith shook his head. "Might scream. Ravi?"

The hologram cleared its throat, a quaint little trick to convey humanity. "The legionnaires are currently being given a series of bogus orders to keep them unfocused and busy while we conclude our business. Wraith's… particular access allows us the time to have this conversation. But they will no doubt investigate the hysterical screams of a girl child. Republic standard operating procedures require them to look for what the House of Reason calls 'heroic moments for purposes of publicity.'"

"That's an impressive trick," Rechs said. "Telling legionnaires which way to go."

"Only lasts long enough for them to get chewed out by their CO," Wraith said.

"So who else are you?" Rechs asked. "Under that armor. Your momma didn't name you Wraith, boy. And I'll bet she didn't name you whatever fake name you're about to give me, either. That is, *if* you're kind enough to oblige an old fellow former leej before I kill you."

"Asking me to take off my helmet is against the code," Wraith said.

Rechs gave a dry chuckle. "We both know you're not guild."

Wraith appeared to consider this, then removed his helmet. "The name's Aeson Keel. Captain of the *Indelible VI*."

"That probably means something, like Wraith does... but I stopped paying attention to everyone who wanted to kill me a long time ago. Sorry—never heard of ya."

Keel gave a lopsided grin. "That's the idea."

"Okay then." Rechs's fingers moved slowly toward the hand cannon at his side. It was foolish of Keel to give him an opportunity for a kill shot. Trying to play to what was most likely a young man's ego and hot temper hadn't worked enough to get the kid to do something stupid. Rechs decided to just go ahead and see this thing out. The odds were in his favor. Even now.

"So what happens—" Rechs began.

In a blur of speed, he went for his sidearm. But no sooner had his hand gripped his weapon than Keel's blaster was already drawn and leveled squarely at Rechs's head.

The wobanki let out an impressed purr. Even the coder gave a low whistle.

Keel grinned widely. "Ravi estimated we'd draw even." He almost giggled. "A true fifty-fifty. I told him he was crazy. No way you're as fast as the stories. Only I'm that fast."

He smiled.

When was the last time someone got the drop on you, Rechs? Had it ever happened?

He knew what this was about. Galactic gunslingers always wanted to test his mettle. This young gun needed to prove to himself, and to the galaxy, that he wasn't just the guy who laid a snare for big, bad T-Rechs; he had to prove he was *better* than the old man. The new bad-as-you-please sheriff.

"So that's that, huh?" Rechs said. "Go ahead and pull the trigger. You tracked me, roped me, and the reward is all yours now."

"Reward?" Keel asked, as if it was the first he'd heard of it.

"Don't play stupid," Rechs spat, feeling his temper get the better of him. "Two hundred grand."

"Listen," Keel said, re-holstering his blaster. "I just landed over *ten times* that just for finding the last surviving Maydoon." He waved his hand at Prisma. "There's an admiral bringing his entire fleet here, right now."

Rechs sighed. "So that's the real bounty, eh? Find the girl, find me. Get me alive, so I can be brought before the Senate and House of Reason. Do me a favor and pull the trigger."

Annoyance flashed on Keel's face. "I might," he said. "Look, this admiral is a piece of twarg dung in a white uniform. If it weren't for the sheer amount of money, I'd have told him to find Prisma on Kublar and then I'd've put a blaster bolt in his head the moment he got off his shuttle. He doesn't want *you*. He wants to find her because he thinks she'll lead him to someone named Goth Sullus."

Prisma gasped.

"Sullus," Rechs repeated slowly.

"You know him?" Keel said. "Great. See, that's what I need to know. What makes finding Goth Sullus worth so many credits? Who is he, exactly?"

"And you're not here to kill me?" Rechs said.

"You? You're a fossil. Where's the fun in that? I'm here for myself. There's a lot more credits in this than what I've got so far. And so far, I've made a fortune."

"Then... you're for hire," Rechs observed.

Keel seemed to think about this new tack for a brief second.

"So let me hire you," continued Rechs. "Sullus is here. We want him too. I'll pay you—twice what your last job was, if you work for me to kill him."

Keel's eyes widened. "Sullus is *here*?" He laughed and rubbed his hands together. "Well, I thought there'd be a little more to it than that after finding the girl and the bot. Ravi, let our... *friend* Lao Pak know where to find Sullus. Make sure Lao Pak gets payment *before* he delivers Sullus's location to our client. And make it clear that I'm not here."

"I made you an offer," Rechs said.

"I know you did," Keel said, turning back to him. "But let me help you with the math. I'm getting paid two hundred and fifty *million*. You're prepared to double *that*?" Keel crossed his arms, as if daring Rechs to actually try to lie to him and tell him he had that many credits.

The wobanki's ears flattened, indicating a longing for such impossible wealth.

Ravi raised a finger. "Technically you are only being paid half that sum, per your agreement with Lao Pak."

"Semantics, Ravi," said Keel.

"Fine," Rechs said. "I'm good for it."

"Oh, well then!" Keel rocked on the balls of his feet and looked to his navigator. "Hear that, Ravi? He's *good for* it. Well, Mr. T-Rechs, in that case..."

Rechs carried on, unperturbed. "All I need is for you to watch the girl here while I go on ahead to kill Goth Sullus. Then you can claim the prize. I just want him dead, and then we disappear. I'm going out there, into the citadel. You get back to your ship and watch for the *Siren of Titan* to try to get off the landing platform."

Keel looked at the old bounty hunter suspiciously. Trusting this guy was stupid, but it was also a lot of money. "That's it?"

"And let the wobanki, the bot, and the girl go. They've got to make it back to my ship. Yes, that's it. More or less. Consider yourself on retainer."

Keel almost laughed. He'd apprehended his share of bounties, and he knew the sorts of desperate ploys they would come up with when backed into a corner. But no one had ever just up and offered him five hundred *million* credits. *That* was ballsy. The idea that this fossil had that kind of money was so absurd… it almost had to be true.

And if he *was* telling the truth, it'd be the easiest five hundred million credits anyone had ever earned. Plus, he'd *still* have earned the two hundred fifty million for the original job. He'd found Sullus, hadn't he? It wasn't his fault if Sullus was killed by this old man before the admiral could talk to him.

Besides, Keel had no intention of letting Admiral Devers talk to *anyone* much longer.

He looked to Ravi. The hologram shrugged.

In the end, greed won. No, not greed. Sound fiscal strategy. Keel was going to buy a luxury yacht. The kind that could sail on waves as easily as in space.

Keel returned his gaze to Rechs. "Okay. But I'm gonna hold you to all of this. And obviously I know how to find you, trap you, and kill you. But until then… partners. Agreed."

"No," said Rechs, and suddenly the hand cannon was pointing at Keel's head. "Not partners. You work for me now, kid."

24

The kid—Wraith—was good, Rechs thought. Better, maybe. If he made it out of this gunfight alive and got everyone back to the ships, then he was probably great. Or would be someday if he lived that long.

But that was yet to be seen.

But the new question was: why was some Repub admiral interested in Goth Sullus? A minor edge thug no one had heard of. And why was a minor edge thug pulling a big job on a sector defense capital? In broad daylight?

For Rechs, killing Goth Sullus was about Prisma—but he knew it was about more than just that now.

Hang out near the edge. Wait.

Maybe the waiting was over.

He pulled the heavy blaster from off his back and made his way forward under heavy fire, moving toward the citadel. He stalked and shot down legionnaires like some jungle predator. The kid with Wraith had given the leejes a dozen contradictory orders, and Rechs was moving in and among them like a shark smelling blood in the water.

He reached the grand colonnade, a series of Senate-worthy steps that led up into the center of local Republic power. Grand and opulent Tyrasian marble. No expense was ever spared to keep up the facade of power the Repub needed to maintain control of a starving galaxy at constant war with itself.

As Rechs ran up the steps, he pulled a flashbang bolo from his utility belt and separated the attaching wire from each connected ball. Ignoring all the incoming blaster fire, he twirled the bolo overhead and lobbed it into the main entrance to the citadel.

A loud *bang* echoed off the marble caverns inside. If all went well, the flash had killed some dead and stunned the rest by optically scrambling their brains. Rechs raced into the entry hall, blasting at the survivors.

Four legionnaires poured into the entry hall at the far end, reinforcing the breach. Legion Comm had proba- bly been restored by now, guessed Rechs, and these men were being called back from the ongoing battle with the Brotherhood on the floors above—called in to stop this new counteroffensive coming at them from below.

Rechs stitched three legionnaires with heavy blaster fire and butt-stroked the fourth as he came at him. The last guy tried to bring his N-4 up in a useless attempt to get off a gut shot, but Rechs kicked it out of his hand and smashed the leej in the bucket a second time for good measure. Incredibly, the leej's bucket cracked. The guy went down.

"Don't make 'em like they used to."

Rechs slipped into the elevator, dragging one of the dead leejes with him. He pulled a micro-lock from a utility pouch and slammed it into the door controls.

"Override controls and lock doors," he shouted at the device.

Using a multi-tool, he pried the protective plate off the leej's update socket port, then ran some fiberwire from his helmet into the port. A moment later he was reading all transmissions to and from some idiot named Antullus to the rest of the platoon. He quickly got the gist of it: basically the point was getting everyone killed by trying to respond everywhere at once instead of using the principles of focus and mass, as every leej was taught according to the training Rechs had once mandated long ago. He felt bad for all the kids he was about to kill. They'd been led by an idiot. But that had been going on for years.

Whatever it takes to make sure you don't feel bad about that, that other voice reminded him. *About the kids you're going to kill now. Don't feel bad, Rechs.*

Rechs hit the elevator button for the Defense Network Vault access. From the leej traffic he'd read, it looked like that was where the Brotherhood was focusing their effort.

Why was some local thug interested in anything the Defense Network had to offer?

You're not here to find out why. You're here to kill the man who killed Maydoon. For the girl. For Prisma. That's all. The Republic is beyond saving. Caspo and Telos proved that.

The floors ticked by.

He heard Mara, Mother Ree now, tell him—no, *remind* him—that he was like some knight on an endless quest he couldn't even remember receiving.

Almost there.

Which is it, Rechs? he asked himself.

The doors slid open.

Feel bad, or... play to win?

He was facing the backs of a leej squad engaged in a furious firefight with the Brotherhood far down the length of a corridor that led to the secure rooms of the Sector Defense Administration Building.

He shot the leejes in the back until the heavy blaster he was using got too hot.

One turned and aimed at Rechs. Rechs drew the hand cannon off his thigh quick as a hypersnake and put three slugs into the leej. The kid. Whoever he'd once been to someone.

The kid fell back in a heap, slug holes smoking in his shiny armor.

The Brotherhood killers had paused in their continuous fire to watch this old school Mark I armored bounty hunter drop the legionnaires they'd been trying to kill. Until he started coming for them.

He got his portable defense shield up just in time to reflect three blasts. Keeping it between him and the Brotherhood, he reached out around its ethereal red glow and fired back with the hand cannon. One guy went down clutching his guts and screaming bloody murder. Another's head just disappeared in a sudden spray of red mist. More were flung back by the impacts of the hypersonic depleted-uranium slugs violently tearing through their bodies.

Blasters were one thing. Slug throwers were orders of magnitude more brutal.

The Brotherhood's group leader was on his comm and ordering them to fall back by twos to the vault.

"We're pulling out. Move! Move! Move!"

Rechs advanced, shooting from behind the energy disruptor shield. Thirty seconds later the barrier gave out, but it no longer mattered. Rechs was in and among them, firing point blank into their ceramic-weave armor with one hand and wielding his carbon-edged machete with the other. He shot one ugly Dantha in the face and slashed another killer across the throat when the guy came at him with a wicked vibroknife.

Two more tried to get off blaster shots, but Rechs dodged and threw his machete, sticking it in one shooter's chest. Rechs unloaded the hand cannon on the other. Violence delivered up close and personal in a sudden staccato blare of violent death.

When both shooters were down, he retrieved his blade and advanced through the next layer of defense. He was using the hand cannon on full auto, putting as much gunfire between him and the targets ahead as possible. Ill-aimed blaster fire careened off the access paneling all around him, and smoke and haze obscured the debris-strewn hallway. The whine of blasters mixed with the *brraaaap* of the hand cannon.

Rex switched to IR to target better. He closed in amid the cordite haze and blaster discharge, then hacked and chopped at them as they coughed and tried to run.

One struck him in the left shoulder with a disruptor mace. Fire and pain erupted across his shoulder and down his arm—that whole side of his body felt like it had been filled by a swarm of deadly mummy-bees. The machete dropped from his fingers. His armor gave him a cardio infarction warning alarm. Several heartbeats had just gone missing from his telemetry.

Rechs smashed the guy in the face with the butt of his hand cannon, and shot him for good measure once he was down on the ground.

Then he screamed in pain. The stinging was intensifying into crawling napalm.

He stumbled forward, dragging the left side of his body with him. He fumbled for an anti-toxin injector with his numb hand and slammed it into his thigh. He had no idea whether it would do any good.

It did a little.

Just up ahead, the blast door to the network vault irised shut. Through its diminishing window he could see the gleaming white vault beyond, and within it, two large Brotherhood members and a man in a black cloak and hood. The man stood in front of Sector Defense Master System Planner and was holding a data globe in his hand.

Rechs holstered his weapon and grabbed the door to the vault.

"Full increase!" he roared at the armor.

Hydraulic strength tripled and then redlined as Rechs tore the massive gleaming metal door apart. Suit power was now down to less than twenty percent.

As Rechs stepped through the opening, he was greeted by a volley of high-pitched blaster fire. One shot slammed into his forearm, but was deflected by the suit and struck the ceiling above. Even so, it was a real bell-ringer. He pulled his hand cannon and fired back at them.

The three members of the Brotherhood fell back, exiting toward the catacombs that led to the network nodes. It looked like the inside of some robot insect's hive in there.

Via audio detection, Rechs heard legionnaire boots in the distance behind him. So be it. He moved forward, hand cannon out, and proceeded into the nodes. Two chambers down the length of the corridor he was greeted by crossfire from heavy blasters.

When he saw the holes seared into the walls of the ceramic honeycombed network, Rechs knew these weapons were overcharged enough to punch nice big holes in his armor. It was dangerous to fire blasters on that setting. Which meant they knew something about his armor. Knew it generally stood up to regular blaster fire. In other words, two men working for Goth Sullus, whoever he was, knew about *him*. And knew he was coming for them.

"Warning!" a Network Defense System automated announcement declared. "Unauthorized system breach detected."

Rechs circled around down another corridor tube and came upon one of the Brotherhood who'd had him pinned down in the crossfire. He shot the guy. He took another shot at the guy in position opposite this one, but that shot missed. He heard the guy falling back, cackling maniacally.

"We always knew you'd show, Rechs! Got a big surprise for you!"

Rechs dashed forward. Speed was of the essence now. That threat, a tease, a taunt, had been made to get him to check his rush. Or at least, that's how it had seemed to

Rechs. But even Rechs knew it was also some kind of invitation to follow.

They needed time to do what they were here to do.

But not forever.

Rechs crashed down the core access tube and burst into the main node power grid, ready to fire. Whirling yellow lights and hazard yellow girders warned him of the inherent danger in this room. But everyone was gone. All the terminals had been scrambled to erase whatever access had gone on here.

There was only one thing that mattered here. Rechs had been a general for the Repub long enough to figure that out—along with so much more than anyone would ever know. He knew exactly what the sector defense grids were really for. Defense information for large-scale conflicts. Automated defense plans, codes, and security access. *War.* Not heists, robberies or hijackings, but full-scale inter-galactic war.

That's why Goth Sullus had wanted Maydoon's data globe. That's why he'd killed Prisma's father. The man had some kind of super-secret access to all the levels, even the ones that were hidden.

But once again, why would some local thug looking to carve out a name in contraband on the galaxy's edge be interested in the big picture stuff? Was Goth Sullus looking to cozy up to the MCR? To stand up to a real Repub response, one would need capital warships and an army the size of the Legion even if you had everything in the defense network. You'd still need to respond to the threat of total warfare. You'd need ships, war bots, fighters. You'd need another Legion just to fight the Legion.

And there was no other Legion.

The Repub had all that, and many times over. The truth was, if the Repub decided to crush you, it could make that happen. Easily. Given time.

All a hack of the defense grid would tell you was how it would happen to you.

A cold thought ran through the old bounty hunter.

It's him.

Hang out on the edge. Wait.

Goth Sullus... whoever he is... it's him. But only if you can remember who the "him" is.

Haven't you've known all along?

Except I can't remember what I know. I've lived too damn long!

He charged through the room and down the access tube on the opposite side. He threw himself into the nearest stairwell, and looked up.

High above, a robed figure was climbing up into the dark reaches beneath the roof.

Rechs pushed himself, taking steps two at a time. Gasping for air. Blaster shots careened off the walls around him as he raced upward. He heard the sudden *huuuusssh* of a pneumatic portal and knew his target was through. He kept running anyway.

By the time he reached the portal, they'd locked it. He checked the armor's power and found it diminishing fast.

He pulled his heavy blaster and fired at the door.

Nothing.

Beyond its barrier, the engines of a starship approached departure whine.

He pulled his fragger and slapped it on the door. Pulled the pin and dropped back a few feet. It blew through to the other side in a sudden explosion of energy and heat. Rechs heard footsteps and glanced down. Fresh Republican legionnaires were swarming up the stairs after him.

He was getting a very bad feeling about someone having hacked the defense grid. *Take down that starship*, he told himself. *Stop this before it starts. Stop Goth Sullus before the galaxy catches fire again. Isn't that why you're out here? Isn't that why you were waiting?*

Something unknown had decided to change the state of play in the galaxy. And for all its flaws, the Repub had this going for it: it was the known. It could be worked with. Propped up. But the unknown... well, that was just the point; it was unknown. Who knew what shape the galaxy might take next? There were nightmares, and then there were stark raving mad nightmares. Rechs had seen them out there on the edge, beyond the Repub. Nightmares that were all too real when power was in the wrong hands.

He stepped through the smoking portal.

The *Siren of Titan* was already lifting off from the platform. Rechs ran forward, firing at the most vulnerable spots on the ship's belly, hoping desperately to bring the ship down. But none of his shots found their mark, and the ship hurtled off into the blazing orange twilight of Andalore. Within seconds it was a new star racing into the upper dark of the galaxy. Rechs watched it go.

He heard the leejes below coming for him.

His suit was low on power. He was low on ammo. And he was tired. But he would fight. He would probably fight until he died, which might be in the next few moments. But the Republic was in trouble—and he would do everything, as he'd always done, to protect it for just one day more.

He heard them calling out corners and blind spots over the L-comm, itching to engage, and frightened to get to him.

The Legion was coming for Tyrus Rechs.

25

"C'mon, keep up!" Keel called over his shoulder. He sprinted down a narrow alley outside the government parkscape sector, with only Ravi and the wobanki matching his pace. When he reached the intersection of alley and street, he motioned with his blaster for the catman to take cover behind a toppled dumpster.

Keel peered around the corner into the street, then ducked back. "Four legionnaires," he informed Ravi. "Just standing around. Probably stationed to close off the street."

The hologram twisted his mustache and looked back at the others, who were struggling to catch up. "Captain, you must slow your pace. The others cannot be keeping up. The princess is committed to the girl—who is just a girl— and Garret is hardly an example of athletic conditioning."

Left unsaid was the pondering pace of a war bot. They were built to kill, not for speed.

"Yeah, well, if they don't get going, I'm going to leave 'em."

Ravi frowned. "The girl lost her parents. You are not suggesting abandoning her?"

Keel stole another look at the legionnaires, then leaned against the wall and checked his blaster's charge pack. "Galaxy is full of orphans, Ravi. They're not all my problem."

"Yes, but the money promised by Tyrus Rechs requires that she become your problem."

Keel rolled his eyes. "Hey, Skrizz. You have any idea your fossil of a partner was rich?"

The catman gave a negative hiss.

"But you think he's good for it, right?"

The wobanki mewed uncertainly, then growled in quick, hushed tones.

"Not my fault you didn't negotiate before joining up." Keel turned back to Ravi. "All right, I'll move more slowly. Too many credits to leave on the table. I got an idea."

Leenah arrived, holding Prisma by the hand, both of them out of breath.

"I want to be with Crash!" Prisma whined. The girl had clearly taken a liking to the pink-skinned princess, but that didn't stop her from constantly looking over her shoulder at the war bot.

"Too bad," Keel said bluntly. "That bot is a magnet for blaster fire. You move through the streets with it, and you'll join the rest of your family."

"I don't care. We're in this together," Prisma said, sticking her chin out defiantly.

"And I *do* care," Keel said, bending down to look Prisma in the eye. "I'm making a lot of money to keep you alive. You can be stupid and die on your own time. Besides, I need the bot for..." He stood up. "Why am I arguing with a kid?"

Leenah placed a protective hand on Prisma's shoulder. "We're moving too fast for Prisma."

"Yeah," Garret agreed, joining them. He was practically gasping for air. "For me too." The war bot arrived right behind him.

The coder really is out of shape if he can barely outrun a war bot, Keel thought.

"I've got a solution," he said. He put on his helmet, becoming Wraith again. "Everyone, hide your weapons and hold out your hands like this." He held out his arms in front of himself as if they were manacled. "Except you, uh, Crash."

The entourage followed his command. They tucked weapons inside jackets and waistbands and pantomimed being captured.

Keel motioned for his navigator. "Ravi, use your TT-3 bots to project ener-chains over everyone's wrists."

In moments, holographic restraining cuffs were superimposed over the wrists of Prisma, Garret, Skrizz, and Leenah.

"I am believing I know what you intend," Ravi said, taking on the appearance of a prisoner and causing ener-chains to appear around his own wrists.

"Good," Keel said. "Follow me. Crash, you bring up the rear. Keep your blaster pointed at the wobanki, but *don't* shoot him. Unless I say."

Skrizz growled a warning.

"Relax," Keel said. "It's a joke."

Keel strode into the street, moving in the practiced, disciplined steps of a legionnaire. His train of prisoners followed, their heads down, with Crash clomping along in the rear.

Keel held up a hand. "You four!"

The legionnaires turned, startled.

"Who're you?" asked a leej with sergeant chevrons.

Keel used his helmet to link into the L-comm system for direct communication with the legionnaires. "What does it look like, Leej? I'm dark ops."

"We weren't briefed that dark ops would be planet-side," another leej answered.

"Well, that's the trick," said Keel.

"We need some sort of code clea—"

Keel sent a burst transmission over IR wave directly to each legionnaire's helmet. It displayed on their HUDs as an all-black clearance level, along with a rank and a call sign: Wraith.

The legionnaires instantly stood straight as lasers. "Sorry, sir."

"So here's the situation," Keel said, ignoring the apology. "My team is engaging with Brotherhood mercenaries, but their leader, Tyrus Rechs, is giving them hell. This is Rechs's crew. I'm under real-time orders directly from the Senate council to get them off planet and back to the capital. You four are my new escort."

"Even the kid?" asked the sergeant.

"Whatta you care, Leej?" Keel shot back. "She yours?"

"We have orders from the sector colonel to keep this street clear."

Keel shook his head. "Consider them countermanded. And you're welcome for that. Points are out there making such a mess of things, they'll probably forget you're here and call in a buzz ship strike on your position."

One of the legionnaires stepped forward. "I happen to be appointed as a second lieutenant by the House of Reason and—"

"Then your men know exactly what I'm talking about," Keel interrupted. "Let's move."

He walked on, sure that each legionnaire would fall in line without further complaint. They did, flanking the prisoners, two legionnaires on either side.

The "prisoners" played their parts perfectly, watching their shoes without speaking.

"Uh, sir?" asked one of the legionnaires over the L-comm.

"What is it, Leej?" Keel was brusque, but not so much as to make the soldier feel small for talking.

"Is that a... war bot behind us?"

Keel made a show of turning around, as if to see exactly which war bot the legionnaire was speaking about. "Oh, yeah. It won't bother you if you don't bother it."

They had traveled to within a click of the docking bays when the call came over the L-comm. "Spiral Company, this is Major Bex. Our L-comm system has been compromised by an unknown source. The *Intrepid* will be re-linking your comms in thirty. However, I need to warn you all that a Savage Wars-era war bot has been positively identified with our primary target. Be warned. Be advised. Spiral-1 out. KTF."

The legionnaires stopped in their tracks, and the prisoners stopped with them.

Keel turned slowly to face his hijacked escort. "Probably another bot," he said. "This one is part of my team. Right, war bot?"

"I serve the Republic," Crash thundered in its terrible voice.

"See?" Keel said. He hoped that would be enough to do the trick.

The legionnaires stood in silence for several moments. Then in unison they brought their N-6 blaster rifles to bear on Keel.

"Why didn't you answer us over the L-comm?" asked one of the legionnaires over his external helmet speaker. "It just switched, and you're not answering our hails."

"Well, boys," Keel said, subtly digging his heels in. "I didn't come in on the *Intrepid*, did I?"

"Dark ops or not," said the point lieutenant, moving toward Keel, "we have to check this out and detain you until Rep-Int clears you."

"I understand completely," Keel said. He thumbed the switch on his bullpup for maximum discharge. The way the leejes were standing, he might get another two-for-one.

"Fourteen percent," Ravi said, drawing a look from the legionnaire closest to him.

Fourteen percent? There was no way these legionnaires, unknowingly surrounded by a hostile crew and a war bot, would stand that good of a chance. Unless...

Keel turned around slowly. A platoon of Republic Army basics, accompanied by a pair of combat sleds, was moving down the street toward him.

Ravi's odds made a bit more sense now.

"Yes, I do understand," Keel said, relaxing his posture. "But I can't allow any diversions with regard to these prisoners. I'll go with you, and the bot can come, too. But can a couple of you at least take this bunch to the docking bay? I've got a jump shuttle on standby."

The legionnaires must've been discussing over their private comm, because Keel heard no immediate answer.

"Prisoners," Keel barked. "Move to the opposite side of the street." He pointed to the side of the block closest to the spaceport docking bays.

Leenah hurried Prisma to the side, and Skrizz and Garret did likewise.

"Hey!" the legionnaire point protested.

Ravi stood motionless in the street. Keel nodded at him. Ravi nodded back.

"Oh, no!" Keel shouted in mock surprise. "That one has a sword!"

From out of the folds of the universe, a great, gleaming khanda sword appeared in Ravi's hand. The navigator held it over his head and lunged toward the legionnaires as Keel bolted to join the rest of his crew.

At first, it was as though the threat failed to register in the legionnaires' minds. They just stood dumbly as Ravi whirled toward them. The hologram brought his sword down on the legionnaire closest to him, slicing through the man's reflective armor as if it were made of vapor paper.

The legionnaire screamed and fell at Ravi's feet.

This awoke the other leejes. They fired in unison at Ravi, but their blaster bolts passed harmlessly through him. One of the blasts struck a fellow leej square in the chest and sent him to the ground.

The hologram-projecting TT-3 bots flamed out and fell to the ground like swarthflies crisped by a 'sect zapper as blaster bolts cooked them in passing.

Keel waved for his crew to duck into another alley. "Let's go! Straight for the ships! Don't stop running! Carry the kid if you have to!"

"Wait!" Garret protested. "The TT-3s! He's still fighting—something's—how?"

"Ponder the deep questions another time," Keel screamed, pushing the coder square in the shoulders to get him moving.

Ravi whirled his sword over his head and disarmed his foes with a single great arc. Blaster rifles clattered to the ground, and the two surviving legionnaires held their hands in shock.

"You should run," Ravi advised. "Your lives are more precious than your training would suggest."

The platoon began to move down the street rapidly, but didn't fire—probably for fear of hitting the two surviving leejes.

Two blaster bolts flashed from Keel's side of the street, each one taking down a legionnaire.

Ravi turned to his captain. He looked as if he wished to protest Keel's shooting of the legionnaires, but knew Keel wouldn't hear it.

"Crash!" Keel shouted at the war bot. "Buy us some time against those basics!"

"Acknowledged," the bot bellowed in a voice so low and awful that it seemed to make the ground shake.

The bot raised its arm and sent a thick shower of blaster fire into the ranks. Basics fell backward and forward under the deluge, some returning ineffective fire, others scrambling for the relative cover of porch stoops and alleyways.

Dat-dat-dat! The combat sled opened up with its heavy twin blaster cannons. The shots ripped up the cobblestone streets and flew through Ravi. One hit the bot in its armored breastplate, causing it to take a stumbling step backward to keep from falling.

A high-yield, small-package missile emerged from a compartment on Crash's shoulder. The missile launched with a *whoosh* and a trail of gray smoke. It sped toward the combat sled and impacted just beneath the front repulsor. The explosion sent the sled flipping into the air and sent pieces of soldiers flying in all directions.

"Ordnances expended," the war bot announced. These machines packed a hell of a punch, but one punch was all they had until a supply team could re-arm them for further combat. "Awaiting orders."

"Run!" Keel yelled.

The captain quickly caught up with his crew. Skrizz was kneeling behind a dumpster chute, laying down covering fire for Keel. Keel took cover, then shot at the pursuing soldiers so Skrizz could move forward to the docking bay. "Get to your ship!" Keel shouted.

But the catman stayed put. He blathered in his yowling tongue and held up a remote call cylinder.

"Surefire way to get your ship shot down," Keel said. "I don't care how sophisticated your AI."

Ravi was walking calmly toward Keel, which was good. The basics continued to fire at the hologram, no doubt wondering why they never seemed to get a clean hit. It kept those blaster bolts from sizzling around Keel's head, which was just fine with Aeson Keel.

The bot lumbered forward to join the captain and the wobanki, sounding like it cracked the streets with each heavy footfall. Still programmed to participate in the fire-move-fire retreat, it merely stopped and announced, "Ordnances expended."

"Yeah, I know." A blaster bolt hit the wall just above Keel's head, sending masonry debris and sparks showering down. "Stay here and do what you can to get Skrizz on his ship."

Keel turned to the wobanki. "She coming in to land in the intersection behind us?"

Skrizz growled an affirmative.

Keel nodded. "Okay. We'll link up in orbit and share jump coordinates."

The wobanki growled a question at Keel.

"No," Keel said, rising to his feet. "She comes with me. A little insurance to make sure Rechs pays his debts. I'd take you, but the old fossil seemed more interested in her well-being than yours, no offense."

Skrizz yelped that none was taken, and continued firing as Keel sprinted the remaining distance to the *Indelible VI*.

26

Keel ducked his head as the ramp of the *Six* closed behind him. He tossed his helmet onto the deck and moved toward the cockpit.

"Everyone strap in, this is gonna be tricky!" he shouted—then stopped short when he saw that all of them were already secured in their jump seats, even the little girl. "Oh, good."

"Where's Crash?" Prisma demanded. Her tone was impetuous, though her voice was tiny. Like a rich girl demanding an answer from her servants.

"He's helping your cat get on board the old man's ship," Keel said, shedding layers of armor as the *Six*'s pre-flights ran in the background. Ravi, he knew, would have jumped his intelligence onto the ship, likely leaving behind whatever TT-3 bots remained.

"What?" Prisma exclaimed.

"Hey, it's okay," Leenah said soothingly. "We're not going to hurt you. You're safer this way."

"No!" Prisma protested, struggling against the restraints. "I should be in the *Crow* with Crash and Skrizz and Rechs! I'm being kidnapped!"

Keel bent over and stuck a finger in Prisma's face. "No! Kidnappers *want* to take their victims. *I* can't wait to give you *back*!"

Prisma attempted to bite Keel's finger, but the captain's reflexes were too quick.

"You shouldn't bite," Leenah scolded her.

Garret waved his hands to get Keel's attention. "Captain Keel, I saw Ravi perform without his TT-3 bots, and he appeared on the ship without them a few moments after we boarded. How—"

Keel waved him off. "You probably did a better job with the bots than you realized, and he was able to lose a few. He can jump from the bots to the ship in an emergency—don't ask me how. So you'll have to build some new ones."

"I'm not sure there's time—"

"I'm out of chit-chat time myself," Keel said. He left for the cockpit in a rush.

Ravi was already in the cockpit, as expected. Keel dropped into the captain's seat as Ravi guided the *Six* up out of its docking bay and into the sky.

A pancake-shaped light freighter moved in a straight line past them. It was old and beat-up, with a center-placed pilot's cupola latticed in metal. Its engines howled as it lowered into the intersection near Skrizz and Crash. The remains of the basic platoon were advancing on their position.

"Let's give them a little covering fire and get into orbit," Keel said.

Climbing and then nosing the flight controls over and down, Keel moved the *Six* in position for a strafing run across the city. The belly guns sent bright blaster fire down the middle of the Repub-Army-crawling street like a runaway freight rig. Basics scattered to get away as the *Six* tore the sky apart with its howling engines.

"Okay," Keel said calmly. "Let's exit atmosphere."

A beep sounded, accompanied by a flashing red light.

"Sensors read pursuit by a Republic buzz ship," Ravi said, his hands moving across the controls. "Engage?"

Keel throttled forward. "Let's outrun. But not too fast. Don't want them to lose interest and stick around for the wobanki."

"You like this man-cat?" Ravi asked, one eyebrow arched.

"He's got a certain reverse charisma," Keel admitted. "Showing up to deals with a little crazy at your side never hurts."

The *Indelible VI* roared through the cityscape, flying just above the roofline of lesser structures and through the enigmatic Repub skyscrapers erected in the name of pride and progress. The buzz ship struggled to keep up, remaining just out of its effective range of fire.

"I am reading that the wobanki's craft has lifted off," Ravi announced. He looked at Keel. "But the ship is not making its way to orbit."

"Probably picking up the old man," Keel mumbled. "That's their prerogative. Let's get into deep space before the destroyers start showing up."

With a blue flash, a chime sounded.

Ravi moved to answer the comm transmission. "I am wondering who this might be?"

Before the navigator was able to bring the call online, Rechs's voice sounded over the cockpit speakers.

"Wraith. Follow the fast-attack cutter entering orbit north-northwest of your position. Don't lose track of it under any circumstances. Goth Sullus is on board, and he needs to be taken down. I'm serious, kid, if I don't make it out, the galaxy is about to go from bad to worse real quick."

Keel rubbed his chin. "You know, I usually get half up front for this sort of work..."

"Check your account, kid. I pay on the handshake."

Keel rolled his eyes and looked to Ravi as if to say, "Yeah, right."

The navigator pulled up their off-moon account and let out a whistle. "I do not know how he so quickly determined your identity and the location of your account, but..." Ravi superimposed the account status in front of Keel as a target-alert warning howled and chimed urgently.

The captain's jaw dropped. He swallowed several times. "We're rich, Ravi. *Rich* rich. Buy-a-planet-and-retire rich."

"Don't wet yourself over all those new zeros in your bank account," Rechs said. "It all ends up being meaningless in the end. Trust me."

"Oh, sure," Keel replied. He rolled his eyes at Ravi. He didn't believe the old bounty hunter's wisdom for a second. He muted the comm. "All right, Ravi, let's hunt down the"—he read the ship's readout on his monitor—"*Siren of Titan*. You'd better punch it if we're going to catch up with that ship before it makes the jump."

Ravi piloted the *Six* through the mesosphere. When they came within hailing range of the *Siren*, Keel didn't move for the comm. "Let's see if we can get close enough to attach our homing beacon to the hull without drawing any attention to ourselves."

Ravi nodded. "We are just a harmless freighter looking to get away from whatever new mess the Republic brought to this planet."

"Exactly."

A streak of green blaster cannon bolts raced toward the *Six*, impacting in brilliant flashes of light as the ship's shields absorbed the blasts.

"Not even a warning shot? Well, that's just rude." Keel banked hard to avoid further hits. He throttled to near top speed, only holding back what was necessary to get the beacon shot off.

The *Siren*'s turret-fire streaked behind *Indelible*; its targeting was unable to effectively lead Keel's speeding ship.

"Detecting a core flush," Ravi said, urgency in his voice. "They are preparing to jump."

"Just a little closer..."

Keel barrel rolled the *Six* and fired the beacon on a best-guess trajectory. "There!"

Ravi's fingers danced across the terminal. "Locked to hull. Reading is strong."

The incoming fire ceased as the *Siren* disappeared into the folds of hyperspace, leaving the *Indelible VI* alone. Keel was surprised that no Republic ships had scrambled to intercept. Perhaps the Brotherhood had taken out their star ports?

"I am calculating likely trajectories." Ravi pulled on his beard, pondering the data in front of him. "Wait...

Something is wrong. I've lost the signal. Captain Keel, I do not have enough data to draw a reasonable conclusion!"

Keel hissed in frustration. "Must've ionized their hull at the jump. Good way to take care of any homing beacons. Well, plan B. What's the most likely planet from what you've got, Ravi?"

The navigator shook his head. "There are three hundred and seventy-two potential destination planets all within acceptable margin of error."

Keel threw up his hands in exasperation. "Great. Just great." He rested his chin on his fist and thought. A memory came immediately to mind. Mother Ree. "Tusca. Ravi, set a course for Tusca."

"I am not showing that as one of the potential destinations."

"It has to be. Back at the monastery... That old woman might be a lot of things, but she wasn't wrong about much."

"Yes, Captain. Course plotted for Tusca."

Keel reached out and launched the ship into hyperspace. "We'll want to jump short and make sure they don't see us arrive."

Ravi nodded.

Keel leaned back in his chair as rippling waves of folded space rushed past the cockpit window in ethereal shades of blue. "Ravi," he said, tapping his chin with the steeple of his fingers, "did you salvage enough TT-3 bots to go off ship again? I could use your backup."

"I am afraid not," the navigator said. "We are back to the first square."

With precision that no nav-bot could match, Ravi dropped the *Six* out of hyperspace. Another couple of seconds and they would auto-stop before striking the planet. Now they had two hours to prepare during the subspace flight toward Tusca.

When the comm relay caught up with the craft, Keel scrolled through text messages and pulled up one from the wobanki. "They found our beacon. Should be about an hour behind us, unless they jump straight to the planet."

"They are not so stupid," Ravi said.

"No, they're not."

The comm chimed, and Keel frowned. "Lao Pak."

"May as well get it over with."

Keel brought up the pirate king on screen. Lao Pak immediately launched into an opening salvo of profanity. Keel listened silently, doing everything he could not to further aggravate the foul-mouthed pirate. Keel already had his money—now he just had to see about keeping the coder and maybe getting a little bit more.

Lao Pak finally seemed to notice that the conversation was one-sided. "You gonna say something back, or you too scared of me, 'old friend'?"

"Look, Lao Pak," Keel said, holding his hands out plaintively. "I'm sorry."

"I knew you say that!" Lao Pak exploded. "I knew you say—wait, what you say?"

"I said I'm sorry." Keel gave his best impression of an orphaned terro pup. "I promised a good friend that I wouldn't steal his coder, and then I broke my promise. I'm sorry."

"And you not answer my calls!"

"That, too." Keel said. He held up a finger. "But I *did* listen to them. Wraith told the admiral that Prisma would be on Andalore."

"Yeah," Lao Pak said, making it clear that this was, to him, old news. "Admiral Devers there right now."

"That's the thing," Keel said, his voice still hinting at repentance. "Maydoon *was* there. Now she's on Tusca."

"Tusca!" Lao Pak let out a new stream of vile oaths. "Why she on Tusca? That place nowhere."

"I don't know." Keel added sarcastically, "Maybe Andalore didn't have nice enough hotels."

"Why you say 'she'?" asked Lao Pak. "Maydoon a man."

"The man's dead. I tracked down his daughter, but trust me, this is who the admiral is looking for."

Lao Pak considered this. "She pretty?"

"She's a little girl," Keel growled.

"She a pretty little girl? Gomarii will take her, you know? Pay extra. More money to split."

"You'll have to come get her yourself," Keel said.

"Okay, focus on main thing. I call admiral, tell him go to Tusca."

Keel gave an exaggerated nod, as if to a king. "That's all I'm asking. Plus one other thing."

"What thing? You no try double cross? Again!"

"No!" Keel protested. "We're pals, remember?"

"Sure. I *remind* myself to remember."

"I need you to tell the admiral that Wraith won't be there to collect. Make it very clear that Wraith *won't* be in the system. Tell him that Wraith took a job on the other side of the galaxy. Have him send the money directly to you."

Lao Pak eyed Keel suspiciously through the holo screen. "Why you trust *me* with money? I could disappear. *I* not trust me with this much money."

"Well, *I* trust you, old friend. Besides, we both know Wraith would track you down and kill you if you crossed him. Just get it done, and the split can be sixty-two thirty-eight."

"I get big part, right?"

"Yeah."

"Okay." Lao Pak licked his lips. "You make bad deal. This easy work for ten million credits."

Keel gave a half smile. "You always were good at math. That's why I'm keeping your coder as part of the deal."

Lao Pak opened his mouth to protest.

"Or the deal's off," Keel threatened.

The pirate king narrowed his eyes. "Fine. He not worth that much money. You stupid, Keel. Not like Ravi. He smart. But you, you stupid. You die one day of being stupid. Then I laugh, 'ha ha.'"

"Pleasure doing business with you, Lao Pak." Keel switched off the transmission.

"I am not seeing your plan in this," Ravi said with a shake of his head. "We are filthy rich, yes, but you should not throw away so much money for no discernable reason.

There are a number of charitable organizations that deserve these credits more than Lao Pak."

Keel shrugged. "Admiral Devers needs to think Wraith is far away."

"Why is this?"

"So I can kill him."

27

Keel landed the *Indelible VI* just behind a natural bluff that overlooked Tusca's main spaceport. He'd flown in low and quiet, taking advantage of the last fleeting hours of Tuscan darkness.

The ship's jammers and stealth plating didn't hurt, either.

Garret followed Keel out into the waning night and to a high point. Keel carried with him a long, black case with the word "Twenties" painted on the surface.

"I thought," gasped Garret, panting, "we were going to fly atmospheric to the port and look around."

"We are," Keel said. "After this."

He knelt down and opened the case, revealing an N-18 long rifle that looked as though it had seen more than a few battlefields. Keel began assembling the weapon, screwing on the barrel and attaching the interlocking stock and grip.

"What's that for?" Garret asked, looking over Keel's shoulder.

Keel looked up at the coder with a coldness in his eyes. "Killing. Always make 'em pay."

"Oh."

The rest of the sniper rifle was assembled in relative quiet. Even Garret's heavy breathing had died down by the time Keel finished.

Lying on his stomach, Keel peered through the augmented scope and zeroed in a grand fountain at the center of the spaceport. "All about impressions, right, Devers?"

"Huh?" Garret asked.

Keel got to his feet, satisfied. "You finish up with those TT-3 bots?"

"I'll have one of them done by the time we're refueling in the star port. I just need to raid the mech-shop for a few parts. Ravi won't be able to leave the ship until then."

Keel nodded and headed back to the *Six*.

The scene on Tusca was nothing like Andalore. It was quiet here—ordinary. Apparently Sullus and his crew intended to keep a low profile. Perhaps the spaceport served as their base of operations?

True to his word, Garret had gotten a single TT-3 bot operating well enough for Ravi to join Keel off-ship. Even better, the kid had agreed to fly with Keel and Ravi for a while once the current job had ended. In fact, he'd jumped at the chance. Of course, that was *after* he'd heard just how much money Keel now owned. No sense leaving the company of the wealthy when you're looking to get rich.

Keel leaned against a wall, soaking in the sunlight. Ravi stood at his side, crossing his arms and watching as the spaceport's streets slowly filled.

They waited.

Five minutes later, Leenah appeared, holding Prisma by the hand. As they passed by Keel, the princess gave no indication she even knew who he was. Prisma, on the other hand, tried to kick Keel in the shins.

"You should put your kid on a leash, lady," Keel called out to Leenah as she walked toward a breakfast café.

Leenah didn't look back, but did make an ancient hand gesture telling Keel what she thought of his advice.

Keel laughed at the insult.

"You almost sound happy," Ravi observed.

"Lots to be happy about, Ravi." Keel used his foot to push himself off the wall and into the street. "C'mon, let's take a look at things before Rechs shows up."

"Or the Republic," Ravi added.

"*Especially* them."

Ravi strode at Keel's side. After a moment, he said, "I am being very much convinced that it is unwise for you to carry out your plan."

Keel stopped in the middle of the street, forcing pedestrians to pass him on either side, like an airstream moving around the hull of a ship. "I have very few regrets in life, Ravi, but letting that..."

He realized his temper was rising, and people were starting to stare. He calmed himself and lowered his voice. "That miserable excuse for an officer needs to die."

"Then why haven't you killed him before?" Ravi asked.

Keel continued down the street. "Just drop it."

"I apologize," Ravi said, jogging to catch up.

"It's fine," Keel said, swatting away the apology with a wave of his hand. "You still have the docking bay number Garret gave you?"

"Yes. The *Siren of Titan* is making use of docking bays thirty through forty."

Keel shook his head. "For the life of me I don't know why anyone would fly something that requires more than one bay."

"Presumably this is in order to fit all the many mercenaries accompanying Goth Sullus."

"Yeah, I know, Ravi." Keel smiled. "That's why we're rich now, though. *We* can get the job done on our own."

They arrived at docking bay forty. A few Brotherhood mercs loitered about the entrance, apparently just passing the time.

"Wonder what they're waiting for?" Keel said. "Let's walk the length of the street and see what we see."

He mixed in among the spacers and crew moving eagerly from dock to cantina. He was careful to dodge the wrecks who stumbled back drunkenly to their ships, all of them reveling in a promise kept—a promise to not quit drinking until day broke.

He caught glimpses of the *Siren* as he walked past each open bay hangar. The ship was surrounded by dockhands of various species, all of them working under the watchful eyes of some Brotherhood men. Nothing out of the ordinary. In fact, if Keel hadn't witnessed the chaos at Andalore, nothing here would have suggested to him that he was looking at anything other than a traveling guild, landing for repair and resupply.

And then he saw the legionnaires. Not the standard-issue, watered-down Legion of today. No. They didn't wear the Republic's "inspired" reflective armor. These men's armor looked like Keel's—only darker and without the modifications. It was a polished black, with red running from each shoulder epaulet down the arm in a bold stripe.

"Ravi," Keel said, nodding toward the leejes. "What do you make of that?"

"Dark ops?" Ravi suggested.

"No, I don't think so. The red wouldn't fly. Too visible. This is something else."

"Something else like what?"

"I'm not sure. When I shook down that Kimer fellow back at Corsica, he mentioned legionnaires that looked just like this. I figured he was just confusing some mercs with painted knock-off armor. These are definitely with Sullus."

Ravi stroked his beard. "And are they legionnaires indeed?"

Keel didn't have an answer. And even if he did, the opportunity to give it was taken away by a call over his comm.

"Wraith, this is Rechs," the comm barked.

"Go for Wraith," Keel said.

"Where's the girl?"

"She's fine," Keel said, making himself sound wounded at the insinuation that she would be anything but.

"She'd better be," came the menacing reply.

"Yeah," Keel said, every bit as annoyed with this conversation as he was curious about the odd legionnaires in the docking bay. "Because I agreed to take an obscene amount of money off your hands just as an excuse to do the one thing that would make me lose it."

"Lotta sickos in the galaxy, kid."

Keel muted his mic. "I know, I'm talking to one."

Ravi hooted at this.

"What do you have on the *Siren* and Sullus for me?"

Keel flicked the mic back on. "I'm watching the *Siren* now. No sign of Sullus though."

"Why not?"

Keel rolled his eyes. "I don't know. Maybe his quarters have a vibrating bed. I've been here since before the sun came up, and nothing has left the docking bay."

"Did you do a cross-sectional particle scan? Check against the *Siren*'s radiation signature?"

"Of course," Keel said impatiently. He muted the comm again. "Did we, Ravi?"

The hologram nodded.

"Good," said Rechs. "So where's the *Siren*?"

"Docking bays thirty through forty. I'm looking at it right now. Sullus seems to have recruited his own legionnaires, too. Black armor. They're all lined up in parade rest inside, by the ship."

"That's lucky." Rechs's voice was almost drowned out by the roar of the *Crow* as it came in low and fast. It hovered just above Sullus's hangar. "And where is the girl, exactly?"

"Having breakfast by docking bay ninety-eight."

"Perfect."

A swirling cannonade of missiles jumped from the *Crow* and erupted on the docking bay's roof. This was followed up by a scorching barrage of blaster cannon fire. Spacers ran in panic. Ships violated every safety protocol in the book, taking off in an attempt to avoid the coming fight.

The *Crow*'s ramp lowered, and Rechs leapt from the ship, firing thrusters to slow his descent. He hit the ground with a thud, his ponderous MK1 armor leaving a dent in the paved street. No sooner had he stood than two Brotherhood mercs came running for him. Rechs put two gaping holes in them with his hand cannon as he turned to Keel. "You shoulda worn your armor."

"I was incognito!" Keel protested.

Blaster fire sizzled past the trio.

"Not anymore. Besides, KTF, Leej. What else did you think I would do?"

The old maniac seemed to be enjoying the chaos. In fact, he seemed lost in it. Aim, shoot, kill. Aim, shoot, kill. It was like he was an unthinking machine.

And above it all the *Obsidian Crow* hovered, pivoting and firing, at mercs and the strange dark-armored legionnaires.

Keel drew his blaster and leveled a pair of dark legionnaires. The holes he left in their armor caught fire. He looked down at his blaster. "Looks like the new armor still can't quite stop you, eh, girl?"

"We go inside the ship," Rechs ordered, running toward the docking bay.

Keel gladly allowed the armored Rechs to draw most of the lead fire and pick off Brotherhood and Legion alike with well-placed shot after shot. Ravi's sword wreaked havoc on any combatant who drew too near. Dying men screamed in bewilderment about the phantom they could not touch, but who could touch them only too well.

"Perhaps *I* should be the Wraith, yes?" Ravi crowed.

Rechs and Keel reached the inside of the hangar just as the scattered mercenaries and soldiers began to regroup. A volley of counter-fire by the legionnaires sent the invaders diving for cover behind a massive recharge cell.

"If these are the real deal," Rechs said as he loaded archaic bullets into his archaic slug thrower, "they're gonna try to get around us on either side. Flank—"

"—and spank," Keel finished. "I'll take the left."

The pair fired at the advancing dark legionnaires, dropping soldiers before those soldiers were close enough to get a clear shot.

"If it were me out there," Rechs observed between reloads, "I'd have tossed a fragger."

"They are probably afraid of the damaging our 'cover,'" Ravi suggested. "Were they to damage this recharge cell we are hiding behind, it would cause a feedback detonation large enough to level the entire docking bay."

"Right, but I have *good* armor, see?" Rechs said. "So I'd toss the fragger anyway."

"Good for you. What I have right now is thin and prone to paper cuts," Keel shouted, sending a blaster bolt into the forehead of an advancing Brotherhood merc, dropping him in a heap. "So if you've got any grenades, send them *that* way."

"I'm saving those," Rechs said. "But our equalizer just showed up."

The massive frame of the war bot darkened the docking bay's door. A medium-range frag-launcher popped from its chest and sent a series of explosives into the legionnaire lines.

"Oh dear," the war bot whined in its servile house-bot voice. "This all feels... so unnatural."

Skrizz loped into the hangar, viciously blasting anyone who attempted to crawl to safety after the blast. Every bit the evolved predator.

Rechs holstered his slug thrower and stood. "Your coder did a superb job taking control of the war bot. Took me a while to undo it," he said to Keel. "I consider myself more of a tinkerer than anything else. But with time, you become a master of lots."

Keel followed Rechs toward the carnage. All the firing had stopped. The Brotherhood sentries and legionnaire guard had been made entirely inoperative. "So what now? Board the ship? You'll notice that reinforcements didn't come running down the ramps once the fighting started."

"Which probably means that Sullus is locked up," Rechs called over his shoulder. "That, or you lost him."

Skrizz growled and waved Rechs over. The wobanki stood on top of a battered Brotherhood merc.

"Survivor, huh?" Rechs asked.

The wounded mercenary was struggling for breath. Skrizz seemed to revel in grinding its paw into the wounded man's chest.

"Let him up," Rechs ordered.

The wobanki obeyed, and the merc gasped for breath.

"Goth Sullus," Rechs said, his voice spectral through his helmet speakers. "Where?"

The mercenary wheezed a profanity in a language Keel couldn't identify.

Rechs nodded. "You're not wrong." He bent down, grabbed the merc by the throat, and lifted the wounded being until its feet dangled helplessly off the ground. "Sullus," he commanded a second time. He squeezed, and alien cries of pain issued from the merc.

"*Korba che Sullus*," the merc rasped. "*Suma lerich che.*"

Rechs dropped the merc at his feet. "That wasn't so hard, now was it?"

Before the merc could answer, Rechs fired a bullet from his slug thrower into the merc's head.

He turned to Keel. "Looks like Sullus left 'with the others' before the sun came up. You sure you were watching for him?"

"Yeah," Keel said. "Must've been before we landed."

"Would you like for me to clean up this mess?" the war bot queried.

"Leave it." Rechs moved outside into the warm morning sun. And froze. The ground rumbled. Then rumbled again. And again. And again.

Keel followed the old bounty hunter's gaze and heard himself gulp. Down the street, a four-story-tall HK-PP mech, bristling with heavy cannons above its squat torso and oversized legs, loomed above a veritable army of black legionnaires.

"We will enjoy a fifty-six percent greater chance of survival if we fall back to the *Indelible VI*," Ravi.

"Yeah," Keel said, taking a few steps backward. "Let's do that."

Rechs made no argument. A Hunter-Killer Planet Pounder would make Swiss cheese of even his MK1 armor. Soon the whole entourage was running headlong toward the ships while blaster fire ate up the ground at their heels.

28

The dark legionnaires were practically on top of them.

Rechs pushed through the terrified crowd stampeding around him. He'd lost sight of Skrizz and Keel, but those two could take care of themselves. And the bot... no one would bother the bot.

Rechs dashed down a side alley, dropped a proximity mine, and sprinted away. He heard its telltale whine just before it exploded. He didn't pause to assess the damage. He quickly made his way back to the high canyon walls of the docking bays and the warrens of maintenance corridors that ran like arteries for vagabond ships.

Above the street, the massive mech seemed to be firing at random targets. Its huge cylindrical blasters moaned and whined, and large sections of the star port went up in sudden debris clouds.

He needed to get Prisma out of here. Needed to be sure she was alive and that she could reach safety. And he needed to kill Goth Sullus. For her, and for the Republic.

More of the dark legionnaires poured into the crowd. No sign of Sullus. But the sound of an Intec heavy blaster alerted Rechs that Keel was nearby. He saw five leejes fall in rapid succession. The kid *was* good, no doubt about it. And as long as he saved the girl, he could call himself the greatest. Rechs wouldn't argue. All that didn't mean anything in the final balance.

Keel was swapping out a charge pack while his holographic navigator did some technological wizardry with a sword, somehow slicing through armor that was meant to be impervious to melee weapons. Something about the way the Sikh moved reminded Rechs of... of... nothing, probably. What was real, and what was a product of his aging mind and memories that belonged to who-knew-what? It was all jumbled together now, into a life he could no longer piece through. Not with any reliability.

The Sikh was fighting, and fighting well. That was enough. Mercs and a few legionnaires were going down like harvested wheat at summer's end.

Some dim vision tried to force its way into Rechs's mind. Some memory of a day when the wheat had been cut and harvested and there'd been a rocket's red glare.

Aren't you tired of the memories? the voice asked. And the voice was himself. As it had been all along. Drawing him back from a past he didn't want to remember, a past he missed at the same time.

"The past is gone," he swore at himself as he ran.

And the future is right now.

Forward for what remains of the time left.

He spotted Keel sprinting toward his ship's docking bay, blaster fire chasing his every step. Then the kid paused and covered for Rechs as he did the same. They found the agile Skrizz and the behemoth war bot hunkered down behind cargo modules outside the docking bay.

"Where's the girl?" Rechs asked Keel. He looked around almost frantically.

Ravi held up a palm as if to calm the old warrior down. "I am communicating with the *Indelible VI*. She is safely inside."

"Good," Rechs said. "Get her out of here. All of you. Get out now. I'll lead them away from the bay. Get clear and get out of this system now."

Skrizz growled a query.

"Yeah, you too."

Keel pulled out his blaster and fired it into an advancing squad of legionnaires being rallied by an officer. "You can't handle all these on your own."

"Have to, kid. I think there's no coming back from this one." Rechs pulled a fragger from his belt, cooked it, and hurled it at the oncoming troops. "But you work for me now, remember? So get going and don't look back."

Dark legionnaire squads swarmed the maintenance corridor leading to the bay. The blaster fire was instantly overwhelming. Keel hesitated only a moment before running toward the docking bay where the *Six* waited.

Rechs blasted straight into the air. He was careful to conserve jump fuel, but he wanted to get both elevated and visible. He fired down at the swarming legionnaires below, picking off several and causing the rest to scramble. He disappeared onto a high overhanging rooftop before they could return fire.

He looked up. High above, in Tusca's burning blue sky, the dim outline of a fleet of destroyers appeared in orbit.

The admiral had arrived.

Keel ran toward the *Six*. The war bot had already lumbered aboard. "You joining us?" Keel asked the wobanki.

Skrizz held up his remote slave cylinder and shook his head. Already Keel could see the *Crow* moving in a straight line on approach for a quick pick-up.

"Suit yourself."

Blaster fire struck the walls around them. Rechs had distracted most—but not all—of the mercs and legionnaires. The wobanki and Keel returned fire.

Keel was about to offer to stick with Skrizz until the ship landed when the wobanki began to shake and smack the slave cylinder. Rather than landing, the ship turned and moved in the opposite direction. The catman hissed its jabbering expletives.

"Told you," Keel said. "C'mon!"

Skrizz dashed up the ramp of *Indelible* while Keel stopped to send two more blaster bolts into the advancing legionnaires. When the wobanki was safely aboard, the captain disappeared inside his ship as well. The dark leejes were now struggling to set up a medium blaster cannon.

"Go! Go! Go!" Keel screamed as he ran up the corridor. Ravi, already in the cockpit, waited for Keel to strap in.

"Everyone is on board," the hologram announced.

"Punch it!"

The *Six* lifted up on repulsors, rotated, and roared out of the docking bay hangar, its repulsor backwash sending the legionnaires and their partially assembled blaster cannon flying.

The wobanki and Leenah joined Keel and Ravi in the cockpit.

"How nice," Keel said, dodging anti-starcraft fire. "A party in my cockpit."

The wobanki growled in nervous, stuttering tones.

"Not yet," Keel answered, pushing the throttle hard and putting distance between the ship and spaceport. "I need to tie up a few loose ends before we leave Tusca. How's the girl?" he asked Leenah.

"Frightened," the pink Endurian princess replied. "She's with her bot, and that seems to have a calming effect. Garret is showing them some tricks with the machine that Prisma didn't know about."

Keel nodded and gave Ravi control of the craft. "Speed us out on a southerly course, Ravi, then swing back around to the spot. But take your time. Not so fast that they see us come around."

"Garret told me about another trick," Leenah said, grabbing Keel's arm before he could depart. "The one you're looking to pull. You're honestly planning on staying planetside during a Republic invasion by an entire sector fleet?"

"Yeah." Keel looked down at the hand gently gripping his arm. He tugged himself free and strode quickly to his quarters, locking the door behind him and removing any chance for further discussion.

As *Indelible* raced across the planet, Keel slowly put on his—Wraith's—armor. Legs and boots, torso, shoulders and arms. All that was missing was his helmet. He moved to the old chest at the foot of his bed and pushed aside the heavy wool blanket. Two helmets stared up at him. The first, his merc gear: optimized for combat, near indestructible. The second, his old leej bucket: black, unworn for years.

He put the old bucket on his head.

Small cylinders of black smoke rose from the spaceport. The HK-PP was still rampaging through the streets, and legionnaires swarmed toward a central point. From the cockpit, Keel had a pretty good idea who they were swarming.

Shuttles were landing, sent planetside by the Republic fleet in orbit. But the legionnaires and basics that issued forth were not hostile toward Sullus's forces. There seemed to be an eerie, unspoken truce. It didn't smell right, but none of that mattered to Keel. He was out of the *Indelible VI* the moment it landed. He moved with determined speed to the sniper's nest he'd built earlier that morning. The one that overlooked the dead star port.

All that mattered—the *only* thing—was being here now, before the shuttle carrying the admiral landed.

Keel dropped to his stomach, picked up his weapon, and looked through the scope at the scene some five kilometers away. No one was around. Had he miscalculated? Arrived too late?

The crew of the *Indelible VI* crept out from the ship behind him. Keel knew they were there. He could hear their breathing above the silent desert, where only the barest of breezes crossed. It didn't matter now.

This mattered.

"Just a little while longer, boys," Keel whispered to all the ghosts of his past that had followed him in the days since Kublar. "I promised."

As if on cue, the shadowy figure of a commander in high-shine armor strode onto the scene, rallying legionnaires to a focal point in the battle down there. He was accompanied by an honor guard of dark legionnaires with high-speed, low-drag weapons, their armor still gleaming.

Keel ripped his gaze away from the man and looked skyward.

There!

There was the Elixir-class shuttle. The admiral's preferred transport.

Keel watched through the sniper rifle of an old friend, long in the grave. He watched and knew that Admiral Silas Devers, "the Hero of Kublar," was descending in that shuttle.

Part of Keel wanted to squeeze the trigger then and there. To shoot until the landing craft spiraled downward into a fiery crash.

Twenties could have made that shot.

Keel knew what Devers was after. He wanted Sullus. Wanted an alliance. Was willing to pay a quarter billion credits and hand over a sector fleet to get it. The old man was right. This was all bigger than they'd ever imagined. This was the beginning of the end of the Republic. This was regime change, and that scumbag Devers wanted to meet the new boss first. Sullus would be a fool to turn down such an offer from a sector admiral. Instant fleet at his command.

And the moment the agreement was made, Keel would end Devers's life.

The shuttle drifted down. Almost achieving landfall.

Almost…

Keel's vigil was interrupted by the distinct thrum of an overhead troop transport very close at hand. He could feel the dust fly up around him. Could hear Ravi and the others screaming for him to get back to the ship. But he wouldn't take his gaze away from the scope. He couldn't if he tried. It was an addiction now. A drug that had to be fed. A song that had to be finished. Watching the shuttle. Waiting for Devers. Ending Devers…

He would not let them down again.

He would make it all right.

29

Ravi shouted for Keel's attention as Republican legionnaires fast-roped down from their troop transport. "Captain, we must leave now!"

It was no use. Keel was deaf to all entreaties, caught entirely by the lure of his revenge.

Blaster fire sizzled around the ship as the legionnaires closed in. Skrizz and the others were forced to retreat inside the *Six*, but Prisma found herself cut off somehow, lost in the sudden confusion of a chaotic firefight among the main landing gears. A pair of dark legionnaires lunged for her, and she screamed.

"Maydoon! Surrender!" one of the legionnaires shouted over squad audible. His electronically amplified speech made him sound soulless and machine-like.

Crash appeared. He fired two single blasts from his wrist cannon that freed both legionnaires from their appendages. Prisma felt sick at the sight. She looked away, and saw Ravi coming to her, cleaving his way through armored killers.

More legionnaires were swarming around the ship now. One swung around the ramp and fired an EMP shotgun at the bot, shutting down its primary drive systems. They'd come prepared.

Prisma cowered behind Ravi as he flashed his brilliant sword at any legionnaire who dared approach—and many did dare. They fell. Scores of them. Confounded by this ghost among men, the legionnaires fired, aiming high to avoid hitting Prisma.

Even as he fought, Ravi sought to assure Prisma. "There is a four percent chance that we will survive. And even against such odds, there is still room for hope."

Prisma was dazzled by his every stroke. Until the blaster fire thickened. Until he flickered and wavered. Until the TT-3 bot exploded in a shower of sparks and it seemed like Ravi would fade away. And then he *did* fade away, growing thin and stretched like a dusting of snow on too much ground.

The legionnaires closed in around Prisma. This was the end. She was going to die while Sullus and the rest of the galaxy lived on. It wasn't right for Sullus to live and for her daddy to... be dead. That darkness wasn't right.

And then, Ravi came back.

He was so thin that he had all but disappeared, but he came back. Came back and fought the legionnaires, forcing them to fall back.

"I don't want to die," the little girl screamed.

Ravi graced her with a kindly smile. "The body is mere clothing for the soul and is discarded at death. Look at me..."

And then a darkness stirred in the sky—and Ravi again flickered and faded.

And Prisma saw him no more.

The legionnaires swarmed toward her, their blasters raised.

Prisma screamed again.

Buy time for them, Rechs thought as he waded out into the last gunfight of his life.

Goth Sullus was headed for Breakheart Pass out in the Salt Desert, somewhere across the rocky, barren wastelands of Tusca. There, high on a granite ridge, the sleeping ruins of the Ancients had waited long before the first humans had ever jumped out into the Big Dark. Why some old scout or desert rat had decided to call the place Breakheart Pass, no one would probably ever know.

Rechs knew the kid, Wraith, would be doing everything he could to get them out of here now. *That's the best I can do for you, Prisma.*

And then he began to shoot down as many dark legionnaires as he could, falling back a block at a time. Making them pay for each yard. One last battle for the T-Rex of the Legion.

But these guys weren't stupid. They weren't making sudden flanking rushes or firing in the open. They were moving low and slow and calling in for support from the big AK-PP. Hidden behind cover, they'd take shots and cover for another squad to shift forward, forcing Rechs back a block at a time. Snipers were shooting at him from the tops of habs and warehouses, and from well back within dark spaces. Not hanging out of windows where he could shoot them down.

They were pros. They'd been trained just like he and Caspo had trained the first leejes. Back in the early days. Before the Golden Age, as some had once called it.

Whatever this Goth Sullus was up to, he'd hired the best. Or at least the pretty good.

Rechs's next shot struck a Brotherhood gunslinger mixed in with the dark legionnaires. The hulking killer went down onto the sand-swollen street, bleeding out in the dust of this ancient world.

Blaster fire careened and ricocheted all around and off of Rechs. He took a certain satisfaction in each missed shot. *His* legionnaires would've gunned him down for wading out into the open like this.

His armor's integrity was dropping, though.

He saw the *Indelible VI* blasting out of the hangar bay and climbing off above the street battle.

They made it.

Rechs fell back another block. Moving farther and farther from the empty hangar Wraith's trick ship had just left. He hacked the bucket of a dead dark legionnaire and found out exactly where Goth Sullus had gone. A place called Breakheart Pass deep in the Tuscan desert. Ancients' ruins marked the spot.

Now he ran down a cargo-strewn street.

"Lyra," he said into his comm as he ran for his next firing position. "Land at the port. Pick any open dock and stand by."

He continued his slow retreat.

It wasn't long before the Brotherhood and the dark legionnaires had him pinned in a crossfire. There literally was no easy way out of the spot they'd run him to ground in. He passed some kind of reflection pool and backed into the ancient chapel beyond. He pulled his last fragger and tossed it through the open portal at them. Its explosion seemed to check their rush.

His right arm was on fire. A direct hit from a blaster had destroyed the armor there. He quickly ripped off the melting impervisteel turning to slag and tossed it aside. His neoprene suit below was burned through. Burnt flesh greeted him underneath.

The suit told him how bad it was.

It was bad.

Rechs crouched down behind some shipping containers someone had piled in the old chapel. Heavy blaster fire from the rooftops was coming in through the old stained-glass windows, the glass shattering into warm sprays of colorful shards.

There was no way they were letting him leave this building alive. There was no way they were letting him reach the ruins out in the desert, or Goth Sullus.

Why?

Who was Goth Sullus?

And then the ground began to shake. And shake. And shake again. Shards of stained glass began to rain down onto the floor of the old place.

The HK-PP had arrived.

He heard the mechanical whine of massive servos hauling the feet of the Cyclopean mech toward the battle. Through one of the high smashed windows he saw its terrible head across the rooftops. It fired—and tore off the upper reaches of the ancient chapel.

Mercs and leejes rushed the building.

Rechs swept their ranks with his hand cannon on full auto, cutting them down as they came for him.

The entire building was coming apart around him as the HK-PP closed in for the kill. Through the gaping hole in the wall he could see its immense guns and massive legs sweeping toward him.

Rechs killed three more, but it seemed as though twenty dark legionnaires immediately took their place, crawling forward through the disintegrating building. Their fire was concentrated on his position, pinning him down. Waiting for the mech to deal the death blow.

The Mark I wouldn't stand up to that level of firepower.

He crouched down behind cargo containers and cycled through his suit menu, looking for an old trick that hadn't worked in years. *When was the last time you used this one?* The image of Mother Ree when she'd been the girl Mara appeared on the wonky old hard drive of his mind.

Long time indeed.

It hadn't worked since then. He'd tried to have the energy disruptor batteries recalibrated since, but no one had ever been able to fix that fantastic tech from long ago. Still, occasionally—and this was what he was hoping for now— the suit's enigmatic nano-tech would just fix itself when it felt like it.

The blaster fire stopped. They weren't interested in coming in to get him. Once the giant mech was finished, they'd come in and get the body. What remained would do for their purposes.

He found the menu.

Incredibly, the old trick was active. A personal energy field disruption bubble. It used to hold for a full five minutes. Who knew how long it would work now.

Who knew anything?

"Lyra," he said into his comm.

"Here, Captain."

Rechs had never been sentimental. And he wasn't now. "Detonate the Romula nuclear mine."

The killers hovered around what remained of the building, crouching behind cover, screaming at him to come out and die now.

Rechs activated the energy disruption bubble.

"As you wish, Captain. Goodbye."

The ship detonated the weapon, taking the star port and about two miles of everything else with it.

30

"No," Keel said to himself. "Not like that."

He had just watched Devers's shuttle abruptly scream away from the star port—and then Tusca had erupted in a small nuclear explosion.

He had seen it all in slow motion. First, a blink-of-an-eye wave of energy passed through every structure—and then the blast seemed to chase this wave, carrying everything with it out into the lifeless desert. And finally, the cloud began to rise.

It wasn't even a mushroom when Keel turned his head, bereaved and utterly lost.

He became vaguely aware of danger. He looked for his ship, but where it had stood in the distance, he now saw nothing other than a pile of dead legionnaires.

And then a scream filled his ears over the distant din of the coming fallout. The scream of a little girl.

Keel bounded down the hill. Prisma was running for her life, and a squad of legionnaires was giving chase. The few clouds above appeared to join in the race, swept away by the advancing shock wave.

"Set for stun," called out one of the dark legionnaires.

This was a trick. Something to get him to lower his guard. Keel raised his rifle and sent a powerful blast through the soldier. The legionnaire's comrades dove to the ground, and Keel could see their minds processing this new threat.

Keel ran at a pace unknown to most legionnaires. As he rushed right through the startled leejes, he dropped a fragger in their midst. They scrambled to escape the blast. Keel just kept racing toward Prisma.

He scooped the girl up in his arms and ran. Prisma screamed, apparently mistaking Keel for a legionnaire. She smashed her tiny fists against his helmet in a feeble attempt at resistance.

"Knock it off, huh, kid?" he said through his bucket's external speakers.

Prisma wrapped her arms tightly around his neck and began to sob.

The *Indelible VI* appeared from behind a boulder, hovering before them.

The shock wave hit. Dark leejes behind Keel were swept away like toys suffering the tantrum of some massive child beyond understanding.

The *Six* hovered languidly, waiting as long as possible for Keel and the girl. Keel reached up into the gear well and grabbed hold of the landing gear.

The air turned into a sudden scream, and the ship literally rocked over onto its side, its spatial hydraulics unable to fully compensate.

"Ravi!" Keel screamed into his comm. "Get us out of here! I think that crazy old man just nuked himself and everyone else. Don't raise the gear until we get inside the internal maintenance hatch."

Instead of Ravi, the wobanki growled an affirmative.

As Keel felt his feet fall away from the ground, the blast from the nuke tried to suck him out into the maelstrom. He held on tightly to the landing strut with one arm, pushing Prisma, her hair whipping across her face, up closer to the maintenance hatch with the other.

The internal hatch locks popped, and the maintenance door spiraled open. Leenah and Garret helped them inside, and the ship took on altitude.

Keel tossed his bucket to the deck. Leenah's eyes had told him everything he needed to know. Ravi had not jumped back into the ship.

Leenah took care to strap in Prisma. The girl looked with concern at Crash, who lay motionless on the floor.

"We'll get him up good as ever," Garret said.

Leenah strapped herself in next to Prisma and looked up at Keel. "Skrizz is going to take us to hyperspace as soon as we clear Tusca's atmosphere. You'd better just strap in back here."

Keel gave a lopsided grin. "No way I'm letting some *cat* fly the *Six*." He disappeared into the cockpit.

Rechs ran through the apocalyptic maelstrom of irradiated dust and dirt that was rapidly turning into a mushroom cloud above him. Even with the disruption bubble active, the suit was struggling to maintain its heat sink. He ran hard, knowing the shield wouldn't hold for much longer.

It didn't. He was mostly out of the crater when it collapsed, but still within the whirling cyclone of irradiated debris and dust. Temps were approaching two thousand degrees. He fired his jump jets and roared off through the storm, navigating only by temperature, his arm on fire, the flesh melting as though the hottest white poker of all time and ten of its buddies were beating on that exposed piece of flesh.

He emerged from under the stalk of the mushroom cloud. It towered high above him, already rising above ten thousand feet. The jump jets gave out, and he smacked hard into the burning, blackened landscape, rolling several times through ash and fire.

Unconsciousness reached for him like the mouth of some hungry being from the outer dark, threatening to swallow him whole.

"No," he grunted. To pass out now was to die of heat and radiation poisoning.

He'd had the *Crow* for a long time.

He struggled to his knees. As the cloud climbed higher and higher, he fumbled with a skin pack. He slapped it over the exposed area—little good it would do—and felt the tranqs shut down all the pain centers. It would try to save the flesh and fight infection, but the arm was gone. Rechs knew that. It hung limply at his side, useless.

All around him, the scrub and low twisted trees of Tusca had been blown to the ground in one direction. And everything was on fire.

Rechs stood. He halfheartedly saluted what remained of the *Obsidian Crow*—irradiated particulate matter rising higher and higher into the atmosphere. In time it would settle and drift across this dead world.

And over your body, he thought.

His armor easily handled the radiation. It was space-rated, so rads were nothing for it. In fact, ambient radiation was converted to energy via the energy recharge cells.

Rechs brought up a map and found a weigh station to the east. He set the course on his HUD and began to trudge toward it.

The twin suns beat down on Rechs's armor. He turned at the top of an iron-gray ridge and looked back at the remains of the star port. Wildfires were sweeping up and away, driving a thousand black, smoky torpedoes and the remains of the mushroom cloud out over the desert.

He faced forward once more. The weigh station he'd been heading for was visible far below.

He would find transport there.

And then he would find Goth Sullus.

31

The lev cycle was the only thing that still worked in the dusty old remains of the place. The weigh station hadn't been an actual station in years. More recently it had apparently been the crash pad of some old H8 junkie who'd probably wandered off into the desert on a binge, never to return. Who knows how many years ago that was.

But the lev cycle still worked. It was a junky old Hogg cobbled together out of a hundred different other hoverbikes. Rechs sat down within its wheel-shaped frame and kick started the ancient engine. It whirred to life, and moments later he was pedals up and flying across the desert toward the granite ridge his HUD told him was called the Breakheart.

To the west, one of the suns was falling into the desert, and the landscape was turning a burnt orange. Twisted trees, bent low by the wind, seemed to watch him pass. He felt an urgency to finish this before Goth Sullus got off planet. Sullus's ship, the *Siren of Titan*, had gone up with everything else in Tusca, but there was still a Republican fleet overhead. Rechs was taking no chances.

When he made the winding road leading up into the Breakheart, he expected to find some kind of vanguard waiting to ambush him.

Instead he found nothing and no one but the silence of the lifeless desert.

No Brotherhood.

No traps.

No war bot in ambush mode.

He scanned the red rock above for signs of life. When he saw none, he swallowed some pain meds and continued on. He climbed the twisting pass, doubling back in and out of the low saw-toothed mountains, and emerged onto a high windswept plateau.

He'd caught sight of the Ancients' ruins as he was racing along the curves below. They were massive, like they all were. Angular and strange, enigmatic and weird, like all the ruins they'd ever found on any of ten thousand worlds throughout the galaxy.

But why had Goth Sullus come here?

Just another madman who thought the Ancients had given him some kind of prophecy with which to light the galaxy on fire? That had been done before.

Or...

... was this all just a trap?

Rechs made the burning ridgeline and looked out at the complex of ruins spread across it. As with all the Ancients' ruins, the only structures present were squat, leaning pyramids of no apparent purpose. No door had ever been found to lead within these structures. They were impervious, though they were seemingly made of ordinary stone; the rock used in their construction was always native to the world. But it was impossibly tight-fitting rock, almost hyper-compressed, or even fused together. Completely inviolable.

No telegraphy or radar had ever been able to probe the secrets of these structures. So the galaxy had ultimately disregarded them and moved on with its business. Yet there they sat, always watching from just beyond the perimeters of all those tiny outposts out in the Big Dark.

Rechs brought the Hogg to a stop on the wide flagstone-paved court before the main and most alien pyramid. There was no one here. He dismounted. The soft hush of the wind came to him through his armor's local ambient audio detection. It made the same ghostly whisper it always did around the ruins.

He spun about, facing one of the smaller pyramids. He had that overwhelming feeling he was being watched. That sixth sense every leej gets when they know there's a sniper drawing a bead on you from some hidden place. But there was nothing beyond the sigh of the wind and the silent pyramids.

"Rechs!" shouted a voice.

But when he turned, there was nothing there.

Except now he could hear some kind of low, furtive whisper. And then a chorus of whispers. And more. The whispering threatened to drown out the world and his sanity as it crescendoed. He slapped the side of his helmet to make sure it wasn't a bucket malfunction. He told it to run an audio diagnostic. Everything was in the green. Yet he could still hear that low, whispering chorus. Or was it the wind?

He took off his helmet and held it under one arm.

The ghost whisper chorus stopped. Everything was dead silent again.

The wind felt cool on his face. He could smell the old, yet familiar, smell of the alien desert. It smelled of sage and dust and burnt wood, as all deserts do. A low, pulsing energy surged through the air. He tilted his head and concentrated, trying to detect its source.

He never would have anticipated what happened next.

A small section of the grand pyramid ahead folded in on itself brick by brick. Across its face, the ancient rocks unstacked themselves and fell inward toward nothingness—like some event horizon had swallowed them. What lay beyond them was only a waiting blackness. It had the feeling of being not just empty space... but a sort of mind-bending *nothing*ness that rational minds could not comprehend.

And then that voice spoke again. The one that had been speaking to him all along and for so many years. The voice of an old friend long forgotten. Near and at hand. A voice so known it had almost seemed his own.

Maybe because of all the guises they'd been forced to wear, he hadn't recognized it. But hearing it now...

It was Admiral Caspo.

And Asper Sulo.

Daq Sula.

Jasen Solis.

John... John *something* from way back when, in the age of nuclear fission light-huggers hauling out into the first worlds. That had been on Outer Vangora. During that war... where all those people died.

Josh Sulliman.

Mars. No, not yet.

On Mars he'd been... Sullivan. Casper Sullivan.

Lieutenant Commander Sullivan, NASA. First Officer on the *Intrepid*.

Sullivan was the voice. And the whispers. And the calling from the dark within the Ancients' pyramid.

"It's been a long time... old friend. A very long time."

Rechs started slowly toward the gaping maw, staring in utter disbelief at the darkness within. Some part of him wanted to go... to finally know all the secrets that haunted the forgotten places of the galaxy.

What was within these Ancient places was the knowing of such things.

And yet how could it be anything other than destruction?

He stopped. He felt drugged by the pain meds, or the calling void, he didn't know which.

Even now his mind, or what was left of his mind, was coming apart at the seams, as though the event horizon were whispering and pulling at the same time. How else could he hear his old friend's voice coming from within there?

"You're dead!" he shouted at the darkness.

A dry chuckle. It reminded Rechs of all the grave dust that ever waited on all the tombs of all the dead. It came from that blank space in the universe... the space waiting in front of him.

I'm losing my mind, he thought. *That's all this is.*

"No, you're not, Rechs." The voice was clear as day. "You're not. And this is as real as it's ever been. I didn't go down with the ship that day on Telos. I let her burn up once she hit atmo. It was a nice place to exit... stage left. It was a perfect time to disappear and begin my search."

"Why?" Rechs asked. Why?

"You know why!" The voice rang out through the forgotten rooms of his mind. "I was tired of watching what you and I and the others had built with our sweat and lives get ruined by the meddling herd of do-gooding scolds. The pack animals were finally in charge, and they no longer needed the lions."

"Where... where have you been, Sullivan?"

That dry grave whisper chuckled again.

"Do you remember the Quantum Palace, old friend? I followed all the clues you chose to forget, Rechs. I'd been working on it all along. I unraveled what that place really was and what it had done to us, and I followed those clues. I found something wonderful out there beyond the edge of the galaxy. Way out there in the emptiness between here and far Andromeda. It's forever out there, Rechs. The distances are mind-numbing. On a tiny planet orbiting a lost star, I found the answer to all the galaxy's problems. And now I've come back to heal, and to destroy. I've come back with the power to do everything that needs doing."

"Why?"

"You know why. You know exactly why, my friend. And you have this chance to stand with me, right now, and make things right one last time and forever... even though, let's just say, oldest of friends, let's just say I already know the answer you'll choose."

The wind began to hush and whisper. The sky turned a bloody red as the last sun began its final descent. The hot day was done, but the fading heat remained.

"You're going to take over the Republic, Sullivan."

Goth Sullus.

"No, Rechs. I'm going to destroy it. It's dead anyway."

The wind hushed and moaned, crossing dusty flagstones and picking up small swirls of grit to shift along a few inches more.

"And then I'm going to build an empire the likes of which the galaxy has never seen. The strong will protect the weak as it always should've been. I'm going to do all the things that need doing, Rechs. Just like I always said I would. It'll last ten thousand years... and so shall I."

The desert winds of evening began to rise. The last sun remaining in the sky touched the horizon and began its final descent. Out over the desert, everything, even the pyramids and the paving stones, was washed in rusty, dried, ancient blood.

The end of the day on Tusca.

The end of everything.

"Choose, Rechs." Pause. "But I think we both know how this plays out now."

"Maydoon?"

"He was one of the best spies the Republic ever made. Quite an assassin, too. He knew where all the bodies were buried. All the access codes were his for life. They kept him as a sort of failsafe against themselves... if you can wrap your mind around that sort of dithering foolishness. Typical herd thinking. They never wanted any one of them to have too much power over the others. Afraid someone might rock the boat and do a little good. So he was the insurance. An ambitionless man, given all the secrets, so he could protect them from themselves. His data globe gave me access to the sector defense network. The orders that guard the Republic from itself, and stand ready against unimaginable boogeymen from the outer dark."

Rechs thought of Prisma.

He wasn't perfect, but he was my daddy.

"Well... their boogeyman is here now. But there is a way for you to live through this, my oldest friend. You can join me, and we'll rule the galaxy together. But for that to happen, the Maydoons have to die. *Have* to. He buried a chip inside her. A chip that contains the location of the WarMind. An AI-driven bot army and fleet that circles the galaxy, ever asleep and waiting to protect the Repub against a doomsday scenario just like this one. Choose now, Rechs. Choose whether you can be the general you once were... or just some down-and-out bounty hunter on retainer for something as base as petty revenge. We can do great things together, Rechs, you and I. We've been through too much to not do the big things that always needed doing. I would hate for it to be any other way. I would hate for it to be without you."

Rechs waited, considering all that Sullivan had said from inside the void in the pyramid's face. Whether it was true or not, it didn't matter. He'd seen too many tyrants and genocidal potentates who'd had their way in their low little nightmares. Too many times he'd been ordered to put them down.

Too many times he had seen that power corrupts.

And ultimate power... corrupts ultimately.

There would always be those who thought they could rule over others without the consent of the governed. There would always be tyranny and tyrants. Always...

And then there was Prisma.

"He wasn't perfect. But he was my daddy, and I loved him."

Rechs raised his helmet like some old knight going out to the lists once more, one final turn, then fitted it back over his head. It locked in place and sealed with a slight *hiss*.

He heard that whisper in his head, coming from the blank space in the galaxy that shouldn't be.

"I see you've chosen, old friend. Stupid... so very stupid." That grave whisper that was once a friend chuckled dryly again. "Then it's time you met your replacements, Legionnaire."

Targets appeared on Rechs's HUD. Four of them. He wasn't getting any kind of reading on their armor, but he could see that their weapons were ready. He turned to the right and saw the first one materialize as if dropping from some sort of cloaking device.

Leej armor, but far better than the new stuff, or even the stuff of those other dark legionnaires back in Tusca. Skinned in black with no red stripe.

Rechs turned and saw another one of them appear on top of a smaller pyramid. Same armor, and this guy had a heavy sniper rifle that practically spelled out the word "lethal at long range." The next one to appear had some kind of bionic rig to help stabilize the largest, most wicked-looking heavy blaster he'd ever seen. It looked like a tri-barrel N-50.

The last trooper stepped right out of the event horizon darkness within the face of the pyramid. He was all in black, and carrying a hand cannon just like Rechs's. A hard-caliber slug thrower. Except this weapon was new, and somehow its graphite appearance made it seem much more deadly.

"Allow me to introduce my legionnaires, Rechs. The armor is just like yours... but not really. I'll be honest—it's as close as we can come. Yours... yours was once in a lifetime. Nothing like it. But this will do against the legionnaires of the Repub. They, as they say, ain't what we used to be—are they, old friend? I'd like you to meet my legionnaires, General Rex. I call them shock troopers."

Rechs simultaneously keyed his jump jets and fired at the leej with the tri-barrel. The sniper fired a high-density energy blast, but missed—just barely. A series of blasts from the N-50 chased Rechs across the burning red sky. He landed behind the guy with the hand cannon in a swirl of grit and dust. The blaze from the tri-barrel centered on that trooper and ventilated him in seconds.

Rechs pulled the hand cannon out of the dying man's hand, dropped to the ground, and rolled, firing at the trooper with the subcompact blaster. He had to use his left hand—his right was useless.

The trooper deployed an energy shield and closed, crouched and firing, as Rechs put ineffective rounds on target. As many of them as he could. The trooper's shield collapsed, and he switched to a two-hand firing position, bearing down on Rechs. Rechs closed and put six rounds all across the guy's armor. Six smoking vapor trails raced off into the red desert behind that trooper as he tumbled to the flagstones.

Rechs surged into a run, and the sniper atop the smaller pyramid nailed him with a high-powered charged shot. Searing hot pain went through Rechs's midsection, and his legs gave out. He tumbled to the pavement of the ancient temple complex.

Suit integrity warnings lit up all across his HUD. Med seals locked in place and began to repair. But the pain was blinding. He could smell his own burnt flesh, and it felt like his leg had been blown off.

It hadn't been.

But it sure felt like it.

The HUD announced that he was down to two bullets in his own hand cannon and half a load in the one he'd taken off the first trooper. He let both weapons fall to the ground and reached into a cargo pouch for a pain tranq. He slammed the whole load in above the thigh of the shrieking leg.

Not even a second later, all the pain was all gone.

The medicine flooded the damaged area, knocking out local pain receptors all the way up the spine. All he felt now was numb. It wouldn't last, but it would do for what remained.

He heard the hard strike of boots on the pavement, coming for him.

He rolled over onto his belly and tried to push off the ground. Tried to stand one last time.

Instead he got a tremendous kick that sent him sprawling.

He momentarily lost the ability to breathe, but he forced himself to his knees. Warnings on his HUD signaled all kinds of dire things that were starting to matter less and less.

The man with the tri-barrel gun reared back to smash in Rechs's helmet. Both of Rechs's hand cannons were out of reach. One on the flagstone behind him, the other within reach of the useless hand. A distant thought occurred, through Rechs's pain-shrouded brain, that he should reach for his machete.

There was no time. The trooper brought the tri-barrel down, hard, on Rechs's helmet, sending him to the pavement once again.

He was only out for a second, yet his body seemed to scramble and tumble away on some kind of autopilot. As though the will to live that was within him wasn't ready to go, even if he was dead. Or maybe the guy had simply sent him flying with a series of savage kicks.

When he came to, he heard those same hard-soled combat boots coming for him once more. They sounded just like leej boots.

Hell, he thought, *they* are *leejes... just different now. New somehow. But not better.*

Never.

Again he barely pushed himself to his knees.

The trooper raised the tri-barrel to deliver another blow.

But this time, as the heavy weapon ascended, Rechs drew his machete and in one swift motion lopped the man's arms off at the elbow.

The N-50 clattered to the flagstones. The trooper backed away, hyperventilating as he looked at both stumps, then fell onto his back.

The sniper fired, and Rechs threw himself to the ground. The high-energy shot sizzled overhead. Rechs slither-scrambled like a sidewinder across the pavement, toward his dropped hand cannon. It was a race. Could the sniper re-center and re-charge the rifle for the next shot before Rechs reached his weapon?

As Rechs felt his glove wrap around the grip, he knew the sniper's shot was coming. Atop the bloody pyramid, the black-armored trooper was drawing a bead. The dying sun reflected off his telescopic lens.

It was an impossible distance for most hand weapons.

Suit targeting took over and calibrated. Rechs squeezed off one round. There wasn't time for more.

The slug tore through the sniper's throat. The long blaster rifle clattered down the smooth face of the pyramid, and the man fell back and out of sight.

Rechs struggled to his feet, leaning heavily on the one leg that would support him. He turned to face the yawning event horizon void in the face of the pyramid.

Out walked the man in the hooded cloak.

Sullivan.

Or...

Goth Sullus.

Where did he come from in the moment before he was here? Where did that dark nothingness void lead off to?

Nowhere... old friend. And... goodbye.

His old friend was walking out of nothing.

All the questions, thought Rechs. *And all the answers.*

That dry chuckle rose above the last of the day as the last sun finally disappeared below the horizon.

"Well done, old friend. Well done indeed."

Rechs raised the hand cannon and centered it.

The man drew down the hood of his cloak without the least concern for the bullet Rechs was about to put through his skull. Like Rechs, he looked young for a man who'd lived a thousand and more years. Barely middle-aged. A smooth, bulbous head; a high, intense forehead. Iron-gray hair swept forward. And gray eyes that seemed alive with some kind of other life.

Did he always have gray eyes? wondered Rechs in the nano-second before he pulled the trigger.

It doesn't matter who he was. He's Goth Sullus now. And Goth Sullus killed a man. And a debt must be paid.

Rechs fired.

I should have given Prisma the picture back, he thought as the bullet spat forth, racing at Goth Sullus...

... who merely waved one hand absently, sending the slug racing off on some other, unconsidered course.

Rechs's leg gave out. He collapsed onto the still-hot dry pavement of this ancient place, his armor making an understated and pathetic *clunk* as the man who was now Goth Sullus walked toward him.

"I told you," Goth Sullus said, "there's something wonderful out there beyond the edge. Goodbye, Rechs. Second star from the right... straight on 'til morning, oldest of friends."

And then, with nothing more than a gesture of his index finger and thumb, Goth Sullus broke Tyrus Rechs's neck from a distance.

The Mark I armor fell over and lay still.

The first stars were coming out above.

The man in the dark robe began to laugh beneath the lens of the galaxy he would conquer.

And it was a terrible thing.

Epilogue

The strange gray shuttle came down in the night. Its ominous hum rose above the crackle of the bonfire the man in the dark robe known as Goth Sullus had made.

Upon the pyre, the body of Tyrus Rechs was being consumed by flames.

Sullus stood and watched the flames consume his oldest of friends. The burning ash and sparks rose up against the stars of the galactic edge.

The armor lay nearby.

The four admirals exited the shuttle as soon as troopers had formed a defensive perimeter. Cautiously they approached the man known as Goth Sullus. The man in black. His back was turned to them.

"Sir, our fleet has arrived." The admirals, all in crisp, tight-fitting black uniforms, stood aside to reveal a man dressed in the white garb of a Republic admiral. "Admiral Devers of the Republic wishes to speak with you."

Sullus nodded.

Devers stepped forward and lowered himself to one knee, his head bowed. "Sir, I present to you, for the benefit of the galaxy, the Republic's third sector fleet."

The wind keened softly, causing a gust of sparks to leap away into the darkness.

"Good," said Goth Sullus.

He turned to face them all.

"You may commence the attack."

Author's Note

Hey there, it's us, Jason and Nick! We're so glad you made it this far, and we hope you're enjoying our foray into Space Opera and Space Marine fiction. We especially want to thank you for indulging us with this little detour into two of our characters' side stories.

Galactic Outlaws was our version of a Western set in space. We wanted to do this because we're both big fans of Westerns. Jason likes *The Searchers* and Nick's a big fan of *Shane* ("Shane, come back!"). We felt this was the best way to show you the larger story of *Galaxy's Edge*. The series is not just about the foreign wars where brave leejes are fighting the good fight despite the odds; it's also about the places and people they fight for.

And as you've now seen on Ackabar, not every company of legionnaires is like Victory Company. More on that later! It's brutal out on the edge, with enemies trying to tear you apart from without and within. Things get a little bit sharper and a whole lot murkier.

Best to keep your blaster close by your side.

Measure twice, shoot once.

One of the best things about sci-fi is it allows us to explore new areas while reinvigorating existing concepts. Humanity might one day expand across the galaxy, but some things about us will never change. War, the struggle between good and evil... we'll probably find all of that out there, just like we did back home. Except we'll have blasters and fantastic ships. And beautiful alien sirens.

As you read on, you're going to experience a lot of exciting things as the story continues to unfold and expand. We'll be seeing more of what makes the Republic tick (including its seedy underbelly), more of life out on the edge, more of the non-Legion branches of service like Marines, basics, and sailors. And of course, in the very next book we'll be getting back to the characters you love from book one. Chunn, Exo, Ford, and the rest are back as they become the deadliest card in the Legion's hand... a Dark Ops *Kill Team*.

Which is the name of the next book. It's going to take everything the kill team's got to face a deadly military cabal that's growing into a dire existential threat that threatens to change the face of the galaxy forever.

And beyond that? The entire series is complete. An epic, galaxy-spanning military space adventure is just waiting for you to experience it. Plus, in addition to the main series, there are some awesome stand-alone books that explore deeper into some of the characters our readers have demanded to know more about. Don't just take our word for it—check out the Galaxy's Edge Fan Club on Facebook and meet a bunch of fun readers who dig talking about Galaxy's Edge. We're there all the time, answering questions and asking for advice on where we should take the story next. We hope to meet you there too.

Thanks again for reading, and we'll talk again after *Kill Team*.

And as always... KTF!

— Jason Anspach & Nick Cole

PS. Amazon won't tell you when future books come out, but there are several ways you can stay informed.

1. Enlist in our fan-run Facebook group, the Galaxy's Edge Fan Club, and say hello. It's a great place to hang out with other KTF-lovin' legionnaires who like to talk about sci-fi and are up for a good laugh.

2. Follow us directly on Amazon. This one is easy. Just go to the store page for this book on Amazon and click the "follow" button beneath our pictures. That will prompt Amazon to email you automatically whenever we release a new title.

3. Join the Galaxy's Edge Newsletter. You'll get emails directly from us—along with the short story "Tin Man," available only to newsletter subscribers.

Doing just one of these (**although doing all three is your best bet!**) will ensure you find out when the next *Galaxy's Edge* book releases. Please take a moment to do one of these so you can find yourself on patrol with Chhun, Wraith, and Exo for their next gritty firefight!

JOIN THE LEGION

You can find art, t-shirts, signed books and other merchandise on our website.

We also have a fantastic Facebook group called the Galaxy's Edge Fan Club that was created for readers and listeners of *Galaxy's Edge* to get together and share their lives, discuss the series, and have an avenue to talk directly with Jason Anspach and Nick Cole. Please check it out and say hello once you get there!

For updates about new releases, exclusive promotions, and sales, visit inthelegion.com and sign up for our VIP mailing list. Grab a spot in the nearest combat sled and get over there to receive your free copy of "Tin Man," a Galaxy's Edge short story available only to mailing list subscribers.

INTHELEGION.COM

GET A FREE, EXCLUSIVE SHORT STORY

THE GALAXY IS A DUMPSTER FIRE...

ABOUT THE AUTHORS

Jason Anspach and Nick Cole are a pair of west coast authors teaming up to write their science fiction dream series, Galaxy's Edge.

Jason Anspach is a best-selling author living in Puyallup, Washington with his wife and their own legionnaire squad of seven (not a typo) children. Raised in a military family (Go Army!), he spent his formative years around Joint Base Lewis-McChord and is active in several pro-veteran charities. Jason enjoys hiking and camping throughout the beautiful Pacific Northwest. He remains undefeated at arm wrestling against his entire family.

Nick Cole is a Dragon Award winning author best known for *The Old Man and the Wasteland, CTRL ALT Revolt!,* and the Wyrd Saga. After serving in the United States Army, Nick moved to Hollywood to pursue a career in acting and writing. He resides with his wife, a professional opera singer, south of Los Angeles, California.

Honor Roll

We would like to give our most sincere thanks and recognition to those who helped make *Galaxy's Edge: Galactic Outlaws* possible by subscribing to GalacticOutlaws.com.

Marlena Anspach
Robert Anspach
Steve Beaulieu
Steve Bergh
Wilfred Blood
Christopher Boore
Brent Brown
Rhett Bruno
Marion Buehring
Mary Ann Bulpitt
Peter Davies
Nathan Davis
Richard Fox
Peter Francis
Chris Fried
Hank Garner
Michael Greenhill
Phillip Hall
Josh Hayes
Angela Hughes
Wendy Jacobson
Chris Kagawa
Mathijs Kooij
William Kravetz

Grant Lambert
Danyelle Leafty
Preston Leigh
Pawel Martin
Tao Mason
Simon Mayeski
Jim Mern
Alex Morstadt
Nate Osburn
Chris Pourteau
Maggie Reed
Karen Reese
Glenn Shotton
Maggie Stewart-Grant
Kevin Summers
Beverly Tierney
Scott Tucker
John Tuttle
Christopher Valin
Scot Washam
Justin Werth
Justyna Zawiejska
N. Zoss

Made in the USA
Middletown, DE
07 February 2020

84346002R00228